Under the Banyan Tree

Raghbir Dhillon

D1528380

Dedicated to Doris Dhillon, my wife, a noble person who brought joy, cheer, and happiness in my life, and the lives of many persons who came in contact with her. She left this world on March 16, 2007, leaving us behind clinging to her cherished memories.

Contents

My Omnipotent Hanuman God 1
Grandpa's Shindig 10
My Struggle to Become a Preacher 18
Exorcism of My Husband 33
Winning the Indian Derby 52
My Search for Nirvana 62
Reincarnation 75
Keeping One's Pledge 92
College Degree 96
Capturing a Pernicious Ghost 108
American Astronaut Explores Heavens 121
Locust Ate My Cycle 135
Catching a Romantic Ghost 139
Almighty Cobra God 147
Restoring God's Eye 158
My Portent Tiger Hunt in India 172
The Ghost World 185
Snared by Dowry 197
Grandma's Gold Ring 207
Royal Elephants' Dung 217
My Indian Mother-in-law 226
God Parts Heaven for His Believer 235
Hindu Monk and Celibacy 243
A Novel Ritual of Dumping Sins 251
Lynching of the Innocent 262
She Defeated the Yammas 271
Her Tragic Struggle 282
Sledding 293
Jeeto's Sofa 298
My Struggle to Find Love 302
My Search for Life After Death 308
A Smart Polygamist 317

Cruel Hypocrites 329
The Sounds of the Last Farewell 338
I Fought Racial Prejudices 342

My Omnipotent Hanuman God

Two hundred mud huts looked like a bunch of mushrooms sprouting at the feet of the Himalayan Mountains. This was my village, Thati, and it had clean air and fertile soil. We could see the golden sun rising behind the majestic Mount Everest Peaks and hear the soothing music of the ripples dancing in the sacred Ganges River. We were content and happy.

In 1940, when I was in high school, my father told me to get a job in the town or join the army after getting my diploma, since the land, he owned, could hardly feed my siblings. I worked hard and won a scholarship for college. After graduating from college, I left the village with a heavy heart and became a clerk with the central government in New Delhi.

In my windowless office, I was buried under mountains of files, and the overhead fan, croaking like a wounded pregnant frog, further irritated my nerves. It took me six months to get adjusted to my new life. I plodded for two years and then took one month's leave and rode a bus to my village.

My parents were delighted, and my mother kissed my head many times. After dinner I took my string cot on the roof of the home, from where I could see the bright stars in the sky and shimmering lights on the hills. It was a big relief from the Delhi traffic noise and smog, and I slept like an exhausted camel.

At four in the morning, I heard the tintinnabulation of the temple bells and my past association with them flashed across my mind: Every morning, on hearing these chimes, Mom

1

awoke me, and we walked to the temple. Ten days after my birth, she took me to the sacred place, cuddled in her arms. When I became two years old, I started trotting, holding her hand. At age four, I carried the basket for the offering to the temple. Mom always walked with closed eyes while chanting mantras. She never stumbled, and I believed the god at the temple was guiding her steps.

The temple was made with marble, and its dome was covered with gold. When I was five, I was allowed to carry the basket inside the temple. As I stepped in, tightly hugging the basket, I was stunned to see a huge gold statue shimmering under the flickering lights of the earthen lamps. Tendrils of smoke from the incense burning pots and the lamps were curling around the awesome figure, and the sonorous chanting of the pot-bellied priest resonated from the marble walls. I was awestruck. When I moved closer, I discovered the face of the statue resembled a monkey, and it wore a gold crown studded with glittering rubies and sapphires, and beams of light were shooting out from its large diamond eyes. Glancing at the long tail, I felt sure it was a monkey and whispered, "Mom, our god is a monkey."

She slapped me and scolded, "Never say those words again. He is Hanuman God and not a monkey. Always keep in mind he's our savior and is omniscient."

I wiped my tears and mumbled, "I'm sorry."

From then onwards I was afraid of the powerful god who looked like a monkey and lived in a huge home made with marble and gold.

At the age of seven, I had to go to the temple at five in the morning, carrying mother's basket, come home, and walk to a school in the neighboring village. The teacher told us that there were more than a million gods and goddesses, but I always believed that my Hanuman God was the most omnipotent. Mom carried flowers from our garden to the temple, and once a week she took costly Burfee (sweets made with milk and sugar). I marveled at the god who enjoyed

2

thousands of sweets everyday, while we could taste it only once a year on the Diwali festival. At the sight of Burfee, my mouth watered and my belly begged, but I could stifle my desire. Finally I succumbed and decided to steal one piece. Next morning, while walking to the temple carrying Mom's offerings, I joined mother in singing and slowly slipped my hand in the basket, took out a small piece, and concealed it in my pocket. Mom presented the basket to the priest who touched one piece to the god's mouth and took the rest into the inner chamber. It was impossible for Mom to find one piece missing, but I was scared. With great anxiety, I watched her facial expression and was relieved, when on our return trip, she patted my back and said, "Bir, you're a good worshiper; I'm glad you have memorized the sacred hymns and can sing beautifully."

"All this is due to the grace of our Hanuman God," I responded.

I went to school, occupied my desk, and tried hard to listen to the teacher. But my mind, dreaming of the piece of Burfee, failed to focus. I repeatedly felt the piece in my pocket and was glad when the classes ended. I sprinted out of the school and stopped near the banyan tree, stretched on the ground, and relished the delicacy, while enjoying the singing of the birds. I reached home full of bliss and helped my father to feed the animals and sang praises of Hanuman God. At night, when I was alone, fear attacked me: Hanuman God is going to punish me for this theft, and I'm going to become sick or even die. I prayed feverishly to Hanuman God not to mind my having a tiny piece, since he gets thousands.

Since I didn't become sick and no calamity struck me, I felt sure Hanuman God was not mad at me. For two years I enjoyed the sweets without feeling any guilt. Now I was enthused about going to the temple, and mother didn't have to awake me; I was up and ready.

When I was nine, I noticed hundreds of silver rupees piled at the god's feet. I rarely saw a silver rupee in my father's hand. The rich city people, however, made their offerings in silver coins, instead of flowers and sweets. My heart pumped faster at the glimpse of the huge wealth and begged me to secure one coin from the rich god. After a great deal of planning and rehearsing, one morning I pasted glue on my left hand and was ready for my adventure. Mom made the offering, and I prostrated before the god, placed my palms near the god's feet, and prayed. After a few minutes, I stood up, folded my hands and sang loud praises of Hanuman God. I kept my hands locked, and when Mom was not looking at me, I managed to pocket the rupee which had stuck to my left palm. Now I felt like a Crorepati (millionaire). One silver rupee could buy many things in those days. I converted the rupee to passas and buried them near the cremation ground. I was sure no one would dare to dig near the place where ghosts danced all the time. I stopped stealing Burfee and could purchase my own.

In my daily prayers at the temple, I thanked Hanuman God for the rupee and begged for his forgiveness, but I always noticed anger in his fiery eyes. I suspected the god overlooked my pinching the Burfee, since it was only a tiny piece of food, but he was upset at my stealing his silver. I felt doomed. I couldn't return the rupee, since I had spent a portion of it, and my father didn't have a rupee in the earthen pot in which he kept his money. One day, while coming from school, I found a cobra, with its raised hood, crawling toward me. The fear, that Hanuman God had sent it to punish me, grabbed my body. My legs turned into jelly, and I couldn't move. I begged Hanuman God to help me, but he ignored my pleas, and the cobra bit my leg. I slumped on the ground and cried. Luckily, our neighbor was returning with his donkeys. He dumped me on one donkey and delivered me to my parents. My father brought the hakim who cut open the blue blister and applied some ointment over it. I experienced a sharp pain from the cut and the scalding ointment. To drive away the Devils, the hakim forced me to smell the red peppers burning on the charcoal. Now I felt as if I had entered hell. As I pinched myself, I felt pain; I was happy I was still on earth. Feeling sure that Hanuman God was punishing me, I thought I must make my confession to have a peaceful end. I asked Mom to come near my bed and whispered in her ear, "Please secure forgiveness from Hanuman God."

"Forgiveness? For what?" she asked with arched brows.

"I have sinned."

"Son, what did you do?"

"I stole one silver rupee from his temple."

Mom's face turned pale, and she slapped her forehead. "Holy cow! I can't believe this. How could you do that?"

I explained my trick. She dabbed her tears and said, "Son, I can see why you are in trouble: Hanuman God asked his assistant, Cobra God, to punish you."

"Mom, I know that and am very sorry for it. Now I beg you to go the temple, offer one rupee, and get me pardoned. Otherwise, I'm sure to die with this excruciating pain," I moaned.

"All right, I'll do that, but promise never to steal a penny from anywhere."

Tears channeled down my cheeks. I wiped those with my knuckles and gave my solemn pledge. Mom went to the temple, placed a silver rupee at the god's feet, and begged. As she told me about her visit to the temple, I was relieved of my worry. Next day I felt better and was sure the god had forgiven me. After getting out of the sickbed, I walked barefoot to the temple and rubbed my nose one hundred times before the god, while Mom sat cross-legged near me. Hanuman God taught me a good lesson, and the temptation of stealing never entered my head.

As I felt a tap at my shoulder, the flashback ended. I opened my eyes and saw Mom standing next to my cot. "Bir, time to go to the temple."

I took a hurried bath and accompanied Mom for the worship. During my entire vacation I prayed with Mom at the temple and felt great peace and joy. My vacation ended, and I returned to my job. I was still a bachelor and wanted to marry an educated girl. However, before I could do that, I had to save money to buy a decent home. Through frugal living I could lay aside two thousand rupees in five years and was searching for a place.

One day my friend, Mastan, arrived at my residence. He dropped out of school in the second grade, and I had not seen him after that. He told me that he had come to invite me to his marriage. I accepted his invitation. Mastan left after lunch.

Two days before the marriage, I took leave from my work and reached Mastan's place on the border with Pakistan. I was astonished to see his two-story mansion complete with electric fans, fancy lights, and a marble fountain. He welcomed me and showed his house and the adjoining big barn where he kept several fast Arabian horses.

I noticed he had invited more than sixty families. It was impossible to provide cots to all the guests. Therefore, the furniture from the living room and the five bedrooms was stacked in the barn and each guest was given a mattress, a pillow, and a sheet. I managed to make my bed in the corner of the living room. Amongst the guests, I met my classmate, Kishan, who was working for Mastan. Kishan greatly admired Mastan's largesse.

"Mastan must have made a mountain of money," I remarked.

"Bir, in his business money crawls to your feet."

"What business?"

He scratched his chin. "I thought you knew."

I shook my head.

"Mastan is the king of the smugglers and controls two hundred miles of the border."

"What does he do?" I asked.

"His fast horses slip through the border at night with tubes attached to their bellies. The border guards don't suspect the horses without riders."

"Kishan, what do those tubes contain?"

"They carry whiskey and bring back opium. Whiskey is banned in Pakistan and opium in India. Mastan is making a huge tax-free income."

"Did he invite his smuggler friends?"

"Yes, all the guests except you are members of his trade. You're a college graduate, and Mastan wanted to impress his father-in-law by your presence."

The marriage was performed with a lavish feast and fireworks. I walked with the bridegroom in my three-piece silken suit and a flashing tie. During the night there was dancing, singing, and heavy drinking. I hated boozing, therefore I congratulated Mastan and retired early to my bed. Next morning, I got up at five to catch the train for New Delhi. As I rolled up my bed, I was stunned to find a bundle of hundred rupee bills. I had seen several of the inebriated guests flashing their stacks of currency, and anyone of them could have hid this money thinking it was his bed, and in no way could I locate the real owner. I remembered my pledge to Hanuman god, but I managed to convince my heart that I was not stealing, but simply picking up the money dropped under my pillow. I stashed the money in my pocket and returned to New Delhi.

In the morning I went to my office. For eight hours, seated at my office desk, I struggled to concentrate on my job, but the dreams of buying a big home and marrying a pretty educated girl, clouded my brain. In the evening when I returned home, I made sure about the money which I had concealed in my pillow. After dinner, I prayed to Hanuman God, went to my bed, and fell asleep. Suddenly, I had a terrible dream in which I saw Hanuman God standing near a red hot stove, with a spear in his hand, and yelling, "Bir, you're a thief. I'm going to roast you over burning charcoal."

7

Under the Banyan Tree

I tried to run and landed with a big thud on the floor. Drenched in sweat, I was trembling, and my heart was trying to burst out of its cage. I scrambled up, went to the bathroom, took a cold shower, prayed to Hanuman God, and returned to my bed. I dozed off and the horrible dreams reappeared—I saw an army of demons, riding mosquitoes, buzzing around me. With loud chuckles they pierced my body and enjoyed dancing in the fountains of blood. I woke up trembling and jumped out of the bed. The demons vanished, but I was afraid to go back to the cot. I moved to the sofa, closed my eyes, and my mother's image appeared.

"Son, you're a thief! You stole the money," Mom rebuked.

"I didn't steal. It was lying on the ground under my bed, and I just picked it up."

She peered into my eyes. "Did you earn it?"

"No."

"Then it is not our money; you should have returned it to its owner," she scolded.

"There were many guests, and I could never locate the real owner."

She wiggled her finger. "If you take anything for which you have not worked or was not given to you, you commit a terrible sin."

"What should I do now?"

"Son, this money is poison for you; get rid of it."

"How?"

"The proper place for it is Hanuman God's temple. The priest will use it to feed hungry mouths," she explained.

"Please secure my pardon from our god. I'll deliver the money to the temple tomorrow."

Mother kissed my forehead and vanished; I felt better and slept without any dreams.

Next morning, I took two days leave and visited Hanuman God's temple in a disguise. I couldn't openly throw the big bundle at the god's feet, so I packed it in an old, brown bag and sat cross-legged in the temple, waiting for the opportune moment. When the priest left his seat near the statue, I surreptitiously placed the packet, bowed, and left without meeting anyone. I returned to my work with a light heart.

Thirty days passed without any incident, and I felt sure the money had fed many starving persons. One morning, I read in the newspaper: "The priest's helper in Hanuman God's temple had been arrested for passing counterfeit hundred rupee bills. The culprit confessed to the court that he found ten thousand rupees in a brown bag near the god's feet and could not control his temptation."

I folded the paper, closed my eyes, and thanked Hanuman God for appearing in my dream and saving me. If I had kept the money and tried to use it, I would have been behind bars with a ruined life.

I purchased a two-bedroom home and married a girl who had a high school diploma. Soon I was promoted to a post where I could easily make thousands in kickbacks. I was an exception among the group of officers who openly collected bribes. I, however, was content and kept my promise with Hanuman God. With easy money, my fellow officers overindulged in wine and women, and many lost their health and jobs. I advised them to worship Hanuman God and seek his help, but they ridiculed me and my god.

Faith can move mountains and work wonders. My staunch belief forced Hanuman God to emerge from the marble statue and save my life. Look, my god is not a monkey, but is an omniscient power which pervades the universe.

Grandpa's Shindig

245 Hanuman Road, New Delhi

"Nathan, my lingam (penis) has started doing pushups," Dev, a seventy-year-old man, whispered in his friend's ear.

"Tighten your loincloth and crush it down," Nathan, an emaciated man with grey hairs said under his breath.

Dev struggled with his dhoti and mumbled, "All right, I've pinched it hard and hope this will work."

"It must. You can't create a scene here," Nathan said. "Remember, we're leading my grandson's marriage procession."

Dev spewed from the corner of his mouth, took out a gold box from his pocket, lifted a betel leaf, and started chewing.

"Sorry, when I hear a marriage band, it reminds me of my marriage, and my libido gets out of control," Dev said. "Anyhow, with fully compressed lingam, I'm feeling better."

"Good, calm down for a few hours. After the marriage, I'll take you to my room, and we'll plan our shindig."

"Shindig!" Dev exclaimed. "I'm all for it."

Dev and Nathan were walking behind a white stallion which was decorated with shining brass jewelry and bells. Nathan's grandson, wearing a pink, plumed turban was sitting on the horse, and a servant in white uniform was struggling to hold a tall canopy over the rider's head, while trying to avoid the swishing tail of the skittish horse. Playing the local favorite tunes, a forty-piece-brass-band was marching in front of the horse. A party of two hundred men and women followed Dev and Nathan. The women were singing, and the betel-chewing men were chuckling and cavorting.

In one hour the procession reached the bride's decorated house. The marriage ceremonies ended at seven in the evening. The marriage party, along with the bride, returned to Nathan's house in limos. Nathan, the richest man in India, was delighted, since the bride brought more dowry than he had expected. He measured the success of a marriage on the size of the dowry and paid no attention to the bride.

Nathan took Dev into his room and locked the door.

"Do you want some tonic?" Nathan asked.

"What tonic?"

"It's whisky in a cough syrup bottle," Nathan winked and said.

Dev took a sip, smacked his lips, and said, "I used to love it, when I was young."

Nathan patted Dev's hand and said, "Now let's discuss your problem."

"I've already told you that the marriage festivities remind me of my marriage and unleash my libido which I have been struggling to control," Dev moaned.

"I pity you. You lost your wife, and the gods don't permit you to have a woman."

Dev scratched his chin. "Look, most of the gods have big harems, and they can marry even when they are centenarians. Why don't they permit us to marry again?"

"Well, we can't question the gods who are Nehkalank (above worldly sins). You better pray for help at their temple."

Dev shook his head. "It doesn't work."

"Why?"

"Nathan, when I see the dancing breasts of the young priestess, as she raises her arms to make an offering to the goddess, my body is set on fire, and instead of worshiping I dream of dragging her to my bed."

Nathan touched his sacred thread (cotton thread necklace worn around the neck to protect from sins) and said, "Ram,

Ram, Ram. Sex with the holy priestess. Shame on you. Control your dirty thoughts. Remember, you are a great-grandfather."

"Age doesn't extinguish the fire in a human heart," Dev moaned. "Come on, you're of my age. Be honest with me and tell me, how do you feel when you see a gorgeous young girl taking a dip in the sacred river?"

Nathan took a deep breath, adjusted his sacred thread, and whispered, "I close my eyes and chant mantras. But I have to admit that I peep through half-closed eyes and long to undress her."

Dev stood up, ambled to the Goddess Laxmi (goddess of wealth) marble statue, and touched her feet with folded hands. When he removed the old garland from the neck to put a fresh one, he yelled, "Holy Cow! What have you done to the breasts of our goddess?"

"Calm down," Nathan whispered. "Every morning when I place a fresh marigold garland around her neck, my hands slip to her firm breasts and play with them. I don't hurt her; she has been so kind to me."

Dev patted Nathan's back and said, "Well, then you, too, are a hypocrite, facing a losing battle."

"Yes, I am. My wife died ten years ago. I've been sleeping alone and posing as a celibate saint," Nathan said and moved closer to Dev. "Can you keep a secret?"

"Certainly, we've been friends for more than fifty years, and I've never let you down."

Nathan grinned. "Every night I sleep with a different, gorgeous, young girl."

"Hari Krishna! How do you manage that?"

"I've a calendar of naked girls."

Dev's beady eyes sparkled. He smacked his lips and shouted, "You dirty rascal; how could you secure that?"

"Dev, one day I overheard my grandson talking about a naked girly calendar with his classmate. Next day, when my grandson was at college, I sneaked into his room and found the calendar of naked American beauties, concealed under his mattress. I pinched it and stuck it in my pillow."

"What about your grandson?"

"He can never imagine my stealing it and suspected the servants. He, however, couldn't dare to say a word about it, since he knew I whipped any child who even brought the picture of an Indian actress in my house," Nathan smirked. "Well, now every night I can select one of the girls from the calendar, and make her sleep with me."

Drops of drool dripped from Dev's lower lip, and he licked those with his tongue. "Can you loan it to me for one night?"

"I can, but it won't help you," Nathan said.

"Why?"

"The dumb pictures will pour gasoline on the burning fire, and your heart will beg for a warm body."

Dev rubbed the rosary to his forehead. "Well, we have no choice but to suffer; we can't break the traditions and marry again."

"I have been dreaming of a rendezvous with a young girl," Nathan said. "You're so smart; can't you think of a way to quench our lust with the real thing?"

Dev closed his eyes and scratched his head. After a few minutes, he blinked with a smile and said, "I've a plan, but it needs some courage."

"Spit it out; I'm all for it," Nathan blurted.

"Tomorrow, you arrange an all night prayer meeting to seek Goddess Parvati's blessing for your grandson and his bride, and we can have our rendezvous without causing any suspicion."

"Dev, how are you going to arrange that?"

"I'll hire a bewitching, young dancing girl who sings like a bulbul (Indian singing bird), and send a taxi to bring her to the Rest House near the Nehru Dam. This place is completely isolated from the public, and we'll be safe. I know the attendant and can easily bribe him to secure the biggest room reserved for the Chief Minister."

13

"How did you discover that place?"

"When I was young, I used to take whores there," Dev said with a gleam in his eyes.

Nathan pulled up his dhoti to choke his lingam and said, "Hurry up, make all the arrangements and don't worry about money; I'll pay all the bills, since it's for my grandson's marriage."

"Okay, it's all settled. Tomorrow at nine in the evening I'll pick you up in a taxi."

"Dev, why not use our limos?"

"We can't trust our chauffeurs."

"Good, a smart move," Nathan said and started chanting mantras, and Dev joined him.

Nathan escorted Dev to the gate, where Dev's limo was waiting for him.

Next day, Dev arrived in a taxi at nine in the evening, and Nathan took him inside his room.

"I've told my children that we're going to worship all night at the temple and will return at sunrise. They all are delighted," Nathan said.

"I, too, didn't have any problem convincing my family that you need help in this noble job," Dev said. "Nathan, do you remember my cousin, Amar?"

"Yes, what about him?"

"He begged to join us, but I told him, I have to ask you."

"No problem, I'm inviting my friend Chandan, too. Four of us will have a real good time," Nathan added. "By the way, have you made all the arrangements?"

"All set, let's move," Dev said.

Nathan and Dev left the house, while singing praises of the goddess. They sat in the taxi which picked up Amar and Chandan, and soon entered a huge bungalow which was surrounded with beautiful gardens. The attendant opened the door, and the party of four old men lumbered into the spacious living room. This room was full of rose bouquets, and their fragrance was dancing around the room. The attendant pocketed the hefty bribe and left with a deep bow. The four men removed their turbans and adjusted their dhotis. They stacked the furniture in the corner and made ample room for the hired girl to dance.

After ten minutes, another taxi arrived. Dev emerged from the Rest House and escorted three musicians and a young girl who was wearing a diaphanous dress. On entering the living room, the girl greeted the group with a wink and a smile. The four old men sat cross-legged on the floor, forming a circle. The musicians tuned their instruments, and the whore tied brass bells to her ankles, wrists, and waist. She giggled, checked the bells, and started singing and dancing. As she twirled near the old men, they inserted one hundred rupee bills in her brassier. Soon her brassier was over stuffed. The enchanting music, the exotic dancing, and the fragrance of flowers supercharged the old men, and they tried to grab her, but she was agile and too fast for them. After one hour the singing ended. The four old men, scrambled up, tottered, and lurched to embrace her. She pushed them back and said, "I can satisfy one man at a time. Sweethearts, I'll go into the bedroom, remove my clothes and get ready to entertain you, but there's one hitch."

All shouted, "What's that?"

"Look, you're highly respected men and will never reveal your names. So I can't call you by your names. Give me your rings. I'll take those inside the bedroom, get ready, and then I'll show the ring near the door, and the owner of that ring can step in and have a good time."

They were businessmen who always wore costly diamond rings. On hearing this, they were discombobulated. Nathan, however, couldn't control his fire, and he was the first to drop his ring. With some trepidation all the others followed his example. She picked up the rings, winked, and sashayed inside the bedroom. Soon a ring appeared through the parted door. It belonged to Dev. He threw away his walking stick

15

and dashed in like a bull chasing a concupiscent cow. After thirty minutes he staggered out, holding his chest with one hand and lingam with the other. The grin on his face showed he had thoroughly enjoyed his investment. In two hours all four men had their flings. They were exhausted, but there was a gleam in their eyes, and mirth danced on their faces.

The whore put on her clothes, kissed each old man, and said her farewell.

The old men washed their lingams with sacred Ganges water. Then they took showers, painted their foreheads, clicked their rosaries, and recited Scriptures for a few minutes. It was three in the morning. Nathan removed his glasses and said, "Dev, that was a real elixir; now I can see better without my glasses."

Dev danced a little jig and exclaimed, "No pain in my legs. See what a sixteen-year-old damsel can do for us."

"I agree, we should do it again."

"My grandson is getting married next month, and I'll take care of that shindig. Do remember to wear a cheap ring on that night," Dev said. "Now let's go to the temple, thank the goddess and take home a few garlands as the proof of our praying at the temple."

Nathan scratched his ear. "Good thinking, but how can we explain the missing rings?"

Dev smiled. "Very simple. We'll tell our families, we threw those at the feet of the goddess to secure a good future for the newly married couple."

"Excellent idea, let's go," Nathan exclaimed.

The taxi took the four old men to the temple. They rubbed their noses and obtained forgiveness for their tiny sin. The rejuvenated old men reached home at sunrise with temple garlands around their necks.

Nathan had bought two more large marigold garlands. As the newly married couple touched his feet, he placed the garlands around their necks, and addressed them, "Children, I prayed all night to the goddess at her temple. She touched my

16

heart and wanted me to make a big donation. I didn't have the cash, so I gave her my ring. I'm sure you will have a happy married life."

"Thanks Grandpa, you are the best. You spent all night praying to the goddess and even sacrificed your diamond ring," the grandson said.

Nathan clicked his rosary and said, "I'm glad I could do it. The worship was great. Though I was up all night, yet I don't feel tired. After touching the goddess, my heart rejoiced, and an electric current ran through my body. Now I'm looking forward to the coming marriage of your younger brother."

My Struggle to Become a Preacher

On the sultry afternoon of March 29, 1913, a half-blind midwife struggled to deliver me into the world. The sounds of her grunts and my mother's moans seeped out through the slit in the closed door. My father, a tall man with salt-and-pepper hair, stood in front of the door, and clicked his rosary. The midwife pulled me out, wiped my nose and mouth, held me upside down, and slapped my bottom. I screamed. My father heard my cry, dashed in, felt my water-spout, and yelled, "It's a boy!" I howled louder. Without making any effort to pacify me, he scooted out of the room and started singing and dancing, and all other members of the family joined him in the merrymaking. Had it been a girl, there would have been gloom and sorrow, since the girls with their dowry problems meant a big financial loss.

The place of my birth, Khara Village, located in Northern India, had eighty cow-dung-plastered mud homes which belonged to the farmers. In the center of the village stood a marble temple, and the adjoining brick home was owned by the Brahmin priest.

My mother was an orthodox Hindu who didn't eat anything before praying at the temple. So, when I was five-days-old, she took me to the temple at five in the morning, and I never missed a day after that.

I was taller than the other boys of my age, and when I became three-years-old, I started helping my father: At noon Mom placed me on the back of the black mare, and I carried food and drinks to the workers in the fields. My first ride was horrible, and I had a sore bottom, but soon I got over the pain and began enjoying the work.

Every morning I accompanied Mom to the temple and saw the priest, who wore a spotless white dhoti and sat cross-legged near the feet of the marble statue. A marigold garland dangled around his neck, and three white lines covered his forehead. His melodious singing of hymns enchanted me, and he looked like a heavenly saint to me. I admired and worshiped him.

When I was five-years-old and Mom and I were standing in the temple, I grabbed Mom's hand, gestured toward the priest, and said, "Mom, someday I'll be a priest like him."

"You can never be a priest."

"Why?"

"Son, this work is allotted to Brahmins, and you're not a Brahmin."

"What should I do to become a Brahmin?"

Mom patted my back. "It's impossible. The gods arranged the caste for you, and you have to live and die in it. You're a Vaisya and should plan to become a good farmer."

My dreams were shattered, but I managed to mumble, "All right, I'll try to enjoy plowing the fields."

One evening, I heard a heated discussion between my parents:

"Bir is six now; I want to send him to school," Dad said.

"Ram! Ram! Ram! We shouldn't break our traditions. The gods never gave us proper brains to study books. Bir should help you and learn our trade."

"Woman, I don't plan to send him to college. I want him to be able to read and reply to my letters. I'm tired of going to the shopkeeper and paying him for this work. Moreover, after his education Bir can help me in keeping account of the money and the seeds."

Mom dabbed her tears with the end of her sari. "Poor Bir doesn't have a good brain, and we shouldn't force him."

"Let's give him a chance."

Next day, Dad took me to the school in the nearby village, and I joined the classes. Every morning I walked with the priest's son, Kishan, to the school. At school, I discovered I did have a brain, and it could work better than some Brahmins.

Nothing special happened to me for eight years, and I reached the eighth grade. By this time God Brahma had given me three younger brothers. One evening my father asked me to sit next to him. From the look on his face, I guessed he was facing an emotional turmoil.

"Son, you have gathered more than enough knowledge which we need for our work. I'm short of a working hand and want you to quit school after this grade and help me."

"I like books and want to become a preacher," I pleaded.

"Impossible!"

"Why?" I asked.

"You're not a Brahmin. The gods made us Vaisyas to farm the earth, and we can't change the rules. If you do good deeds, the gods will make you a Brahmin in your next birth, and then you can become a preacher."

"The gods never made these rules—a Brahmin, Manu, fabricated them," I asserted.

Dad's face turned red, and he yelled, "Shut up; stop that blasphemy. The gods spoke to Manu and revealed the truth, and the poor fellow wrote that to guide us."

"What truth?" I asked.

"God Brahma created Brahmins from the flesh of his head and gave them proper brains for teaching and preaching. He constructed Kshatriyas from his arm muscle and made them great fighters. He developed us from his thigh and gave us good bodies to produce food. We're lucky we're not Sudras who were made from the feet and are meant to do menial jobs," he explained.

My Struggle to Become a Preacher

I knew it was all a mythology concocted by the heated brain of a Brahmin, but I didn't want to break my father's heart. "Sorry Dad, I was wrong."

Next day, while at school, I told Kishan about my decision. He held my hand and said, "Buddy, I'll miss you, but you've made the right choice. God Brahma gave farmers strong bodies without any brains for the hard work and reserved the brains for us."

I was doing better than him at school and didn't like him to call me a dunce, but I couldn't fight against the traditional beliefs and said, "Kishan, I do have a brain and am going to ply that in the coming years."

"Wish you good luck," he said. "When you come to the temple, please do see me."

I nodded. We shook hands and parted.

I quit school. Now every night I yoked my two buffaloes and plowed the fields or worked the Persian well to water the crops. I enjoyed the stars and the singing crickets which tried to keep consonance with the music provided by the jingling bells on the necks of my buffaloes. These placid, cud-chewing beasts could easily understand my commands, and the people admired the perfect straight lines which they created with the plow. I felt tuned to Mother Nature and experienced the presence of God in everything surrounding me. In the evening I spent hours in reading the books which I could borrow from the headmaster. In spite of the back-breaking hard labor, I never gave up my dream of becoming a preacher. I thought of changing my identity and going to another province. But for preaching, I had to master Sanskrit, since the Scriptures are written in that language. Sanskrit, however, couldn't be learned in any school—the priests taught this to the members of their clan. The only way I could learn Sanskrit was to trap a priest and force him to help me. It was an unattainable dream, but I was undaunted.

21

Kishan graduated from the high school and then went to a college in a distant town; I lost touch with him.

Five years slipped away. One morning, as I returned to the barn, tired and covered with dust, I noticed a tiny person in a white cotton dhoti, standing near the gate. His forehead was covered with white lines, and he was spinning a rosary. He rushed to grab my hand and said, "Bir, nice to see you."

My chin fell, but I controlled my anger by biting my lower lip and asked, "Why are you missing your classes?"

"I dropped out in the third year."

"What are you doing now?"

"Bir, like you, I've entered my father's profession and am working as a priest in Durgiana Temple."

"Good for you," I said. "What is the reason for your this surprise visit?"

"Bir, can we sit somewhere?" he said. "I would like to discuss something with you."

"All right, let me take care of my buffaloes."

I tied the buffaloes, dumped fodder in their troughs, washed my hands, and took Kishan inside the barn. We sat cross-legged on the jute mats, and I said, "Look, after our last encounter, I told you I would never see you again."

"I'm sorry for what transpired," he said. "With your help, however, I could achieve the goal of my life."

"Fornication!" I yelled.

"Bir, please calm down, you were my best friend and classmate for many years."

"You bamboozled me. I thought I was helping you in your fire worship and was clobbered."

He sucked in a blast of air, released it with a sigh, and said, "Sorry, I wasn't honest with you. I told you that if we worshiped behind the temple, we'd get good grades. You agreed, and I took you to the rear of the building and lit a fire. Actually, this was a signal to the old priest's young wife who appeared behind the bushes."

"Damn it, I thought you were doing the fire worship, and I was guarding the sacred ritual, but you always slipped away for thirty minutes with an excuse of answering the call of nature. One night, while you were gone, an old priest with two thugs attacked me. They rebuked me for helping you in the seduction of a young lady."

"I'm sorry. I was sure you could handle them, and you did beat them off. Anyhow, I thanked you, dressed your injuries, and begged you to accept one hundred rupees. You refused the offer and cut me off. Anyhow, the sacred worship did help you, and you stood first in the class."

"Look, you tricked me into many things, but that was the limit."

He adjusted his sacred thread (Hand-spun cotton necklace worn around the neck to protect from sins) and started singing something in Sanskrit. His melodious singing with tearful eyes touched my heart, and I asked, "Kishan, what are you singing?"

"The sacred Scriptures."

"I know that, but it's in Sanskrit, and I don't understand a word of it," I said. "Translate it for me."

"'A man of lower caste must never refuse forgiveness to a Brahmin.' I beg you with folded hands."

I didn't want to go against the Scriptures and said, "All right, but promise not to deceive me again."

He raised his rosary hand to the sky, and then pointed to the Brahmin cow in the barn and said, "I promise, and that sacred cow is my witness."

"Let's go in the house and have some breakfast."

"Bir, I don't have time; I have to rush back to the temple. I came here to ask you one favor."

"What?"

"Do you remember the emaciated priest who attacked you?"

"Yes, what about him?"

"He's impotent and sixty years older than his child bride. With my help and God Brahma's blessings, he has a son now. He's ecstatic, and his wife has induced him to hire me as his assistant," he said. "Bir, that's the richest temple in the state, and we get tons of offerings. I'm earning more than a Deputy Commissioner."

"I'm sure you can easily do that. You are smart, and you can easily hoodwink people with your knowledge of Sanskrit, a clever Brahmin brain, and mellifluous singing. Enjoy your life."

"Thanks, everything is fine, but now I'm facing a big problem."

"What's that?"

"Bir, the old priest wants me to perform the pilgrimage to the sacred river."

"Ganges River is only twenty miles from here, and you can easily walk there and take a dip."

"I've done that many times, but those don't count. This time I have to cover the distance to the sacred river with my bare body."

"You are only five-two. Holy cow! How are you going to stretch yourself?" I snickered.

He laughed and said, "I won't extend my body, but it has to cover every inch on my way to the sacred river."

"How?"

"I have to wear nothing except a tiny loincloth, draw a line, stand in front of it, recite a prayer, prostrate on the ground with my extended arms and folded hands. Then I mark a line where the tips of my fingers touch the earth, stand up on this line, recite a mantra, and repeat this process all the way to the sacred river. After completing the ritual, I'll pray there for five days and then walk back barefoot."

"Kishan, this will kill you; you know our scorching summer sun and the burning earth."

"Yes, I know that, but I have no other choice, otherwise I'll lose my job," he said. "You're the only person, I know, who can save me from the weather and the thieves."

"How can I help?"

"Accompany me and carry water and food. If I become sick, you can bring me home."

"I can't do that; you better hire a servant."

"Bir, a hired-hand can rob me and run away. Moreover, he won't have the strength to face the thugs. Look, it's your sacred duty to help a priest; I'll pay you one hundred rupees. You'll also be able to wash your sins."

I gazed at the ceiling and suspected some kind of trap.

He again started singing in Sanskrit, of course.

"Holy Cow! What are you chanting now?"

"Any person, who denies help to a Brahmin in his sacred ritual, will end up as a fecal worm in his next birth."

I shuddered, since I firmly believed in Scriptures and transmigration. Surely I didn't want to become an insect in human stools.

"All right, I'll help you," I said. "When are we going to start?"

"Come to my home tomorrow at four in the morning and bring a satchel with your clothes, light bedding, and your stick."

We shook hands. Kishan left after blessing me and thanking me in Sanskrit. I took care of the animals and entered the house. My parents were delighted to learn about my mission and begged me to pray for them and bring a bottle of the sacred water.

I got up at three in the morning and went to Kishan's home. A huge crowd of his relatives and friends had gathered there. I took hold of Kishan's luggage, a bag of food, and some utensils. For protection against robbers, I had brought my six-foot-long bamboo stick, reinforced with brass bands, and with it I could defend myself against more than five persons.

25

Kishan was naked, except for a tiny rope covering his lingam (penis). He stood before a white line, rubbed his body with ashes brought from the temple kitchen, recited a mantra, and stretched on the ground. People shouted his praises and rained flowers on him. The worship commenced, and after walking a few yards with us, the crowd went to their homes.

Kishan took a breather after every thirty minutes, and I gave him water and fanned him. Soon the sun rose from behind the tall Himalayan Peaks and began baking the poor earth. Kishan's fair skin started turning red, and soon blisters appeared. I applied the ointment and encouraged him. We managed to cover nine miles and camped for the night. During the night, I heard him moaning with pain and mumbling something in Sanskrit.

We started early in the morning, and in ten hours we could see the shimmering line against the horizon—the sacred Ganges River. At five in the evening we entered the Hardwar City, and reached the temple. A middle-aged, bald person, with triple chin, rushed to hug Kishan; he was Kishan's maternal uncle. This person's girth was more than his height and appeared to be rolling on the ground. His white cotton dhoti, slipped from his huge paunch, and swept the floor.

He patted Kishan's shoulder and said, "I'm glad you decided to perform this sacred ritual."

Kishan introduced me to his uncle, Jagan Nath.

Jagan Nath said, "Kishan, take your friend to my home and rest. Tomorrow morning you both can assist me. My two assistants have become sick, and I'm losing my business."

"My friend isn't a Brahmin," Kishan stuttered.

"Don't worry. He will never recite any Scripture, but will eat the food. From his size, I'm sure he can eat three times more than you. Thanks for bringing him."

At four in the morning, Kishan and I took our baths with the sacred river water. Jagan Nath came, painted white lines on my forehead, gave me a thick cotton thread to wear around my neck, and I was directed to dress in a thin cotton dhoti. After dressing, I looked in the mirror and smiled—I did look like a tanned Brahmin priest. Jagan Nath, the holiest priest in Hardwar, took us to the temple on the bank of the scared Ganges River, where we joined his two assistants and sat cross-legged behind him. People came with trays, loaded with sweets, and placed those near Jagan Nath's feet. He quoted the price. After receiving and putting the money in a steel box, he asked the name of the deceased person. Then he ate one piece, chanted the name of that individual and threw water toward the sun. He told the people, who were sitting with folded hands and tearful eyes, "The deceased has received your gift, and he thanks you."

Then Jagan Nath signaled us, and we pounced upon the delicacies. The other assistants were impressed with the amount and speed at which I could consume the food. When the trays were cleared, the worshipers bowed their heads and left thanking the priest. I enjoyed costly sweets which a farmer couldn't afford to purchase, and in so doing I earned money for the priest.

One old lady, loaded with jewelry, brought a bottle of imported whisky and begged, "My husband couldn't live without his daily drink, and he must be miserable. Please deliver this bottle to him."

Jagan Nath took a sip, chanted a mantra, and said, "Your husband is delighted and thanks you. I'll convey the rest of the bottle to him during the night."

Smiles wreathed the lady's face, and she touched his feet and left singing his praises.

At sunset a huge crowd gathered with folded hands and Jagan Nath announced, "Children, rejoice. I've transported all the food to your dead relatives."

Jagan Nath's assistant stood up and said, "The holy priest has delivered all your offerings to the Heaven. I can vouchsafe for it, since the holy priest never passes any stools."

The crowd applauded and threw flowers at Jagan Nath.

Everyday Jagan Nath and his assistants sat cross-legged on the bank of the river and plied their trade. All went to the toilets and then resumed their seats, but Jagan Nath never walked to the comfort station. It appeared to be an impossible feat to me, and I started watching his movements. Jagan Nath, like other priests, took a dip in the sacred river after three hours. One afternoon, when Jagan Nath dived for his swim, I sneaked behind him. I was a good diver and could easily hold my breath under water for several minutes. I saw him swimming downstream and ducked after him. When he was far away from the worshipers, he released his loin cloth, and I saw the feces coming out of his bottom. I caught him by the neck and pointed to the floating product. He was completely stumped and begged me to swim to the opposite bank where there were no worshipers. When we sat on the embankment, he caught my feet and begged, "Don't destroy me and the faith of thousands who believe in me."

"You've been cheating."

He placed his gold necklace around my neck and said, "I beg you to have this and forget the whole thing."

I shook my head. "I don't want this necklace, but I need your help in one matter."

"What's that?"

I peered into his eyes and said, "Teach me Sanskrit."

"I can't; you're not a Brahmin."

"You disguised me in a Brahmin's dress. and I'm performing the sacred ritual. No one ever objected to it."

He closed his eyes for a few seconds. Blew out a blast and said, "I can help you, but Kishan knows your identity and that poses a big problem."

"Don't worry about Kishan; he will never be able to recognize me. I'll grow whiskers and come with identity papers of a Chaturvedi Brahmin (a Brahmin belonging highest order)."

"If you can do that, then I'll hire you as my assistant and teach you the Scriptures. You must keep the necklace as my gift, though."

We shook hands and swam back to the bank where the temple was located and resumed the worship. Jagan Nath told Kishan and his assistants, "Kishan's friend has faithfully served me. I offered him money, but he refused to accept anything. Then I ordered him to have my necklace as a gift from the temple. I'm glad he agreed."

It was a costly present. I glanced at Kishan and saw dark clouds on his face, but the fellow managed to curl his lips.

The worship period ended. I purchased one glass bottle, and filled it with the sacred river water for my parents, and we started our homeward journey. Owing to the bleeding blisters, Kishan was dragging his feet and moved at a crawling speed with my support. After covering ten miles, we reached a small village. He slumped on the ground and said, "I can't go further. Let's camp here; we'll resume our journey early in the morning. I'll purchase milk from the village, and we'll cook rice pudding. You make the chapaties."

I collected a few stones, built a chullah (open hearth), lighted wood sticks, and baked some chapaties. Kishan arrived with milk, and we cooked the rice pudding. I tasted it; it was delicious.

We ate the chapaties with mango pickle. Kishan looked at the pudding, smiled, and said, "Let's play a game."

I was surprised and growled, "What game?"

"We won't eat the pudding now, but in the morning we'll compare our dreams, and the person, who can describe the best dream, will win the game and eat the pudding."

He placed one hundred rupees on the pot and said, "Look, we'll make it more interesting by betting one hundred rupees."

I mumbled, "I only have ten rupees."

"You can bet the necklace."

I realized it was his clever trick to get the necklace. When I closed my eyes, the gears in my brain worked fast and gave me a good plan. I smiled, placed the necklace on the bills, and said, "All right, I agree."

At five in the morning, Kishan got up with a big smile. We sat cross-legged near the pudding. He started describing Heaven and how he met many gods and goddesses. He elaborated about their thrones, the assisting angels, and their transports. I was impressed; I didn't know the names of most of the gods whom he described. With a triumphant look, he asked me about my dream. I said under my breath, "I didn't have any pleasant dream."

He grabbed the necklace and the money and lifted the spoon.

At this I said, "Wait, don't remove the cover from the pot. I did have a horrible dream."

"What was it?"

"God Shiva, with his eyes shooting flames, poked his spear in my chest, and ordered me to finish the pudding and never gamble the sacred necklace. I couldn't refuse his orders; you know his cantankerous temper, and he is the most powerful god of destruction and death."

Kishan's chin fell, and with some trepidation, he handed over the necklace, cleared his throat with a painful effort and said, "I had plans to secure my uncle's necklace, but you outsmarted me this time. I never thought a simple farmer could beat a clever Brahmin."

I smashed my fist on the ground. "Well, you broke your promise and tried to cheat me again."

He dabbed his tears with the end of his dhoti and begged, "I'm sorry; please forgive me. Let's be friends."

I couldn't refuse forgiving a Brahmin, and I shook the proffered hand.

Deep in my heart, I was delighted because it was the first time in my life I could beat this crafty Brahmin and his uncle.

My Struggle to Become a Preacher

We reached Kishan's place at six in the evening. He paid my wages, and we parted with an embrace. When I entered my home, I gave the sacred water to my parents. Mom was surprised to see the glittering gold necklace around my neck and asked, "Where did you get that?"

I grinned and said, "The holy priest gave it to me for my services."

"Son, take it off; you know only a Brahmin priest or a woman can wear that. We'll keep this for your wife," she said.

I placed it around her neck and said, "The gods have arranged this for you."

I pivoted toward Dad, grabbed his hands, and said, "I have one request."

"What's that?" he asked with a surprised look.

"Now you have four more sons to help you; please permit me to chase my dream."

"What do you plan to do?"

"Become a preacher," I said.

Dad and Mom were stunned. Then I explained my scheme.

Mom wiped the tears with the end of her sari and said, "We assure you that whenever we visit your temple, we'll never reveal a word about your identity, but will touch your feet like other worshipers."

Dad was delighted. "Thanks God Brahma. My son will be a preacher and help us in the next world."

After nine months I purchased a birth certificate of a Chaturvedi Brahmin. My beard had grown to six inches and a bushy mustache concealed my lips. Completely changed in appearance, I reached Hardwar and became Jagan Nath's assistant. I worked very hard and became famous for my scholarly sermons. After eight years I was selected to head the Banaras Temple, the biggest in India. Now, as Shri Madan Lal Chaturvedi, I taught Brahmin seminary students, and my sermons at the temple drew huge crowds.

Every year I ordained more than two hundred priests, but they were all Brahmins. I longed to change the system, but couldn't stop the juggernaut. In 1940 Mahatma Gandhi started his Harijan movement against the caste system. I invited him to my temple, and he asked me to admit some non-Brahmins in my class. I accepted four non-Brahmins. The temple authorities didn't have the courage to refuse Mahatma. I steadily increased the number of non-Brahmins.

I had become the most famous and respected priest in India, and with Mahatma's help I could destroy the caste barriers for the priesthood and hundreds of non-Brahmins became preachers.

When I turned eighty, I wrote this story of my life and sealed it with instructions that it must be opened after my cremation.

On June 8, 2003, however, while I was sitting cross-legged on the bank of the sacred river, watching the setting sun, I heard the dancing ripples whispering to me, "Bir, you're ninety, and soon your ashes will join us. Wake up, get your story published. You have done nothing wrong by pretending to be a Brahmin. Rather you have lived a celibate saintly life, enlightened thousands of minds, and the details of your struggle will inspire many truth seekers."

I stood in knee-deep water and recited a prayer of thanks to Mother Nature. Then I rushed to my office and mailed this story to different magazines.

Exorcism of My Husband

125/Sector 36D, Chandigarh, India. March 9, 1962

"Your husband must see an exorcist," my friend and neighbor, Satwant, a tall white-haired lady, grabbed my hand and said.

"Why?" I asked with a puzzled stare.

"He's possessed by an evil spirit."

"Satwant, how could you conclude that?"

"Look, so far he has been madly in love with you, but today he tried to kill you. There is no other logical explanation for his bizarre behavior," she said.

"I believe he found his old flame and wants to get rid of me."

"You're wrong," she said. "Well, now tell me how this incident started."

"We were enjoying our breakfast. Suddenly he shot out of his chair, grabbed my neck, and tried to strangle me. I broke his hold and shoved him. He tumbled down on the floor, and I sprinted to my bedroom, locked it from inside, and moved the dresser against the door. He pummeled the door, shouted profanities, and pledged to kill me. After thirty minutes, he left, and it became quiet. I parted the door and heard loud snores from his bedroom. I packed my things and came to you through my back door. I'll call a taxi, go to New Delhi, stay in a hotel, and get the first flight to America."

"Look, his sudden flare, without any provocation, shows the evil spirit has captured him. You must pity the poor fellow and help him; please don't run away."

33

"Satwant, I can't delay; I'm afraid of losing my neck. I'll never see him again, and when he comes to America, he will receive the court's restraining orders and divorce papers."

"Please calm down and stay in our guest room for two days, and let's verify the whole thing. If he's not possessed, the general will drive you to New Delhi," she said. "I beg you; I love you both."

"I can't take a risk," I said. "What about Rughby attacking me in your house?"

"Impossible! Look, the general is six-seven and weighs 300 pounds, and he can lift Rughby with one hand. The general will warn Rughby who is afraid of the general's Herculean strength and volcanic temper."

"All right, I'll postpone my departure for two days," I said.

"Emily, I suspect something."

"What's that?"

"If Rughby is captured by an evil spirit, then he must be visiting his friends during the night."

"What friends?"

"Evil spirits at the cremation grounds," she said.

"It can't be true, since I've not seen him leaving from the front door of our house during the night."

"He can easily jump from the rear window," she said. "I'll request my husband, and we will watch Rugby during the coming night."

General Tara Singh, a towering giant with white beard, returned from his walk, Satwant explained her plans, and he agreed to help us.

Suddenly, there was a loud banging on the door, and the general slightly parted it.

"I've come to get the bitch," Rughby yelled.

"I don't have a dog," the general smirked.

"I meant Emily."

The general lifted Rughby in the air, swung him around, and threw him on the lawn.

"Young man, watch your tongue. Never step in my house without my invitation. If you do it again, you won't be able to walk."

Rughby turned tail and ran back to his house.

After my M.A. from Drew University, I was teaching in Cleveland High. Rughby had done his Ph.D. at Ohio State University and was teaching mathematics in the same school. He courted me for two years, and we got married in 1958. We had wonderful married life and came here on our summer vacation. We rented the furnished bungalow from a general who was visiting his sons in America. For ten days, I enjoyed the place, and then this tragedy struck me.

After dinner, the general, Satwant, and I sat in chairs on the balcony and watched Rughby's bedroom and the front gate of my house.

At midnight we saw a shadowy figure jumping out of Rughby's bedroom window, and we surreptitiously chased him. This person had Rughby's height and build, but in the darkness we couldn't clearly see the face. This individual sprinted like a rabbit that has seen the hounds, and we had a rough time to keep up with him. Somehow we managed to stick to the chase, keeping an adequate distance so as not to arouse any suspicion. When this figure entered the well-lit crossing, we recognized Rughby.

I held my breath and killed my shriek.

Rughby left the town and beelined toward the cremation grounds. On reaching there, he avoided the gate and jumped over the five-feet-high compound wall at a secluded corner. We tagged him. I was scared and grasped Satwant's hand, but the general was unfazed. He helped me and Satwant to climb the wall. We slid down on the other side and hid in the bushes, and he followed us. When we landed inside, I saw ten pyres sending curling flames mixed with smoke and sparks into the dark moon-less sky. The priests, tending the fires, were using long bamboo poles to stir the logs. The smoke and the smell of burning cadaver attacked our noses. Then I saw Rughby dashing to an unattended fire, carving out a piece of flesh from the burning corpse, sprinting to the banyan tree near the boundary wall, drawing a circle on the ground, and placing the smoldering piece in its center. The general crawled forward and could recognize the smoking piece. He skulked back and told us, "He has carved out a heart from the corpse."

Rughby removed a brick from the wall, took out a woman's dress and slipped into it. Then three horrible looking women joined him. They placed their smoldering meat in the circle and hugged Rughby. Then the group danced around the circle. In twenty minutes the dance ended, and they sat cross-legged on the ground. All picked up their pieces and started gnawing them, while smacking their lips. At that time smoke began shooting out of their ears, noses, and eyes, and they looked like a pugnacious Devils.

"Who are these women?" I inquired from Satwant.

"They are either witches who practice voodoo, or persons possessed by evil spirits."

On watching Rughby, a strict vegetarian, eating cadaver, I was terrified and a painful knot grabbed my stomach.

The three witches kissed each other and Rughby and left. Rughby changed back into his clothes, concealed the dress and the knife in the hole in the wall, replaced the brick, jumped over the wall, and sprinted toward his home. We followed him and saw him slipping into his bedroom through the open window.

I felt as if I was hit by a freight train and tears trickled down my cheeks. Satwant made tea and we sat in the living room.

"This shows Rughby is mentally sick, and I must take him to a good mental institution in the States," I said.

"That's impossible. He would refuse, and you can't carry him in chains," Satwant asserted.

"Then help me to get him treated in a mental hospital here," I pleaded.

"Trust me, he's not a mental case."

I buried my head in my hands and cried, "Oh my God! I'm completely befuddled."

The general addressed me, "Emily, don't worry, I know Principal Harbans Lal who can exorcise. I'll invite him tomorrow, and he'll treat Rughby."

"Let's have some sleep," Satwant said.

It was three in the morning, and we left for our bedrooms. I prayed and went to sleep.

In the morning, we had our breakfast at nine, and the general phoned the Principal who agreed to come at five in the afternoon.

At 4:30 p.m. the general told me, "Let me bring Rughby for the meeting."

I wondered how the general was going to accomplish it, but soon the general returned with Rughby. The general sat on the sofa, and reticent Rughby scrunched in the corner chair. Now the general, Satwant, Rughby, and I were sitting in the general's living room. Three ceiling fans were churning hot air and billowing the thin blue curtains. Framed war trophies, military awards, and five pictures of the general getting his gallantry medals from the President of India were hanging on the walls.

The doorbell chimed. The general got up from his chair and opened the door. I saw a tall, thin man in his late fifties, with white hair, moving toward us. The general made the introductions and gestured to an empty sofa. The visitor removed his sandals and sat cross-legged on it. I was impressed by the kindness and warmth in the visitor's eyes.

With hands locked behind his back, the general paced in front of us. After a couple of rounds, he stopped near Rughby, speared into Rughby's shifty eyes and said, "Look, I've invited

Principal Harbans Lal to spend a few minutes with us, and I want you to listen to what he says."

"General, I know the principal and don't want to be checked by him. There's nothing wrong with me. I've been examined by Dr. Vohra, the best in Chandigarh," Rughby snickered.

The general brushed off Rughby's remarks and said, "Rughby, now we are all going to play a simple game."

"What game?" Rughby moaned.

"We will hold five cloves in our fists."

"General, I'm in no mood to play silly games; I'm dead tired and can hardly keep my eyes open."

The general shook Rughby's shoulder and said, "Young man, you better behave. This will take only five minutes."

Rughby acquiesced with a groan.

The general requested the principal to proceed. The principal uncoiled himself, stood up, gave five cloves to each of us, and asked us to close our fists and shut our eyes. After spraying holy water on each fist, he recited some mantras in sotto voce. Suddenly I heard a thud. When I opened my eyes, I found Rughby sprawled on the floor in a lifeless form. His light brown skin had turned into a pitch-black color; his face was distorted and thick white saliva had gathered at the corners of his swollen, convulsing lips. I noticed hardly any sign of breathing, and his motionless eyes were focused on the ceiling.

I thought Rughby had a heart attack, and I rushed to help him, but the principal stopped me and said, "Don't touch him; I'll take care of him."

The principal chanted a mantra and touched Rughby's forehead. Rughby blinked and slowly his eyes came to life, and the black color of his face started fading. In a few minutes he regained his normal features and color.

I was sure this was not a hoax—Rughby could never put up this show. I was baffled and couldn't believe what I had seen.

The principal patted Rughby's back and announced, "This test has revealed to me that this young man is possessed by an evil spirit."

I grabbed Satwant's arm and asked, "What should I do now?"

The general overheard me and answered, "Emily, let's request the principal to get rid of the dirty spirit."

I nodded.

The general pivoted toward the principal and said, "Please drive out this spirit."

The principal shook his head and said, "I can't; she's too strong for me."

"All right, do you know anyone who can castigate it?" the general asked.

"Yes, the saint at Mukatsar can easily handle it. Don't delay the visit. This dangerous spirit has less than a month to complete her mission of killing its prey."

Satwant wrapped her arm around my shoulders and pleaded, "We must go there."

At this point, I was far away from my parents, relatives, and friends, and agreed to try something which I had ridiculed all my life. Rughby, however, was adamant and rebellious and shouted, "All this is absurd; I'll never go there. I'm not possessed; I need some rest."

The general eyeballed Rughby and said, "You'll go; you have no choice."

Rughby shrugged and mumbled, "Yes, general."

Rughby tried to approach me. But being afraid of the evil spirit in him, I ignored him, and the general saw him off at the door.

Next day, the car was ready for the trip. The general brought tottering Rughby and made him sit on the front seat near him, and Satwant and I occupied the rear seats. The car crawled out of the driveway. At this time a cool breeze was blowing, and the sun was hiding behind the hills. As usual the general's driver, Kalu, sang as he drove, but his singing was low-toned and depressed. He recited the names of several different gods in his singing.

After traveling for two hours on the bumpy, dusty roads, we reached Mukatsar, and the general pointed to the temple. I saw it had no domes, filigree, or decorative paintings. It was a simple, two-story, concrete structure. When we came closer, I could hear the hum of the fans and the click of the hand pumps.

Kalu parked the car under a banyan tree, and we stepped out. It was required to go barefoot, so we removed our shoes near the car. For going inside the temple, everyone had to cover their heads. Satwant gave me and Rughby scarfs; she had her dopata, and the general was wearing his turban.

After entering the arched gate, Satwant asked a volunteer, "Where can we reach the saint?"

He pointed to the steps and said, "Those steps will lead you there."

We climbed up the steps, entered a large room, and joined a long line waiting to enter a smaller room in which the saint received the patients. When our turn came, we stepped into the room and saw an old man with a long, white, flowing beard and matching turban, seated cross-legged on a marble dais. I was impressed by the glow on his face. We bowed and stood with folded hands.

The saint asked us in a soothing voice, "My children, what's your problem?"

"Holy saint, my brother is sick, and we beg for your help," Satwant replied.

The saint smiled and said, "Children, you should always beg the Almighty God. We all are beggars, and I'm one of them. Let me approach Him and find what's wrong with your brother."

Then the saint took out a bottle, gave it to Satwant, and said, "Ask your brother to fill this bottle with water from the hand pump and bring it to me."

Satwant turned to Rughby and whispered, "Go down into the courtyard, fill this bottle and hurry back."

Then she addressed the general, "You better accompany him."

Soon Rughby, escorted by the general, returned with the bottle full of water and gave it to the saint. The saint put his little finger in the bottle and said, "Let's all pray to the Almighty."

I closed my eyes and heard the ticking of the wall clock.

After meditating for five minutes, the saint gave the bottle to Satwant and said, "Child, take your brother into the meditation room. All of you sit cross-legged there, and let him take a few sips from this bottle."

We bowed and moved to a small adjoining carpeted room, sat cross-legged, and Rughby took a swig. As soon as he did this, he started talking like a woman. I recognized the voice, since I had heard it when he shouted profanities while trying to strangle me. His face became distorted, the color of his skin changed, and foam appeared on his swollen lips. This was the same face which I had seen when the principal tried his exorcism. Rughby's head started spinning like a Buddhist prayer wheel, and his body was twisting and turning.

Satwant and I ran to the saint, leaving the general to control Rughby. Satwant, with misty eyes, told the saint what had happened.

The saint said, "Child, I've found what's wrong with your brother. Don't worry, he will be over this spell in a few minutes. When he was under the spell, the spirit controlling him was communicating with me. The spirit's name is Bhagwati, and she is one of the meanest I've ever tackled."

Satwant asked, "Holy saint, how could this evil spirit manage to enter Rughby's body?"

"She was a prostitute and developed leprosy in her old age. When she died, there was no one to perform her proper cremation. The employees of the public service department dumped the corpse on the burning pyre and ran off. This unattended cremation gave a chance to a witch to steal Bhagwati's burning heart, and turn it into ashes while reciting evil tantras. Thus Bhagwati's spirit became a slave of that witch. Someone bought the ashes from that witch and gave those to your brother. Since Bhagwati led a filthy life, she won't hesitate to do any despicable thing."

"Please castigate her," Satwant pleaded.

"I will, but she will not leave with prayers and sacred water. I'll have to torture her, and this will take at least seven days. If your brother decides to get treatment here, you have to help him; he won't be able to manage by himself."

We paid our respects to the saint and rushed back to Rughby. By this time he had recovered from the spell, and Satwant narrated what the saint had told her.

"Rughby, you must come here for your treatment," Satwant asserted.

Rughby began shaking his head, while wiping the foam from his mouth. I was bewildered and sat wordless. The general grabbed Rughby's shoulders, shook them, and said, "Young man, no excuse; you're coming here."

Rughby rubbed his eyes and mumbled, "Yes, general."

Satwant looked at the general and said, "I must come with Rughby and Emily; Emily can't handle this alone."

My knees had turned into jelly, but I managed to hug Satwant and said, "Thanks, I do need your help."

"Then it's all settled, I'll accompany you, and we both will sleep on the marble floor near Rughby and work in the Langar (free kitchen). I'll also bring my maid servant, Kanta, to assist us," Satwant said.

We moved into the second hall that housed the patients and their families. There Satwant contacted the volunteer and reserved a small space where four persons could sleep. Then we left the temple, returned to the car, put on our shoes, and the homeward journey started.

Now I felt I was being sucked into strange cryptic rituals, but I didn't mind, since I was determined to save my husband.

Next morning Satwant, Kanta, the general, Rughby, and I arrived at the temple. We entered the prayer hall, and Kanta made our beds on the marble floor. Satwant looked at the clock and told me, "We better hurry to the meditation room."

We rushed to join the other people undergoing treatment. I was surprised to find a two-year-old boy talking perfect English with a British accent. I was amazed and asked Satwant to speak to the mother of the child. After meeting her, Satwant told me, "The boy can't talk even in his native language, and his parents are illiterate."

"How can he do this?" I asked.

"Simple; he's possessed by the spirit of an English woman."

At this stage, I tried to analyze the whole affair, but my mind failed to offer any logical explanation for what I had seen and heard. Definitely it was not a hoax.

We snaked through the gathering, located an open spot, and sat cross-legged on the floor. Rughby followed the saint's directions and took a swallow from the water bottle. As soon as he did this, his voice underwent a complete transformation. The evil spirit took hold of his body, and he started screaming, "I'm Bhagwati. This body belongs to me, and I'll kill any bastard who tries to expel me."

I scrutinized Rughby and found his lips weren't moving, and his face muscles were frozen, but the screams were coming from somewhere inside his chest. Two hefty volunteers rushed to pin down Rughby to stop this violent outburst, but the spirit still continued vomiting curses.

The saint arrived, placed his stick on Rughby's shoulder, and said, "Bhagwati, what are your intentions?"

The woman's voice in Rughby replied, "I've been ordered to slowly kill and am doing my job."

The saint admonished, "You should know this man is under God's protection. God is more powerful than any Devil; you can't do any harm now."

"Yes I can, I'll complete the job allotted to me," the spirit yelled.

The saint raised his stick and clobbered Rughby's back with a big force and said, "You're leaving me no alternative, but to take harsh steps. I order you to leave and spare yourself from my beatings."

On hearing the swishing sound and the thud of the stick, I glanced at Rughby's back, and saw blood dripping from red welts. He neither flinched a muscle nor showed any signs of pain. I was perplexed.

At each blow the spirit cried, cussed, and shouted profanities. After fifteen lashes, the saint again ordered her to leave, but she shouted back, "Old fool, you better open your clogged ears and listen: 'I've finished many people and am doing the same here. I'll fight you with all my strength, using all the tools of my trade. I've been given such a beautiful body to enjoy and am not going to leave. You better watch your step.'"

Suddenly we heard a distant hissing sound. The saint ran around Rughby and threw ashes from his pouch, while chanting mantras. The hissing sound became louder, and I saw a black cobra crawling toward Rughby. The stolid face of the general showed no emotion, but Satwant and I were petrified and held our breath. The black cobra came near the line and tried to jump over it. It fell back with a big thud, as if it had hit a steel wall. It moved to the right side and tried again, but collapsed, hurting itself. It attempted to enter from all directions and failed. The saint was watching all this with a smile. He touched the black cobra with his stick and scolded, "Look Bhagwati, you have seen for yourself that the power of God is much stronger than the tricks of your Devil."

The black cobra evaporated, and I heard an old woman crying, shouting, sobbing, and cussing from inside Rughby's body. I wanted to rush and hug my husband, but local customs forced me to crush my feelings. I closed my eyes and prayed. The saint asked Satwant to collect the ashes and put them in his pouch. I helped her, and she gave the bag to the saint. The session ended with a short prayer.

The saint left us to treat others. After a few minutes Rughby looked almost normal and told us, "I felt I was pushed out of my body, and an old woman had taken hold of it. I tried hard to resist, but she was too strong."

I asked, "The saint pummeled your bare back with his stick which left red welts and oozing blood. Didn't you feel any pain?"

"No, I didn't feel anything?"

Satwant questioned, "Rughby, you were talking in an entirely different dialect. I couldn't understand several words you used; where did you learn those?"

"I don't even know what I said," Rughby replied with a confused look.

He was drenched in sweat and looked depleted. Satwant and I assisted him to the bed, gave him a cold drink, and he fell into a sound sleep.

The general took his leave, and Kalu drove him back to Chandigarh.

The normal practice required the relatives of the patient to help in the Langar, while the patient was sleeping. We left Kanta in charge of Rughby and went there. When we entered a large compound, I noticed several huge brass pots cooking on wood burning brick stoves which were sending curling smoke and sparks into the air. A gangly, old man, with shoulder length white hair, greeted us with folded hands and said, "Welcome to the God's free kitchen. My name is Kundan, and I take care of this place."

Satwant said, "We've come to volunteer our services."

"God bless you. This place is run by people like you, and it daily feeds more than eight hundred persons. Let me show you around and then allot work to you."

He gave us a tour of the area and then conducted us to the place where steel dishes were being washed and said, "I request you to start washing dishes; we're short of help here."

Under the Banyan Tree

We relieved two volunteers. After two hours we were replaced by other helpers, and we returned to our resting place. Satwant recited her own prayers and told me to read the Bible which I had brought in my bag. She explained, "Prayers will help Rughby. I strongly believe there is one and only one God, and He has many assistants. He is sitting on the top of the mountain, and we are taking different paths to meet Him. Any path or action, which moves the soul to the top, is sacred, no matter in what language and under what religious guidance it is spoken. Emily, your Bible reading will certainly help you and Rughby."

I took my Bible and started reading, while Satwant recited Gurbani (Sikh scriptures). After thirty minutes, we stretched on the beds, and sleep took hold of our tired bodies.

Rughby went through three more sessions, but the beatings and prayers failed to dislodge the adamant spirit.

On the fifth session, before starting the treatment, the saint told us, "This spirit is vicious and obstinate, and I have to use red-hot rods. You will see and smell burning flesh, but you shouldn't worry. It will only hurt the spirit, and the young man won't feel any pain."

When I saw the flames shooting out from the stove which was rolled in by the volunteers, I was horrified and prayed. Several glowing steel rods were resting on the burning charcoal. Rughby sat cross-legged on the floor and took a sip from the bottle. The spirit took hold of his body, and a woman's voice started screaming and cursing. The saint pointed to the red-hot rods and said, "Bhagwati, look at those rods; they are ready for you. I'm asking you one more time. Are you prepared to leave?"

I heard a woman yelling, "No way; you old son-of-a-bitch!"

Then the saint ordered his assistants to touch Rughby's chest with the rods. I closed my eyes and heard the hissing sound of the singeing flesh and the screams of a woman. The

46

session ended after thirty minutes. The spirit was crying and fulminating, but refusing to leave. I opened my eyes, and my heart sank as I noticed burnt skin and blood on Rughby's chest. He was dazed, but showed no signs of pain. Satwant and I helped him to walk to our resting place. I applied balm on the bleeding wounds, and soon he fell asleep. We rushed to the kitchen for our volunteer work.

After two hours we returned, completely drained. We weaved around the people to reach our beds, and I was frightened to see an old witch sucking blood from Rughby's chest. I screamed, and Satwant grabbed me before I hit the floor.

"Emily, what's wrong?"

My knees were shaking, but I managed to say, "Look at Rughby. An old witch is drinking blood from his chest."

She lifted her head and glanced at Rughby. "Yes, I do see her. She's grinning with blood dripping from her lips, and her eyes are shooting fire. I'll get her."

Satwant dashed and jerked the woman's hair. The witch vanished, and Satwant's hands were covered with cobwebs.

Kanta heard my scream and sprinted to us. She saw our ghastly faces and trembled.

"Sorry, I left Rughby; I had to rush to the latrine," she stuttered

I wiped my eyes and said, "Kanta, we saw a witch sucking blood from Rughby's chest."

Kanta mumbled, "I'm very sorry."

Satwant searched around and asked, "Where are our holy books?"

"I put them in the corner while cleaning the place and forgot to bring them back."

Satwant admonished, "You made a terrible mistake, luckily we came before too much damage was done. The saint told me to keep the holy books near Rughby, and I forgot to tell you. The spirit is scared of them. In the future, never move them away from Rughby."

Kanta said, "I didn't know about that. From now on the holy books will always remain near Rughby's head."

I said, "Satwant, now I can see what was happening to poor Rughby. When he was alone, the spirit had been drinking his blood and draining his strength."

"Don't worry, we know the problem now. I'm sure the saint will get rid of the spirit, and Rughby will be your charming prince again."

Satwant and I began reading the holy books, and the livid wrinkles on Rughby's face started fading away.

The sixth session started at nine in the morning. When the spirit in Rughby's body again saw the hot rods, she cried, "This punishment is getting too much for me; I'm an old woman and can't bear it anymore. I'm willing to leave provided you meet my demand."

The saint, standing next to Rughby, asked, "What do you want?"

"Five pounds of rice pudding made with Brahmin cow's milk. Mind it—not a drop of buffalo milk."

"All right, your rice pudding will be here tomorrow at nine in the morning, and you should be prepared to leave at that time."

The spirit groaned, "Yes, I will, after I finish my pudding."

The saint turned his head toward Satwant and said, "Arrange five pounds of rice pudding and use the milk from a Brahmin cow."

Satwant bowed with folded hands and the session ended. Then we walked to the public phone near the post office, and Satwant dialed the general and said, "Good news. The spirit has agreed to leave tomorrow, but she wants five pounds of rice pudding made with Brahmin cow's milk. Don't use any other milk. Let Kalu bring it before seven in the morning."

I heard the general's jubilant voice popping out of the receiver: "Don't worry. I'll get the milk myself and have the pudding cooked in my presence. I'll bring ten pounds; the spirit may need more."

Satwant placed the receiver on the hook, and we walked back. When we entered the hall, I found Rughby dozing and joshed, "Get ready to finish five pounds of rice pudding tomorrow, so we can go home."

He grimaced. "You know I hate rice pudding; I can hardly eat a few spoonfuls. I'll never be able to finish five pounds."

"Don't worry, that isn't for you. Bhagwati wants it."

In the evening we finished our duty in the kitchen, recited our prayers, and went to sleep. I was still skeptical and couldn't believe what I had been witnessing. The whole affair appeared like a nightmare.

In the morning, the general arrived with two buckets of rice pudding covered with white sheets. He kept one bucket in the car and directed Kalu to carry the other to the treatment hall.

The general exchanged greetings with us, and we moved to the treatment area. The saint arrived, and we stood up with folded hands and lowered heads. The session started promptly at nine. Rughby took the water, and the spirit took command of his body.

The saint touched Rughby's chest with his stick and asked, "Bhagwati, are you ready to leave?"

"Yes, give me my pudding first."

The saint removed the cover from the bucket, placed it in front of Rughby, and said, "Here's your pudding. Now I want you to convince these people, particularly the American lady, that you have left this man's body."

"What proof do you want?"

"Do you see the banyan tree in front of our window?"

"Yes," the spirit smirked.

"I want you to break the top limb as you leave."

"Okay, I'll do that after finishing my pudding."

The saint said, "Bhagwati, enjoy your food."

Now Rughby started using both hands in dumping the rice pudding in his mouth. Soon he finished and even licked the bucket. There was a loud burp, and the spirit bellowed, "Watch! I'm leaving and will break the limb of the banyan tree. Tell the American lady to never doubt our existence."

After the spirit said this, I felt a blast of cold air shooting out of Rughby's body. The window flew open, and the big limb from the banyan tree crashed down. My eyes had been focused on the tree top. There was not any breeze and no animal or bird was sitting on the limb which fell on the ground. I was overwhelmed and couldn't believe my eyes. I rushed to hug Rughby, but prevented by Indian traditions, ended up holding his hands. Smiles appeared on Rughby's face, and he looked almost normal.

The saint placed his hand on Rughby's shoulder and said, "The evil spirit is gone, and you'll recover your complete health in a few hours. Remember to hold daily prayers in your home."

Satwant touched the saint's feet, and I followed her example. Rughby and the general bowed with folded hands. I donated five thousand rupees to the free kitchen. We reached the car and the homeward journey started. Now Kalu's singing could be heard for miles around. He was thanking all the gods and goddesses. I counted more than two hundred different names in his recital.

The general dropped Rughby and me in front of our house. As we entered, Rughby took me in his arms and begged with misty eyes, "Darling, I learned from Satwant that I was mean to you and even tried to kill you. I apologize; kindly forgive me."

I chuckled and said, "It was Bhagwati and not you. She gave you a tough time, too."

He turned serious and said, "In this exorcism process, there are many incidents for which I can't find a logical or scientific explanation. Thank God the nightmare is over."

"Look, there are several things which I can't understand either: your eating the rice pudding; the two year old boy talking in perfect English; your speaking like a woman; the appearance of a black cobra; the breaking of the tree limb; your feeling no pain when they scorched your skin and lashed your back. All this is beyond my comprehension. Frankly, these don't bother me at all. I'm glad you're healthy now, and the spirit has been exorcised."

The news of the exorcism reached Rughby's relatives and friends, and they all visited us. We decided to cut short our stay and leave after four days.

Next day, as we were watching the sun setting behind the hills, Rughby said, "I want to find the person who gave me the cursed stuff."

"Forget it. The longer we stay, the more we become targets of that evil individual. Let God take care of it."

Rughby took a deep breath and exhaled it with a sigh. "All right, I'll accept your advice."

Time for our departure arrived. The general, Satwant, Rughby's relatives, and several friends came to see us off at the airport. I heard the roaring engines and Pan Am took off. When we were in the air and sipping coffee, I squeezed Rughby's hand and asked, "What do you think about your exorcism?"

"After undergoing the treatment, I'm forced to conclude—the evil spirits are there, and they can capture a human body."

"Well, I used to poke fun at the people who believed in spirits and exorcism. Now I'm a firm believer and am certain that evil spirits and exorcism are facts and not fiction."

Winning the Indian Derby

March 5, 1962, Bombay, India

As a black stallion galloped across a painted white line, Baldev, a husky man with walrus mustache, clicked the stopwatch, and shouted, "Hari Krishna! Two minutes and three seconds."

He adjusted his gold necklace and inserted the stopwatch in the inner pocket of his flashing Nehru-jacket.

Though it was nine in the morning, yet the Indian summer sun was strong enough to squeeze out channels of perspiration. He wiped the sweat from his forehead with his silken handkerchief and dabbed his diamond earrings.

A pint-sized jockey returned with the horse, saluted, and said, "Maharaja Sahib, how did we fare?"

"Excellent, keep up the good work."

A flock of chirping parrots, bound for the neighbor's mango grove, flew over and deposited hot dropping on Baldev's bald head. He cursed the birds, wiped his head, and kicked the gate.

Baldev was the eldest son of the Maharaja of Barda who died in 1960, and the title of maharaja ended with his death, but Baldev still insisted that his servants must address him as Your Highness or Maharaja Sahib. Anyone who failed to do that lost his job.

He left the stables and sauntered back to his two-story brick bungalow. When he stepped in the living room, an old servant, dressed in an over-starched white uniform, rushed in, and made a deep bow. Baldev relaxed on the throne-shaped chair, and the servant removed the maharaja's shoes and socks and rubbed the feet. After a few minutes Baldev waved his arm, and the servant gently placed the feet on an ottoman and left.

The stuffed-animal-heads, popping out of the walls, stared at Baldev, the hunter who had traveled all over the world to kill them. Three ceiling fans, which keened like young lady mourners, billowed the saffron-colored curtains.

Baldev's personal assistant, Major Ram Singh, an old man with a huge paunch, entered the room, bowed with folded hands, and said, "Namaste, Maharaja Sahib."

Baldev nodded with a smile and gestured to a chair next to him, and Ram adjusted in it.

"Thanks, Your Highness."

"Ram, I've great news."

"Your Highness, what's that?"

"The black stallion, we bought yesterday, can fly."

Ram raised his folded hands to the ceiling and said, "Thank God Brahma."

"I hope the gods will help me to win the Derby," Baldev said. "Well, let's talk about Goddess Laxmi (goddess of wealth). Have you received the lease payment from American Hilton Hotels?"

"Yes, your Highness. I got the check yesterday and deposited it in your account in the Bombay Bank."

"Fine, I'm distressed in leasing the Marble Palace where I was born and raised, but I've no other choice."

"Your Highness, it, too, breaks my heart, but we can't afford to keep it. The electric bill is more than twenty thousand rupees per month, and the maintenance staff costs more than eighty thousand."

Baldev took a deep breath and released it through his pursed lips. "I had five passions: hunting; racing cars; pretty foreign women; mujra parties; and horse racing. I gave up all except horse racing. Then to chase my dream of winning the Derby, I left Barda and bought this bungalow near the

Bombay racetracks. It was tough, but I'm slowly getting used to it."

"Your Highness, you made the right decision."

"I could have easily won the Derby before 1947, when we had fast horses and unlimited resources."

"Your Highness, your father, God bless his soul, was a pious man and believed that the Scriptures spoke against horse racing and betting."

"Yes, he was religious and orthodox. Well, do you have anything else to discuss?"

"Yes, Your Highness, yesterday when you were out, the Maharaja of Nabha called."

"Holy cow! What did he say?"

"Your Highness, he wanted to fix the marriage date for his daughter."

"I don't like this setup, made by my father, but I'll honor my father's promise. The marriage, however, has to wait till I win the Derby. Can you make some excuse to postpone it?"

"Your Highness, it won't be easy. Last time I promised him that you wouldn't delay it again."

"Make some sort of excuse about my birth stars."

Ram rubbed his head for a few seconds. "Your Highness, I think I can manage it by sending our astrologer who is a smooth-talker. I, however, request you to get married after the Derby."

"All right, I'll get hitched then," Baldev groaned. "Let's focus on racing. Well, I've heard Nathu is a big man in the horse racing. Do you remember him?"

"Your Highness, how can I forget. I hired him in 1918, after we lost two food-tasters from food poisoning. He was an obsequious sycophant and could easily win favor with your father. For twenty years he milked more than eight hundred people in the palace and then left."

"What a fickle karma! When Nathu worked as our servant, every morning he used to touch my feet. Now he's the richest man in India and lives in a palatial home with many servants."

"Your Highness, everything is preordained by our stars. Do you know he was a loan shark?"

Baldev shook his head.

"Your Highness, he didn't have any family. He ate at the palace and invested all his salary in loans to others. He charged horrendous rates: He told borrowers, 'I charge a nominal interest of one passa per day for a one rupee loan.' On hearing one passa, people fell into his trap and ended paying more than three hundred percent annual interest. He could also bamboozle several concubines, and they were forced to sell their jewelry to him at dirt cheap prices to pay for their loans."

"I remember, he painted three white lines on his forehead and posed as a pious person. I can't understand why he's indulging in this sinful horse racing."

"Your Highness, to make money. He'll even go to Hell, if he sees gold there."

"Do you know anything about the horse he is entering this year?"

"Your Highness, he met me at the temple and was boasting about his new white stallion, Agni."

"Can that horse run faster than my black horse?"

"Your Highness, I don't know much about horse racing, but can check for you."

"Look, today my horse ran one mile in two minutes and three seconds. His brown horse won the race last year in two minutes ten seconds. Find out how fast his Agni is."

"Your Highness, I'll drive to his place and check his stables."

"Wish you good luck," Baldev said. "All right, you're excused."

Ram stood up, bowed, and left.

Ram returned after one hour and found Baldev studying horse- racing news. He bowed and said, "Your Highness, bad luck."

"Spit it out."

"Your Highness, Agni can run one mile is less than two minutes, and it'll beat our horse."

Baldev's chin fell, and he started pacing the room. Suddenly, he stopped and said, "I want to win the Derby, and this may be my last chance. Can you do something?"

"Your Highness, I'm at your service."

"Do you know any witch who can destroy his horse by her Tantras (black magic)?"

"Yes, Your Highness."

"Then use her."

"Your Highness, give me two days."

"Go ahead and hurry up."

Ram made a deep bow and left.

For two days Baldev anxiously waited for the results of the black magic. On the third day Ram reported, "Your Highness, I bought a potion from the witch at the cremation grounds and sprayed it on the stable wall. But it failed to work."

"Why?"

"Your Highness, Nathu has a priest who chants prayers after throwing sacred water on the horses, and the evil spirits can't go near them."

"Then kill his horse."

Ram held his breath. "Your Highness, we've limited resources, and we're not above the law now."

"Then do it surreptitiously."

"Your Highness, before 1947, I could have eliminated any person within two hours. Now it will need some tact and time to kill this dumb animal."

"Go to the temple and seek help from the gods."

"Your Highness, I'll go there and then rush to Nathu's stables."

Ram left and returned with disappointed looks.

"Well, did you have any luck?"

"No, Your Highness, bad kismet. Disguised as a beggar, I took a poison packet, and tried to slip into Nathu's stables, but was stopped by his guards."

"There must be some way to handle him. He has won the Derby five times. You were his boss; can you induce him to skip this year?"

"Your Highness, he's a tough nut, but I'll try my best. He might have some gratitude for the largesse shown to him by your father."

Ram drove to Nathu's place, returned after three hours and reported, "Your Highness, Nathu is an avaricious, heartless skinflint. I requested him to let the Maharaja win the Derby, but he shook his head. I offered him a handsome bribe, but he refused to accept it."

Baldev closed his eyes and rubbed his forehead. After a few seconds he blinked with a smile and said, "All right, meet him again and arrange a card game with him."

"Your Highness, where do you want to play this match?"

"In the Mud Palace. Nathu would love to sit at an equal level with me at a place where he served as a servant."

Ram's mouth flew wide open, and he mumbled, "Your Highness, I hate to say that Nathu is a smart player and will easily beat you. Moreover, he never plays without a wager."

"I'll gladly make a bet."

"Your Highness, what do you have in mind?"

"The loser won't enter his horse in the Derby."

"Your Highness, this won't induce him, since he's sure of winning the card game and the Derby."

"Then tell him that if I lose, I won't enter my horse and will give him the Royal Necklace."

Ram's face turned ghastly pale, and he stammered, "Your Highness, not the Royal Necklace. It's worth crores (millions) of rupees and is your sacred trust."

"Don't worry, I'm not a bad player; I hope to beat him, win the Derby, and achieve my dream."

Ram acquiesced, drove to Nathu's place, and arranged a match which was to take place after fifteen days in the Mud Palace.

Baldev left Bombay, moved to the Mud Palace, hired one smart fellow as his punkhaman (fan bearer), and spent all his time playing cards with him.

Fifteen days flew away and the day for the match arrived. Nathu, a hunchbacked old man wearing a white cotton dhoti, came in his limo to the Mud Palace and kissed the ground from which he had sucked his wealth. This palace had no electricity since Baldev's grandfather had refused the introduction of the devil's contraption, and pankhamen were used to fan the maharaja and his guests.

Ram escorted Nathu to the living room. This room had freshly painted cow dung on the walls which were covered with gold framed paintings of several different gods. A marble statue of god Shiva stood in the corner. Nathu touched the statue's feet and then shook hands with Baldev. They sat cross-legged on thick rugs. A punkhaman stood behind each player and slowly waved the matted fan with one hand.

"Before I start the game, I want to see the Royal Necklace," Nathu said.

 Baldev took out a huge, diamond studded necklace from his pocket and placed it in front of Nathu. Nathu's beady eyes sparked; he chanted a mantra, and the game started. Ram and Nathu's beautiful, young secretary sat down at some distance and watched the show.

Nathu won the first two games and had to win the next game to win the match. Ram's heart sank to the bottom of the Indian Ocean, and he fervently prayed to the gods. He had given his pledge to the late Maharaja that he would take care of his prodigal son, and he was looking at the impending disaster.

Baldev's face was covered with beads of sweat, and he wiped his forehead with the back of his hand. At this, the punkhaman in front of him touched his nose with one hand. The third game started and Baldev won. Then the other two games lasted for a long time, and in the end Baldev managed to prevail. Baldev picked up the Royal Necklace, placed it around his neck, and said, "Nathu, it was my lucky day. The goddess of luck stood right in front of me and guided all my moves."

Nathu wiped his tears with the end of his dhoti and lamented, "The goddess did favor you, and you won the bet. I promise not to enter my Agni."

"Look, I want to be one hundred percent sure about your horse not competing in the race."

"I'm a man of my word," Nathu asserted.

"Then you won't mind if I bring your horse to my stables and return it to you the next day. Your trainer can sleep near it."

Nathu closed his eyes and began scratching his ear. On noticing Nathu's hesitation, Baldev handed over the Royal Necklace to him and said, "Keep this as insurance, and I'll retrieve it after returning your horse."

Nathu placed the Royal Necklace around his neck and grinned. "All right, I agree; my Agni will easily win next year. I give you one tip."

"What's that?"

"I've heard the horse owned by the Birlas is faster than your horse; try to purchase their jockey."

Baldev nodded with a smile.

"Okay, I wish you good luck," Nathu said and scrambled up with Baldev's assistance.

While holding his secretary's arm, Nathu entered his limo which shot out of the palace, leaving behind a tail of dust and smoke.

After Nathu left, Major Ram Singh said, "Your Highness, I'm glad you could win, but you took a big risk."

Baldev chuckled. "No risk at all."

"Frankly, Your Highness, I don't get it."

"The whole scheme was all well planned and perfectly executed. The punkhaman facing me was trained by me, and he signalled the cards in Nathu's hands by touching his lips, hair, eyebrows, forehead, et cetera. When I wiped my forehead with the back of my hand, he acknowledged the signal and started working. I could have easily won in a few minutes, but I prolonged the game to make Nathu feel comfortable and avoid any suspicion."

"Your Highness, I'll go to the temple and pray for forgiveness for this sin."

"There's no sin on my soul."

"Your Highness, how?"

"Look, I told the truth to Nathu—the goddess of luck stood before me and managed my every move."

"Your Highness, you're right; I do remember you telling this to him. But our horse is still facing a challenge from Birlas' horse."

Baldev winked with a grin and said, "I've a solution for that, too."

A day before the Derby, Baldev brought Agni to his stables, and Nathu sent his trainer with the horse. In the evening Ram gave a bottle of rum, laced with soporific material, to Nathu's trainer. Next day Baldev and Ram came to the stable early in the morning, while Nathu's man was snoring, and worked on Agni. Nathu's trainer got up at ten and saw the black stallion leaving the stables. He didn't check his horse which was housed at the distant end of the stables and sprinted to the racetracks; he had laid heavy bets.

At the Maha Laxmi Racetrack, all saw Baldev's black horse, entering the race and Nathu's white horse, Agni,

missing. They learned Agni was sick, and Nathu had
withdrawn it. Nathu stayed home, since he couldn't bear the
pain of watching another horse winning the Derby. Thousands
cheered, yelled, and screamed as Baldev's black horse won the
race by six lengths, breaking the track record. The band
played, cameras flashed, and many congratulated Baldev.
Next day Baldev's picture with his winning horse appeared on
the front pages of all the Indian newspapers.

Nathu's trainer was devastated, since he suffered heavy
losses at the races. He slipped back to his cot in Baldev's
stables and found a bottle of imported whisky near his bed. He
finished the bottle and turned to stone.

After the victory celebrations, Baldev brought the winner to
the barn near his house. He gave big rewards to his jockey,
trainer, and the stable boy, who were in his loop. They took
the winner to the shower and scrubbed hard to wash off all the
black color. Then they wiped it thoroughly so that there was
no trace of the black charcoal paint. Baldev thanked the
goddess and enjoyed a sound sleep.

Next morning Nathu came in his limo, returned the Royal
Necklace, and his staff took away his horse and its trainer.
After they left, Baldev patted Ram's back and said, "I have
achieved my dream. Let's go to the temple and thank the
goddess."

After Baldev and Ram returned from the temple, Baldev
said, "Ram, no more racing for me; I can't afford it. Sell the
horses and this bungalow, and we'll move to the Mud Palace
in Barda and take care of the family farm."

"Your Highness, should I call the Maharaja of Nabha?"

"Go ahead. I'm above forty, and it's high time to get
married and produce an heir to the throne."

My Search for Nirvana

March 29, 1917. Shiv Temple, Utter Pardesh, India

"It hurts my Lulli," I cried, as my dad fixed a gold statue on my lingam (penis).

He patted my back and said, "Calm down, son, you have to go through this sacred ritual."

"Why?" I moaned.

"Look, you're the son of the head-priest of Shiv Temple, and our god wants us to wear his statue."

"Dad, I can hang this from my neck."

"No, the neck is not the proper place for it. For eons your ancestors had practiced this, and you have to follow their footsteps."

I wiped the tears with my knuckles and said, "I don't like it; it hurts."

"When you become eighteen-years-old, I'll explain everything to you about this ritual. Meanwhile, you have to wear this ornament during your worship at the temple; get used to it."

I was four-years-old and had no other choice, but to crunch my teeth and tolerate the pain. Dad was built like a bull and was quick to use his whip. He helped me in tying my dhoti, and I sat cross-legged near God Shiva's statue.

Two years slipped away. I reached the age of six and joined the public school. In our land of rigid caste barriers, I was lucky to be born as a high caste Brahmin, Chateurvedi, meaning master of all four vedas. I was seated in the front row near the teacher, and the back rows were reserved for lower castes. When I was not permitted to play any contact games, I felt disgusted. I was told that the gods gave me a sacred body, and I can't contaminate it by touching a Sudra.

One evening I asked my father. "Dad, why can't I play with Sudras?"

"They are untouchable!"

"They're not sick and look like us. Why are they untouchable?"

"Son, the gods gave them a lower caste, and it's a great sin to touch them."

"You told me that god Brahma created all of us from the same material."

"Yes, he did, but some objected to what God Brahma had made them. This annoyed our god, and he punished them by turning them into Sudras, and they have to atone for their sin by serving the higher castes," Dad smirked. "Well, don't pollute your mind with this rubbish about equality. The gods have laid down the rules, and we have no right to question them."

I was not satisfied with the Dad's explanation. But when I saw his fiery eyes, I succumbed and said, "All right, I'll be careful and avoid Sudras."

The best student in my class was Kalu, a Sudra. I sought his help with my homework, and he protected me from the class bullies; we became friends. One day on the way to school, I held Kalu's hand, and a member of our temple congregation saw us and reported this to my father.

In the evening, when Dad came home for his dinner, he was erupting like a volcano. Without questioning me, he laid me on his lap and grabbed his whip.

"You touched a Sudra and are going to destroy the sacred Brahmin family," he yelled.

"Forgive me, I'll never speak to him again," I cried.

"You have to be punished," he shouted.

63

I closed my eyes, heard the swish, and felt sharp pain as the whip landed on my bottom. After ten swipes, he laid me on the floor.

"Rub your nose on the ground," he shouted.

I began drawing lines with my nose.

After I had rubbed my nose twenty times, he flicked sacred water over my body, chanted a mantra, and said, "Go to your room and remember your punishment."

While wiping my tears with my knuckles, I shambled to my room, and Dad ambled to the temple, chanting mantras.

For several days I found it difficult to sit on my seat. I never again spoke to my friend, Kalu.

After school hours, I studied Scriptures from the temple priests. By the time I turned fifteen, I had read all the Scriptures and could easily perform the temple services. One morning Dad told me, "Bir, from tomorrow onwards, I want you to help me with the evening worship."

"Yes, sir."

So I began conducting the temple services. A gorgeous girl, who was a few years older than me, always came to the temple at the time I was on duty. When she gave me her offering for the god, she always managed to touch my hand. Her smile, the exotic perfume, and her touch, shot electric currents through my body, and I winked at her. One day, when I was passing through the dark alley of the temple, she grabbed me in her arms and kissed me. I was astounded, but felt a great thrill in my heart; I kissed her back. After that we started meeting in the dimly lit corner of the temple. Our good days, however, didn't last long: Dad saw me smooching her.

One evening, as I reached home after performing the temple service, I found Dad was waiting for me. Without saying a word, he conducted me to the prayer room in our house. I saw flames shooting from his red eyes, and he was fiddling with the whip. I had grown taller and stronger than him, and stared back at him with a rebellious stance. He dropped the whip and said, "Sit down, you dumb idiot."

I sat at his feet. He placed his hand on my shoulder and said, "I saw you messing with a girl in the temple."

"Dad, I was not messing: I was just explaining the Scriptures to her."

"Damn it! You were kissing. I saw this with my own eyes."

"I'm sorry."

"Stop doing that. I warn you that fornication is a great sin, and the gods will punish you for that."

"How can the gods do that?"

"They will make you a larva in the human stools in your next birth."

I shook my head. "I can't understand this."

"Millions of years ago, the gods formed 8.4 million species, placed them on the earth which they had made, and gave them souls. The soul starts from a microbe life, slowly advances to animal life, and finally enters a human body. If, as a human being, you do evil things, then you're punished and sent to the lower form of life."

It was hard for me to accept this, since I had studied the Darwin Evolution Theory at school. I closed my eyes and became reticent.

Dad's yell: "Don't go to sleep," landed me back to face my problem. I opened my eyes and noticed his flinching face muscles.

I knew it was impossible for me to explain that I liked the girl and there was nothing beyond kissing, so I chose to make peace with him. "Dad, I'm sorry; I'll never kiss any girl again."

Dad sprinkled sacred water over my head, chanted a mantra, and said, "Your sin is absolved. Look, after two years you will be eighteen, and you'll have a wife. Then you can perform your conjugal duties and kiss her as much as you want."

During all the years of my working in the temple, I was not allowed to perform Shivling worship in the basement. I had seen Dad taking the ladies there for twenty to thirty minutes. My curiosity piqued. I hid behind sacks of corn stacked in the corner of the basement room and held my breath. Soon Dad entered with a young girl, locked the door, bowed his head to a cylindrical marble stone, and placed flowers over it. Then he threw away his dhoti and stood stark naked. I was stunned. After removing the golden statue hanging from his lingam, Dad patted his lingam which shot up to an enormous size. The lady kissed his lingam and removed her sari. He recited a mantra and entered her body. After twenty minutes, he washed the lady's pudenda with sacred water, kissed her, and said, "With the blessing of God Shiva, you're sure to get a son."

The lady thanked him with a big smile and tied her sari. Dad began chanting mantras, opened the door, and climbed the steps. The lady followed him with folded hands.

After watching this, I was completely devastated: My dad, the revered head priest, was fornicating in the temple. A few months ago he had strongly condemned my kissing. I couldn't believe my eyes and ears.

Now a big tornado churned my heart and a painful knot grabbed my stomach. I came out from my hiding and slipped back to my duty. It took me six days to simmer down, and then I decided to question Dad about this strange affair. I concluded if I failed to get a convincing explanation, I would leave this hypocritical profession and search for Nirvana. One evening after the prayers I asked my dad, "I've some questions."

"About what?"

"Your worship in the temple basement," I replied.

"Well, it's a sacred ritual of worshipping God Shiva's lingam."

"No, it is copulation."

He scrunched his face to control the throbbing muscles and said, "Why do you say that?"

"I've seen the whole affair with my eyes."

"When?"

"Six days ago, when you took a young girl wearing a blue sari to the basement."

"Impossible, the door was closed."

"Dad, I was hiding behind the corn sacks."

He turned ghastly pale and said, "Well, this is a duty allotted to us by the gods. I wanted to explain this, after you became eighteen-years-old and got married. Your lingam is being prepared for that, and that's why you were made to were a gold statue which pulls it down and extends its size. All right, you only saw me performing my scared duty."

"What's sacred about it?"

"This holy ritual helps the impotent and sick husbands and their families. A woman can't get a divorce even if her husband is impotent, sick, or in jail. This woman comes to the temple for help. She gets a child without any guilt on her soul and isn't condemned by the society. It hurts no one, but helps all the parties involved."

"What were you doing with the cylindrical stone?"

"It's not a stone, but a part of God Shiva's lingam. I invoke its blessing and perform my noble duty."

"Dad, how can this stone be a part of our god?"

"Let me explain its history: Once God Shiva, our powerful god of destruction, came to his bed and found his wife, Parvati, in a bad mood—she had a terrible headache. He, however, wanted to have fun and started fondling her breasts. She shot out of the bed and flew toward Heaven. He was not interested in getting up from the soft bed and chasing her. So he started extending his lingam which became many miles long and penetrated Parvati's body. Dangling in air in an awkward posture, she cried with pain. When god Vishnu, the preserver of the world, noticed her terrible suffering, he threw his weapon which broke the lingam into millions of pieces and

67

those turned into stones. The stone we have in the basement is one of them."

I was perplexed, but couldn't question this mythology and get into more trouble. So I said, "Thanks, Dad, for explaining this."

"Well, next year I'll prepare you for this part of your duty."

"How are you going to do that?"

"You'll be given a potent medicine which is rich in zinc, and your lingam will be rubbed with a special oil. You'll have a wife to practice this ritual. You'll relieve me from some of the basement worship: I'm getting too old to handle so many worshipers."

So far I was virgin, and this completely befuddled me. "Thanks Dad, for enlightening my mind," I said, bowed my head, and left.

I continued spying on Dad's basement worship and was amazed at his hypocrisy: When an ugly woman came for worship in the basement, he simply rubbed the stone on her private part, threw sacred water, and blessed her with loud chants. The worship was entirely different for a pretty woman.

Now I felt sure that we, the Brahmin priests, were cheating the world and ourselves. I could never take his place and do this type of Shivling worship and preach hatred for a fellow man. I wanted enlightenment, so I decided to run away and search for Nirvana. One night I left a note on my bed and disappeared.

I traveled to Patna, Bihar, and from there took a bus to Sanchi Hills. For a few days I prayed on the banks of the Sacred Ganges River near the place where the Bodhi Tree used to exist, and Buddha received his enlightenment under that fig tree. Then, like him, I moved to the place which had barren, black, granite hills. It was summer and the temperature rose above 120 degrees. There were hot springs which threw steam in the burning air, and the place looked like Hell. I could see why Buddha chose this site to torture his body. There was only one cold water spring, and I camped near it. Every other day I found an old man with white beard coming to fill his pitcher. This man had a rare glow on his face, and I decided to seek his advice. I grabbed his feet and begged, "I'm searching Nirvana, but don't know how to proceed."

"Come along with me," he said.

I followed him, and we reached a place where there were four thatched huts. He entered his hut, sat cross-legged on the floor, and gestured me to sit in front of him.

"What do you know about Nirvana?" he questioned.

"Nirvana is the salvation of the soul."

"Yes, that's a Hindu definition called Mokhsha or Mukti. Lord Buddha, however, defines it as achieving a state in which you rise above human passions. It's an enlightened state of mind which can be attained by defeating the five enemies: lust, anger, greed, pride, and attachment to the worldly things. In your battle you must have proper belief, aspiration, speech, action, livelihood, effort, thought, and meditation, to tackle them."

"How can I achieve all this?" I questioned.

"Practice perfect self-control, seek unselfishness, knowledge, and enlightenment."

"What if I fail?"

"You won't, if you follow Lord Buddha's instructions."

"What are those?"

"Torture your body to subdue the wild soul. When you achieve Nirvana, your heart will be filled with love that knows no anger, hatred, or ill will, and you'll do good to God's creatures and love your enemies."

I folded my hands, bowed, and said, "Can I camp near your place?"

"I've three other disciples and you can join them. We've strict rules here, and if you break them, we'll ask you to leave."

69

I touched his feet and left. I returned with my backpack, built my hut, and the old man became my Guru. Next day I began torturing my body. I fasted and ate a few parched grams every other evening and focused on the Almighty. In one month I lost thirty pounds; my soul, however, felt much better. I prayed naked in the burning heat in front of a fire. After ten months I felt the presence of God near me, and noticed Him in the humming flies and the stinging mosquitoes.

I met the other three disciples, but all observed silence and rarely spoke with each other. One of them was Gopi who was my age and looked like my twin brother. I liked him, and we became friends.

After four years I told my Guru, "I think I've achieved Nirvana and would like to go back to the world and preach."

"Come with me, we'll worship at Devgari Temple on the bank of the Ganges River, and I'll give my decision after our trip."

Next morning Guru and I undertook our journey. We were wearing torn saffron robes and carried our water and food in bags. We covered twenty miles. One evening, as we were passing through a large town, I saw a ruby, glimmering under the rays of the moon. When I stooped down and tried to pick it up, my hands were dirtied with the spit of a person who had chewed a betel leaf.

He noticed me and remarked, "You have failed in one test."

"Guru, I never wanted it for myself, but chose to secure it and give it to the poor and needy."

"Son, when you achieve Nirvana, a ruby is like any other stone, and you never bother about it."

"I'm sorry."

We resumed our journey. He flicked his rosary, and I tried to concentrate on the Supreme Power. When we reached the river, we saw a beautiful damsel, seated on the bank. She sobbed with tears running down her cheeks. When she saw us, she rushed to us and begged with folded hands, "My husband was to come here, but he hasn't arrived. I don't know how to swim and can't cross the river. If I remain on this bank, I'll be eaten by the wild animals. I beg you to help me."

I ignored her, but my Guru asked the girl to ride on his shoulders. The girl sat on Guru's shoulders and embraced his head. He swam ahead of me, deposited the girl, and walked away without saying a word.

I hadn't experienced the touch of the fair sex for many years and wondered how my Guru felt, while the girl's soft thighs wrapped around his neck. I thought he should have avoided this temptation.

"You shouldn't have bothered about carrying that woman," I said.

"For me she was like a bundle of hay. I dumped her and never thought about it again. You're still carrying her in your mind. When you achieve Nirvana, a woman will be like a sack of potatoes for you. You won't be bothered by her touch and won't mind helping her. Son, you have to work harder to achieve your goal."

We prayed at the temple and returned to our huts. I had failed and realized that I still had to cover a long distance.

One day while meditating, I heard Gopi's shrieks, sprinted to him, and found he had been mauled by a tiger. I carried him to the Guru's hut and laid him on the floor. The Guru placed his hand on Gopi's head and said, "Son, time for you to meet Lord Buddha."

Gopi grabbed my hand and begged, "Please cremate me and carry my ashes to my mother and wife. It will give peace to my soul and solace to my family. My house is in Palka Village, and the diary in my hut gives the details about my life; I intended to write my biography after attaining Nirvana."

I looked at my Guru, who nodded, and I gave my promise to Gopi.

There was contentment on Gopi's face, and he smiled as his spirit left his body. We collected a pile of wood. Gopi's body was reduced to ashes, and I packed those in a small cotton bag.

Next day, I recovered the diary from Gopi's hut, skipped through it, and began my trek to Gopi's village. I covered forty miles in two days and entered Palka. When I stopped at the public well, I was surprised to find the people, who stood near it, greeted me with folded hands. The leader said, "Gopi, great to see you back. Your family needs you."

"What is the problem?" I asked.

"Your house and land are to be auctioned tomorrow."

"Why?"

"After you left, your father-in-law mortgaged them. He couldn't pay back the loan, so those will be auctioned."

"I never gave him the right to mortgage my property."

"Then you can easily stop the auction."

"Thanks, I'll meet the judge tomorrow."

While I was moving inside the village in my saffron robe, people bowed their heads with folded hands. Now I was in a big fix—how to locate Gopi's house. Chanting mantras, I walked slowly in the street and prayed for Divine help. Suddenly a seven year old boy ran toward me, grasped my legs, and said, "Dad, you're back."

I lifted the child and said, "Let's go home."

The child hugged my neck and said, "I missed you very much."

After two minutes, he pointed to a wooden gate in a six-foot-high mud wall. When I opened the gate, an old lady ran to me, grabbed me in her arms, and said, "Son, the gods have brought you back. Had you not come, we would have become homeless tomorrow. Now you can save us."

She kissed my forehead, and I felt her hot tears on my face.

We entered the house, and I sat on the string cot. I drank cold water to push down the frog in my throat.

A beautiful woman, in her early thirties, rushed in and touched my feet.

"Swami, thanks for coming to your family."

I patted her head and said, "I'm back, and Lord Buddha's blessings will be with you forever."

Then I addressed the mother, "Look, I've taken a pledge of celibacy and will stay here only if I'm allowed to sleep in the barn and keep my promise to Lord Buddha."

"Son, we will help you. We need you here," the mother said in a firm voice.

The wife wiped her tears. "I agree, I'm glad you're alive, and I can wear the red mark on my forehead."

"Ramu mortgaged your land and told the people that he knew where you were meditating, and he obtained your signatures," the mother explained.

I'd never seen Ramu coming to our camp, so I said, "He never met me and simply forged my signature. I'll meet the judge and save our property."

"What about Ramu?" the mother asked.

"We'll forgive him."

Then I saw an old man jumping the wall and running away.

She pointed to the sprinting figure and said, "There goes Ramu; grab his neck."

"Forgive him, and let God take care of him."

My wife came with a basin of cold water and washed my feet. After dinner, I went to the barn with Gopi's diary and thoroughly studied the details about Gopi's birth, growing up, and his renouncing his home. Now I was fully prepared to act as Gopi and save a family.

I placed my string cot near the snoring buffaloes and went to sleep. Next morning I met the judge who canceled the mortgage, and I didn't press charges against Ramu. Surreptitiously, I walked to the river and dumped Gopi's ashes with a prayer.

Soon I was plowing the fields with placid, cud-chewing buffaloes. It was a bone-breaking job which was difficult for a Brahmin, like me. Daily I got up at three in the morning, yoked my buffaloes, and God gave me the strength to draw perfect lines while tilling the land. Though my body took care of the fields, crops, and animals, yet my mind was always in perfect tune with God.

After the day's hard work, I cleaned the village bathing places, and helped in the temple kitchen. I still wore my saffron robe, and the villagers came to seek my help in their mental and spiritual problems. I came home late, touched the mother's feet, patted the wife's head, hugged the son and helped him with his homework.

After dinner, I moved to the barn and communicated with God. Now I felt love, joy, contentment, and peace filling my heart: I was not attached to any worldly thing; the gorgeous woman didn't arouse my passions; the hard life and body torture didn't bother me; my soul always felt the presence of God; I had no enemies, and I loved and served all creatures.

I had achieved Nirvana.

Reincarnation

Thati Village, Punjab, India.

"Oh, my God! That man is torching my son," my wife, Emily, screamed, as a tall priest with flowing white beard lighted a cluster of hay and thrust it into the pyre.

I grabbed her trembling hand and struggled to stifle my tears. Tongues of flames shot out of the logs, and crackling sparks mixed with smoke twisted toward the sky. Two hundred relatives and friends, who had gathered around us, moaned: Men whimpered under the tent of their hands, and the ladies cried while beating their chests. The priest circled the pyre and threw cow's butter over the hungry flames.

When the roaring flames swallowed the shroud and engulfed the corpse, Emily tottered and swooned. I caught her before she hit the ground and gently laid her down. My sister rushed with a glass of water from the nearby hand-pump, and I sprinkled cold water over Emily and fanned her. After a few minutes, Emily shuddered, and fountains of tears gushed out from her deep blue eyes. I tried to talk to her, but she had turned into a statue.

The idiosyncratic chants of the priest, the raging fire consuming my son, the wailing crowds, and the sight of my agonizing wife shattered my heart. A big knot grabbed my stomach, my mouth went dry, and I felt like sinking in a quagmire.

I took a deep breath, released it through pursed lips, and asked my younger brother to sprint to the barn and bring the tractor-trailer. In ten minutes the tractor arrived. I lifted

Emily, adjusted her in the trailer, placed her head on my thighs, and fanned her. The noisy tractor moved over the bumpy mud roads, and its jolts shook the bones. I looked at Emily: She was still dazed and didn't utter a single word. I held her hand with tears in my eyes, but there was no response. It appeared to me that a huge chasm had opened between us. I begged for God's help.

The tractor reached the family home, and I carried Emily inside the bedroom. There were no cots, since according to our mourning customs those along with the other furniture had been stacked in the barn. My sister rushed to spread a sheet on the floor. I gently laid Emily on it and propped her up with several pillows. Then I sprinted to the kitchen and brought a glass of cold skimmed buttermilk, and my sister assisted me in forcing Emily to consume it. After five sips, Emily opened her eyes, sat up, and cried hysterically with choking hiccups. I held her shoulders, but didn't restrain her from crying, since I was sure this emotional eruption would serve as a safety valve for her pent-up emotions. I squeezed her hand, and she recognized me. I laid her back and began waving the matted fan over her.

"Thank God, Emily is feeling better. Now you take care of her, and I'll join mother," my sister said and left the room.

I continued fanning Emily, and after fifteen minutes she adjusted her shoulder-length blond hair and asked, "Where are the ladies?"

I was delighted to hear her voice and replied, "They are in the living room."

"What are they doing?"

"Keening."

"I want to join them," she raised her chin and said.

"Emily, you can't."

"I will; they are mourning for my son."

"All right, I'll take you there, but promise to watch them and pray."

"Okay, let's go."

I helped Emily to stand up, escorted her to the living room, and we sat cross-legged on the floor and observed the keening ritual; my mother and sister took turns to lead the group. The leader sang praises of the deceased and let out a shriek. Then the ladies moved in a circle behind the leader, while wailing and pummeling their chests. After five rounds, they paused for a few seconds. Then the leader sang another eulogy, and the group started pulling their hair. In a similar manner they slapped their cheeks and thighs. It was painful torture, and I saw blood oozing from their cheeks, and their blouses were soaked in sweat and blood. Emily watched them with tearful eyes.

"They are hurting themselves. Can't you stop them?" she asked.

"No, it will break the traditions and their hearts."

I noticed Emily's quivering hands and the tremor in her voice and said, "Well, you have participated in the mourning; time for you to take some rest."

She groaned, but I pulled her up, forced her to walk back to the bedroom, and laid her on the sheet.

She sighed. "My heart has been shattered."

"We lost our only child; I'm devastated, too," I said. "Well, I warned you about the hot weather and the mosquitoes, and requested you to leave Timmy with your parents."

"I regret, but it was my dumb idea to bring Timmy here to see his father's parents."

"Don't blame yourself. All this was written in our karma," I said. "Anyhow, my parents were ecstatic, and Timmy enjoyed riding the horse and the camel."

"Yes he did, but you shouldn't have cremated his body here," she moaned.

I grabbed her hands and pleaded, "When we married, we promised to respect each other's faith and never try to proselytize. I went to your church, and you visited my Gurdwara (Sikh temple). My parents wanted to perform the cremation with the reading of the Holy Book to secure peace for the departed soul, and I have to respect their wishes."

"We should have taken the body to America for services at my church."

"Christianity does not forbid cremation. We will carry half the ashes to America for the church services, and I'll throw the other half in the sacred river here."

She stifled a sigh. "Hard to believe: Timmy has left us forever."

"No, he is still here."

"Why do you say this?"

"Emily, according to my beliefs, humans are made out of four elements: water, earth, fire, and air. After death the body turns into these basic elements, no matter whatever method is used for the funeral services. The everlasting spirit, however, leaves the body and waits for its reincarnation."

"Reincarnation? I don't believe in your theory of life after death."

"We'll discuss that later. You're tired; please close your eyes."

"I'm hungry."

"I'm starved, too, but we can't eat."

"Why?" she asked.

"Our customs: No cooking can be done in this house, and all have to fast. I, however, can bring you another glass of buttermilk, since drinking liquids is permitted."

"Thanks, I consumed enough of it."

She closed her eyes. I shut the door, stretched on the floor near her, and watched her breathing. Soon her tired body yielded to sleep. I prayed for my wife and the child's spirit, but at this stage I felt as if a part of my heart was dead, and the other portion was slowly withering away. I begged God for His intervention. While I was praying, slumber crept in and took hold of me.

Next morning, I woke up early and glanced at Emily. She was still asleep, and her breathing was normal. I thanked God, took my bath, sat cross-legged in the living room, and listened to the priest reading the Holy Book. After one hour, I returned to the bedroom and awakened Emily. Her eyes were swollen, and her face looked paler than a mustard flower, but she was in a better mood.

I thought it would calm her if I took her away from the house which was filled with gloom and sorrow.

"Let's go to the farmhouse," I suggested.

"Will your parents permit it?"

"They won't mind. At this time we get a cool breeze from the hills, and a walk in the open fields will help us."

She acquiesced with some hesitation.

I told my plan to my sister who was delighted; she adored Emily and was greatly worried about her health. I helped Emily, and we ambled out of the village. The sun was genuflecting behind Himalayan Mountains, and the cool breeze was shaking the corn tufts. Droves of chirping parrots flew over our heads. Emily was an avid bird-watcher, but today she didn't even raise her head. I pointed to the farmers who were plowing the fields while singing and cussing their buffaloes, but she ignored it and trudged on. Finally, we reached the tube well, sat near the concrete basin which was receiving the sparkling, clear water, and washed our faces. There was a small shed near the tube well. The farmhand, who lived in it, was at our house, helping my father. I went inside the hut, lighted a fire, made tea, brought two cups, and gave one to her.

While sipping tea and watching the ripples making tranquilizing sounds, we sat wordless, battling with our emotions. After ten minutes, she dabbed her tears and said, "I miss Timmy."

"I miss him, too. But I think his spirit is alive, and we can communicate with him."

"Don't be ridiculous. I've already told you, there's no life after death."

"Emily, you're wrong. There's life after death," I said. "Can I tell you about my personal experience?"

"Go ahead."

"It happened when I was nineteen and was studying in college. During the Diwali holidays, I decided to come home. My train arrived at three in the morning. I was the lone passenger who disembarked and had to walk one mile to my village. It was a full moon night, and I could see the bats and owls flying in the sky and hear the singing of the frogs and crickets. I was full of life and trotted over the winding path which snaked through the fields. After fifteen minutes, I reached the village pond and found my grandfather watering his horse. Thinking he was going somewhere, I dashed to him and offered my greetings. I was surprised to find him in a sour mood. He patted my back and said, 'Bir, tell your father, I have stored carrot seeds in the pitcher in the storage room. This pitcher is the third from the bottom, in the fourth row from the left corner.' Before I could give my reply, he jumped on his horse and galloped away. I returned home and was surprised to learn that Grandfather had died yesterday.

"I asked my father, 'Are you looking for carrot seed?'

"'Yes, Grandfather forgot to buy them.'

"'Come on, let's check the storage.'

"We entered the large room, and I located the pitcher specified by Grandfather. When we removed the pitchers on its top, we discovered it full of carrot seed. My father was stunned and asked, 'How could you pinpoint this out of the sixty pitchers?'

"I described my meeting with Grandfather at the village pond. All were convinced that I must have seen my deceased grandfather, since no one, except him, knew about the seeds."

"I think you must have suffered some sort of mental hallucination."

"No, I did see him with my own eyes, clearly heard his voice, and he patted my back," I said. "Darling, spirits do exit. Timmy might be sitting right next to us."

"Please stop all this fictitious talk," she snapped.

"All right, do you see television images and sound waves floating in the air?"

She shook her head.

"They are always there, and the television can pick them up and produce the picture and the sound. Similarly, spirits do exist, and we need a good medium to communicate with them. Before we leave India, I want to talk with Timmy."

"Don't be crazy."

I grasped her hand and begged, "All right, I'm crazy, but please do give me a chance."

She pondered for a few seconds. "Okay, to make you happy, I'll go along with your fantasy."

"It's not a fantasy. Have you ever read the book, 'Edmond' by Sir Oliver Lodge?"

"No, who is Lodge?"

"He's the father of radio and is one of the greatest British scientists. He experimented with the spirit of his son, Edmond, who was killed in World War I, and wrote this book about his research. It's a fascinating book, and there are two copies in our library in Cleveland."

"All right, when we go back, I'll read that; I've an open mind."

"Then it's all settled. Tomorrow we will start the search for our son's spirit."

I washed the cups and placed them in the hut, and we started our homeward trek.

When we returned home, the recitation of the Holy Book had been completed, and the musicians were singing the hymns. My sister rushed to me and said, "I'm glad you have come; I was just going to send somebody to fetch you. Both of you have to be present at the closing ceremony."

We sat cross-legged on the carpeted floor in front of the gathering. The singing ended, and the ceremony was completed with a prayer. Furniture was brought back in the house, and a fire was lit in the kitchen.

Next day we hired a taxi for one week and started the search for our son's spirit.

I had heard about a Mullah who performed séances and established contact with the dead at midnight in the Muslim graveyard. We took the taxi to the gate of that place and walked in the dark night, crisscrossing the unmarked graves. It was tough, since no tombstones were permitted, and the graves were just heaps of earth. The tiny crescent moon was helpless in lifting the dark veil from the face of the earth, and we stumbled frequently. We entered the tent and joined the group which was seated on the ground in front of an old man who had a dyed-red beard and was wearing a green robe, and six shining butcher knives rested on a grave in front of him. There was complete silence, and we could hear the croaking of the frogs from a distant pond. The Mullah pointed to the grave and said, "This grave belongs to my friend, Jammal, who was killed by a camel while he was on a hajj in Mecca. Since the fellow died at the sacred place, Allah bestowed him with great powers."

Then the Mullah recited verses from the Koran, grabbed one knife, plunged it into the grave, and shouted, "Jammal, I request you to come here."

When he ended his yell, we felt a blast of air and heard a moaning sound. All trembled, and Emily grabbed my hand. The Mullah placated us, "Don't be afraid. Jammal is here to help you. Come one by one and ask your questions."

When our turn came, we made our offering and requested him to contact our son. The Mullah thrust another knife and murmured a few words in sotto voce. Then he told us that Jammal doesn't know English and our child can't speak Urdu, hence there was no communication between them.

I was disappointed. We stood up, bowed, and came out of the tent. When we sat down in the taxi, I began suspecting the whole setup. I slipped back into the graveyard and crawled to the place from where the moans were emanating. I found the Mullah's assistant with a large blower and a tape player, hiding in the bushes. After the signal from the Mullah, this factotum used the tape and the fan for creating the hoax.

I was disheartened, but was not prepared to abandon my search. I returned to the taxi and told Emily, "This Mullah is a chiseler."

"How do you know that?"

I described my discovery.

She grasped my hand and said, "Let's forget this wild goose chase and go back to the States."

"I'm not going to give up; there must be some good mediums."

"You're too stubborn," she moaned.

We stayed in a hotel and located a Hindu medium and attended his séance. We found he was a fake, too. He told us his spirits can't cross the ocean and contact our son's spirit in America, because they are forbidden by his Veda. We paid the fee and left his place.

We located a Sikh medium, and a taxi took us to his ashram. We entered a large hall and saw an old man, with a flowing white beard, seated cross-legged on a tiger skin. We laid our offering at his feet, and he gestured us to sit in front of him. I explained my problem.

"I need the mother's help to reach the child," he said and grasped Emily's hands. After five minutes he shook his head. "Timmy is reticent and refuses to communicate. I, however, can force him, but it will take seven days. Stay here and let the mother come to me alone at ten in the night."

I had noticed lust in his snake-charmer's eyes, while he was holding Emily's hands and decided to avoid him. We made the donation and left. We learned later on that this fellow was a

83

police constable and was dismissed for corruption, rape, and adultery. Now with this flimflam, he was making tons of money and seducing young girls.

When we stepped out of the hall, I said, "All right, I give up. It's impossible to find an honest medium."

"Good, I'm glad you're ending your search," she said. "Well, we're in Amritsar; I'd like to see the Golden Temple before we go to your village."

"Fine, it'll give me great solace to offer my prayers for Timmy's soul."

The taxi dropped us in front of the Golden Temple. We removed our shoes and socks, dipped our feet in the concrete basin full of water, and passed through a huge Oriental arch. Emily was impressed by the sight of the golden dome shimmering in the huge pool surrounding it. Before entering the main building, the worshippers have to complete the circle around the temple. As we were walking, suddenly I saw my old professor, Gurlal Singh. He was now in his late seventies, and his whiskers had turned gray.

I greeted him, introduced Emily, and asked, "Sir, what are you doing now?"

"Meditating, I've become a disciple of Annie Basant."

"Who is Basant?"

"Daughter of the famous British admiral."

"Basant is an Indian name; how can she have that?" I said.

"That's her adopted name; she was raised as Anne Woods."

"What's her religion?" I asked.

"None, simply love and serve God's creatures. Thus one can keep his faith and follow her rules. So I'm a still a pukka Sikh."

"That's great. Can you tell me a little more about Mother Basant?"

"Well, she was the president of the World Theosophical Society and could communicate with the dead and trace the journey of the spirit through many previous births."

Reincarnation

I thought God heard my prayers and arranged this meeting. "Where can I see her?" I inquired.

"She died in 1940."

"Sorry to hear that. Did anyone else take charge of her work?"

"Yes, her assistant, a German lady who has adopted an Indian name, Amrit, which means a nectar, has taken her place. She has the same powers, since Mother Basant's spirit is guiding her."

"Where can I meet her?" I asked.

"In an Ashram near Mount Everest in Bhutan State; I spend two months every year there."

"Can you explain how to get to that place?"

Gurlal described in detail: the train-ride to Silighuri, bus to Thimpu, and a five mile climb to the Ashram.

I thanked Gurlal, and we completed the circle around the temple and entered the worship place. I prostrated myself before the Holy Book and begged God to help me in my enterprise of contacting my son's spirit. We returned to the hotel, and after my lengthy pleading, Emily agreed to visit the Ashram.

In the evening we took the train to Silighuri, and reached there next day at four in the afternoon. From there the twenty-mile journey to Thimpu was a bone-shaker in a jam-packed, rattling bus. With great difficulty, we located the only hotel in the town and were lucky to get the last room. This room had one string cot and a small wooden chair. The musty, fetid smell and beree smoke saturated the place. There was a small window facing the tall peaks. I opened the window and requested Emily to stand next to me, and we admired the awesome, majestic beauty of the snow-clad peaks. I learned from the hotel manager that the guides from the Ashram came in the morning at eight to receive the guests at the bus stand.

We got up early, had our breakfast, and walked to the bus station. At eight two girls, with four sherpas, arrived at the crowded place. One was tall, slim, with freckled face and red

85

hair, and the other was short and stout and had shoulder length black hair. We introduced ourselves and sought their permission to accompany the group. They welcomed us and took hold of our suitcase.

Soon a honking bus arrived, bringing a storm of dust and smoke with it. Ten foreigners emerged and were received by the two guides.

The tall girl addressed the group, "I'm Tresha and next to me is Susan. Susan has just arrived from Italy and can't speak fluent English. We'll try our best to make your trip to the Ashram as pleasant as possible. It's a five mile steep climb, and we'll adjust to your pace."

Three sherpas took hold of all the luggage. Tresha lead the polyglot group, and Susan guarded the rear. The slow and steady climb started.

After ninety minutes we reached the bank of a river and could see the clear blue, sparkling water, flowing in a twenty foot deep gorge.

"We'll take a breather here and make Indian herbal tea. We can supply coffee, too. I, however, suggest you try our tea; it will help your body and provide the extra energy needed to climb in thin air," Tresha said.

All nodded with smiles.

Tresha ran down the hill like a mountain goat and brought a bucket of water. I noticed a stone Chullah (open hearth) with dried wood stacked near it. Susan packed twigs in the Chullah, lit the fire, and the flames shot out underneath the pan. The group stretched on green grass and admired the clear, blue sky, and the snow-clad peaks. While making tea, Tresha, and Susan sang hymns in their melodious voices. We had tea in steel cups which warmed our hands. I looked at Emily; she appeared to be enjoying the trip. The mist, rising from the cups and the mouths of the group, made angelic figures. All felt rejuvenated and thanked Tresha and Susan, and the climbing resumed.

After trekking for one hour, we could see the dome shooting out of the pine trees. Tresha pointed to it and said, "That's our Ashram. Cheer up; only a two-hundred-feet ascent is left."

The climb became steeper and the pace became slower. All trudged forward, and finally we entered the large compound.

Tresha explained, "The large building in the center is our prayer and meditation room. The cottage next to it belongs to Mother Amrit. The other cottages, away from the main building, are for the devotees and Ashram staff. The building, with the large chimney, is the kitchen, and the dining hall is next to it. Do you have any questions?"

A tall man with a big paunch asked, "Can we cook our food?"

"No, all the food is cooked in the kitchen and served at specific hours which are posted in the cottages."

An old lady with a cheerful red face questioned, "How do you manage your food supplies?"

"We are almost self sufficient. We are vegetarians and grow our vegetables and fruits. We, however, purchase the other needed things once a month. Our goats provide us with milk and trim our lawns," Tresha replied. "Remember, no smoking or drinking of alcohol is permitted in the Ashram area."

We moved further and stood in front of the prayer hall. I got whiffs of the tantalizing smell from the kitchen, and my hungry stomach growled, but Emily's stoic face showed no emotions.

Tresha and Susan took every member to the allotted cottage. They escorted us to our place and opened the door. I smelled fresh hay. They gave us a sheet and two blankets, and helped us to make the bed over the hay bundles. The small cottage, ten by eight, was made from local granite, and it had a small window. The only furniture was a wooden stool.

"You have seen the dining hall; dinner will be served at eight. You must be there in time. If you are late, you will miss your meal," Tresha said.

"Where are the toilets?" Emily asked.

"There is one toilet for the sick. All healthy persons are to go deep in the forest away from the Ashram and seek comfort there."

"What about showers?"

"Again we have one shower for the sick, and all of us take our baths in the nearby stream. We collect rain water in tanks and use it for cooking and providing a shower for the ailing persons."

We thanked Susan and Tresha, and they left.

"Emily, I admire these young volunteers. They have conquered the worldly passions and have found peace in their souls and hearts."

"Yes, they are wonderful."

She stretched on the bed and closed her eyes. I stared at the shaft of light shooting through the window and studied the motes dancing in a zigzag manner, like humans drifting in life without any purpose. My thoughts turned toward Timmy and my wife, and I feverishly prayed for them. I glanced at my watch: 7:45. I touched Emily's hand. She rubbed her eyes, adjusted her hair, and stood up. We walked to the dining hall and sat cross-legged on the floor among a group of sixty persons and were served beans, vegetables, and bread on steel plates.

"This is the best meal I ever had," Emily whispered to me.

"This food is prepared with love and prayers."

After dinner Tresha took the group to see Mother Amrit. We entered a big hall and found more than forty monks, dressed in saffron robes, seated cross-legged before their earthen lamps. The figures, created by the flickering wicks, were dancing on the walls. The hall smelled of fresh flowers, burning incense and mustard oil. The only audible sound was that of human breathing and the flick of the rosaries. We stood with folded hands before a marble dais and saw an old lady with snow white hair seated cross-legged on it. Her oval face, without any wrinkles, glowed, and I noticed a halo surrounding her head. I thought the halo was my mental hallucination; I rubbed my eyes and scrutinized again. It was still there.

We stood in silence with bowed head. Tresha presented the group. The Mother raised her rosary hand and said, "Children, you're tired after a long journey; go and rest. Come tomorrow morning at six. May God's peace be with you."

We shuffled out of the building and went to our cottage.

"I felt a strange force radiating from Mother Amrit," Emily said.

"I had the same experience. Did you see the halo over her head?"

"Yes, I did see something like that," she said.

"Well, let's go to sleep. In order to be at the prayer hall at six, we should get up at four in the morning."

Emily opened her Bible, and I closed my eyes in a silent prayer. After fifteen minutes, we stretched on the bed and were sound asleep.

We woke at four, sought comfort among the wild flowers, faraway from the temple, and walked two hundred feet down to the river. I dipped my hand in the water. It was biting cold and sent shivers through my body. I turned my head and noticed several monks standing on one leg in knee-deep water, chanting mantras. Evidently, their minds had taken full control of their bodies and the cold didn't affect them. We washed our faces, arms, and legs and started climbing back. Exercise brought circulation to our numb limbs, and we felt better. I was glad to find my wife in a better mood.

At six, we were among the group of fifteen persons who were escorted to see Mother Amrit. When our turn came, we stood with folded hands, and I said, "We want to contact our son's spirit."

Mother Amrit gestured us to sit down, and we sat cross-legged on the floor. Then she closed her placid, deep blue eyes, and went into a trance.

I heard the pitter-patter of tiny feet and felt a blast of cold air. The wicks, burning in the oil lamps, quivered. Mother Amrit opened her eyes and said, "Look, Timmy is standing next to you. Timmy, hug your parents."

Timmy always hugged me in a particular manner—one arm on my shoulder and the other around my chest with his head pressed to my heart. I felt the familiar embrace, and my heart jumped with joy. Then I noticed a smile on Emily's face, as she kissed the air.

"Timmy, how are you?" Emily asked.

"Mom, I miss you, Dad, and my dog."

"Don't worry about Buddy; we'll take good care of it."

"Mom, the Mighty Power has given me orders to go back to you. The carrier of the dead made a mistake in taking me away."

"Wonderful, how will you do that?" Emily asked.

"One year from now you will give birth to me."

Emily wiped the tears of joy running down her rosy cheeks and said, "Honeybun, we'll be waiting for you."

"Sorry, I've to leave now; I'll see you after one year."

I again felt the hug and then heard the sound of the tiny feet moving away. I glanced at the luminous dial of my watch: 6:32.

Emily was glowing and so was my heart.

We touched Mother Amrit's feet and made a place for the next devotee. When I came out, I wrote down in my pocket diary the time and date of this meeting: 6:32 a.m., July 15, 1997.

Next morning the guides took us to the bus stand. In two days we were back in my village. My parents were surprised to find joy and happiness in our eyes.

We returned to Cleveland and resumed our teaching jobs. Emily was not morose, but full of joy and hope. When she

90

bought a big load of baby boy stuff, I was surprised and said, "You should have waited till you became pregnant. You know, for four years we have tried hard to get another child and have failed."

"I want to keep my word with Timmy; he's sure to come," she said with a determined look.

"Then you believe in reincarnation."

She smiled. "Certainly, I do."

"Good, let's do our part to help Timmy."

I lifted her to the bedroom, and she conceived on that night. This time she didn't have any morning sickness, and she looked radiant and cheerful. Every morning, before leaving for her job, she dusted and kissed Timmy's picture.

On the night of July 13, 1998, I got her admitted in the hospital, and she gave birth to a male child at 5:32 in the morning. It was 6:32 in the morning of July 15 in the Ashram. I checked my diary and confirmed that one year ago Timmy had met us at this exact time in the Ashram.

We were thrilled in this reincarnation and named our child: "Timmy".

Keeping One's Pledge

Thati Village, Rajisthan, India

Ramu, a sixteen-year-old, wiry nomad, parted his black hair and coated it with scented oil. He wore his white cotton dhoti and made a red mark on his forehead.

Fully spruced up, he went to his mother and touched her feet.

"Son, it appears you're ready to go somewhere."

"Yes Mom, I'm going to bring Kanta from her parent's village today."

She glanced at him and asked, "Where is the necklace, you got from Kanta's parents?"

"It's in the box under my cot."

"Son, get it and put it on, otherwise your in-laws will think you have pawned it. Moreover, as a son-in-law you must wear the big dowry gift to show them that you appreciate it."

He scurried to his cot and returned, wearing a shining silver necklace.

She kissed his forehead and said, "Go to Goddess Parvati's temple and then go for your bride. I'll be praying for you."

He went to the barn, patted his camel's neck, and said, "Bhoora, be good. I'll feed you the best corn on our return."

He rode the camel to the temple, tied it to the fence, sprinted in, and rubbed his nose near the feet of Goddess Parvati's statue. He looked up and was delighted to see the goddess's lips which had curled in a smile.

He took hold of his camel and traveled on a sandy path in the desert. After one hour he reached the oasis and decided to drink some water. The sight of trees loaded with dates enticed him. He decided to pick up this delicacy for his young bride. He secured his camel, removed his dhoti, tightened his loincloth, and climbed up the tree.

Up in the blue sky, he sang while harvesting the crop. Suddenly the area was struck by a sandstorm. Under the blasts of the ferocious wind the sixty-foot-high tree swayed like an inverted pendulum. On noticing the Yammas (carrier of the dead) with their nets, his bones got chilled; he trembled and tightened his arms around the tree and prayed.

With tears in his eyes, he begged, "Goddess Parvati, if you save me from this storm, I'll give you the silver necklace which I'm wearing."

Suddenly, he experienced the presence of Goddess Parvati, and even felt the soft touch of her hand. The demons, which were dancing in the storm, screamed, the Yammas dropped their nets, and the storm lost its strength. He found a lull in the howling wind and managed to slip fifteen feet down. His heart slowed its pounding, and he felt better.

He crawled down twenty feet.

"Goddess Parvati, you don't need a cheap silver necklace, since you have many gold ones. If you help me land safely on the ground, I'll bring twenty rupees to your temple," he said.

While trembling, he crawled down like a caterpillar and managed to lower himself twenty feet more. The tree, however, was still shaking from the thrusts of the howling wind. He looked down and was cheered to see his camel, but his heart sank when he discovered his dhoti had flown away.

"Goddess Parvati, I have to deduct the loss of my dhoti, so I'll bring ten rupees to your temple," he said.

He chanted Goddess Parvati's name and inched downward. When he was six feet above the ground, he smiled, and said, "Goddess Parvati, you get thousands of rupees from rich people, and you don't need ten rupees from a poor man. To thank you, I'll rub my nose ten times before your statue."

When his feet touched the ground, he was euphoric—he had tricked the goddess. As he untied the camel, he heard the roar of a desert lion. The camel brayed, broke the rope, and bolted. He pivoted his neck and saw Yammas grinning while holding their nets. His legs turned into jelly, and he couldn't climb up the tree. Now his heart told him that he had cheated Goddess Parvati, and she was punishing him. To atone for his sin, he dropped on his knees and begged with tears, "Goddess Parvati, forgive me. I tried to cheat you. I'll never ever do that again."

Suddenly, a hunter's bullet buzzed over his head, and the lion vanished. He was happy that Goddess Parvati forgave him and came to save him. He thanked the goddess and searched for his camel. Soon he found it near the spring.

Now he was naked except for his tiny loincloth, and he couldn't go to his wife's place in this condition. He rode straight to the temple, placed the silver necklace at Goddess Parvati's feet, rubbed his nose on the floor, and said, "I promise never to break my pledge with you."

When he came out, the silver necklace was not around his neck, but there was peace and joy in his heart. When he reached home, he found his wife and her father had just arrived. He touched his father-in-law's feet.

"Son, I was going to Ganga Nagar, and thought on my way I should drop Kanta at your place."

Ramu's heart was bubbling with joy, and he said, "Thanks, Dad."

At night, when Ramu and Kanta were alone, he said, "You passed by the oasis, did you see any sand storm there?"

"No, it was a clear day without any wind."

Now he was sure the storm was created by the goddess to teach him a lesson. He narrated his experience and said, "I don't want to tell this to my parents. They're bound to inquire about the necklace; what should I do?"

"Mom gave me money which is enough to buy a necklace. Tomorrow you ride to the town and purchase another necklace similar to the one given by my parents."

He kissed Kanta and said, "Thanks Goddess Parvati for giving me a wonderful wife."

"Look we both should thank the goddess. She saved me from becoming a child widow who lives and dies in hell, and taught you a good lesson."

They sat cross-legged on the floor and prayed to the goddess.

College Degree

March 8, 1939, Thati Village, Punjab, India

"Look, Nargas, we both have to struggle to keep Surat in college. Soon he will get his degree, secure a big job, and we'll retire," Puran, a tall, muscular man with flowing white beard, spoke to his placid, cud-chewing buffalo which he had named after the famous Indian actress, Nargas. The buffalo shook its head, swished the tail, and continued plodding at its leisurely pace. Puran was disgusted, but he had no other choice. Whipping and shouting would have further antagonized the buffalo, and it would have stopped.

The sun, which had been hiding behind the tall Himalayan Peaks, shot up, and the cool breeze turned into a hot blast. He completed the plowing, released the buffalo from the yolk, lifted the plow on his shoulder, and began trudging toward the village, tagging his buffalo. The buffalo, relieved from the yolk, snorted, and picked up speed. After covering half a mile on the dirt road, he reached his barn, stacked the plow in the corner, tied the buffalo, and threw fresh fodder in the trough. The old buffalo buried its head in the chopped corn stalks, and its tail swished continuously to ward off the hordes of flies.

As he was drenched in stinking sweat and coated with black soil, he rushed to the public well, the bathing place for men. He removed his clothes, laid those on the wooden bench, grabbed the wheel, and started pulling the water bucket. He felt a tap on his shoulder, pivoted his neck, and saw Buta, the neighbor's son.

"Uncle, let me help you," Buta said.

Puran handed over the wheel.

Buta vigorously turned the wheel, pulled the bucket out of the well, and poured it over Puran who rubbed his body with a smile.

"I admire your big muscles," Buta said.

"I worked hard to get those."

"Dad told me you were the champion wrestler."

"Yes, that was fifteen years ago."

Puran rubbed soap on his body, and Buta poured another bucket on him.

Buta looked into Puran's eyes and asked with some trepidation, "When's Surat going to finish college?"

"I don't know; it's a tough job."

"He's taking more time than others."

Puran remembered his son's explanation and said, "He's smarter than them and is working harder to acquire all the knowledge."

"Puran, it looks strange to me."

"Why?"

"Surat's classmates got their degrees and are on their jobs, but he's still stuck there."

"They are unripe and didn't master the full education. Surat is trying to become ripe and acquire all the wisdom," Puran said. "Well, did you go to college?"

"No, I dropped out in the first grade."

"Buta, so we both know nothing about college and can't comprehend the hardships involved in college studies."

"I admit I'm a birdbrain. Frankly, to me the words on the books look like buffalos grazing in the fields. It must be tough to chase those herds. I, however, think there's no harm in your checking Surat."

"It seems to be a good idea," Puran said and then shook his head. "Oh, no! He's working hard; I shouldn't disturb him."

Puran thanked Buta, wiped his body, donned his clothes, tied his turban, and went to the Gurdwara (Sikh temple). He rubbed his nose before the Holy Book and begged God to speed up his son's education; it had drained all his resources.

While walking home, Puran's mind mulled over Buta's suggestion. When he stepped in his house, his wife, Guro, a thin middle-aged woman with a charming face, greeted him with a smile. She placed a mat on the floor, and he sat cross-legged on it. Then she brought two chapatis and an onion on a brass plate and laid those in front of him. He glanced at the onion and asked, "Where is the omelet?"

"We don't have money to buy eggs."

He stifled a sigh, since he had mailed the money from the sale of his crops to his son and was left with no cash. He turned reticent and finished his breakfast without saying another word.

He wiped his hands, took a deep breath, released it through his pursed lips, and said, "Guro, we have no other choice, but to make these sacrifices for our son's degree."

"I agree, but it's very painful."

"Cheer up, after he completes his studies and gets a big job, I'm going to redeem your jewelry from the pawnshop."

She shrugged her shoulders and mumbled, "I'm too old now and don't care for it."

He grabbed her in his arms, planted a kiss, and said, "Your pretty face doesn't need any help, but I do want to see your dangling earrings and hear the jangle of your gold bangles."

"Stop this romantic stuff," she blushed and said. "I'm worried about one thing."

"What's that?"

"Our son is taking too long."

"Be patient, soon he'll be out of college," he consoled.

"Kundan, our neighbor's son, has finished college and has become a police inspector."

"It bothers me, too. This morning Buta asked me to visit Surat. I think I should do that and check how Surat is progressing."

Her face turned ghastly pale. "Oh no! You shouldn't. Surat will be mad. He has warned you against disturbing his studies."

"Woman, I won't bother him at all. I'll meet him for a few minutes and rush back."

"You know better, but be careful and don't waste his time."

"I'll be prudent," Puran said. "All right, then it's all settled. I'll finish my sowing in two days and then walk to his college."

He scrambled up, washed his hands, and ambled to the large wooden dais under the banyan tree in front of the Gurdwara. This was the meeting place for the farmers. Here he found two groups playing cards, and several men were sprawled and snoring. He greeted the group, sat cross-legged, and watched them. He was in no mood to join them, since his mind was thinking about his son. On hearing the jangle of the bells, he pivoted his head, and saw the postman who had tiny brass bells tied to his ankles and was carrying a huge mailbag. The card games stopped, and the postman delivered letters to the outstretched hands. Puran got one letter and rushed to the village shopkeeper who always read the letter and wrote the reply.

The shopkeeper looked at the postmark and said, "It's a letter from your son."

Puran's heart started thudding, and he yelled, "Hurry up, open it and tell me what it's speaking."

The shopkeeper opened the letter and read: "Dear father, please mail one hundred rupees without any delay. I want to buy a book which contains information about the whole English language. Your son, Surat."

Puran's face lost the rosy color, and he blurted, "One hundred rupees! There must be some mistake. Please read the letter one more time."

The shopkeeper read the letter again.

"That's a huge amount," Puran said and rubbed his forehead. "Well, he wants to buy a mighty book which tells everything about English. I think it must be costing that much, since English rules the world."

The shopkeeper knew the English dictionary would cost only five rupees and the poor farmer was being bamboozled by his son. He felt pity for Puran, but he didn't want to break old man's heart by revealing the truth.

"Puran, you better go and check your son."

"Today I was thinking about it," Puran said. "Will it hurt my son's studies if I see him for a few minutes?"

"Not a tiny bit. Look, the college is only ten miles from here, and you can take a bus which will take you there in twenty minutes. Spend a few minutes with him and hurry back."

"Do you think it's proper for me to do that?" Puran asked.

"Most of the parents do meet their sons. You can also give him this money, and it will save you the postage expenses."

For a few seconds, Puran's hand wrestled with his mustache. Finally, he said, "Okay, I'll leave right now. I can easily walk to that place in less than two hours," Puran said. "Can you loan me one hundred rupees?"

"Sure, but you have to pay the normal interest."

"I accept your terms."

The shopkeeper wrote down the loan, and Puran fixed his thumb impression on the spot shown to him. Puran tied the money in his handkerchief, inserted it in his inner pocket, and thanked the shopkeeper.

Puran went straight to his home and told his wife about his decision.

"I'm confused," she stammered. "You planned to complete your work in two days and then go there. Why are you changing it?"

"Today, I got a letter from Surat asking for some money, and I can easily postpone sowing to help our son."

"How much does he want?"

"One hundred rupees."

Her chin dropped. "One hundred! We don't spend that in a year."

"Woman, he badly needs a powerful book. I'll give him the money, stay for fifteen minutes, and rush back."

"All right, I'll be praying to Satguru for you."

"Good, but do pray for our son so that he can complete his studies."

He kissed his wife and started walking toward his son's college. The road was jammed with traffic. The smoke, dust, and noise didn't bother him, since he was dreaming that his son was driving one of those fancy cars, and he had retired in his son's big bungalow with many servants.

After two hours he saw the mammoth building which had several domes and minarets, and a huge clock was popping out of the central dome. He was awestruck and puzzled; he had never stepped into such a gigantic structure. When he entered the steel gate, the clock chimed two times.

He was perplexed to find hundreds of erudite students running like bees in a hive. All looked scholarly to him, but he was not intimidated, since he was much taller and stronger than them. He stopped near a young man and asked, "Do you know Surat?"

"Which one; there are so many Surats here."

"He's from Thati Village," Puran added.

"Oh yes, we all know that son of a rich landlord. The fellow lives like a maharaja."

Puran felt a big knot in his stomach, but he caged his emotions and asked, "Where can I reach him?"

The young man pointed to the hostel and said, "He lives in Room Number Ten in that building. You can't miss his room—it's highly embellished and is always loaded with fragrance and music. Your ears and nose will lead you straight to it."

Puran was devastated to hear all this and prayed to God that this young man might be talking about some other Surat and not his son. When he entered the hostel, his olfactory senses

101

and ears pointed him to the room, and he didn't have to ask anybody. He knocked at the door. His son, Surat, a short, corpulent young man dressed in a three-piece silken suit with a gold necklace dangling around his neck, parted the door. Puran bit his lower lip, controlled his anger, and stood there, staring at the unbelievable figure.

His son quickly pulled him inside and bolted the door.

"Dad, you promised never to visit me. Why have you come?"

"To give you the one hundred rupees which you wanted," Puran said and handed over the money.

Surat stacked the money in his inner pocket. "Thanks for the trouble; you should have mailed it."

"I thought you were in a big hurry."

"I could have waited for two days. Please stretch on that bed, and I'll bring some food. In the evening I'll take you to the Golden Temple."

Puran noticed his son's ghastly face and was sure that the fellow wanted to conceal him and then smuggle him out in the darkness. He ignored his son's remarks and paced the room, examining the pictures of naked girls hanging on the walls. He adjusted his huge shoulders, peered into Surat's shifty eyes, and shouted, "Your place looks like a Devil's den."

"Dad, I have to create the proper atmosphere for my hard work."

"Damn it. The naked girls can't help your brain; they set fire to your libido. Our Scriptures forbid us from ogling them."

"The modern scientists have discovered that these pictures energize the cells in the brain without affecting the sex urge," Surat explained. "Dad, you should have put on some new clothes."

"I came to meet my son and not the Deputy Commissioner," Puran smirked. "Now tell me more about the book you want to buy."

"You know English controls the whole world and this book contains all the information about it."

"Can you show it to me?"

"I can't."

"Why?"

"I have to order it from England."

Puran patted Surat's back, "Now tell me, when are you going to complete your degree?"

"Dad, you're a farmer and know that it takes time for any fruit to ripen."

"Your classmate, our neighbor's son, graduated this year and is a police inspector now."

Surat chuckled. "That dumb was unripe and could only become an inspector. When I come out, I'll be fully ripe and start at the top as superintendent of police."

On hearing his son's rosy remarks, a smile appeared on Puran's face. "That's great, but how many more years will you take?"

"Only a few more."

"Son, we're getting at the end of our finances. Can't you speed up?"

"I get only three hours sleep and plow the books all the time. Don't worry; I'm doing my best."

"All right son, keep up the good work. Your mother and I daily pray at the Gurdwara for you."

As Puran turned to leave the room, Surat grabbed his father's hand and said, "I can't accompany you to the gate; I want to finish my college project."

"Don't bother, I can find my way out."

"Please avoid all the students and don't ask them any questions about me. They're all jealous of my achievements and will tell you wrong things."

Puran said his farewell and moved out of the hostel.

When he was near the gate, he saw the young man whom he had met earlier. This fellow greeted him with a smile and asked, "Could you meet Surat?"

Puran nodded.

"Boy! He's lucky."

"Why?" Puran asked.

"His father has a mountain of wealth and doesn't mind his son spending money like water. He failed in his class three times; no father will ever tolerate this."

Puran's heart started hammering its cage, and he couldn't believe what he had heard.

"Are you telling the truth?"

"You can ask any person on the campus. Are you his rich father's hired hand?"

Puran walked away without giving the reply. He still thought the young man might be making up all this stuff, and he decided to check it with his old friend, Professor Atma Singh, who hailed from the neighboring village, and was living on the campus. Puran asked one student the location of Professor Atma Singh's office. After following the directions, he met the Professor.

"Sat Sri Akal (Sikh greetings), Atma."

"Sat Sri Akal, Puran. Nice to see you. You were a great wrestler."

"You were good in wrestling with the books."

"Puran, what can I do for you?"

Puran cleared his throat with some effort and said, "I want to know when my son is going to get his degree."

Atma adjusted his seat, bent forward, and whispered, "I want to be frank with you. Surat will never be able to get his degree."

Puran's mouth flew wide open. "Why? He's working very hard."

"Didn't he tell you that he failed three times in the first year class?"

"No, he never revealed this to me. I just learned it from another student and came over to you to confirm it."

"He failed and lied to you. You're simply wasting your money. Look, your son is not cut out for books, and he should help you with the farm work."

"All this is hard to swallow," Puran said. "Atma, I've one more question."

"What's that?"

"Can you tell me the value of the book which gives full information about English?"

"Five rupees."

"Are you sure?"

Atma took out the dictionary from his bookshelf and said, "Here's the book. It costs less than five rupees."

"Do you order it from England?"

"No, it's sold at the college bookstore."

Puran felt as if he was hit by a freight train. His son turned out to be a worthless goof, a cheat, and a liar. He managed to control his anger by crunching his teeth.

"Thanks Atma," Puran said and shook hands with his friend.

He rushed out of the office, scurried to a wooded area, broke one branch of a mulberry tree, and made a club out of it. Armed with this, he dashed toward Surat's room.

When Puran entered Room Number Ten in the hostel, he found his son listening to the music, while sipping wine. When Surat saw his father, he jumped up, and snapped, "Dad, you're back; what's wrong?"

"Everything! Pack up your stuff. You're coming with me."

"I'll be worthless without a degree," Surat moaned.

"You'll never be worth anything. Shut your mouth and start packing."

Puran was much stronger than his son, and he twisted Surat's ear and said, "I give you ten minutes."

"Please wait, we can leave during the night," Surat implored.

Puran ignored the request, destroyed the dirty pictures with his stick, and threw the bedding on Surat's face.

"Bundle it up," Puran yelled.

With tears rolling down his cheeks, Surat gathered all his things in a big sheet. Puran placed this bundle on Surat's head and shouted, "Move, I'll carry your suitcase."

They stepped out, and Puran heard the chuckles and taunts of the students.

"Here goes the maharaja with a load on his head, and a farmer in dirty clothes chasing him with a club," one student yelled.

Surat lowered his head and walked fast. When they were outside the steel gate, Surat said, "I can't walk ten miles. We should rent a Tonga (one-horse-drawn buggy)."

"Damn it. We're poor farmers and can't afford it."

Surat moaned and started trudging. Puran let Surat stop for a breather at a few places, but didn't speak a word to him. Finally, they reached home. Puran sent his son to the bedroom. Then he explained the whole thing to his wife who covered her face with the tent of her hands and cried.

She dabbed her eyes and asked, "What do you plan to do with our son?"

"This fellow is like a Funder (barren buffalo). You give it good food and pamper it, and it becomes fat and turns barren. You make it plow the fields; it loses the excess fat and starts yielding milk again. Look at the scoundrel's big paunch. He'll have to work with me in the fields."

"What about his education?"

"Forget it. He's not meant for it. We sacrificed our needs, and you even pawned your jewelry to help him in college. This spoiled brat lived like a maharaja and never touched the books. He's going to become my farmhand, and in one year he'll get rid of his potbelly."

Puran fixed a lock on the bedroom's door and told his wife, "Go and make supper; I'm starved."

Surat started moaning loudly, expecting his mother to intercede.

With a heavy heart, she listened to the whines for three hours, and then she went to her husband and pleaded, "Our son is starving. Let me feed him something."

"Don't mess up everything by giving him food; he has enough fat. Let him apologize first and promise to work in the fields."

Surat sobbed, whined, and waited for his mother to sneak in with luscious food. He, however, was disappointed and had to starve for two days. On the third day, Puran and his wife went to the Gurdwara, leaving moaning Surat locked in the room. When they returned, they found Surat banging at the door and begging. Puran left for the barn.

"Mom, please let me out," Surat pleaded.

"Are you willing to apologize?"

"Yes, hunger pains are killing me."

"All right, I'll ask your father; he has the key to the door."

She returned after ten minutes and opened the door. Surat rushed to grab his father's feet and begged, "Dad, I'm sorry for my past misdeeds and promise to help you."

"Well, I can't trust your words, but from hence onward I'll let your actions speak for you."

Puran sold Surat's gold necklace, bought another buffalo, and named it College Degree. In the morning Surat yoked the new buffalo under his father's supervision, and they left to plow the fields.

The old farmer thanked Satguru and sang hymns of gratitude: He had tamed his prodigal son, and the College Degree, for which his son had wasted so much money, was now plowing his fields.

Capturing a Pernicious Ghost

March 29, 1944, 22 Hanuman Road, New Delhi, India

"Prem, I want you to capture a ghost for me," a tall man with flowing white beard and blue turban barged into my office, occupied a chair in front of me, peered into my eyes, and demanded.

I was annoyed, but couldn't insult an old man from my community, so I said, "Sardar sahib, you're at the wrong place. I'm a detective and not a ghost hunter."

"I know that. God bless your father's soul; he used to be my friend and classmate," he said and then stretched his hand. "My name is Sucha Singh."

I shook the proffered hand and said, "Nice meeting you."

"To please your father in heaven, you must take up my case and subdue the ghost."

"I don't believe in ghosts which exist only in the mind of an opium-eater, while he's riding high."

"Prem, I'm sure with your education and training in America for fifteen years and your powerful gizmos, you can easily capture this ghost and find out for yourself that ghosts are there."

"Okay, I'll investigate it after I return from my vacation in Simla Hills."

"How long are you going to stay there?" he questioned.

"Ten days."

"It won't work; I'll be dead by that time."

"You look healthy. How can you be sure of your death?"

"I'll be murdered by the ghost who has given me three days to settle my worldly affairs."

I took a deep breath, released it through my pursed lips, and said, "All right, I'll cancel my vacation and take up your case."

He took out a bundle of hundred-rupee bills from his pocket and said, "I'm rich and will pay your fee plus a big bonus."

"Keep it with you; we'll talk about it after I've handled your ghost."

He pocketed the money.

"Well, did you try our exorcists?"

"Yes, Muslim, Hindu, and Sikh exorcists failed to castigate it."

"Please describe the ghost."

"After her cremation, Taro, my step-mother has turned into this ghost."

"Where is your father?" I questioned.

"He passed away last year."

"How old was he at the time of his death?"

"Eighty-nine."

"When did your step-mother die, and what was her age?"

"She was cremated on the pyre of her husband, and she was sixteen."

I jumped from my seat and shouted, "Damn it, you performed sati and roasted her alive."

"No, Prem. I never did that. She was a pious person and wanted to become a sati, and I didn't stop her. But instead of going to heaven to warm my father's bed, she turned into a ghost," he said and dabbed his eyes. "I should have dragged her out of the pyre."

"Look, sati is banned by law, and you can be sent to an iron cage for twenty years."

"Impossible! All the villagers will declare that she had a heart attack, and the village doctor has certified it," he said. "I'm sorry for what I did in the past; please help me."

"All right, now tell me why her ghost is after your blood."

"She blames me for her tortured death. I performed three Bhog ceremonies, readings of the Holy Book, and fed thousands of hungry people to appease her soul. I was happy it worked. But on the fifth anniversary of my father's cremation, the ghost appeared on the cremation grounds, and after that it continued doing that at irregular intervals."

"Did the ghost do any harm?"

"Yes, on its first visit, it killed my favorite stallion. Five years later it murdered my son, and now it has set its sights on me."

"When did your mother leave the earth?"

"She's still alive."

"Then your father was a polygamist."

"Yes, it's our family tradition. He had three, but I'm content with two."

"How was your relationship with your step-mother?" I inquired.

"Fine, though she was younger than me, yet I touched her feet, and she patted my head."

"Who negotiated this marriage?"

"My mother, who was old and sick, arranged her friend's daughter, Taro, for her husband. Taro and I played together as kids, and she used to giggle, as I pulled her long braids."

"If she liked you, and you were a dutiful son, then why is she harming you and your family?"

"That's what I want you to discover. I've always carried out the ghost's orders," he said.

"What were those?"

"It wanted me to start a school for girls. Much against my beliefs, I complied."

"What are your beliefs?"

"Women are created by God to cook and raise children, and education spoils the whole process."

"You are wrong there. I think the ghost did a noble job."

"Noble, ha! It's a sin for a girl to go to school. Educated girls are destroying the fabric of our ancient civilization—

getting divorces, selecting their husbands, and demanding equal rights."

"There is nothing wrong with those rational demands," I said. "All right, what happened next?"

"The ghost commanded me to stop lashing my wife."

"Sardar sahib, I'm distressed to learn that you're a wife-beater."

"Prem, a wife is like a buffalo, and one has to use a stick to make it work. My wife is stubborn. I tried my best to control my anger and pleaded with her, but failed; I was forced to whip her. The omnipresent ghost saw me beating my wife and cursed my horse which fell dead next day."

"It might have been bitten by a cobra."

"No, it was killed by the ghost's curse, since there was no blue blister to show the snake bite."

"Did the ghost visit you again?"

"Yes, it did appear before my son's marriage and ordered me not to accept any dowry. I didn't take any furniture and goods, but secretly accepted cash. The ubiquitous ghost learned about it and murdered my son."

"Why didn't it kill you instead of your son?"

"Prem, it wants to torture me and enjoy my suffering."

"Hard to believe, anyhow, what did the ghost do on its next visit?"

"One unmarried girl in my village became pregnant—an unpardonable sin. I ordered the father of the girl to remove the black spot on our village name. The ghost learned about it and ordered me to stop the murder."

"You should have done that and helped the girl to get an abortion."

"Impossible! It was a question of our sacred traditions and family pride. The girl was asphyxiated and cremated. The ghost appeared and threatened to kill me. I begged for mercy, and it gave me three days. So here I am."

"I know the police here, and we can lock you inside a cell where the ghost can't reach you."

111

He shook his head. "It won't work; the ghost can turn into smoke, a snake, an ant et cetera and can easily enter the jail."

I realized there was a no way out for me, and I had to accept his case.

"Let's move," I said. "Well, I prefer using my motorcycle in your case instead of my jeep, since I'll be able to crisscross over the fields and chase the ghost. Sit on the rear seat of my motorcycle and order your driver to bring your car."

At 7:35 P.M. my motorcycle thundered through the dusty streets of Ratul, Sucha Singh's village. I dropped Sucha near his house and went to the guest rooms in the village gurdwara. After eating at the temple kitchen, I went to sleep.

Next morning, I met the priest and asked him, "Did you perform the cremation ceremony for Sucha Singh's father?"

"Yes, I recited the Scriptures."

"When did Sucha Singh stack his father's young wife over the corpse?" I questioned.

"Before igniting the hay in the pyre."

"Was she alive or dead?"

"Dead. Sucha Singh told me that her heart had failed."

"Look, you are telling a bunch of lies. The truth is that Sucha Singh performed sati and you helped him," I said. "Husband and wife are always cremated on separate pyres and never on one pile of wood."

"Mister, don't send me to jail. I was young and would have lost my job, if I had opposed Sucha Singh," the priest moaned.

"I think Sucha Singh gave you a huge bribe. You have sinned and helped him in the murder."

He dabbed his eyes and said, "Satguru have mercy on a poor sinner."

I knew he would never confess this to the police, and no one in the village would come forward to contradict Sucha Singh, so I ended my conversation.

"Go and beg Satguru to forgive your sin for assisting the murder of an innocent woman," I said and left.

The sun had taken a dive behind the distant hills. I decided to inspect the cremation grounds and question the attendant. I fixed my backpack on my shoulders, wore tennis shoes, and walked to the final resting place for the villagers. I noticed a ten-feet-long and two-feet-high brick wall erected on the corner of the cremation area. Evidently it was a Smadhi, a monument for some person cremated there. I flashed my light on the wall and tried to read the inscription, but rain had obliterated it. An earthen lamp rested on the ground in front of this wall, and its flickering wick created ghostly figures. A cremation was in progress, and a young man was throwing wood over the burning corpse and stirring it with a long pole. He was unsteady on his feet.

When I reached him, he threw his sarong on a half-full whisky bottle and continued working.

I greeted him and asked, "Can you spare a few minutes?"
"No, I'm busy."

I flashed a twenty rupee bill and said, "I'm willing to pay for your time."

He dropped the pole and said, "I'm ready."
I pointed to the wall and asked, "Whose Smadhi is that?"
"A sati."
"What's her name?"
"Taro."
"Sucha Singh's step-mother?"
He nodded.
"Well, who lights that lamp?"
"Sucha Singh's servant, who comes here every evening, sweeps the place, and ignites the lamp."
"Did the sati say any farewell words?"
"No, she was comatose."
"Do you see any ghost?"
"Yes, I always see the ghost of every person I cremate."

113

"Have you seen Taro's ghost?"

"Yes, many times, but it doesn't bother me. I hide in my hut and drink."

I gave him the money, and he thanked me.

I examined the area and searched the bushes; no trace of the ghost. I returned to the gurdwara and slept.

To check the cause of Taro's death, I visited the Village Hakim. I saw an old Brahmin, with a freshly oiled clean-shaven dome, seated behind a battered wooden table which was covered with bottles, herbs, and animal parts.

I greeted him, and he said, "Extend your arm. I'll diagnose your sickness from your pulse."

"I'm not sick, but want to ask you a few questions."

"Mister, my time is precious."

I laid three ten-rupee-bills on the table and said, "I think this can buy ten minutes of your time."

He nodded with smile and pocketed the money.

"What was the cause of Taro's death?"

"Heart failure; I checked her." he said in a firm voice.

I knew I wouldn't be able to shake him and changed the topic. "Did Sucha Singh's father purchase any aphrodisiac medicine from you?"

"Yes, he was above eighty and his wife was sixteen, and he sought my help. I gave him my potent medicine which costs only sixty rupees per ounce. If you want to convert your lingam into a steel rod, try one ounce."

"Thanks, I don't need it."

"Did your medicine produce any results?" I asked.

"No, his lingam was a dead leach. I can make a horse run fast, but can't put life in the dead."

I thanked him and left the shop.

I went to Sucha Singh's house. He rushed to grab my hand and asked, "Prem, have you traced the ghost?"

I shook my head. "I spent one night at the cremation grounds and found no sign of a ghost."

"Wait for two more days; the ghost is bound to come there."

"I'll do that," I said. "What statement did Taro make before jumping into the fire?"

"Not a single word."

"I've learned that she didn't walk to the cremation grounds," I said. "What was the reason?"

"She begged me to help her in her anguish, and I offered her whisky. She drank a full bottle and passed out."

"Then you murdered her. She never had a heart attack."

"Her heart failed after she got drunk," he said. "You can verify this from our Hakim."

"I did that," I said. "All right, my investigations have revealed me that your step-mother entered the next world as a virgin."

"My father was potent and did a good job."

"Stop telling lies. I've discovered this from the Hakim."

His chin dropped, and he mumbled, "My father did have some problems."

"I'm not interested in your father's potency," I said. "Anyhow, I've fixed my devices and gadgets in the cremation grounds and will trap the ghost."

"Thanks, tonight is the anniversary, and it will be there. I can loan you my rifle."

"Don't worry, I always carry my revolver," I said and ambled to the gurdwara.

At nine, I fixed my backpack, checked my revolver, and walked to the cremation grounds. The area in front of the wall was swept, and a marigold garland rested near the burning lamp. I planted my microphone behind the wall and climbed the banyan tree, not far from the area.

At midnight, the microphone picked up the sounds of rustling clothes, and I saw a shadowy figure emerging from the bushes. It had a pitch-black face with red flaming eyes. Its long tongue covered with blood was sticking out of its fanged teeth. The cremation attendant ran to his hut and closed the door. I examined the apparition with my night binoculars. It came near the lamp, lifted the garland, and sat cross-legged.

I climbed down the tree, hid under my blanket, and crawled toward the ghost.

"Don't squirm. Nothing can save you," it yelled.

"Have mercy upon a poor man," I whispered in faked Sucha Singh's voice.

"Where was your mercy when you raped me while my husband was lying on his death bed?"

I was stunned at this revelation, but mumbled. "I'm sorry."

"You showed no compassion, when you drugged me and laid me on the burning logs."

I stuffed leaves under the blanket and pussyfooted to the bushes in the rear of the wall, while the apparition stared at the stuffed blanket. I made a swift, noiseless move, and pounced upon the ghost. The mask fell down and revealed the scarred face of an old woman. She was calm, and I saw warmth in her placid eyes.

"Who are you?" she asked.

"I've been hired by Sucha Singh," I said. "Well, who are you?"

"I'm Taro, Sucha Singh's step-mother."

"You're supposed to have turned to ashes with your husband."

"Satguru saved me."

"How?"

"Guru Nanak intervened and protected me. You can see what flames did to my face and body," she spoke with firm conviction.

My heart cried as I studied her hands and face.

"Please release the grasp on my hair; it hurts."

I dropped my hold and sat in front of her. She stuffed the mask in her bag and said, "Let me explain everything, and then you can decide. When I was fifteen, Sucha Singh's father purchased me for ten thousand rupees. Though my husband was older than my grandfather, I remained faithful to him. My husband became sick and couldn't get out of the bed, and I went daily to the gurdwara to pray for him. During this period, Sucha Singh dragged me to the basement and raped me. I begged him, but he laughed and didn't stop this torture. I was devastated, but was helpless and couldn't reveal this to my husband; it would have broken his heart. When my husband passed away, I told Sucha Singh that I longed to go to my parents, complete my education, and become a teacher. He refused my request and wanted me to become his third wife."

She paused to clear her throat and continued, "I told him that I'll never do that. Then he requested me to become a sati."

"Didn't you tell him that Sikh Scriptures forbid sati?"

"Yes, then he told me that it was only a suggestion, and he was not serious about it. I had a severe headache, and he gave me some medicine, and I passed out. As the flames scorched by body, I regained consciousness. I found myself in a burning pyre, lying over the corpse of my husband. Suddenly, thunder and lightening covered the sky. Sucha Singh and his family left and directed the cremation attendant to complete the job. Strong winds removed the burning logs from my body and rain doused the fire. I managed to crawl out and hid in the bushes. I was stark naked and bleeding blisters covered my body. The rain stopped, and the attendant again lighted the fire. I crawled to his hut, took out one sheet, and walked to the Golden temple and joined the beggars and lepers. With my open bleeding sores, people thought that I was a leper. After fifteen days, I saved enough money to buy a ticket to Hardwar to join the Nirmla Sikh Ashram under a new identity."

"Why did you come back to the place where you suffered so much?"

"To help the women. We are sold like cattle and treated like buffalos. I purchased a mask, appeared on the cremation ground and sent for Sucha Singh who trembled as he stood before me. I ordered him to start a primary school for the girls, and he agreed with some trepidation. I told him that I'll visit him on the cremation anniversary and check him. On my next visit I ordered him to upgrade the girls school to high school level, and he did it."

"You did a noble job," I said. "Why did you kill his horse?"

"He promised not to beat his wives. When I learned from a villager, who visited our Ashram, that he had not kept his word, I had to do something to scare him. I knew the secret passage to the barn, slipped through it, and poisoned his horse."

"All right, killing an animal is not a crime. Why did you break his son's neck?" I asked.

"I didn't hurt his son who came to the cremation ground to see me in place of his father. He was drunk and tried to pierce me with his spear. I screamed and hit the horse with my mask, and the skittish horse bolted. The young man tried to control the horse, but failed. The horse galloped under the banyan tree, and the rider's neck broke as it struck a big limb. Had he been sober, he could have easily avoided this. I took advantage of this accident and told Sucha Singh that I punished him for accepting dowry."

"When did you visit again?"

"I didn't come for six years. Then I had to arrive here to save one young girl's life. This unmarried girl had sinned by becoming pregnant, but the punishment of her sin should not be her death. I told Sucha Singh to send the girl to Nirmla Sikh Ashram and people there will take care of her and the child. He, however, ignored my request, so I came here and told him that he will be killed in three days."

"How are you going to achieve this?"

"My prayers and his fear and guilt will do the job. I'm sure about it," she said.

"I've full sympathy for you and your noble work. You have achieved great things, and it's the time for you to quit. Let's contrive your exit and also help your cause."

"How do you plan to do that?" she said. "Look, I don't need a penny. I enjoy my life of meditation and prayer and will be delighted to meet Guru Nanak any time."

"I'll tell Sucha Singh that you have agreed to stop coming here, provided he gives twenty thousand rupees every year as scholarships to the girls entering college."

"And wife-beating is stopped, no one accepts dowry, and if a girl makes a mistake, she should not be murdered," she added.

"Good, please state these four demands in a clear voice, while I tape it."

As she cleared her throat with a dry cough, I pressed the button on my tape-recorder. She finished her statement, peered into my eyes, and said, "Young man, I count upon you to keep your word. Mind it, our Satguru is always watching us."

She stood up, waved her arm, and left.

I rushed to Sucha Singh's house.

"Did the ghost come?" he asked.

"Yes, it was determined to kill you. I pleaded with it, and it accepted my deal."

"What's that? I'll do anything to save my neck."

"The ghost has just arrived, please listen to it," I said and played the tape which was concealed in my pocket. Sucha Singh listened to it with open mouth. When the ghost's statement ended, he touched the ground with folded hands and said, "Respected sati, I fully agree to your demands and will never break them."

With tears running down his cheeks, Sucha Singh rubbed his nose on the ground.

"Sardar sahib, your obeisance is in the wrong direction. Turn you head to the right," I said.

He pivoted to the right and bowed his head. "I don't see the ghost."

"It doesn't want to reveal its face to you. It stood there, made its statement, and then turned into smoke. Didn't you recognize your step-mother's voice?"

"Yes, are you sure that it won't visit me again?"

"Absolutely, it will come only if you break your promise."

"I pledge by the Holy Book that I'll keep my word."

"Sardar Sahib, I solved your ghost problem," I said. "Call me, if it bothers you again."

He thanked me, and gave me a bundle of bills. I returned the money and said, "Please use these to help the needy girls."

In the evening the village council met and the chairman, Sucha Singh, made the council pass the resolutions which complied with the ghost's demands.

In the morning, I took hold of my motorcycle. When I passed the cremation grounds, I lowered my head toward the wall to honor the noble lady who suffered under the cruel Indian traditions and impersonated as a pernicious ghost to improve the fate of women.

American Astronaut Explores Heavens

June 4, 2026, NASA Mission Control Center, Texas

"NASA Mission Control, Astronaut Gopal speaking. Do you hear me?"

The technician on duty picked up this faint message. He was stunned and said, "Yes, I hear you. Please offer more details about you."

"I was one of the astronauts in the space shuttle which exploded on March 26, 2006."

"I can't believe you. No one survived on that mission."

"I did," Gopal asserted.

"Stop fibbing. We are busy and can't afford to waste time on your hoax."

"Look, I'm alive and want to tell my story to the world," Gopal explained.

"All right, from where are you speaking?" the technician asked.

"The Heavens."

The technician burst into peals of laughter and felt sure that he was speaking to a lunatic. He, however, couldn't ignore the whole affair without verifying it.

"Wait, let me contact my boss," the technician said.

"Who is your boss?"

"John Carpenter."

"He knows me; give him my regards."

John Carpenter joined the conversation. "Gopal, how are you?"

"Fine."

"Well, what is your social security number?"

"781-40-1899," Gopal said. "Well, I give you more information to clear your doubts: My Texas State driver's license number is D6745322. I was born May 4, 1950, in Ludhiana, Punjab, India; I did my Phd. at Purdue University, in 1970. My wife's name is Sita."

"Gopal, wait for two minutes. Let me verify all this."

Soon John checked the computer records and found the information was correct. Still he thought, the identity theft was common, and this smart fellow had stolen Gopal's records and was bamboozling him. He ordered his technician to record the message, so that later on they could analyze and compare with the recorded voice of Gopal.

"Gopal, thanks for waiting. We are recording your message," John said.

"Good, please see that it's published in the major American newspapers. It will benefit and help the human race."

"I'll do my best," John said. "All right, we are ready, go along with your message."

"On March 29, 2006 our space shuttle was hit by flying debris which made a big hole in the spacecraft. This ignited the fuel and flames engulfed us. There was a complete pandemonium. Somehow I managed to eject in my capsule and after traveling two months, I entered the Heavens."

"Stop there. What you say is not correct. We saw the shuttle blowing into tiny pieces and its debris was scattered all over America—from Florida to California. The funeral services were performed for seven astronauts who lost their lives and that included you," John said. "It happened twenty years ago. Why didn't you contact us earlier?"

"I could not, since I was searching for God. Finally, I met Him and immediately decided to reveal His message to the world. I took out my transmitter from the storage at the gate of Hindu Heaven. I tried, and it worked. God was helping me. So here I'm telling my story."

"I don't buy that. Anyhow, go ahead with your story," John said.

"Well, when I noticed the debris hitting the shuttle, I pulled the red lever and shot out. It was a split-second action. Luckily, it worked for me, but my six colleagues missed it and blew up with the shuttle. My capsule worked smoothly for fifteen minutes. Then it started spinning and tumbling. I tried hard to correct it, but failed. I was doomed, since I was traveling at more than twenty times the speed of sound and had no control over my transport. After eight hours I felt a big jolt with a fierce suction effect and suspected I had entered the black hole. I studied the instrument panel and found it was stuck at the right end of the dial. Evidently I was traveling faster than it could display. I was drenched in sweat, and my heart was pounding like the hammers of the gold-leaf crushers. This torture lasted for two hours, and then my capsule stopped shaking and the travel became much smoother. I guessed my capsule was shooting through some kind of vacuum. This eased my nerves, and I checked my provisions. There were food capsules and water to last for twenty days. I reduced my intake and the supplies lasted for fifty days. Fifty torturous days passed, and then I was without food and water for six days. I became weak and could hardly move my arms. I had mental hallucinations and saw faces of Yammas (carrier of the dead) staring at me. I prayed to God and begged Him to end my misery.

"I was dizzy and half-awake. Suddenly there was a jerk and my head hit the dashboard. I glanced at the speedometer and found it alive—the needle hovered around the fifty mark. Thinking I had entered the next world, I rubbed my eyes and pinched myself and found that I was still alive. Soon pitch darkness disappeared, and I saw four suns covering a beautiful landscape in which tall trees loaded with fruit and flowers were kissing the blue sky, and beautiful bushes were waving their arms.

"My capsule came to a shaky halt before a huge arch which was made out of pure gold and studded with flashing diamonds. Men dressed in saffron-colored-uniforms were patrolling the gate. I saw long lines before fifteen turnstiles. People, in white robes, showed their white slips and were conducted to different waiting vehicles. I glanced at the vehicles and was surprised to find those worked without creating any sound or smoke. When I examined further, I discovered their exterior shells were covered with solar panels. I concluded that the solar energy was running them.

"My reverie was shattered, when one soldier jerked me out of the capsule and stared at me with fiery eyes. I trembled and felt sharp pain in my arm.

"'What the hell are you doing here in this funny gizmo?' the soldier yelled after slapping me.

"A ten-foot-tall man, wearing a white robe, and having a white beard which touched the ground, appeared on the scene. With a glow on his face and corona on his head, he looked like a saint to me.

"'Drop him,' he ordered.

"The soldier dumped me on the ground and resumed his duty.

"I grabbed this saint's feet and washed them with my tears.

"'Get up son. Excuse my soldier's conduct. He has never seen a man in your strange outfit. The carrier of the dead takes the souls to the admission halls where the angels check their records. Very few get white slips to enter Heaven, and they arrive here, wearing white robes. We check the slips and transport them to the Heavens allotted to them.'

"He lifted me and touched my head. My exhaustion and weakness disappeared.

"There was no trace of dust, smog, or smoke. The air was free from the smell of burning coal, fuel oil, and gasoline. I filled my lungs with the clean air which was saturated with the fragrance of flowers. Though there were four suns, yet the temperature was in the low seventies, and the cool breeze enhanced the comfort.

"I blinked. 'Sir, I'm finding it hard to adjust my eyes to the glare from the four suns.'

"'It will take you some time to get adjusted. Come in my office; you'll feel more comfortable there.'

"I collected my gear and followed him. The gravitational pull was much smaller than on the earth, but I was trained to adjust to it and had no difficulty in walking behind him. We reached his office and sat on golden thrones. He looked at me and said, 'To which Heaven would you like to go?'

"I was delighted and asked, 'How many Heavens do you have?'

"'We have many: Christian, Muslim, Buddhist, Hindu, Sikh, Jewish, Jain ....'

"Being a practicing Hindu, I thought I would be comfortable in a Hindu Heaven and replied, 'Hindu.'

"He snaked his fingers through his long flowing beard. 'It will take me a few minutes to send you there. Have you any other questions?'

"'Sir, is there any Hell here?'

"'No, but the space, a million miles down this path, belongs to Hell. It's overcrowded—most of the humans land there. You're lucky; we spotted you and pulled you out, otherwise you would have gone there.'

"I touched his feet and said, 'Sir, thanks for saving me. Will I ever be able to see my family?'

"'Time will bring no change in you and your body. If your wife leads a noble life and can earn passage to Heaven, you might see her, but she will be an emaciated old lady.'

"Tears rolled down my cheeks.

"The saint patted my hand and said, 'Calm down. It's all written in your karma. Now get ready to go to the Hindu Heaven.'

"'Sir, I've one more question.'

"'What's that?'

125

"'Sir, how do you keep peace among the different Heavens?'

"He pointed to several barracks and said, 'My soldiers live in those. We report directly to God and stop any effort by any Heaven to infringe upon the rights of the other.'

"'Sir, it must be a tough job. Down on earth religion has caused great death and destruction.'

"'No trouble for me. Here our action is swift and severe.'

"I scratched my head. 'Where can I see God?'

"'He's not confined to any church, temple, mosque, Gurdwara, or any place of worship. He's ubiquitous and is standing right near us.'

"'Doesn't He have a Heaven?'

"'No, He fills all the spaces in the worlds, Heavens, and Hells.'

"'Sir, can you take me to Him?'

"He shook his head. 'No, you have to seek Him yourself.'

"'Can you give me some advice?'

"'Yes, don't get lost in the comforts of the Hindu Heaven, but keep your mind focused upon God. Pray daily, do noble deeds, and someday you'll feel His presence right in your heart.'

"I was thrilled. 'Thanks, now I'm ready to leave.'

"He snapped his fingers, and a two-seater transport parked in front of the door. He seated me and waved his goodbye. Then he punched some keys on his hand-held-control. The hatch closed. The transport shot up without making even a slight whisper. On the dashboard, I saw a highly sophisticated computer flashing its lights. I, however, couldn't fully understand the working of the engines. From the transport's outer surface solar panels and the connecting wires, I concluded these were running on electricity generated by sucking solar heat. After ten minutes the transport stopped, the hatch flew open, and I heard the message: 'You have reached Hindu Heaven. Good luck.'

"I scrambled out, the hatch closed, and the transport flew back.

"While I was trudging along, I met a herd of beautiful Brahmin cows with shimmering golden horns. I bowed with folded hands. Their leader shook its head, and the gold bells around its neck made melodious music. I was surprised when I heard from its mouth: 'Child, welcome to Hindu Heaven.'

"A loud snorting sound ripped my ears. I pivoted my head and noticed a white bull, bigger than ten elephants, flying in the air. I was sure it was Nandi and the person ridding on it was God Shiva, the destroyer. On moving closer, I noticed God Shiva had cobras curled around his biceps and neck, and flames were shooting from his blazing eyes. Several snakes were peeping out of the mountain of black hair which covered his head. Flashes of lightening mixed with roaring thunder appeared underneath the bull's feet.

"Thousands of men, dressed in black robes, were coming in groups of four. I could easily conclude that those were the Yammas. The leader of each group read the statement, and God Shiva nodded. The group bowed and left. The whole process was somber, scary, and depressing. I didn't like God Shiva's Heaven and decided to travel to some other Heaven.

"I covered a few miles and saw a huge marble complex. The sign at the gate announced: 'God Brahma's Heaven.' I knew God Brahma is the creator, and expected better things there. I found workers in white robes busy in their jobs. God Brahma was seated cross-legged on his gold throne. Moon crescents shimmered in his black hair, and he was meditating with half-closed eyes. Workers presented the list of births, and the god nodded with a smile. Everyone was serious and worked like a machine. This looked like a boring, monotonous occupation, and I chose to proceed further.

"Soon I entered God Vishnu's Heaven. God Vishnu is the preserver, and his responsibility is to feed the world. I smelled food and different kinds of spices. Many assistants were arranging and cooking food. I was delighted by the enticing smell, but I had stomach ulcers and decided not to join.

"I was dejected and trudged along with lowered head. Suddenly my ears picked up the soothing music of a flute. I knew God Krishna played it and concluded that I must be reaching his Heaven. I loved music, singing, and dancing, and thought I would be happy there. I sprinted toward it. Soon my olfactory senses rejoiced at the fragrance of flowers and burning incense. I stopped before the gate, and the gatekeeper asked me, "What do you want?"

"'Join god Krishna's staff.'

"The gatekeeper studied me from my head to shoes, gave me an orange robe, pointed to the showers, and said, 'Go there, take your bath and get into this robe.'

"When I came out, the gatekeeper examined me and said, 'What are you wearing under the gown?'

"'My underwear.'

"'Pull it down. You are not permitted to wear anything under the gown.'

"I removed my underwear and felt almost naked in that thin transparent robe.

"The gatekeeper took hold of my clothes and gear, placed those in a large box, gave me a slip, and said, 'In case you want to leave this place or are fired, remember your things are in box number ASD176589. Now follow the signs and go to the prayer hall.'

"I entered the hall, bowed with folded hands, and sat cross-legged on the marble floor. This mammoth hall was illuminated with hundreds of multicolored flashing chandeliers, and soft music was drifting around. The beating of the drums started, and God Krishna emerged with his flute. I was hypnotized and stood up like the others and started dancing and singing. God Krishna selected twenty young girls to dance with him on the stage. It was a soul inspiring spectacle to watch God Krishna playing the flute and frolicking with frisky damsels. More than four hundred women, who had assembled here, were called Gopees. They belonged to God Krishna, and no other man could dare to touch them. I was transcended to a much higher spiritual level and thoroughly enjoyed the prayers, ignoring all distractions. The session ended, and I was escorted to my room which was small, but nicely furnished. I was told to report in the morning to the manager who would allot me a job.

"Next morning the manager studied my papers and said, 'With your training in transportation, you're selected to work on the god's vehicles.'

"'What are those?' I asked.

"'Our god uses ninety chariots, and you have to assist in maintaining those.'

"I had never seen a chariot in my life, but at this stage, I was prepared to accept any work.

"So I joined the team which took care of the horses, and washed, polished, and repaired the chariots. It was a backbreaking job, but the evening prayers always touched my soul, and I felt rejuvenated.

"After ten months my prurient hormones began fluttering, and I longed for the company of a woman. God Krishna had hundreds of wives, but we were not allowed to kiss anyone. Those beautiful women lived in a separate building, far away from men, and we could only watch them in the prayer hall in their transparent robes. I thought it wasn't fair.

"One day I decided to slip into the god's harem. It was a dangerous move, but I had lost control over myself. I crawled to the gate and found it guarded by a tall, muscular man who was holding a flashing sword. When I approached him, he shouted, 'Stop there!'

"I stood with folded hands, trembling. He looked me over and said, 'You must be new to the place; this is out-of-bounds for men.'

"'I didn't know about it. I'm an astronaut and have just come here.'

"He arched his brows. 'What is an astronaut?'

"'A person who travels by special flying machines to the moon.'

"He laughed and said, 'You must be drunk. No one can dare to step on the moon.'

"'I did,' I said with determined looks.

"'You are weaving fairy tales, and I like them. Come on, sit on that stool, and tell me your stories.'

"I described the rockets and other space vehicles, and how those can reach the moon. After I completed my narration, I asked him, 'When did you come here?'

"'1924.'

"'From which part of the world?'

"'India.'

"'Which state?'

"'Palta.'

"I exclaimed, 'I also belonged to the same place, so we are brothers.'

"He extended his hand, and I shook it. My hand cried over the grip from a steel-vise.

"I asked him, 'What were you doing in India?'

"'Exactly the same which I'm doing here—guarding a harem.'

"I knew the Indian maharajas always hired eunuchs as controllers of the harems and asked, 'How could you get the job?'

"'When I was young, I loved ogling beautiful girls and good food. The harem-controller's job provided all those benefits. My physical strength impressed the maharaja, and I was selected. Before joining my work I was castrated, and the palace doctor verified it.'

"'Too bad, you lost your sting.'

"A wry smile appeared on his face. 'Well, the benefits I got more than compensated for the loss.'

"'How was the job?'

"'Terrific! I became an expert and could easily read a woman from her face, body movements, and speech. I controlled five hundred women, young and old, and never a single one went astray.'

"'How did you come to God Krishna's Heaven?'

"'I was killed in a car accident in 1924, and my soul was brought by Yammas to God Shiva. I requested God Shiva to give me another chance in a human body. God Shiva shouted, 'That's Brahma's job.'

"'Kindly let me plead my case with him,' I begged.

"God Shiva nodded with a big scowl, and I appeared in God Brahma's durbar. I caught the god's feet and cried. God Brahma opened his eyes and said, 'What do you want?'

"'Chance to have a human birth.'

"'I gave you a strong healthy body, but you defiled it and hindered my procreation.'

"I wept and pummeled my head on the ground near the god's feet and begged, 'Please give me one more chance. I'll never lose my potency and will produce more than one hundred children.'

"The god glanced at the ledger and said, 'You have not earned enough points to become a man.' I held his feet and petitioned, 'Then please make me a Brahma bull in India, and I'll bless many sacred cows daily.' God Brahma smiled and was ready to grant my wish. At this, God Krishna's secretary rushed in and pleaded, 'God Krishna requests you to send this man to control his harem. With his many years of experience, this person can correct all our problems.' God Brahma couldn't refuse his friend's request, and I landed this job.'

"'Don't you crave for a gorgeous juicy woman?' I asked.

"'I did, but God Krishna, who can read each human heart, noticed the storm in my ticker, took me aside, and enlightened me. When he patted my back, all my craving for women vanished, and I could see a woman like any other creature.'

"I held his hand and requested, 'I'm in deep trouble and can't sleep. Can you help me to secure God Krishna's blessings?'

"'Yes, come after two hours when my shift ends, and I'll try to help you.'

"I thanked him and slipped to my job in the stables.

"After two hours I met the guard who took me to the private chambers of God Krishna. Through the half-parted door, I saw God Krishna sprawled on a huge bed, and young girls were rubbing his one side with their firm breasts, and the god's toes were twirling the ivory breast of a buxom lady. There was soft sitar music and melodious singing. I looked at his other side and found it was immersed in boiling mustard oil, and the awful stink of burning flesh and oil was choking the air. I was dumbfounded and asked the guard who explained, 'You can see for yourself, our god's body is above any pain and pleasure.'

"The guard went inside and returned after ten minutes. When I stepped in, I found God Krishna seated on his throne. I latched onto his feet and implored, 'I want to get rid of my libido and find contentment and peace.'

"The god patted my back, chanted a mantra, and said, 'Remove your gown.'

"I shed my robe. The god clapped his hands, and two naked beautiful girls appeared and embraced and kissed me, while rubbing my lingam (penis). I felt cool inside and my lingam didn't budge a fraction of a millimeter.

"I thanked God Krishna and left for my job. The lust had vanished from my heart, and I found no difference between a naked girl and a bush.

"I was at peace with myself, and the desire to meet God took hold of my heart. I remembered the advice given to me at the gate to the Heavens and began focusing on God. After my shift, I went to the kitchen and washed the dirty dishes. I slept four hours and devoted my spare time to help the needy and sick.

"Many years slipped away, and I continued my efforts to reach God.

"One day I saw an ugly old leper, with bleeding wounds, begging for help. He had slipped in the cow dung storage pit and was sinking. I stood there for a few seconds and saw many Heaven dwellers passing by without offering any help. On hearing the leper's cries, they lowered their heads, and moved faster. I threw off my gown, jumped into the stinking mess, and dragged out the leper. Then I used my gown to clean him. When I finished wiping, the whole area was flooded with light, and the leper vanished. I heard a soothing voice, 'Son, you have passed the final test. I grant you Nirvana.'

"I was completely transformed. All hatred, worry, animosity, and prejudices had disappeared from my heart, and I felt lighter than air. I was engulfed in peace, love, and eternal joy and saw and felt God in everything. I learned that God doesn't have any form or shape. He is omniscient, omnipotent, and exists in His creation. If you are good to His creation, you're serving Him and can feel His presence."

Gopal paused to clear his throat.

"Hard to believe all this," John said.

"Look, John, I tell you that these are the facts, since I don't gain anything by fibbing. When my friends, including you and other persons, enter the next world and are lucky to get into a Heaven, I request them to reach me at god Krishna's Heaven and verify my statement. I'll be glad to welcome them. They, however, should remember that I'm working at the stables, and my cubicle number is 98675. That ends my message. Thanks for listening."

"Goodbye, friend," John said.

John and other experts analyzed the taped voice and found it perfectly matched with the messages recorded by Gopal in his previous flights and reported their findings to the NASA administrator who reported it to the President. The President consulted his advisors and decided to conceal the incident from the public. Gopal's name, on the wall built for the astronauts who lost their lives in space, was not removed, and NASA staff was ordered to keep mum about the whole affair.

On July 17, 2030, when John Carpenter was lying on his death bed, he decided to keep his promise and revealed Gopal's message to the press and TV.

Locust Ate My Cycle

"Stop pouting, you'll get your cycle," my dad, a towering giant, snaked his fingers through his salt-and-pepper beard and said.

I hugged him and asked, "When?"

"Next month after we harvest our crops."

"Will I get Raleigh, similar to what Nathu has?"

He nodded with a smile.

"Dad, will you buy me a shining bell with it?"

"Yes."

I thanked Dad, and my heart started dancing.

I was nine-years-old, and we lived in Thati Village, located at the foot of the majestic Himalayan Mountains. My school was four miles away, and I had to trudge to it. Nathu, the chief's son, had a cycle, and he refused to let me touch it. Daily, as I lumbered on the dusty road, he whizzed by me ringing his bell.

Today, as usual, I took hold of my book bag and began my journey to the school. I was flying in the clouds dreaming about my cycle, and I smiled and waved to Nathu, as he swished by me.

I reached the school which was a twenty feet by forty feet mud room and greeted my teacher, an emaciated man with a perpetual frown. He simply groaned. I joined the class, and we sang the multiplication tables. Then we sat down on jute mattresses and did our mathematics on our slates. Four grades were separated by white lines, drawn on the mud floor. It was 1905, and there was no electricity in our villages. One large mat fan, hanging from the ceiling, cooled the class. Students took turns to pull the rope which ran over a pulley and worked the fan.

In those days we didn't have paper or pencils. All students wrote on a quarter inch thick board which was eighteen inches wide and three feet long. At lunch we rushed to wash the board in the pond near the school. After clearing the writing, we pasted the board with yellow clay and placed it along the school wall. In one hour they dried out, and our writing pads were ready.

At lunch, I gave my good news to Nathu, but he smirked, "I'll only believe when I see you riding."

"Don't worry, I'll race with you," I said.

We walked to the pond. Nathu started throwing stones at the frogs, and the board slipped from his hand. Two buffalos sloshed near us and moved the board into deeper waters. Nathu couldn't swim, and he begged me.

"I'll get your board, provided you promise to teach me how to ride a cycle," I said.

"Okay, I agree," he snapped. "Hurry up and get my board."

I removed my clothes, splashed into the water, swam to his board, and retrieved it. After the class he helped me to ride the bicycle. In six days I mastered riding and was ready for the grand moment of my life—ride my cycle.

The sizzling month of June arrived, and our crops were getting ready to be harvested. Every morning at three Dad and his hired hand went to the fields. I took breakfast to them at seven and then went to school.

One day Dad rushed home and told my mother, sister, and younger brother to get ready to fight the armies of locust which were coming toward our village. He gave us large pans and steel rods and said, "Use these to scare the locust and yell at the top of your lungs."

I had never seen a locust and thought it must be bigger than a lion, since Dad was so terrified. We ran to our fields and practiced our action.

Dad pointed to the sky and said, "Get ready, they're coming."

I was stunned, since I was expecting an attack on the ground. The sky became dark, and the sun was covered by the noisy insects. The armies of locust raided our crop. I scared them, and they hopped forward. When we cleared one batch, another wave arrived.

I cussed the tiny insect which always rubbed its legs on the wings and created cacophonous noise. This two-horned monster ate with its mouth and excreted from its bottom at the same time and kept singing. We shrieked, banged the pans, and kicked the locust. After six hours the locust left our fields, leaving behind their dead and our ruined crops.

We slumped on the ground with sore throats and tired bodies. My three-years-old brother, however, continued hitting the dead locusts, and Mom calmed him down.

We drank buttermilk, and Dad patted my back and said, "The dirty locust have eaten your cycle, and you have to wait."

"How long?"

"Two years. This year I've to take a loan to make both ends meet. It will take me two years to pay back the loan, and then I'll buy your cycle."

Uncontrolled tears trickled down my cheeks. "What will we do if these critters attack us again next year?"

"They won't bother us for thirteen years."

Mom wrapped her arms around my shoulders and said, "Wipe your tears; you're my brave son."

I smiled and said, "Mom, I'm fine."

In my heart I cussed the locust which ate my cycle and blamed God for creating it.

Frazzled and covered with dust, we returned home. Dad took his bath and Mom cooked food. We ate without saying a word, completely buried under the lava of our emotions. My dad could face any trouble and danger, but today his eyes were misty and his voice was choked.

After dinner Dad went to bed, and Mom told me, "Come Bir, we must thank God."

I was dumbfounded and shook my head. She pulled my arm, and we walked to the temple and prayed.

"Mom, why are you thanking God who has destroyed our crops?"

"Son, we must thank God for the things He has provided for us and not moan over the loss of the crops. Next year He will give us bigger crops, and you'll ride your cycle."

"Mom, why did God create this destructive locust?"

"God has made eighty-four million species, and He is the only one who knows the reason."

During the night I dreamt I was riding my cycle and an army of locust was attacking me. They chewed up my cycle, and I fell flat on the ground. I screamed and Mom rushed to comfort me.

Catching a Romantic Ghost

Thati Village, Punjab, India, March 29, 1952

"Bir, I'm a moth who is rushing to embrace its flame and nothing can stop me," my cousin, Mohan, a muscular man in his early twenties, laid his flute on the ground and said.

I grasped his hand. "Don't be a fool. Forget Kanta; she's now married to the ruthless chief."

"I can't," he moaned.

"I'm meeting you after two years," I said. "Tell me, why you left college and where have you been hiding."

"Sorry, I didn't confide in you; I wanted to protect Kanta. I needed money to elope with her. In the wanted pages of the newspaper, I saw a job in the mines. This job was risky, but it paid a very good salary. I told this to Kanta who promised to wait for me," he said and dabbed his eyes. "I can't see why she didn't keep her word."

"Look, the chief's wife died, and he could easily purchase Kanta's father," I explained.

"Damn it, she was sold like a cow. The chief is fifty years older than her," he said and banged his fist on the ground.

"The poor girl has already suffered enough in this forced marriage; don't throw salt on her wounds."

"I want to see her alone tonight. If she's happy in her marriage, I'll go back to the mines which are two thousand miles from here and will never bother her."

"Mohan, be careful. The chief would never allow you to seduce his child bride, and if you're caught, he will chop off your head."

"I'll surreptitiously climb the back wall of the chief's compound during the middle of the night and take my chance."

"Wish you good luck," I said.

He grabbed me in his arms and said, "I'm taking this plunge. If I'm killed, my ghost will always be playing the flute at this place. Please promise to come here on a full-moon-night and hear me."

"All right, whenever, I'm in the village, I'll visit this place on Puranmasi (full-moon-night)."

We turned reticent and watched the moonbeams dancing on the ripples and listened to the moaning wind cavorting with the bushes.

Mohan was a musical prodigy—he could cut a piece of bamboo, make a few holes in it, and touch the product to his lips. The music that came out of this crude flute could halt the birds from chirping and mosquitoes from buzzing.

I wanted to stop him, but it was impossible for me; he was much stronger. I embraced him, and his hot tears dripped on my shoulder. I said goodbye, left the sandy bank, and trudged home with a heavy heart; he started playing the flute.

I went to bed, but couldn't sleep and prayed for my cousin. Early in the morning, I went to Mohan's house and learned from his father that Mohan had not returned from the river. I sprinted to the chief's mansion and knocked at the door. I was told by the servant the chief and his wife were sleeping. Then I hurried to the river and started searching. Soon I was joined by Mohan's father and other villagers. Five hundred yards downstream, we discovered Mohan's clothes, and a suicide note. Divers and nets failed to produce Mohan's body, and all thought the river had swallowed him or the crocodiles had eaten him. Mohan's parents cremated his clothes and his picture, and threw the ashes in the sacred river. I was devastated.

The full moon night came after five days, and I went to the place where Mohan had promised to play his flute. I strongly believed in life after death and was sure to hear him. I sat cross-legged and listened to the singing crickets. I looked at my watch: 12.02. I thought Mohan's spirit must not have been released by the Yammas (carriers of the dead). Suddenly, I heard the mellifluous music of a flute and thought Mohan's ghost was there.

"Thanks Mohan, how are you in the next world?" I shouted.

There was no response, and the melodious music continued.

I thought I was dreaming, so I scrambled up, washed my face with the cold river water, and returned. The music was still there. Nobody in the village could play a flute like this, so I was certain Mohan's ghost was keeping his promise. I sprinted to the village and brought Mohan's parents, and they all heard the flute. According to our beliefs, the persons who commit suicide are not welcomed in the next world, and they become malevolent and pernicious. Therefore all the villagers were scared and none dared to come to that part of the river bank during the night. I, however, kept my promise and visited the place on full moon nights and enjoyed the music for two hours.

Next year I completed my degree and immigrated to America. I completed my Ph.D. at Ohio State University and started teaching at Cleveland High where I met Emily, a science teacher. I courted her for two years, and we were married in 1962.

One evening, Emily and I were watching the TV program: "Ghost Hunters."

"Emily, have you ever seen a ghost?"

"No, how can you see a thing that doesn't exit?" she said.

"My father did see my grandfather's ghost who told him the location where he had buried gold coins and stored the carrot seed. After we dug the coins and found the seed, everyone was certain about the identity of the ghost."

"Well, did you ever have any encounter with a ghost?"

141

"Yes, before coming to America, I heard my cousin's ghost playing a flute."

She peered into my eyes and asked, "Did you see and touch the ghost?"

"No, I heard his music."

"Someone must be using a tape."

"Emily, this is impossible, since nobody in our village has a recording device."

"I think it was your mental hallucination," she said.

"Let me tell you the complete story, and then you can decide."

I narrated the whole incident.

"It looks strange," she said. "Well, I'm a science teacher and would like to explore the haunted place."

"We're visiting my parents during the coming summer vacation, and I'll show you that site."

"Good, I'll carry my gizmos and catch that ghost."

During the summer vacation of 1964, we took PAN AM to New Delhi, and a taxi brought us to my village. After we recovered from jet lag, I looked at the calendar and found the coming night would have a full moon.

I addressed Emily, "Tonight I can show you the place where Mohan's ghost plays the flute."

"Good, to explore it I've brought my sound measuring tools and devices to check the magnetic and electrical impulses."

At eleven in the night, I took out my family sword, since I firmly believed that ghosts are afraid of the swords, and guns can't harm them. Emily attached to her shoulders a backpack full of her devices, and we trudged to the river and sat on its bank. There was complete silence which was frequently punctured by the hoots from the owls.

"I don't hear any flute," she said.

"Wait till it's midnight."

After fifteen minutes the flute music entered my ears, and I rejoiced, "Do you hear the music?"

"Yes, let's trace its source."

"There is not a soul on this bank. Now you must believe that Mohan's ghost is playing his flute."

"Stop talking and follow me, as I use my tracking devices," she said and fixed her headphones.

She walked ahead of me, and I saw the needles shaking on her meters as she walked forward. She covered five hundred yards and stopped near thick shrubs.

"The music is coming from inside this cluster of bushes," she said.

I parted the bushes with my sword and said, "Look, there's nothing here."

She ignored my remarks and continued snaking through the thorny bushes. Finally, she stopped near a place and said, "Remove these branches."

As I dropped my sword on the ground, the music went dead. I pulled away the thorny branches and found a wooden trap door.

"Your ghost lives in a cellar here," she said.

"Let me open the door and step inside with my sword."

I lifted the door and smelled perfume and incense. I flashed my light and found steps leading down. After I descended eleven steps, I saw a large room with a costly rug covering the floor, and its walls were plastered with local lime. A shaft in the ceiling provided fresh outside air, and a lamp was burning in the corner near a large bed. A shadowy figure rushed toward me with a knife. I beamed my light on his face and yelled, "Mohan!"

He threw away the knife and rushed to hug me.

"Bir, I know you went to America. When did you come to Thati?"

"Three days ago, and I came here to keep my pledge with you," I said. "Let me introduce you to my wife."

I turned my flashlight toward the steps and said, "Emily, come down. I've captured the ghost."

143

I assisted Emily to climb down, and introduced Emily and Mohan to each other.

We sat on the rug, and I said, "Mohan, you created a big hoax. We all thought you were drowned in the river, and your ghost was playing the flute."

He cleared his throat with a painful effort and said, "I'm sorry, but I've not hurt anybody."

"Does Kanta know that you are alive?"

"Yes, she and her husband are the only persons who know that I'm not dead."

"How did you manage all this?" I asked.

"Let me start from the beginning: After I said goodbye to you, I waited for one hour and then left for the chief's house. I climbed the courtyard wall and discovered the rear window of the bedroom was open. I sneaked into the room. Kanta was awake, and she flew into my arms. I found the chief was snoring and his mouth was covered with blood. I knew he had performed the voodoo ritual to cure his impotency. Open tins of opium and aphrodisiac paste were lying on the floor near the slaughtered chicken. The chief had made use of all these things to arouse his lingam (penis), but it still looked like a dead leach. The chief opened his eyes and saw me.

"'Kanta, do you see Mohan?' the chief stuttered.

"'Yes, I do see him.'

"The chief shot up from the bed and said, 'Let me get my gun to shoot him.'

"Kanta and I tied him to the bed, and I said, 'Listen to us and don't make any noise, otherwise I'd be forced to wring your neck.'

"He agreed and Kanta addressed him, 'Husband, I've been true to you, but you have failed to perform your conjugal duty, and I'm still a virgin. You want me to give you sons without performing your part of the job. I can't bear all this and want to run away with Mohan and lead a normal life.'

"'I'll kill you both,' the chief yelled.

"'You can't; you're in our grip. We'll give you a heavy dose of your opium. Tomorrow you would be found dead with your drug, and none will blame me for your taking an overdose. Mohan will slip away and hide somewhere. After your cremation, I'll sell your lands and go with Mohan to a far away place,' Kanta said.

"Tears trickled down the chief's eyes, and he begged, 'Please spare my life. Kanta, I love you and implore you to show mercy. I'm willing to do anything you want.'

"'I'll stay, provided you permit me to spend nights with Mohan. We'll give you nice children.'

"The chief stuttered, 'I can't; it will hurt my family pride.'

"I stepped in and said, 'Your pride will never be tarnished.'

"'How?'

"'I'll stage my death and my ghost will live in a room which I'll dig on the river bank and play my flute. On hearing a ghost playing a flute, the people will never come near my hiding place. You bring Kanta to me during the night, and she'll return to you early in the morning. You'll get handsome sons. Nobody will know the part played by me, and you can proudly display your offspring.'

"The chief grinned. 'I love that. Kanta will still be my wife, and I'll have sons.'

"So I staged my drowning. When my parents threw my ashes over the river, I was hiding in the bushes and was devastated to hear their keening and cries. Thus I turned into a ghost. Now coming back to the present: Slowly I expanded my hideout into a comfortable home. The chief had been providing me with all the luxuries of life, food, wine, clothing, and a wonderful woman, and I enjoy my flute. During the night I come out and swim in the river. I've produced two sons, and another child is on the way."

Mohan took a deep breath, released it with pursed lips, and said, "Bir, all have benefited from my turning into a ghost. If you expose me, it will destroy many lives. The chief adores

145

his sons, and they worship their father. Kanta is respected and admired as a devoted wife, and I'm ecstatic about it."

I turned to Emily and said, "Don't you think that we should allow this ghost to continue playing his flute?"

"I agree, this is a good ghost who is helping several people. I, too, enjoyed his music."

Mohan bowed with folded hands towards Emily and said, "Bhabi (sister-in-law), I'm sorry to have met you under such strange circumstances. I do love your husband, and we have been good friends."

With tears in our eyes, we shook hands with Mohan and climbed out of the hole. I closed the trap door and covered it with branches.

Emily and I sat on the river bank and watched the waves and shimmering stars.

I wondered how Karma leads humans to different paths, lands, situations, and ways of life. Mohan was destined to lead the life of a ghost.

Almighty Cobra God

"Nath is dying and the chief wants you to come to his house immediately," said the chief's farmhand who had come running and was out of breath.

I placed my camera in my pocket, cycled at my top speed, and reached chief's two-story brick home. I heard the sound of the drum and the jangle of the bells and thought some sort of prayer ritual was in progress. I entered the living room, stood in the corner, and noticed the curtains were fully drawn, and the dim light was provided by the flickering wicks of two earthen lamps. Incense burning in two large brass pots tried to mute the fetid smell. The twisting tendrils of smoke shot from the pots and curled toward the ceiling, creating ghostly figures on the walls. The furniture had been removed, and there was one string cot on which my classmate, Nath, was lying. The chief and his wife, seated cross-legged on the floor, struggled to stifle their sobs.

A bald man with a huge paunch bunny hopped around the cot, and a black cobra, curled around his neck, hissed and flicked its tongue. He wore a tiny loincloth, and a channel of perspiration flowed down from his head to his forehead, nose, chest, bellybutton, and then sprayed the floor. The bells tied to his ankles, wrists, and waist made jarring sounds. I knew his idiosyncratic chants were meant to scare the Yammas (the carrier of the dead) and to appeal to the Cobra God. I recognized the dancer: He was the head priest of our Cobra God Temple.

Nath and I were pre-med students at Santam Dharam College, Ambala, forty miles from our village.

I grew up with blind faith in the Cobra God, but after studying four years in college and interacting with students of other religions, I had my doubts about this archaic ceremony for treating a snake bite. In India eighty percent of the snakes are not poisonous, and their bites caused a slight fever. The priest could claim success of his ritual in those cases. Where he failed, he concocted an excuse that the patient had incurred the wrath of the Cobra God. So my people had unshakable trust in this ceremony.

I couldn't dare to stop this ritual and get clobbered, so I kept mum, hoping the priest would take a breather, and then I would meet the chief and check my friend.

"Cobra God has rejected my petition, and nothing can save Nath," the priest stopped dancing and announced.

Nath's parents slapped their foreheads and cried, "Cobra God have mercy on us."

The priest wiped the perspiration from his forehead with the back of his hand, smudging the three painted white lines. Then he dabbed his tipple chin with the end of his dhoti and slumped on the floor. The black cobra, which had been circling around his neck, raised its hood, hissed, and jumped into his lap.

Nath's mother, a lady with white hair, grabbed the priest's feet and asked, "Why has the god turned down your request?"

"He is mad at Nath."

"Please make another petition," she begged.

The priest shook his head, pointed to the blue blister on Nath's arm, and said, "Look at the stamp implanted by the god; I can read the message written on it."

"What is the message?"

"Nath fornicated in the temple in presence of our god," he said.

"Nath would never do that, since he worshiped the Cobra God and knew god's punishment," she said. "I think someone else, who resembled Nath, was sinning inside the sacred temple, and our god mistook him for Nath."

"Impossible, our god is ubiquitous and infallible," the priest said. "All right, I've done my best. Resign to the god's will and make arrangements for the cremation."

The chief nodded with a sigh. The priest clambered up, coiled the cobra around his neck, and left.

I greeted the chief, and he told me, "Nath wanted to see you."

"When I got your message, I cycled here. My bad luck, I missed talking to Nath. Let me take his pictures."

"Go ahead and hurry up," The chief said.

When I flashed the camera, I noticed Nath's breathing. I felt his pulse; it was still throbbing.

"Nath is not dead," I shouted.

"Why do you say that?" the chief questioned.

"Feel his pulse."

The chief checked the pulse and said, "It's weak and fading away. Our Cobra God has punished him and no power on earth can save him."

"Sometimes a drowning person can be saved by a straw," I said. "Let me bring Doctor Lalu."

"All right, you can try, but I don't trust him. He has no medical degree. He worked as a peon in the army hospital. When he retired, he opened his bogus practice," the chief dabbed his eyes and said. "Go and bring our snake-charmer. He can handle a snake bite."

I wanted to explain my reasons for getting the doctor but gave up the idea, since it wouldn't have changed the chief's decision. I've seen snake-charmers treating snake bites and thought he might be able to save my friend.

I took hold of my bicycle and shot to the mud hut which was located outside the village boundary. As I knocked at the door, a tall man, with black shoulder-length hair, opened it.

"Mangu, the chief wants you to come to his house immediately."

"Why?" he smirked.

"His son has been bitten by a cobra."

He caressed his walrus mustache and said, "Well, well, well, the mighty chief is in a fix."

"Yes, and he needs your help."

"Look, I'm too tired, but I can't refuse him. Wait a minute; let me get my equipment."

I adjusted hefty Mangu and his baskets on the back seat of my cycle, and in five minutes we reached the chief's house.

The chief rushed to grab Mangu's hand and said, "Mangu, heal my son."

"Don't worry chief, I'll do my best."

Mangu opened a small cane basket, took out a white bead, and addressed me, "Hurry up, bring a cup of Brahmin cow's milk."

I sprinted to the kitchen and brought a glass of milk. Mangu washed the bead with milk and said, "Mani is ready to suck the poison."

He punctured the blister, placed the Mani over it, and said, "Let me request Cobra God to grant power to my Mani."

He tapped the edge of his bigger basket, and a black cobra crawled out of it. Then he pressed his lips on his Beena (wind instrument), and enchanting music filled the room. The cobra raised its hood and started swaying, keeping time with the music.

Nath's mother whispered, "Holy cow, the Cobra God is listening to Mangu's pleading and is waving his approval."

I knew it was merely a show. The cobras are deaf, and they raise their heads and swing to protect themselves from the swinging Beena.

After ten minutes, the music stopped, and the cobra crawled back into the basket. Mangu lifted the bead, pressed it, and moaned, "My Mani has failed to suck the poison."

"Why?" the chief asked.

"Your son is punished by our god, and my Mani can't go against the god's orders," he said. "Sorry chief, I'm helpless in this matter."

Then Mangu faced me. "Carry me back to my home."

The chief nodded, and I took Mangu to his mud hut. When the cycle reached the door, I found his daughter waiting for him.

"Dad, how is Nath?"

"Bimla, yammas have arrived for him."

"Could you do something for him?"

He shook his head.

I noticed tears in her blue eyes. She covered her face with the end of her sari and dashed into the house.

Nath had confided to me that Bimla was one of his trophies. I knew Nath could charm a young girl faster than a snake-charmer can attract a cobra. He was God Brahma's perfect creation: He had chiseled features on his honey-colored face and was an expert flute player. He was also the champion wrestler, and it puzzled me how he could make better grades than me.

I dumped Mangu and shot like a tornado to the chief's house. When I stepped in the living room, I saw the chief and his brother had lifted Nath and were going to place him on the floor.

"Lay the body back on the cot. Nath is not dead; let me check," I screamed.

They placed the body on the cot, and I felt the pulse. It was faint, but still there.

"Chief, Nath is still alive. Please let me bring Doctor Lalu now."

"Go ahead."

I raced my cycle to Doctor Lalu's shop. At the door, I met, Kamla, Lalu's young daughter.

"Is Doctor in?" I asked her.

"Yes," she dabbed her heavily painted face and said. "Bir, you look like a ghost. What's wrong?"

"Nath is dying."

"What is his sickness?"

"A cobra bit him."

A sigh escaped her lips. "Ram, Ram, Ram, let me get Dad."

She sprinted into the house which was at the rear of the shop. A gangly old man, wearing a white coat, emerged with his bag. He grabbed his cycle, and we raced to the chief's house.

Lalu rushed inside the living room, greeted the chief, used his stethoscope on Nath, and said, "Nath's heart is still beating; let me give him anti-venom injection."

As he opened his bag, his chin fell, and he moaned, "Holy Cow! My syringe is missing."

Then he faced me and said, "Bir, rush to my shop and get one syringe from my assistant, Baldev."

I cycled to the doctor's shop and met Baldev who told me, "Doctor must have misplaced it; let me give you a new one."

He unpacked a box and handed me a new syringe. I returned in six minutes and gave it to Lalu who loaded it and punctured Nath's limp arm. I studied Nath's breathing and felt sure Lalu was doing all this to please the chief and collect his fee; poor Nath had already left the world.

Lalu again placed the stethoscope near Nath's heart, slapped his forehead, and said, "Yammas have taken him."

The chief snuffed the wicks of the lamps, thus announcing the death of his son. Then he and his brother laid the corpse on the floor, since now it belonged to the Mother Earth.

The dark room was filled with cries, moans, and sobs. Soon the priest, who performed the cremations, arrived. The corpse was washed with sacred water, wrapped in a white sheet, carried on a bier to the cremation grounds, and placed on a pile of wood. The priest poured ghee in the corpse's mouth, lighted the hay in the logs, and flames started roasting the handsome young man. Tears crawled down my cheeks.

Summer vacation ended, and I resumed my studies. The thought of Nath being murdered, however, haunted me. Nath didn't see the cobra biting him, and I've never seen any person having a bite on his biceps. Nath had been sleeping with Shiela, the priest's daughter, and Kamla, the snake-charmer's daughter. Both girls knew how to handle cobras and could have easily made a cobra bite Nath while he was inebriated. Nath had shattered their hearts by getting engaged to the neighboring chief's daughter. I took one week's leave and decided to investigate the death.

I went to the Cobra God Temple, purchased flowers at the gate, sat in the dark corner, and waited for my chance. After one hour the head priest left for the comfort station, deputing his daughter to take care of the worshipers. I stepped out of the shadows and made my offering. Shiela threw the flowers on the marble statue and blessed me. In her saffron robe, she looked like Goddess Parvati.

"Shiela, can I have a few words with you in private?"

"What do you want to discuss?"

"Nath," I whispered.

She called the assistant priest and requested him to relieve her. We moved outside the temple.

"Our friend met a terrible death," I said.

"I know that, but he was punished by our god."

"I think he was murdered."

"Who did that?" she asked.

"I suspect you."

"Why me?"

"I know you were lovers, and he disappointed you by accepting the hand of another girl."

She dabbed her eyes. "Yes, I was devastated, but I never harmed him."

"Look, Nath told me that you always carry a small cobra in your handbag. Snakes can't harm you, since your family blood has become immune by many snake bites."

"I do carry a cobra with me to protect myself. One evening, while I was cleaning the prayer room, Nath grabbed me, and I scared him with my snake."

"Well, we are sitting in our god's temple, and he is watching us. If you lie, you know the god's punishment," I said.

"All right, Nath met me in the basement of the temple every Tuesday. After his engagement, I took a pledge to kill him, but he didn't show up. I swear by Cobra God that I've told you the truth."

"Does your father know about your relationship with Nath?"

"Yes, Nath always touched Dad's feet and promised him that he will marry me after he got his degree."

Now I could rationalize the priest's behavior while treating Nath. Instead of sorrow, there was gratification in his beady eyes.

I had been examining Shiela's face and the tone of her voice and was convinced that she was not prevaricating. Then I decided to get some information about my next suspect from her.

"Do you know Bimla?" I asked.

"Which Bimla?"

"Snake-charmer's daughter."

"She is a Sudra. I heard rumors about Nath meeting her and cornered him. He pulled his ears and said, 'I'll never touch a Sudra; I don't want to burn in hell.'"

"Well, Bimla has milky skin and doesn't look like a Sudra."

"I know her mother was frightened by a British soldier. So she is further polluted by a foreign blood."

I said my goodbye, and Sheila walked back to the temple.

I rode my cycle to Bimla's mud hut. She was hanging clothes on a line in her yard. I parked my cycle and looked around to make sure that no one was near her.

"Bimla, our friend Nath is gone."

She stifled a sigh.

"Nath told me many times that he was madly in love with you."

"He promised to marry me in a civil court in the town, after he became a doctor, and I believed him," she said. "Look at the stinking dog; he threw me away like a dirty leaf plate."

"He was a docile chicken and couldn't take a stand against his parent's decision."

She dabbed her eyes. "He has created hell for me."

"How?"

"My father saw him kissing me and threatened to kill us."

"Did he use one of his cobras on Nath?"

"Impossible. Father had been away for two days and returned thirty minutes before you came to fetch him," she said.

"I think you took your revenge."

"How could I do that?"

"You know how to handle cobras."

Her face turned redder than her ruby nose-ring, and she said, "Buzz out before I shriek. I tell you in clear words that we have no hand in Nath's death. There are thousands of wild cobras, and anyone of those could have attacked him."

After observing her face muscles and the tone of her voice, I was sure she had told the truth.

I returned to my college and contacted my professor who was doing research on cobras.

"India has the biting type of cobras which bite with their fangs and inject venom. The bite turns into a blue blister which has two clear marks from the fangs," he explained.

I pointed to a tube in a stand and asked, "Sir, what's in that tube?"

"Cobra venom. snake-charmers call it 'Sanom'."

I sniffed the tube and said, "Sir, it stinks."

"Yes, it has a distinctive foul smell."

I thanked the professor, came to my dormitory, enlarged Nath's picture, and examined it with a magnifying glass. I was stunned to find the blister had only one hole in it. Evidently, someone had injected the poison with a syringe. Only three persons in the village could do that: Doctor Lalu, his daughter, and his assistant. I ruled out Lalu, since he was surprised at his missing syringe. So Kamla or Baldev might have committed the crime. I decided to handle Baldev first.

I explained my findings to the chief, and we both went to the police station. I offered my proof to the inspector, and the chief requested him to make a surprise raid at Baldev's home. The inspector agreed.

When the police jeep parked in front of Baldev's house, Baldev looked befuddled, and said, "Namasteh, inspector and chief. What can I do for you?"

"I want to search your place," the inspector replied.

"Why?"

"I'll let you know after a few minutes."

We entered the cluttered one room apartment and ferreted for fifteen minutes. I found a syringe, wrapped in a paper bag, under his bed.

I showed the syringe to the inspector who asked Baldev, "What is this syringe doing under your bed?"

"I brought it with Doctor's permission."

I turned toward the inspector and said, "He's lying. Doctor Lalu was surprised to find his syringe missing, and he sent me to his shop where this fellow opened a new package."

"Can I look through Baldev's books?" I asked the inspector.

The inspector nodded.

I removed the books from the shelf and found a small bottle. As I opened the lid, I remembered the 'Sanom' smell in the professor's test tube.

"Inspector, this bottle contains snake venom, 'Sanom'."

The inspector grabbed Baldev's shoulder and asked, "What's this poison doing here?"

"I bought it to kill a dog."

"Don't put me on. No one uses this costly poison to kill a dog," the inspector said. "All right, show me the dog's carcass."

Baldev closed his eyes and became wordless.

I opened the syringe and let the inspector smell the bottle and the syringe.

The inspector sniffed and shouted, "Baldev, it clearly establishes that you used this syringe to kill Nath."

The dam controlling Baldev's emotions collapsed, and he started crying. After a few minutes he wiped his eyes and said, "I confess the murder, but I was forced to do that."

"What was your reason for doing it?" the inspector questioned.

"Nath destroyed Kamla's life. I love Kamla and approached Doctor Lalu for her hand, but he rejected me. Kamla was going steady with Nath who promised to marry her after his medical degree. Nath declared this to Lalu many times in my presence. When Kamla became pregnant, I cornered Nath, but he refused to accept the responsibility for the child. I went to the Cobra God Temple and prayed there. Our god ordered me to kill this bastard."

"How could you do that?"

"After his engagement Nath came to Kamla. She was not in the house. I shook Nath's hand, congratulated him, and offered him a drink which was laced with soporific medicine. Soon he started snoring. I used the syringe and injected the venom. This produced a blue blister. I thought nobody would suspect me, and my soul is clear, since I carried out the Cobra God's orders."

I showed the enlarged picture of the blister and said, "Look at the hole made by your syringe. If you had pricked twice, it would have never aroused my suspicion."

"A silly mistake, but I'm proud of my action," Baldev said. "Praise our mighty Cobra God. Nath got what he deserved."

Restoring God's Eye

Namdev, a clean-shaven young monk and the head-monk were standing near a huge gold statue which had a gaping hole in its forehead. The reflection of the golden dome of the temple shimmered in the water of the sacred Ganges River. The sun had just arisen from behind the snow-covered Himalayan Peaks, and the breeze which had kissed the cold water, was churning the prayer wheels.

"Guru, kindly excuse me from this job," Namdev adjusted his huge shoulders, folded his hands, and said.

The emaciated head-monk with flowing white beard knitted his eyebrows and asked, "Why?"

"Guru, I renounced the world fifteen years ago and don't want to reenter it. Now I own one robe and one langota (loincloth) and nothing else and am content in praying and teaching in the temple."

"Son, I know you had a tragedy: You were devoted to your wife who poisoned you and ran away with your ugly servant. You suffered in the hospital for twenty days. When you came out of the hospital, you overcame your anger and joined us. You proved to be a good monk. Now our god needs your help. It is a golden opportunity for you."

"Guru, what opportunity?"

"If you secure the diamond which formed the eye of our god, millions of devotees will thank you, and on your death, our god will receive you with open arms. If you are killed in

158

the noble task, you will receive Nirvana and get out of the transmigration cycle."

"Guru, I'm afraid to go back and face the cruel world. Can't you use some other monk?"

"Look, you are best suited for the job. You have a college degree and served as a police inspector for ten years. Moreover, none of the monks can match your physical strength."

Namdev closed his eyes, rubbed his forehead for a few seconds, sighed, and said, "All right, I'm prepared to serve."

"Good, all the monks will pray for you, and our god will help and guide you," the head-monk said. "Come into my study, and I'll show you the old records which describe the search for the sacred diamond."

The head-monk followed by Namdev walked to the adjoining room where ancient books were stacked on tall shelves.

They sat cross-legged on the rugs. The head-monk pointed to a steel cabinet and said, "The monks, working on this project, have recorded their efforts in a ledger which is kept in that container. I'll give you the key so you can read the past endeavors and enter your progress."

The head-priest paused to adjust his legs and continued, "All know our god meditated at this place for twenty years and forced the Almighty to appear before him. Our god, however, lost his eyes from the glare of the God's corona, and then God gave him a big eye in the center of the forehead. The diamond in the statue was that eye, and it was stolen by Muslim invaders. The fate of the diamond was traced by our monks and recorded in the books, and you can read it."

"I will. Meanwhile, can you tell me something about it?"

"Son, in the eighteenth century, Ahmed Shaw Abdali, the Muslim invader from Pershia (Iran), ransacked our temple, broke the statue, and removed the diamond. After the invaders left, the devotees rebuilt the temple and erected the gold statue without its eye. When Abdali reached Tehran, he had this diamond fitted in a necklace and gave it to his wife. She wore it on her pilgrimage to Mecca and was killed by a camel. The diamond disappeared during the pandemonium. Later on the necklace with this diamond reappeared on the neck of a bandit in Baghdad. The king of Iraq captured the bandit and beheaded him in the public square. The king got the necklace and gave this to his favorite concubine who was found dead, and the necklace again vanished. The necklace passed through Turkey, Pershia, Iraq, and Syria, causing the death of any person who wore it. Finally, our monk located it in the possession of the royal family in Afghanistan and made a futile attempt to steal it. A few months after the death of our monk, Maharaja Ranjit Singh captured Kabul. The queen, wearing the diamond, was killed and the sacred diamond fell into the hands of Ranjit Singh's general, Ram Singh, who later founded Palta State."

"Why didn't the sacred diamond destroy Ram Singh?" Namdev questioned.

"It did. Maharaja Ram Singh wore this on King George's coronation. Next day, while playing polo, he fell from his horse and broke his neck. Ram Singh's son learned about the curse from a priest. He never placed it around his neck and kept it in a bank in England. Every year he brought this necklace to Palta. The head-queen, dressed as a goddess, wore it and walked barefoot to this temple. After the worship the diamond necklace was flown back to London."

"Why hasn't our god hurt the head-queen?"

"Namdev, our god is merciful; he doesn't want to harm a woman, who dressed as a goddess, walked without shoes to his temple and rubbed her nose at his feet."

"Who is the monk working now on this project?"

"Durga, but he was killed six days ago."

"How did he meet his death?" Namdev asked.

"He went to London and broke into the bank. As he was coming out with the necklace, he was shot dead by the police.

I want you to be careful and don't act rashly like him. Time and God are on our side," the head-priest said.

"How should I proceed?"

"In six months the Maharaja will bring this necklace to Palta, and you should steal it while it's in transit from England to Palta," the head-monk explained.

"When should I start?"

"Wait till I get you a job in the palace. The Maharaja's Wazir (prime minister) is our disciple, and he will hire you on my request. Meanwhile stop shaving and grow a beard. When you enter the palace, you shouldn't look like a monk."

Namdev left after touching the head-monk's feet. He went to the town and bought clothes for the coming job.

After fifteen days the head-monk sent Namdev to Wazir Dewan who presented him to Maharaja Bhoop Singh. The Maharaja was impressed with Namdev's physique and poise and hired him as a personal attendant. On one tiger hunt, Namdev, who had been the champion marksman at the police academy, saved the Maharaja's life from a wounded tiger. The Maharaja promoted him as his bodyguard.

On Sunday the Maharaja's private plane took the royal party to London. As a bodyguard, Namdev, had to accompany the Maharaja, even to the Maharaja's night rendezvous. In the evening the Maharaja went to Gold Diggers Pub and enjoyed the performance of his favorite stripper, Peggy. She was a tall blond who was expert in gyrating her tits and wiggling her hips. After the show the Maharaja went with Peggy to her apartment, and Namdev guarded the place. As the Maharaja was tottering out of the house, he was attacked by two thugs. Namdev jumped from his cover, subdued the rascals, and broke their legs. He saw deep gratitude in the Maharaja's eyes.

Next morning the Maharaja went to the Mercantile Bank and withdrew the necklace, and Namdev carried the steel box from the bank to the royal mansion. Now Namdev could easily steal the necklace, but that would have been a foolish move; he would have been caught. Therefore he decided to wait for the proper opportunity, during the journey back to India. He had become close to the Maharaja and thought of appealing to the Maharaja's inner soul. One evening he broached the subject, "Your Highness, I've heard the diamond in the necklace was the eye of our god."

"That's an absurd mythology concocted by the monks. My ancestor lost ten thousand soldiers to secure it; I'll never part with it."

"Your Highness, I've been told it carries a curse with it."

"Yes, it does. This is nothing new. All big diamonds carry their curses. We, however, have taken care of the curse, and it never bothered us."

"Your Highness, how did you manage that?"

"I never wear the necklace, and the necklace is worn only once a year by the head-queen as she worships in the temple, and after the ceremony this necklace goes back to the bank in London. I'm proud to be the owner of the biggest diamond in the world."

Realizing that it was impossible for him to change the Maharaja's mind, Namdev dropped the topic.

On the return trip to India, Namdev was surprised to learn that the Maharaja wasn't flying back, but taking a special train through France and Germany. In the evening, when Namdev was massaging the Maharaja's feet, he asked, "Your Highness, why aren't we flying?"

"I had to travel by a chartered, white train."

"Your Highness, we've the largest train network in India, and Your Highness has a forty-eight wheel carriage. This costly trip can't beat your travel in India."

"I hate it, but I'm forced to do it."

"Your Highness, why?"

"To keep my pride as the president of the Chamber of Princes. Last year the Maharaja of Barda traveled by train in

Europe and boasted about it in the Chamber. He had two carriages. I'll have four and follow the same route in Europe and show him who the greatest maharaja is."

"Your Highness, I agree the Maharaja of Barda shouldn't have ventured to challenge you; he has a pint-sized state."

The Maharaja raised his arm. Namdev stood up, bowed, and left.

During the travel back to India Namdev became suspicious of Rattan, Dewan's assistant. On prying further, he was surprised to learn that this fellow could not type, didn't know shorthand, and could hardly read English. He doubted Dewan's intentions in hiring this man.

One night Namdev hid in the closet of Dewan's compartment. Soon Rattan came with a bottle. After a few drinks, Rattan smirked, "On your last visit to Bombay, you fell for Actress Nargus and blew tons of money on her. You were bankrupt and begged for five lakh rupees. I gave it to you. When are you going to pay me back?"

"Soon. Are you not having a good time?"

"Yes, but I want my money."

"I'll pay you as soon we reach India," Dewan said.

"Well, where will you get the money?"

"I'll pinch the royal diamond necklace and give it to you. Its market value is four times my loan. You remove the diamond, split it into two parts, and sell it to a jeweler in Bombay."

"That's great. I'll recover my loan and share the balance with you."

They had a few drinks, and then Rattan slipped out of the room. Dewan flicked sacred water on his head, chanted mantras, and went to sleep.

Namdev was shocked at this discovery and decided to watch Dewan.

On Monday morning the Maharaja's party flew to Calais, France. When Namdev stepped in the special train, he was surprised to find the stripper, Peggy, sitting next to Maharaja Bhoop Singh. Peggy looked ravishing and carried a pencil and pad in her hand. He guessed the Maharaja must have hired her as his secretary—the Maharaja was famous for bringing a secretary from Europe, marrying her, and next year giving her a divorce. Most of them were hookers who enjoyed good money and fun.

Namdev carried the steel box and placed it in the living room of the train. He made sure the locks were intact and the key was in the Maharaja's cummerbund. The train shot through the French countryside, leaving behind sparks and a tail of smoke.

While he was sitting in the servants' section, Namdev heard the chime of the bell. He dashed in and found the Maharaja cavorting with Peggy. One empty whiskey bottle was on the floor, and the Maharaja was pouring drinks from another.

"Namdev, bring more drinks and hors d'oeuvre," the Maharaja shouted.

"Your highness, I'll bring them in one minute."

When he returned with the trays, he found Peggy sitting on the Maharaja's lap, and the Maharaja was fondling her breasts.

With some trepidation, he placed the trays on the side table and stood with bowed head.

The Maharaja took the key from his cummerbund and said, "Namdev, get me the royal necklace from that box."

When Namdev opened the box and held the sacred diamond in his hands, he felt an electric current shooting through his body. He recited the sacred mantra in sotto voce and saw his god shimmering in the diamond. Now he was sure he was holding the sacred diamond. He recovered his aplomb and gave the necklace to the Maharaja. The Maharaja showed the necklace to Peggy and whispered to her, "Next year, you will be wearing this to the temple."

164

"Cut it out. You have been telling me this dumb story for many years."

"This time I give you my solemn pledge that you will be my head-queen."

The Maharaja wiggled his finger and said, "Namdev, close the door and see that no one bothers me. I want to give a very important dictation to my secretary."

"Your Highness, I'll make sure about it."

Namdev bowed and left. He told the royal order to all the servants and informed Wazir Dewan.

Namdev returned to the living room, hid behind the sofa, and watched the Maharaja's bedroom.

After two hours Peggy left the bedroom and promenaded to her berth in the train.

Then Dewan tiptoed inside the bedroom, spent fifteen minutes there, and rushed out, holding his slipping dhoti. Namdev felt sure that Dewan came for the royal necklace and took it away in the folds of his dhoti.

Ten minutes later Kishan, a thirteen years old servant, who wore heavy perfume and makeup, appeared carrying a bottle of fragrant oil and a towel. He entered the bedroom and bolted it from inside.

Namdev placed his ear to the door. He heard the Maharaja's grunts, the groans of Kishan, and the squeaks of the bed springs. Thirty minutes later, Kishan came out disheveled and grumpy, carrying something concealed in a towel.

Namdev was shocked to find that the Maharaja, who had many wives and concubines, was also a pedophile.

After some time, Namdev again came near the door and heard loud snoring. He went to sleep on his bunk.

At eight in the morning Namdev took a cup of tea for the Maharaja. The Maharaja didn't stir. He felt the pulse and found the Maharaja had left for the next world. He dashed to Dewan and brought him in. Dewan wiped his tears and took charge of the situation. The semen and whisky stained bed sheets were stacked in a bag, and the Maharaja was dressed in a clean cotton dhoti and carried to the living room. Incense burning pots destroyed the stink, and the Maharaja was placed before God Brahma's marble statue with his hands touching the god's feet.

Dewan asked Namdev and the other staff, "Raise your hands and pledge not to say a word about the British girl being with the Maharaja in the bedroom."

All gave their pledge.

Then Dewan told the staff to leave, and called Peggy. Namdev, guarding the door, heard the conversation between Peggy and Dewan.

"I want your help to save our Maharaja's reputation," Dewan said.

"How?"

"Don't reveal a word about this trip to anybody."

"I will, provided I'm paid my contract money for the year," she said.

"We don't have cash. But I promise to send you check for the full amount plus a bonus of 500 pounds."

"Give me the check now."

"I can't."

"Why?"

"The Maharaja has to sign it. He's dead, and I've to get the signature of the new maharaja."

She rubbed her chin, sighed, and said, "All right, I trust you. I don't gain anything in hurting Bhoop; he was a good friend." Peggy left, and Dewan prayed with closed eyes.

When the train steamed into the Paris railway station, it was shunted onto a siding, where it was surrounded by the reporters who were permitted to photograph the dead Maharaja praying in the living room. The news: Maharaja Bhoop Singh of Palta State, had heart failure, while he was praying to his god, appeared in the newspapers.

Dewan called Namdev and told him to escort Peggy out of the railway station. Namdev took hold of her suitcase, and they left the carriage. After they emerged from the busy station, he hailed a taxi.

"Do you want me to accompany you to London?" he asked.

"No, I know my way; I've visited Paris many times," she said.

Peggy sat in the taxi and waved.

When Namdev returned to the train, he found Dewan sitting cross-legged near the Maharaja's body.

"Sit down and pray with me," Dewan said.

Dewan prayed for five minutes and then explained, "Our Maharaja is worshiped as the son of the Sun God, and we have to maintain his image. I need your help for this."

"I'm willing, but how?"

"We'll tell the press in India that our Maharaja was praying to God Brahma, and we both were sitting next to him. The Maharaja opened his eyes, smiled, and said, 'Children, the God needs my services in Heaven, and I have to leave.' We both begged him, but he replied, 'I can't refuse God Brahma's request.' Then the Maharaja stretched before the statue and was gone."

"All right, Dewan. I'll support you."

A white limousine arrived in front of the railway station and carried the Maharaja's corpse to the airport. From there a chartered plane took off for Palta.

When the plane landed at Palta, thousands of mourners had flocked to the airport. The head-queen led the mourning group and her son, Lal Singh, stood next to her. She placed a marigold garland over the corpse and touched its feet, and this was followed by ninety-five women, the wives of the late maharaja.

Next day a special platform was erected on the palace lawns, and Maharaja Bhoop Singh was reduced to ashes on a sandalwood pyre. Namdev informed his head-monk that the necklace was back in Palta, and soon he would be bringing it to the temple.

The day for the pilgrimage to the temple by the head-queen arrived. Respecting the public sentiment, Namdev decided to steal the necklace after the head-queen's worship. Dewan, accompanied by Namdev, came to the palace with the key. The steel door to the strong room, guarded by two armed soldiers, was opened and the steel box taken to the head-queen's room. Dewan opened the box, found it empty, and fainted. Namdev suspected Dewan had stolen the diamond and was putting up all this show to cover his trail. Lal Singh, the new maharaja, standing next to the box, arrested Dewan.

Namdev rushed out of the palace and traced Dewan's pretend secretary, Rattan, who was staying in Room Number Forty of the Palace Hotel. He thought he must catch Rattan before he left for Bombay with the diamond.

Namdev barged into Rattan's room and found Rattan had packed and was waiting for a taxi.

"Rattan, I know your real identity, but before I break your skull, I want to ask you one question."

"What question?"

"Where is the royal necklace?"

"I don't have it. You can search me and my luggage."

"Dewan promised to give it to you," Namdev asserted.

"Yes, he did. But someone outsmarted him."

"All right, open you suitcase."

Namdev thoroughly searched him and left the hotel.

Now Namdev thought of questioning Kishan, and he rushed to Kishan's house. He found Kishan sitting on a stool in front of his house, playing a flute.

"Kishan, what were you doing in the Maharaja's bedroom in the train?"

"Giving him a massage."

"Don't put me on. I heard your moans and the creaking bed springs."

"Okay, I did provide him some comfort, and he paid me well."

Namdev grabbed Kishan's neck, shook him, and said, "Out with the true reason for your joining the Maharaja's staff?"

"Please don't hurt me; I'll tell you the truth. I'm a goldsmith's son and wanted to steal the royal necklace."

"Could you pinch it?"

"No, I couldn't; someone else had removed it."

"When you came out, what were you concealing in a towel?"

He blushed. "I was stealing a whisky bottle."

Namdev looked at Kishan's facial expression and tone of his voice and felt sure he was telling the truth.

Now only one suspect was left—Peggy. In the special train to Paris, he saw the Maharaja and Peggy alone in the bedroom, and the necklace was resting on the bed. It was quite possible—the Maharaja got stoned, she stole the necklace, and left the room.

Namdev decided to visit Peggy. He resigned his job at the palace, informed the head-monk about the theft of the necklace, and left for London.

It took Namdev ten days to reach London. At midnight, he entered Peggy's apartment through the rear window. She opened her eyes and was stunned to see the Maharaja's servant, who saw her off at Paris, holding a dagger near her heart. She tried to scream, but Namdev was too strong and muzzled her mouth.

"Lady, give me the necklace, and I won't harm you."

"I don't have that. Bhoop placed it in the steel box."

He recited the mantra and saw a flashing light in the pillow. The sacred diamond had magical powers to respond to that mantra.

He snatched the pillow, opened it, and displayed the necklace.

"You were lying," he yelled.

She was trembling with wide open mouth and stared at him like a mouse, confronting a cat.

"Did you ever wear this necklace?"

She shook her head. "I'm not a fool. I wanted to cut the diamond into four pieces and sell it."

"You are lucky for not doing that. If you had worn it, I would have killed you for desecrating our sacred diamond."

He tied her up, gagged her mouth, and covered her with a blanket. Being a trained detective, he had used plastic gloves and wore paper shoes, and thus left no trace behind. He slipped out of the window and rushed to his hotel. Peggy couldn't report the theft of the diamond to the police, since she had stolen it from the Maharaja.

After fifteen days Namdev reached Roshani Temple. Now he was a clean-shaven monk, wearing his old saffron robe. He met the head-monk, and gave him the necklace. The head-monk patted Namdev's back and said, "Congratulations, you have done your duty and earned the god's blessings."

"Guru, how do you plan to proceed now?" Namdev asked.

"We'll keep the whole thing secret. Let me meet Maharaja Lal Singh."

"No use in doing that. Like his father he would never agree to part with the diamond. The Maharaja, however, doesn't know that I was an undercover monk and have recovered the necklace."

"In that case, let's fix the eye of the god. Later on, even if the Maharaja discovers the identity of the diamond, he would never dare to snatch it. He knows that he would be torn into pieces by the devotees."

On Tuesday, the sacred day for Hindus, more than two hundred thousand devotees gathered around the temple.

Namdev brought the diamond on a gold tray. The head-monk offered the tray to the gold statue. There was a loud suction sound. The diamond flew from head-monk's tray and lodged in the hole in the forehead. There were loud cheers and a rain of flowers showered over the statue. Slogans: "Long live our god!" resonated from the temple walls. As Namdev was adjusting the garlands, he touched the forehead of the statue. The diamond was a perfect fit and had become an integral part of the face. He was not surprised at this miracle.

On the advice of his mother, the Maharaja Lal Singh came barefoot to the temple and made his offering to the god whose eyesight had been restored.

My Portent Tiger Hunt in India

March 8, 1939, Barda City, Barda State, India.

"Rughby, let's go back to the States," I adjusted the rebellious strand of my blond hair, dabbed my eyes, and said.

"We can't; it will break my mother's heart," my husband, Rughby, the crown prince of Barda State, grabbed my hand, and pleaded with misty eyes.

"Look, we have been here more than ten days, and your father has not permitted us to step in the palace."

"My mother comes to you three times daily, and she adores you," he said.

"I appreciate that. She, however, has failed to convince her husband."

"My father, the Maharaja of Barda, is worshiped as the son of the sun god, and he has ninety-two wives and sixty sons. But for my poor mother, I'm the only child. I'm sure, if we leave, she would jump in the sacred river. She told me this in clear words," he said.

I saw pain on the tortured face of my husband, a tall muscular man who always wore a dimpled smile.

I acquiesced, "All right, we'll stay for fifteen more days."

He grabbed me in his arms, kissed me, and said, "Thanks, Emily. I'm certain we'll solve the problem before that."

While we were students in Ohio State University, I met Rughby. We fell in love, and after two years of courtship, we got married, ignoring the strong opposition from our parents. My parents didn't approve my marrying an Indian and then leaving the country. I was their only child. Rughby's father wanted his son to marry a royal princess who brought tons of dowry. I didn't have a drop of royal blood and no dowry. As we arrived in Barda, Rajmata, Rughby's mother received us at the railway station. She took us in her gold-plated limo to the Royal Guest House and told us to wait till she could win over the infuriated maharaja.

This morning, we were sitting on the balcony of the Royal Guest House, located at the corner of the palace compound. The palace had a ten-foot-high brick wall enclosing sixty acres. I could see the marble palace shimmering under the rays of the morning sun. I could also hear the murmur of the ripples in the Ganges River which hugged the northern end of the boundary wall. Beyond the river, there were thick jingles which touched the majestic Himalayan Mountains. I could see the mahouts taking care of the maharaja's twenty elephants. The billowing wind showered the fragrance of roses and gardenia flowers.

Suddenly, there was a knock at the door.

"You are permitted to enter," Rughby shouted.

A tall young servant, wearing a white uniform and red cummerbund, appeared with a flashing sword, made a low bow and said, "Maharaja Ram Singh, the mighty ruler of Barda State, wants Crown Prince Raghbir Singh and his wife to appear in the durbar of the marble palace."

"I thank His Highness. Please tell him that the Prince will be there in fifteen minutes."

The servant bowed again and left.

Rughby chuckled and said, "Well, Rajmata must have won over the Maharaja."

"Hope so. However, there was no such indication in the message," I mumbled.

"Hurry up and wear the royal dress, brought by my mother."

Followed by two maids, I entered my bedroom. The maids braided my hair and made a red circle on my forehead. With

173

some difficulty, I could dress in the thick sari which was decorated with figures in gold and silver threads. They helped me to put on tons of jewelry; I emerged from the room and saw Rughby wearing a pink turban with a flashing plume.

"Hari Krishna! You look prettier than our goddess Parvati," he exclaimed.

I pointed to the wall clock and said, "We must rush now."

"Emily, we're on Indian time here. Fifteen minutes can be easily extended to one hour. To please you, I'll hurry up. Let me drive to the palace."

We rushed out of the building. I felt awkward in the sari and the sound of bangles jarred my ears. I was wearing fifty gold bangles on each arm. My neck supported two heavy diamond studded gold necklaces, and my ears wore dangling diamond earrings. I studied Rughby. He, too, had a royal necklace and ruby earrings swinging from his ear lobes.

When we stopped outside, the guards on duty saluted us and pointed to the royal transport.

"His Highness wants you to use this elephant," the captain of the guard said.

We sat on the howdah which had a huge canopy over it. I sank in the thick cushions.

"The palace is only eight hundred yards from here. We could have easily walked to it," I said.

"You know, I wanted to drive my jeep, but the Maharaja wants to keep our traditions."

The ride was smooth, and I enjoyed the music of the bells attached to the elephants' legs.

On reaching the palace, we got down from the elephant, and the soldiers at the door presented their arms. When we entered a huge marble hall, I noticed eight ceiling fans churning the hot air and shaking the tufts of the stuffed animal heads mounted on the walls. The fragrance from flowers and burning incense was saturating the air. We moved forward with folded hands, and I saw a huge man, with a dark, bushy mustache seated on a throne-shaped chair. With his large red eyes and huge turban, he was an awe inspiring figure. Rughby touched his father's feet, but when I tried, the Maharaja turned his legs away with a big scowl. Rajmata noticed this and rushed to grasp my hand and made me sit near her. Rughby, however, stood before his father with folded hands.

A heated discussion between the Maharaja, his wife, and son, erupted. I didn't understand the language, but I could easily read the faces and was sure it was not a cordial family conversation. It appeared Rughby was being chewed up by his father, and his mother was imploring for mercy.

To help my husband, I ambled to the stuffed white tiger which was resting on a marble platform in the corner of the hall.

"Wow! What a marvelous thing!" I exclaimed.

Rughby got the hint, rushed to me, and said in a loud voice, "This is the biggest tiger in the world."

"Who shot it?"

"Maharaja Ram Singh, the champion hunter in the world," he said after raising his voice by a few decibels.

"Holy Cow! I can't believe it," I exclaimed.

Suddenly the scowl and anger vanished from the Maharaja's face. He rose from his throne and sauntered to us. After patting the tiger's back, he said, "Yes, I shot this tiger."

To express surprise, I opened my mouth and widely parted my eye shutters. "Your Highness, did you use a Machan?"

"No, I never use that. I went on foot to kill it."

"I read the Viceroy and the maharajas use Machans," I said.

"Yes, they do. But they are not hunters. They sit on a wooden platform built on tall stilts, play cards, and enjoy drinks. The beaters drive the tiger to a cleared place in front of them. When the tiger presents itself, the expert marksman sets the sights on a rifle which is fixed on a stand. The hunter scrambles up, pulls the trigger, and claims a big hunt. Even a five-years-old can do better."

"Your Highness, hunting your way must be very risky."

"Risky, yes, but there is thrill and excitement in it," he said. "Well, you're married into the family of great hunters. We take pride in our hunting skills. My father hunted with a sword and shield. I, however, carry my rifle with one bullet in it."

I dropped my chin and asked, "What happens if the bullet misses or only injures the tiger?"

He adjusted his broad shoulders and smiled. "So far it has never happened. I, however, always carry a hunting knife to protect myself."

"Your Highness, I can't believe all this."

"All right, I'll arrange a hunt and show you the whole thing."

"Your Highness, I'll be honored to see the greatest hunter in the world in action. I, too, have some hunting experience."

The Maharaja arched his brows. "What?"

"Your Highness, I hunted deer with my father," I said.

"What's your father's profession?"

"A military officer."

The Maharaja chuckled. "Good. A Khashatria (fighter) like us; I like that."

"Your Highness, can you tell me the details of this hunt?"

He parted the hair on the body of the tiger and said, "This is the place where my bullet entered the body and pierced the heart. The tiger died without much pain and its skin wasn't damaged."

"You must be having a powerful rifle; can you show it to me?"

"Daughter-in-law, I've more than fifty guns. Come with me, and I'll show you those and other hunting trophies which I have collected from all over the world."

I followed the Maharaja who started gloating over his hunting skills, and we moved out of the room. There were hundreds of stuffed heads of lions, tigers, panthers, bears, cheetahs, etc cetera, fixed on the walls of the palace. I showed great enthusiasm, as the Maharaja explained the place and how he bagged the animal.

Then he took me to a room where his rifles were stored in cabinets. He selected a few and described their function.

After one hour the Maharaja and I returned to Rajmata and Rughby, and the Maharaja said, "Rajmata, I'm proud of Emily. She loves hunting and has promised to train our son and get rid of his fear of tigers."

Rajmata raised her folded hands toward the ceiling and said, "Thanks Lord Brahma for sending us Emily."

"Move the Prince and his wife to the palace."

"Your Highness, I'll arrange that right now," she replied.

Then the Maharaja addressed Rughby and said, "You and your wife are excused."

Rughby and I touched the Maharaja's and Rajmata's feet and ambled out of the living room. I was bubbling with joy at the success of my mission.

When we reached the Guest House, Rughby took me in his arms, lifted me in the air, swung me around, and said, "You worked a miracle."

"You told me about your father's passion for hunting, and I exploited that. After all I majored in psychology."

"Thanks, before you walked to the tiger, he was thinking of kicking us out of the state, since you were a Sudra."

"Why does he think like that?"

"For him any person born beyond oceans is untouchable. But after you talked with him, he elevated you to our caste of warriors—Khashatria."

"Glad to join your caste," I said. "Well, I understood from his body-language and angry gestures that he was mad at you, and I tried to help."

"You did a good job. Now prepare yourself to hunt with him."

"No problem," I replied. "Well, you'll have to accompany me."

177

"Okay, I'll tag along."
In two hours we were moved into the marble palace.

We assumed our duties: visiting the schools, hospitals, libraries, and civic functions. Two months flew away. The day for the hunt arrived. I was excited but fully prepared for the trip. In the morning, Rughby and I took our baths with the sacred river water and were ready in our hunting outfits at six in the morning. We walked to the front porch of the palace where six jeeps were waiting for us. Soon the Maharaja arrived with a big smile on his face. He drove the front jeep, and Rughby and I sat next to him. The trailing jeeps carried the state game warden and his staff. The convoy traveled on dusty roads and stopped at the entrance of the thick jungle. The Maharaja stepped out of the jeep and checked his rifle and hunting dagger. He ordered the game warden and his staff to follow him at an adequate distance, without making the slightest sound.

"Daughter-in-law, follow me with your rifle, and let me show you the jungle and its inhabitants," the Maharaja said.

The Maharaja moved through the thick bushes like a cobra—agile and fast. I trailed him with Rughby tagging me. He stopped at a few places to point out and describe the birds and animals. I was greatly impressed with his knowledge and understanding of the forest and its occupants. He appeared to know about every creature. His five senses were highly developed, and he could smell, hear, and see things which weren't perceptible to me. After covering some distance, he stopped near a paw print and asked me, "What do you make out of this?"

I shook my head, and Rughby stared at it with confused looks.

Then the Maharaja explained the shape, number, and size of the toes and how this belonged to a seven-year-old male tiger. He turned toward me and said, "I've a book in my library which gives all the details of the paws of different animals.

It's in Sanskrit, but my Wazir will translate it into English for you."

"Thanks, Your Highness," I said.

Pointing to the crows flying in the air, the Maharaja said, "The crows show that we are near the tiger's kill."

"Your Highness, how could you determine that?" I asked.

"The tiger, after making its kill, drags it inside the jungle, lets it rot for one day, and deputes the crows to guard it. The crows don't eat much, but keep watch over the prey. They warn the king of the jungle when some humans or animals are approaching."

As the party moved forward, the cawing became much louder. The Maharaja started crawling on the ground, and Rughby and I followed his example. After we traveled one hundred yards, he raised his hand and pointed his finger. I saw a magnificent, huge tiger munching a calf. The Maharaja aimed and pressed the trigger. While he was doing this, a wasp stung his trigger hand, and the bullet missed and hit the tiger's leg. The tiger roared and jumped toward the hunter. I noticed the Maharaja was struggling with his hurt hand to draw the dagger, and the tiger was looming over him. I aimed and fired. The tiger fell back, rolled on the ground, and dropped dead.

"Good job, thanks for assisting me; my hand was refusing to grab the dagger," the Maharaja said.

We walked to the dead tiger, and the Maharaja exclaimed, "Daughter-in-law, a perfect shot. You're going to give me grandsons who will keep up my family tradition."

I blushed, and Rughby squeezed my hand.

The Maharaja blew his whistle, and the game warden dashed in with his party.

"Send this tiger to my taxidermist," the Maharaja ordered.

I saw several men, with ropes and two long bamboo poles, sprinting to the place—they were the game warden's staff. The legs of the tiger were tied with ropes and bamboo poles were slipped through them. Ten men lifted the heavy load and moved to the edge of the forest. From there a bullock cart carried it to the town. The hunting party returned to the palace where Rajmata was anxiously waiting for us.

"Rajmata, I'm glad our son married a girl who is a good hunter. The gods have heard my prayers, and I'll be able to see our grandchildren following my footsteps," the Maharaja rejoiced.

Rajmata folded her hands toward the ceiling and murmured a prayer.

Rughby and I thanked the Maharaja and went to our section of the palace.

"I'm delighted my father is so proud of your hunting skills," Rughby said.

"I'm happy too."

"Emily, he, however, thinks I'm a chicken and can't hunt."

"Why are you scared?"

"I have developed a fear of wild animals."

"How did that happen?"

"When I was five, the Maharaja took me for a hunt. As I heard the tiger's roar, I lost control of my bladder and fainted. After that I acquired the phobia and refused to go hunting with him."

"You did okay this time."

"On seeing the tiger, I trembled. But after watching you killing it, I've gathered enough courage to hunt with you."

Two days slipped away. One evening Rughby and I were sitting in the garden, watching the birds frolicking in the fountain pool, Rughby said, "Darling, your kill has been stuffed and will be brought to the palace today. Tomorrow the Maharaja is holding a big party to declare you the number two hunter in the world."

"Why all this fuss?"

"Emily, he wants to show his subjects that you're a good hunter and will train me. Moreover, he has arranged another marble platform to place your tiger behind his champion tiger."

"I don't mind this. I, however, feel happy that he has accepted me, and everything is going fine."

"Please write about the whole thing to your parents."

I giggled. "I've already done that."

Next day, as directed by the Maharaja, I wore my hunting dress, and Rughby and I reached the Maharaja's living room. I heard a band playing the local favorite tunes. The Maharaja escorted me to the durbar. As I walked beside the Maharaja, all the durbarees placed garlands around my neck and made deep bows with folded hands. After the completion of this ceremony, the Maharaja clapped his hands. The servants wheeled in the newly stuffed tiger and placed it behind the Maharaja's tiger.

There was a thunderous ovation.

The Maharaja was to make his speech, but he went around the tigers and examined them. Suddenly, his face turned ghastly pale, and he yelled, "Bring in a measuring tape."

The servants rushed in with a tape.

"Measure the tigers," the Maharaja ordered.

The servants held the tape, and the Maharaja checked the size of his tiger. Then the tape moved over to my tiger. When he studied the tape, he slapped his forehead and moaned, "Ram! Ram! Ram! I've lost my title."

He raised his fist and yelled, "Stop the music. The party is over."

All the durbarees knew that the Maharaja's pride had been hurt, and they rushed out, without whispering a word.

Soon the Maharaja, Rajmata, Rughby, and I were standing near the stuffed animals.

"Rajmata, today I suffered the worst humiliation of my life in front of my durbarees," the Maharaja moaned.

"It was your idea to display the tigers," Rajmata said.

"I never thought her tiger would be longer than mine by two inches. I shouldn't have bothered to get her tiger stuffed. Anyhow, the damage is done. Now I can't show my face to my subjects. I'm going to sleep on the floor, eat food on leaf plates, and practice complete abstinence, till I reclaim my title."

"Your Highness, you have back problems and will hurt yourself by sleeping on the ground," Rajmata pleaded.

"I've taken a pledge and don't care for the pain and suffering."

Then the Maharaja faced me and said, "When I see you, my heart gets into trouble. I don't want to get a heart attack. Tomorrow I'll send you to our mansion in London. Stay there till I become champion again."

"Your Highness, I'd like to accompany my wife," Rughby pleaded.

"All right, you both pack up your stuff and take our plane to England."

"Your Highness, you'll not allow me to sleep near you, and I can't see you suffering in the Mud Palace. I beg your permission to go with my son and his wife," Rajmata requested.

"Go ahead," the Maharaja said and stomped out of the hall.

*   *   *

Rughby, Rajmata, and I settled down in Barda Mansion in London. The Maharaja shifted to the Mud Palace which was used by his late grandfather and started his penance. He deputed all his deputies to locate a bigger tiger than the one shot by me.

Slowly and steadily the Maharaja's health began deteriorating. He got up with a stiff back and sharp pain in his body. He made huge offerings to the temples. But all those failed to produce the desired tiger.

One morning he confided to his personal assistant, "Hari Chand, I'm trapped and want to get out of this nightmare."

"Your Highness, I've been worrying about your health. This way you won't last long."

"I'm a Rajput and can't break my pledge."

"Your Highness, can I suggest something?'

"What's that?"

"Your Highness, let me help you bag a much bigger tiger."

"How can you do that?"

"Your Highness, you hunt a tiger and leave the rest to me and our taxidermist."

"That will be cheating."

"Your Highness, you're not supposed to know what I and the taxidermist are doing to extend the tiger. I'll commit the sin and then seek forgiveness from the gods."

"Good, arrange the hunt. I miss my wife, son, and daughter-in-law."

Next day the Maharaja and Hari Chand went hunting. Hari Chand loaded the kill in his jeep, covered it, and brought it to the taxidermist. In four days a huge stuffed tiger appeared in the marble hall, and it was placed near the two other tigers. The new tiger was ten inches bigger than his daughter-in-law's kill.

The Maharaja called his mansion in London and said, "Rajmata, I've won back my title; the tiger I hunted is ten inches longer than the one shot by Emily."

"Congratulations, Your Highness."

"Look, I'm arranging a huge celebration with fireworks, and want you, Rughby, and Emily to take part in it."

The royal plane brought Rajmata, Rughby, and I back to Barda Palace. I found bunting, balloons, and banners flying all over the area. The newspapers printed the Maharaja's picture with his trophy and wrote: Maharaja Ram Singh reclaims his title as the champion hunter of the world.

183

The festivities started at seven in the morning. Rughby and I sat in the front row. I saw the Maharaja sitting on a throne and thousands of his subjects paying their homage to him by touching his feet and throwing flowers at the tiger killed by the Maharaja. A lavish feast followed. As the sun went down behind the hills, fireworks lighted the sky.

I enjoyed all the feasting and celebrations and was glad that I was no longer the champion hunter.

Next day Hari Chand walked barefoot to the sacred river.

The Ghost World

"Rughby, do you believe in ghosts?" my wife, Emily, tamed a rebel strand of her blond hair, and asked.

On the evening of March 8, 1964, my wife, Emily, and I were relaxing on the lawn of our house, 1876 Rocky River Drive, Berea, Ohio. The grinding sound of the traffic was trying to mute the whispering murmur of the water cascading down the river. I was reading Cleveland Plain Dealer, the daily newspaper, and she had buried her head in the book: "Ghosts" by John Alexander.

"Yes, I do," I replied. "Why are you asking?"

She showed me the book and said, "Alexander, the author of this book, describes many ghost appearances. I doubt him. All right, have you ever seen a ghost?"

I nodded with a smile.

"Can you describe it?"

"Certainly, I can," I said and then narrated the following:

I was fifteen and studying in the ninth grade. The classes ended and my friend, Madan, and I were cycling back to our village. The sultry summer afternoon, without any breeze, choked our lungs, and streams of perspiration channeled down our spines. The dirt road, full of ruts and potholes, snaked through the green fields, and we struggled to avoid pratfalls. We approached a herd of placid, cud-chewing buffaloes and tried to pass through them. The animals shook their tails to scare the flies and fully blocked our path. The drover, riding on one buffalo, was playing his flute. We rang the cycle-bells and yelled vociferously, but all this failed to get his attention.

185

We dismounted the cycles and tried to push the buffaloes with one hand, but they refused to part.

Madan pointed to the Persian well and said, "Bir, there's no use in trying to pass these dumb creatures. Let's spend a few minutes near that Persian well, and let the buffaloes hog the road."

I agreed.

We parked our cycles and washed our hands in the cold water from the steel trough. Then, using our book bags as pillows, we stretched under a banyan tree. I could hear the clicking of the wheel, the splash of water leaking from the buckets, and the heated discussion of the polyglot groups of birds. As I heard a stifled sob, I turned my head and saw tears in Madan's brown eyes.

"Something bugging you?" I asked

He wiped his tears and said, "Yes, I'm in a deep trouble."

"What trouble?"

"My girlfriend has been captured by a ghost."

"Madan, don't be an idiot; ghosts exist only in the mind of an opium eater while he's riding high."

"Bir, I pledge by the sacred cow that I'm telling you the truth."

"Okay, but you never told me you had a girlfriend."

"I'm sorry. I had to keep it secret, since I'm a Sudra and she's a Brahmin."

"A Brahmin girl is supposed to avoid your shadow. How could you trap her?"

"Our destined union was arranged by the gods."

"How the gods did that?" I asked.

"We met in the temple, where her father is a priest, and fell in love on our first meeting. I revealed my caste, but she told me: 'You aren't a Sudra; the chief is your real father'."

"Forget the whole thing. You're the top student and are sure to become a Deputy Commissioner. Complete your education first."

"Bir, I'd like to do that, but I can't."

"Why?"

"We have crossed the forbidden river," he moaned.

I was dumbfounded, since I could never imagine him doing this. He went to the temple daily and recited Scriptures all the time. Then I remembered he was helpless—he had the genes of the promiscuous chief, and there was no use in my lecturing him about celibacy. I peered into his eyes and said, "You're dumb. You shouldn't have waded through the no-no river. Anyhow, how many months have passed since she conceived?"

"Two months."

"What about her father and four brothers? Do they know about it?"

He shook his head.

"Buddy, when they discover it, you'll become a bag of mincemeat. You better run to a distant province."

He straightened his chest and said, "Never, I would rather die to save my child."

"All right, then why were you concocting the story of a ghost?"

"That's the truth. Rani, my girl friend, begged her mother to help her in marrying me. When the mother told this to her husband, he hit the ceiling, whipped Rani, locked her in the room, and starved her. Rani, however, refused to change her mind. Then her parents consulted a priest who told them Rani was possessed by the ghost of a Sudra which is inducing her to marry a person of its caste."

"I think the priest concocted this."

"Yes, he wanted to make money and could easily convince her parents. Yesterday they took her to the temple to get her exorcised."

"Madan, when was the last time you saw her?"

"I've not met her for ten days, but we exchange letters through a loose brick in the temple wall. Yesterday her letter, covered with tears, begged me to save her and their unborn child."

"I don't think her father will dare to kill her."

"When he learns about her pregnancy, he's sure to do that."

"Well, what do you plan to do?" I asked.

"Tomorrow our summer vacation starts, and we won't be going to school. I request you to enter that temple and meet her."

"Madan, that's impossible! They know I'm your close friend, and if I ever tried to communicate with her, they'll beat the hell out of me."

"Bir, don't worry: I've a plan."

"What plan?"

"You can pretend to be possessed by an evil spirit, and your parents will take you to that temple. Once inside you can help me to elope with her," he suggested.

"Where will you disappear?"

"I've fully planned it: My father's cousin lives two thousand miles from here. I'll stay with him, change my identity, and marry Rani. I've light colored skin and have acquired a birth certificate and other documents to become a first-class Brahmin, Mohan Travedi. Rani will be delighted, and we'll enjoy a happy life."

The thought of tricking Rani's father and his tough sons sent shivers through my body, and I said, "Buddy, it's dangerous; I'm scared."

He grabbed my feet and begged.

At this my heart forced me to take the risk to save three lives, and I said, "All right, I'll try."

Smiles appeared on Madan's face. "I think we can easily pull it off."

He described his plan, embraced me, and shook my hand.

The herd of buffaloes had left, and we took hold of our cycles and pedaled home. As I thought of the risks involved, a whirlwind started churning in my brain.

Next day the summer vacation started.

As planned, Madan came to my home with his books. He greeted me, and we exchanged signals. I pounced upon him, slapped his face, and yelled, "I want to eat this dirty Sudra."

On watching this my family members were dumbfounded.

While cussing and screaming, I dashed into the living room and brought my father's sword, unsheathed it, and flashed it in the air. My father and two elder brothers rushed to grab me and pinned me down, but I continued kicking and shouting profanities.

My father asked Madan, "Did you have a fight?"

Madan wiped his tears and replied, "No sir, but I think Bir must be possessed by a ghost."

"Why do you assume that?" my father inquired.

"Yesterday while returning from school, we stopped near a pit to take a breather, and Bir went to seek comfort in it. When he returned, he started cussing in a woman's voice and attacked me. I took hold of my cycle and shot out without looking back. This morning I thought the ghost must have left him and came to work on our school project."

My father murmured a prayer, and my mother raised her folded hands to the ceiling.

I continued screaming and yelling. "I'm Bimla, Bimla...."

I had to select a name for my ghost and my best choice was Bimla who used to be our neighbor. She eloped with her paramour leaving behind her two young sons. Her husband, with the help of the police, dragged her back. After three months she died. All the villagers knew she was asphyxiated by her husband, Gopi.

My mother approached me with folded hands and begged, "Bimla, we abhor what Gopi did to you. Please don't hurt my son."

I shrieked in a faked woman's voice, "No way. I'll torture and slowly murder this rascal."

"Why are you so cruel to my son?" My mother asked.

"Gopi cremated me and then instead of immersing my ashes in the sacred river, he dumped those in a barren pit.

Your son defecated over my remains, and I'll teach him a good lesson."

My father instructed my brothers, "Tie him up; we'll take him to the temple to get rid of the ghost."

Though my hands and feet were tied with hemp ropes, still I continued cussing, and blood oozed from my knuckles. I noticed tears in Madan's eyes as he stood with folded hands. Father pinched my nose and asked my eldest brother to pour a bottle of whisky in my mouth. My stomach revolted, but it was impossible for me to stop the process. Soon I passed out.

When I heard the rattling sound of the overhead fans and the loud shrieks, I opened my eyes and found myself resting on the floor of a large hall, and my parents were sitting cross-legged near me. I was sure I was in the temple where the exorcism was performed. I looked around and I saw Rani's brothers and father standing in the hall. The exorcist, a bald man, was going from one patient to another, casting out the ghosts. I studied this chubby person, as he treated other patients and concluded that he was hypnotizing them and making them do strange acts. I decided to dodge his eyes. When my turn came, he poked his stick into my chest and yelled, "Devil, get out!"

I tried to avoid his eye-contact, but failed and lost control over myself. I tore away my clothes and started cursing and shouting. He hit my naked back with his stick several times. I felt sharp pain and thought of giving up, but it was too late. After thirty minutes he sprayed water over me, and my treatment ended for the day. I felt great relief.

There were no latrines in the temple, and all the patients had to go outside in the fields to seek comfort. At five in the morning I went out to answer the call of nature. When I moved away from the temple near the designated spot, I found Madan waving to me from inside the sugar cane field. I slipped in, and he gave me his letter for Rani and explained, "Please give this to Rani; I'm all set."

"What have you planned?"

"I confided my secret to my mother who sold her jewelry and gave me the money for the elopement. I've come with my backpack and will camp here. My mother will tell everyone that I was going on pilgrimage to the sacred temples."

"Will she specify any temple?"

"No."

"That's smart. There are thousands of temples," I said. "Well, with Rani's father and brothers always hovering around her, it will be a tough for me to deliver your letter. Anyhow, I'll do my best."

He thanked me with his tears.

I entered the temple, stumbled near Rani's bed, and dropped my coins. While gathering them, I hid Madan's letter under her pillow. Later when I walked near her bed, she winked, and I thanked the gods.

Next morning Rani didn't return after answering the call of nature. She had eloped with Madan.

When my treatment started, the exorcist came over to me with his big stick. I managed to keep my eyes fully closed, and he couldn't hypnotize me. Then I outsmarted him and began yelling, "I'll leave right now; I can't take this beating."

He appeared to be puzzled and annoyed, but he was left with no other choice but to release me. He chanted some mantras and swung his stick which landed on my back, and I yelled, "I'm going."

The exorcist told my parents that he had castigated the ghost. I returned home, and my family celebrated my recovery.

The summer vacation ended, and I returned to school. Suddenly my troubles started: My neck became stiff and painful, as if someone was sitting on my shoulders and twisting it, and I had nightmares about turning into an old woman. I couldn't tell any member of my family that when I was taken for the exorcism, I was faking, and now I was in real trouble.

The school closed for ten days for Diwali holidays, and I decided to seek help from my maternal uncle who lived like a hermit in a hut and dealt with the Priets (evil ghosts). His village was twenty miles away, and I rode my cycle there. Before leaving I told my parents that I would be meditating on the banks of the sacred river.

Uncle was surprised to see me. He offered me a cup of cold water from his earthen pitcher, and we sat cross-legged on the ground. I described my dilemma. He placed five cloves in my hand and asked me to tightly close my fist. Then he recited strange mantras. I swooned and fell flat on the mud floor. When I opened my eyes, I found him sprinkling water over my face. I felt exhausted and drained.

"Son, you're possessed by the ghost of an evil woman."

"Bimla's ghost. I was only pretending, and that ghost was supposed to be exorcised."

"The trouble is that you got this ghost from that exorcist."

"How?"

"This ghost, Fatto, serves that exorcist. He discovered you were cheating him and ordered her to teach you a lesson."

"Why did she come ten days after I left the temple?"

"She was busy with another person and came after killing him."

"I'm confused," I mumbled.

"Son, ghosts have their own world. After one leaves the human body, he enters the next world. The good people meet the god. The average sinners are given a chance to enter another human body. The evil persons have to suffer and haunt the earth as Priets."

"I can't believe in anything which I can't perceive with my five senses."

"All right, I'll show you their world tonight, but let me get rid of this Fatto first."

Uncle made a circle around me with ashes from his pouch and recited some mantras.

I heard loud shouting and cussing.

Uncle yelled, "Kalu, don't beg; use force."

Then I heard wails and cries of a woman. Soon they faded away. I felt light, and the pain in my neck and burden on my shoulders had disappeared.

"How do you feel?"

"Great," I replied. "Who is Kalu? You were talking to him."

"He's the leader of the ghosts I control."

"Uncle, can you show me the ghosts?"

"No."

"You promised."

He sat wordless for a few seconds and then said, "All right, wait for the sunset."

In the evening we walked to a fallow and sat cross-legged. He chanted some bizarre words, and I heard the rattling thunder of drums. He had brought three bamboo sticks from his hut and made a door with them. Then he showered water over it, while chanting esoteric mantras.

"Bir, when you enter this gate, you will see the world of the ghosts. Don't touch anything and never accept anything from them. If any ghost tries to grab you remember to recite: 'Guru Parbraham.'"

I gingerly stepped inside the gate and heard shrieks and the deafening sound of drums. Horrible looking women with pitch black faces and bloody eyes were dancing and singing. Their hair dragged on the ground like brooms, and blood dripped from their fuming mouths. Their long breasts were twisting and turning like the arms of an octopus. Flies covered their bodies, and a stinking odor permeated the air. I was scared and tried to run, but an elephantine woman picked me up like a toy. A blast of cadaver odor, shooting out from her mouth, hit my face, and I felt that I was being exterminated. She pressed her blood drooling lips on my mouth. I shrieked and recited the mantra. She turned into smoke, and I could hear her moans.

I decided to get out, and as I took a few steps toward the gate, I felt a gust of rose perfume and found a gorgeous girl in a diaphanous dress. She had milky skin with rosy cheeks and her hair was decorated with gardenia flowers. She beckoned me with her index finger, but I shook my head. Then she sashayed to me and embraced me. I lost my self-control, began kissing her, and tried to pull down her dress. She asked me to enjoy some wine and sweets first. I accepted a bottle and spread my handkerchief; she loaded it with sweets. As I was going to take a sip, I remembered Uncle's warning and recited the mantra. The bewitching girl screamed and turned into a smoke tendril which twisted and shot to the sky.

When I staggered out of the door, my nose was attacked by an offensive stench. I examined and found the bottle was stinking urine, and my hanky had human feces.

I was completely worn out and collapsed on the ground. Uncle lifted me up, gave me sacred water, and said, "Bir, did you see the world of the ghosts?"

"Yes, I did. It's horrible! I'm glad I remembered your mantra and could save myself. The ghosts could have killed me."

"I would have never allowed them to do that."

"How could you save me?" I asked.

"I was watching you and my ghosts were ready to pounce in at my orders. But I had no power to stop your messing with the beautiful ghost. I was nervous when you started removing her clothes."

I felt ashamed and said, "Sorry, I was carried away. What would have happened if I had copulated with her?"

"You would have become her slave, and she would have forced you to do strange things for her gratification."

"Like what?"

"Dancing naked in crowded public streets, eating human stools, et cetera."

"Oh my God, I'm glad I could wake up and avoid her trap."

At this stage I was fascinated with the ghosts and said, "Uncle, I want to become your disciple. I'd love to enslave ghosts."

"I would never let you do that."

"Why?"

"It's a dangerous and sinful job. I was lured into it, went in deep waters, and couldn't swim back. The ghosts are my company and won't let me get married and have children. That's why I live in this hut away from the village."

"I thought you chose to be celibate."

He sighed. "People think that, but I know the truth."

I was eager to learn more about the ghosts and asked, "Do the ghosts have leaders?"

"Yes, the most powerful ghost in the state is called the King-ghost."

"Uncle, can you show me that ghost?"

"No, I won't do that."

I grabbed his feet and said, "I beg you and promise not to make any mistake this time."

"All right, let's go to the village pond."

"Why?"

"I need water to protect myself, in case the ghost gets out of my control."

We sat cross-legged near the pond, and Uncle drew lines on the ground, threw a powder, and recited some mantras. All of a sudden a powerful ball of fire, which was ten feet in diameter, came spinning and shooting flames. I was petrified.

Uncle pointed to the fiery ball and said, "This is the King-ghost of our state."

I was frightened and mumbled, "It's going to scorch us."

"Don't worry, I have a contract with it, and it won't harm us and will only dance around us."

"Why is it continuously spinning and making circles around us?"

"It has no other choice. If it stops turning and stands in one spot, it would lose its power, and another ghost will capture its throne."

"What can it do for you?" I asked.

"I can use it to harm any person."

"Can it do some good?" I enquired.

"No, these ghosts never do any noble thing."

"All right, you have seen enough. If you want to follow my path, get permission from your parents, and join me here. Remember, you will become an outcast and a recluse."

I had ambivalent feelings, but the lure of a wife and children conquered, and I said, "Thanks. I, however, want to raise a family and can't accept your hard life."

I helped Uncle to cook the food. After dinner he gave me a mat, and I made my bed on the ground.

After seven days I cycled back home. In five years I graduated from college and immigrated to America. I joined Ohio State University and met you there.

She peered into my eyes and asked, "Are you telling the truth?"

"Yes, I swear it is true."

"Well, I was doubting Alexander, but on hearing your story, I'm convinced about the existence of the ghosts and their world."

Snared by Dowry

Thati Village, Punjab, India

"Son, why are you missing the courts?" an old man with flowing white beard asked.

Baldev, a tall young man with pink turban replied, "I don't have any case today."

"You started your practice six months ago. I thought, by now, you might be having hundreds of murder cases."

"Dad, so far I had one murder case, and I lost it."

"What about the civil suits?"

"Only two cases which didn't pay much."

"Son, I can't understand this. Attorneys are supposed to make big money."

"Too many attorneys," Baldev said. "I can't even pay the rent of my stall."

"Then come here and help me."

Baldev shook his head. "I can't; your work is too hard for me. After spending many years in college and leading a sedate life, it's tough for me to plow the fields."

"I supported you in college for eight years. You have two degrees and should start paying me back. I've to take care of your younger brothers and sisters."

"All right, if I fail to establish myself in one month, I'll move to the village, help you in the morning, and then cycle to the courts."

"I'm glad you're talking some sense. Our neighbor cycles to Amritsar and teaches there, and you can accompany him."

197

Baldev touched his father's knees with folded hands and pleaded, "Dad, can I borrow five hundred rupees?"

"Huge amount. Impossible!"

"Dad, I want to make a safe, lucrative investment and will pay you back with interest."

"What's that investment?"

Baldev produced the Matrimonial Advertisement from his coat pocket, stabbed a circled spot, and said, "I'm going to marry this rich, aristocrat girl. It means a huge dowry!"

"Don't be a fool. No rich aristocrat will ever agree. I'm a poor farmer, and you're a starving attorney."

"I have phoned them."

"What did you tell them about yourself?"

"I'm a leading attorney with a big bungalow, a car, and a few servants."

"That's an outright lie which is a big sin."

"I don't mind sinning. I'm going to trap her, and once we're married, the Indian traditions will forbid her from divorcing me."

"You're incorrigible. Well, what did you tell them about me?"

"You're a rich landlord," Baldev said under his breath.

"Look, if they ever contact me, I'll reveal the truth."

"Don't worry, it will never come to that. I'll hire an actor to pose as my father during the marriage ceremonies."

"What was their response?"

"They were highly impressed and wanted to meet me at my house at Amritsar."

"They would be turned off after stepping into your shabby, one-room dungeon."

"No, they will meet me in a big bungalow and will notice my car and servants."

"How will you manage that?"

"I'll use your five hundred to put on my show."

"Son, that's cheating. I'm sure your bubble will burst, and you will be in deep trouble after squandering my hard-earned money. I recommend that you marry a farmer's daughter who can help us in our work."

"Dad, I beg you. Please let me gamble one time."

"You're building castles in the air. Forget the whole affair."

"Please show some mercy. This man is extremely rich, and he has only one child. I'll be wealthy and promise to help you and my siblings."

"Okay, I'll give you the money, but remember—it's your foolish adventure and your sin, and I've no part in it."

The father walked into the house and returned.

"Son, here's the money. I still think you shouldn't fall into the snares of dowry."

Baldev pocketed the money, hugged his father, and beamed, "Dad, next time you'll find me coming in a big car."

Baldev shot up, jumped on his creaky cycle, darted out of the barn, while ringing his cycle bell and whistling a jovial tune. He didn't care for the girl and was willing to marry even a buffalo, provided it brought a big dowry.

In thirty minutes, he reached his home at Amritsar. He had secured the money and now wanted to arrange a big bungalow, a car, a butler, a cook, and a gardener. During college days he saved his friend, Atma, from drowning in a river. Atma was now a leading attorney. He rushed to Atma and explained his game plan.

Atma chuckled. "That's a ridiculous dumb scheme."

Baldev touched Atma's feet and said, "Remember how I risked my life to pull you out of Ravi River."

Atma looked out of the window for a few seconds and then said, "I do owe you one. What do you want?"

"Loan your bungalow for a few hours."

"I can do that."

Baldev embraced Atma and said, "I thank you for loaning me your house, but I'll also need a butler and a cook."

"I don't have any butler, and my cook left yesterday."

"I beg you to act as a butler for one hour."

"Are you out of your mind?" Atma yelled.

Baldev was smart in turning on the faucets in his eyes, and tears rolled down his cheeks. "Don't ruin my life. After I marry this girl, I promise to pay you one thousand rupees for one hour's work."

Atma sucked in a ton of air, rubbed his chin and said, "All right, I'll help you, but the sin of cheating will be on your soul."

"Thanks, I don't mind the sin. I, however, have one more request."

"Damn it, I've already promised you too much. Don't crucify me further."

Baldev touched Atma's shoes and said, "I can't ask anybody else."

"Spit it out."

"Your wife is a good cook. I'll be obliged if you request her to pose as my cook for one day."

Atma raised his hands in utter disgust. "Okay, I think I can prevail upon her. But if you make one more demand, I'll throw you out of my house."

"Thanks, I've got all I need."

"Baldev, have you settled the date for the visit of the Aristocrat?"

"September 17. I've six more days. Tomorrow I'll bring you a butler's uniform."

Baldev took a hasty leave and cycled to his cousin who was a taxi driver. The cousin agreed to help him. In India the taxis look like private cars, except their license plates bear black letters on a white background, while the private cars have white letters on a black background. Baldev made another set of plates for the day and bought a white over-starched uniform for the driver. The cousin promised to bring his taxi with changed plates to Atma's place on September 17.

The crucial date arrived. Baldev cycled to Atma's bungalow, where he changed into a rented silken suit.

"How do I look?"

"Fine, calm down and don't be so nervous," Atma advised.

At ten a white Mercedes car appeared before Atma's large brick bungalow. The gardener, Atma's clerk, who had agreed to act his part for twenty rupees, saluted and opened the gate. The car crawled on the paved driveway and stopped in front of the porch, next to a shining car. Baldev's cousin, in the chauffeur's white uniform, rushed to open the rear door of the arriving vehicle. A heavyset, middle-aged man, wearing a golden threaded turban, stepped out of the car, and a lady loaded with jewelry followed him.

Atma, dressed in a butler's uniform, made a low bow, opened the door and escorted the visitors to the living room which had three large sofas and several easy chairs. Silken curtains billowed under the waves created by three overhead fans. The air was saturated with the fragrance of flowers and burning incense.

Baldev, relaxing on a sofa, lifted his head, folded the legal magazine he was studying, stood up, and shook hands with the visitor and greeted the lady.

"Sardar and Sardani Karnail Singh, nice to meet you," Baldev said and then gestured to the cushioned sofa. The couple smiled and took their seats.

"Will you have hot tea or a cold drink?" Baldev asked.

"Tea will be fine," the Aristocrat replied

Baldev rang the bell. Atma appeared, bowed, and said, "Hazoor, Sahib."

"Bring hot tea and some hors d'oeuvres."

Soon the butler appeared with a silver tea pot, imported china crockery, and silver plates loaded with sweets and saltines. After adjusting those on the coffee table, the butler left with a deep bow.

The Aristocrat asked, "You told me that you have two degrees. What are those?"

"B.A. in arts and L.L.B. in law," Baldev said. "Let me show the certificates."

Then Baldev pointed to the certificates on the wall, and the visitor glanced at them.

"Good. How is your practice?"

"I'm the best attorney in the province and had to refuse many clients."

The Aristocrat stood up, took his wife to the corner of the room, and discussed for a few minutes. Baldev held his breath with a thumping heart. The couple returned to their seats, and the Aristocrat said, "We approve you. Now we'll show you the pictures of our daughter. She completed her M.A. this year. If you like her, we'll perform the engagement ceremony."

The Aristocrat took out pictures from his pocket and gave them to Baldev who glanced at the ravishing beauty and said, "She looks okay. I accept her."

The lady painted a red mark on Baldev's forehead, inserted a dried date in his mouth, and placed a ring on his finger. The Aristocrat shook Baldev's hand.

"I want an early marriage. Will September 25 suit you?" Baldev asked.

"No, we want a big wedding reception. Let's make it October fifth."

Baldev nodded with a smile.

"Baldev, I own ten thousand acres of farmland, and you will have to manage it. Do you know anything about farming?"

"No problem, I'm fully trained and have a big farm of my own."

The Aristocrat scrambled up and paced the room. After making three rounds, he stood before Baldev and said, "That's fine, but I face one problem."

"What is it?"

"I can't make you the Chairman of my corporation which owns a sugar mill, two textile mills, a steel factory, and several shopping malls."

"Why?"

"The directors of the board are the stock holders and will oppose your appointment unless you own some stocks."

Baldev was stunned; he never expected this.

The Aristocrat patted Baldev's hand. "Son, I can purchase those stocks for you, but it would hurt your pride. You're a rich man and can easily buy those."

Baldev tugged his mustache, grinned, and said, "I can afford it. How much?"

"Fifty thousand rupees."

Baldev's heart sank, but he managed to tame his emotions and said, "I can arrange that by tomorrow."

"All right, tomorrow at ten I'll bring the CEO of the company, and he'll pick up the money and give you the receipt for the shares."

The Aristocrat scrunched his nose, gestured toward the furniture, and said, "You better get rid of this cheap stuff. We have imported all the furniture from England for our daughter. You should bring at least three trucks to cart your dowry."

Baldev's heart jumped with joy, but he kept up his veneer.

The Aristocrat and his wife embraced Baldev and took their leave.

After the party left, Baldev took his friend in a bear hug, flashed the ring, and said, "Thanks, Atma. We've nailed it."

Atma smiled.

"To complete this process, tomorrow at ten, I need your help for one hour."

"Okay, I have to yield, but don't invite them again."

"I'll never do that. On October fifth, I'll be a multi-millionaire."

"I hope it works. You'll be in trouble if they drop at my place before your marriage."

"Please keep my pictures and certificates in your living room. If they visit, tell them that Sahib has gone to New Delhi to fight a case in the Supreme Court."

"This damn thing is getting more and more complicated," Atma groaned.

Baldev dabbed his tears and said, "I owe you so much, but I've just one more hurdle."

"What's that?"

"I need fifty thousand rupees to buy stocks."

"What stocks?"

Then Baldev explained the whole problem and said, "You're rich and can assist me to secure this loan from the bank."

"Look Baldev, I'll help, but I think the lure of dowry has made you crazy."

"After my marriage I'll control millions of rupees. This bank loan is only a peanut."

Baldev and Atma rushed to the bank. Atma provided the collateral, and Baldev got a fifty thousand rupees loan at high interest.

Next day the Aristocrat arrived in his limo. He introduced his CEO, an old man, who was wearing a three-piece silken suit and gold frame glasses. Baldev handed over fifty thousand rupees. The CEO gave him the printed stocks and shook his hand.

The CEO said, "You won't regret this. Our corporation is the richest in India. These stocks give very high dividends— ten times the bank interest."

The Aristocrat pivoted toward the CEO and remarked. "Nathu, now you and other members can't have any objection to my making this stockholder the chairman of my company."

"No, sir. I like your choice, but he has no training in our business."

"I sent you to Harvard for four years and count upon you to teach my son-in-law."

The CEO replied, "Sir, I'll be glad to do that."

Then the Aristocrat gave the address of his residence and invited Baldev to visit him on the coming Thursday.

When the party left, Baldev started dancing and promised Atma to hire him as attorney for his corporation. Baldev said his goodbye and cycled to his place. He couldn't sleep during the night, and time appeared to be crawling like a wounded tortoise. Finally, Thursday arrived. He rented his cousin's taxi which was converted to a private car by changing the plates, and his cousin wore the chauffeur's uniform. After two hours the car reached Ludhiana and stopped in front of a palatial building—the address given by the Aristocrat. Baldev adjusted his tie and looked at himself in the mirror. The chauffeur opened the door. Baldev got out, climbed the steps, and stabbed the bell. He was shocked to see a Muslim, with dyed red beard, opening the door. He thought the fellow must be a servant and asked, "I want to meet Sardar Bahadur Karnail Singh."

"No one of that name lives here."

"Are you sure?"

"Yes, I purchased this house fifteen years ago, and my name is Mushtaq Ali."

Baldev turned ghastly pale, but he managed to thank the person. He thought he might have made a mistake in writing the address. So he rushed to the post office and searched the telephone directory—the name of the Aristocrat was not there. He rushed to the stock market building and learned, the corporation, whose stocks he had purchased from the Aristocrat, didn't exist. Then he went to a jeweler to sell the diamond ring which he had received. He got twenty rupees, since it was a cheap glass.

These discoveries turned Baldev's legs into jelly, his heart stopped beating, and ice spread in his stomach. He staggered to the car which brought him back to his home at Amritsar. He didn't have the courage to face Atma. Therefore he wrote a note to him, and cycled to his village.

The Father was stunned to find his son coming on a cycle instead of a car.

"Where is your car?"

"I've been swindled," Baldev said and then narrated the whole story.

"Son, you wanted to cheat, and God punished you."

"Yes, He did it in a big way. Now I'll stay here to help you and cycle to the courts."

"All right, put your cot and clothes in the barn."

Grandma's Gold Ring

June, 1920, Ratul Village, Punjab, India

"Sorry, I was going to sell you to buy medicine for my back pain," Sita, a middle-aged lady with honey-colored face and brown eyes, kissed the gold ring and said. "I'll never part with you."

She tied the ring in the handkerchief, inserted it in the pillow, and sewed it back.

Her husband, Mohan, a squat man, with a bushy black mustache arrived from the temple.

She tottered into the kitchen and lit the fire. The smoke irritated her eyes and tears channeled down her cheeks. She heard a yell: "Hurry up, I don't want to be late."

"Excuse me, your lunch will be ready in one minute."

She made a cup of black tea and placed it in front of her husband who was sitting cross-legged on the tiger skin. He opened his eyes, smacked his lips, glanced at the cup, and shouted, "Where is the rest of the lunch?"

"Swami (master), this is it."

"Why?"

"We're out of food."

"I do miss the delicious meal," he said with a sigh. "Well, the gods want us to fast, and we've no choice but to resign to their will."

She cleared her throat with a painful effort and said with great trepidation, "Swami, instead of starving, why don't you get another job?"

He scowled. "The gods made me a Brahmin and allotted me the job of a priest, and I'm doing that."

"That job is not bringing any money," she said and stared at him with pleading eyes. "I've one suggestion."

"What?"

"While I was cleaning the chief's house, he told me that he needs a farmhand, and he can hire you for a few hours daily."

He banged his fist on the ground and yelled, "Damn it, I can't dirty my sacred hands which are meant to wash the god's feet. What about your work?"

"Yesterday, while washing the floor, I slipped and hurt my back. So far I've been cleaning the dirty dishes and sweeping the floors of four homes. Now I can hardly walk."

He closed his eyes and his hand wrestled with his mustache. After a few seconds he blinked and said, "Sita, that's too bad. You have been earning the food in times of our great hardship. How is your back now?"

"Terrible."

"Don't worry, I'll pray to the gods to help you."

She groaned. "Prayers won't do anything."

"Woman, have some faith."

He picked up the cup in both hands and started sipping. He took a swallow, smacked his lips, and said, "I love this black tea."

She could easily see through his veneer.

He finished the cup, uncoiled himself, folded the tiger skin, stacked it in the corner, and said, "I'll pray harder to the gods to send some good offering to the temple today."

"Swami, that's only a dream. The people are starving and can't afford to donate anything to the temple."

"I agree they are facing hard times, but they shouldn't forget that one tenth of what they get belongs to the gods. Ten years ago, I used to collect ten rupees daily from the feet of the god and devotees brought tons of delicious food. Now everyone is bringing flowers."

She sighed and became reticent.

She wanted her husband to get rid of his lethargy and do some strenuous work, instead of sitting at the god's feet and singing. Traditions, however, forced her to suffer without complaining.

On noticing her dismal face, he placed his hand on her shoulder and said, "Can I rub mustard oil on your back?"

"We don't have the oil."

"Take it out of the lamp."

"Swami, I can't; we need a light in the house."

He slapped his forehead and said, "Too bad, but don't lose heart. The gods are testing us. Take some rest and pray harder."

He ambled to the temple where he was working as the priest. This temple had seen good days, but now it needed heavy repairs.

She parted the door and saw him entering the temple, lighting the lamp, and pulling the bells with all his strength. A few worshipers arrived, but her heart sank when she found them carrying flowers and marigold garlands. She closed the door and banged her head on the wall.

In the evening when her husband arrived, she was working in the kitchen. She spread the tiger skin, and he crumbled on it. It was the dinner time. She heard the gurgling sounds from his big paunch, and her empty stomach was begging for food, too. She brought a cup of black tea with a handful of parched grams on a steel plate, and adjusted those in front of him. He caressed his mustache, thanked the gods, and then spent a good bit of time in chewing each gram.

She knew her husband was putting up all this show of relishing the food to avoid working in the fields. She was disgusted.

He stood up, washed his hands, and said, "Thanks for the delicious dinner."

Now was the time for the evening worship. She finished her food, sat cross-legged near her husband's feet, and listened to his long windy prayers. Her heart was not with all this—she had concluded that the gods had turned a deaf ear to their begging, and it was just a waste of time and breath. She was glad when the session ended, and she staggered to her bed.

Next morning her husband finished his breakfast and asked, "Sita, are you feeling better?"

She shook her head. "I, however, can't bear the hunger pains; they are much worse than my backache."

"Be brave, pray to the gods and try to do some work."

She was disappointed since she was hoping that by this time her husband would have changed his mind and decided to work in the fields. She killed a sigh and said, "All right, I'll try to work at one house and get some food to feed us."

His face lighted up. "Good, I'll pray for you."

They heard thumping footsteps outside the courtyard wall and saw a letter jumping out of the slit in the door. He rushed to the door, picked up the letter, tore it open, skimmed through it, and his chin fell.

"Bad news?" she inquired.

"No."

"Then why are you upset?"

"I shouldn't, but I am." he mumbled. "Well, my guru is going to visit us."

She took a deep breath, scratched her head, and said, "Swami, what are we going to do? The guru wants costly food and wine."

"I know that. Don't you have any jewelry left?"

"I sold the last ornament to feed him on his previous visit. This time he must starve with us."

He shrugged his shoulders and said, "I can't do that to my guru. I'll burn in Hell. There must be some way to feed him."

She noticed him twisting the end of his dhoti and tears were dimming his eyes. She was sure he would do nothing but pray, and she should do something to tide over the situation.

210

"Swami, don't worry and go to your work. I'll borrow some money from the chief's wife."

She knew it was a lie. The chief, like the other eighty villagers, was fighting hard times, and she had no hope of getting any money.

Color returned to his cheeks, and he stepped out of the house, while chanting mantras. She, however, found sorrow in his tone, and his voice had come down by several decibels.

After her husband was well on his way to the temple, she went to her bed, opened the end of her pillow, and took out the gold ring. This was the family ring which was the wedding gift from her grandmother. She was fourteen at that time and swore to the gods and to Grandma that she would never part with it. She wiped her tears with the end of her sari and kissed the ring.

She recovered her aplomb, grabbed the walking stick, wobbled to the goldsmith, sold the ring, and bought wine, chicken, and other food for the coming visitor. On returning home, she concealed the food and started working on her plan to handle her husband's guru. It was a risky scheme, but she was in a desperate situation. She took out a large rope and a stick. Then she went to the temple dump and picked up a basket of dark red flowers. When she was young, she used to rub those on her cheeks to make them look rosy. This time she boiled those in water and made a red syrup. After placing the rope and stick on the ground, she poured the solution over them. In one hour the solution congealed, and the rope and stick looked as if they were covered with coagulated blood. She scraped the stained soil and dumped it in the nearby village pond. Then she placed the rope and stick in the corner. The preparations for the reception of her husband's guru were complete, and a wry smile mixed with a sigh appeared on her face.

Late in the evening her husband came from the temple with two marigold garlands. They had their dinner—tea with parched grams and went to sleep after begging the gods. She was exhausted and her back was hurting, and she couldn't sleep; she was thinking about her planned adventure.

Next morning her husband had his breakfast and began pacing the room. "My guru is coming during our tough times. Let's pray to the gods to detain him somewhere."

"Swami, we can't alter our karma."

He stopped walking. "Well, you promised to borrow money from the chief. Did you have any luck?"

"Yes, the chief's wife loaned me one hundred rupees."

A gleam sparkled in his misty eyes. "Good, could you purchase all the needed stuff?"

She nodded with a smile.

He patted her back and chanted a mantra. "Thanks Sita, you're a wonderful wife. The gods are sure to reward you," he said and hurried to the temple.

She went to the kitchen and labored two hours to cook the food. Then she stretched on the cot, closed her eyes, and begged Lord Krishna to assist her in her coming project.

She dozed off for thirty minutes. On hearing loud knocking at the door, she got up, adjusted her sari, and opened the door. She found a short, corpulent man with bald head, looking at her with a big grin. She touched his feet. When he raised his hand to bless her, she noticed his huge paunch throbbing like the throat of a monsoon frog. She conducted him to the living room, where she had spread a rug on the cow dung plastered floor. The guru lifted his belly and sat cross-legged on it. The smell of spicy chicken curry was wafting in the air. He sniffed, smacked his lips, rubbed his triple chin, and said, "Food smells good. Where's my disciple?"

"He's busy at the temple and will come for lunch after the noon worship."

"I'm starved. I can't wait for him. I had to walk five miles."

"There's no need to wait. Food is ready, and I'll serve it right now."

She went to the kitchen, brought three bowls and a steel plate, and adjusted those in front of the visitor along with a glass of water. He extended his hands, and she poured water from a jug over them. After this ablution he smiled, wiped his hands with his scarf, said a short prayer, and attacked the food. He took a few bites and inquired, "Where is the drink?"

She gestured toward the glass of water.

"Child, that's not nectar."

She bowed with folded hands and said, "Sorry, I forgot that." She rushed to her wooden chest, brought out the wine bottle, and placed it near the plate.

The guru took out a small bottle from his pocket, added a few drops to the wine and smiled. "This sacred Ganges water has blessed the wine and turned it into nectar, fit for a holy man."

She stifled her tears and watched the butter-ball gobbling up her grandma's gold ring. The shadows of the banyan tree on the wall reminded her that after thirty minutes her husband would be coming for lunch.

The guru asked for several helpings, licked the plates, and emptied the bottle. He patted his belly, burped, and said, "I enjoy blessing this place. The gods have given Mohan a good cook. Child, everything was fine except your chicken needed a bit more turmeric."

She bowed with folded hands and said, "I'll be careful in making the next meal."

It was the time for her to act.

She covered her face in the tent of her hands and began sobbing.

"Child, what's bothering you?"

"Guru Maharaj (respected), you must leave now."

"What's the reason?"

"Your life is in danger."

The guru's chin fell, and he asked, "Why?"

"Your disciple has freaked out. He hates gurus and tortures any guru who comes to our house."

"Ram! Ram! Ram!" he mumbled.

She pointed to the stick and the rope and said, "He uses that rope to tie up a guru and then pulverizes the poor person with the stick, ignoring his begging and my pleas. You can see the blood stains on those. Sorry, I forgot to clean them. Let me take care of it."

She rushed to wipe the blotches on the rope and stick.

The guru, who had been staring at the dangerous weapons, shot up, grabbed his bag, and started to sprint to the door. She stopped him. "Guru Maharaj, I hear my husband's footsteps in the street. To save yourself, you better jump out from the rear window. I'll try to detain him."

She bolted the front door and hurried to the bedroom. The trembling guru tagged her. He tried to wiggle out of the small window and got stuck. Ignoring her back pain, she pushed him with both hands. When he tumbled on the ground, she heaved a sigh of relief. He thanked her and ran. She stood at the window for a few seconds to watch him sprinting across the wheat fields.

She was out of breath and drenched in sweat. She adjusted her sari and wiped the sweat from her forehead. The pounding on the door had grown louder, and she opened it.

Her husband noticed the dirty bowls, a plate loaded with chicken bones, and an empty wine bottle, and said, "Thanks Sita, I see you served proper food to my guru."

She nodded.

"Did he like it?"

"Yes."

"Is he resting now?"

"No, he left."

"Did he give you any reason for leaving?"

"Yes, after eating, he told me he wanted to visit another disciple. I requested him to wait and meet you, but he refused and promised to come back in the evening. Then he made a strange request."

"What was that?"

"He searched our house, picked up a rope and a stick, and wanted to take those with him. I refused and told him that the rope is for my grandson who uses it to make a swing on our tree, and the stick belongs to your grandfather. I'll never part with them. On hearing my reply, he blew his top, yelled at me, and ran out of our home."

"Sita, you should have given him those things. Well, in which direction did he go?"

She opened the window and showed the saffron robe billowing in the fields.

"I don't want to be roasted in Hell for annoying my guru," he said. Then he grabbed the rope and stick, jumped out of the window, and ran after his guru.

She watched the two runners. The gods had blessed both with extra large potbellies and blubber. They huffed and puffed as they rolled on the winding dirt paths which snaked through the crops.

She could hear her husband yelling at the top of his lungs, while waving the rope and stick. She saw the guru glancing back and shivering to notice Mohan carrying the torture implements. The guru was putting forth his best effort to escape from the clutches of a Yamma (carrier of the dead). After twenty minutes, she saw her husband stumbling and falling flat on the ground. She held her breath and was relieved to see him scrambling up and dusting his clothes. The saffron robe disappeared on the horizon. Her husband tottered home and sprawled on the string cot.

She gave him a glass of water and said, "Swami, I'm sorry, I should have given him those things."

"I'm glad you didn't. We can't entertain him every year while we're starving. The gods will forgive us. They understand our situation."

She raised her folded hands toward the ceiling and said, "The gods are merciful. Come on and enjoy the meal. I saved some for us."

After months of starvation they had a scrumptious meal. He took a deep breath, burped, caressed his belly, and said, "I learned something today."

"What's that?"

"I can't run."

"Swami, you have put on too much weight, and I always worry about your heart."

"Yes, my ticker has been bothering me. I do need some exercise."

Her lips curled up. "Swami, then start doing pushups before going to the temple."

"I've a better idea."

"What are you thinking?"

"From tomorrow onwards, I'll close the temple for four hours and work in the fields. This will help my body and bring in much needed money."

She said in sotto voce, "Thanks, Lord Krishna."

Next day he accepted a job with the chief. Soon she felt better and started working, and their starvation days were over.

After fifteen days Mohan received a letter from his guru informing him that he had moved to the south and wouldn't be able to visit him. Mohan was delighted and gave the letter to his wife. She tucked it in the same pillow where she had kept grandma's ring, sewed it up, and said, "Grandma, thanks for your ring. It averted a catastrophe in my life. Please excuse my selling it; I was left with no other choice."

Royal Elephants' Dung

Palta City, India, 1938

"Bir, I've decided to retire and visit the sacred temples," my housekeeper, Ram, an old Brahmin, said with misty eyes.

I was dumbfounded. "Oh no! I can't survive without your help."

"Sorry, you have to adjust."

"What about your promise to stay with me until I got a wife?"

He sighed. "I'm not happy about it. I've been with your family for more than thirty-five years, and you were born in my hands. I longed to see you getting married and then retire."

"Why have you changed your mind?"

He twisted the end of his dhoti and mumbled, "The work here is too much for me."

"You always complained about lack of work," I said. "How has it increased?"

"Well, I have been dumped with extra work which I can't handle."

"What work?"

"I can't describe it."

"Why?" I asked.

"You won't believe it."

"I trust you."

"All right, come here at nine-fifteen."

"Okay, I'll be here, but remember you're not going to abandon me. I'll solve your problem."

217

I finished my breakfast, waved goodbye, and drove to the survey camp.

After graduating from Thompson Engineering College, Roorkee, I joined the Indian railways and my first posting was to undertake the survey for a railway line which would link Palta City, the capital of Cooch State, to Thong Town near the Chinese border. I moved to Palta City and rented a bungalow near the edge of the town. The sixty miles of the proposed line ran through thick jungles which were infested with lions, tigers, panthers, cobras, and ubiquitous flies and mosquitoes. I set up three field camps at twenty mile intervals, and the survey work started. Everyday I got up at five and after a quick breakfast, I drove my jeep to one of my camps. I returned late in the evening, exhausted and covered with dust. So far my life had its normal grind.

On reaching my field office at seven, I hunched over the drawings and tried to check the plotted data. My mind, however, churned over the problem of losing my faithful, trustworthy housekeeper who controlled me like a mother and strictly enforced his rules: no smoking; no drinking; no girls. I was happy, since this kept me out of trouble. I was two thousand miles away from my home province, and if I hired a servant here, the fellow wouldn't understand my habits and language and wouldn't be able to cook the food I liked. The most difficult thing was managing the money—the new servant could easily steal without my detection.

I drove back at nine-fifteen and found Ram, with a scarf strapped to his nose, shoveling huge piles. I got out of the jeep, moved closer, and discovered these were cylindrical pyramids of stinking stuff, each weighing more than fifteen pounds.

"Ram, what is this?"

He removed the cover from his nose and said, "Can you guess?"

218

I shook my head.

"This is the defecation of the elephants."

I had never seen elephant dung. "Boy! These are mammoth piles."

"They have to be. An elephant, a colossal giant, consumes more than six hundred pounds of fodder daily," he said. "Look, I have to clear these and wash this area. This is too much for my weak back."

I was distressed to find an old Brahmin removing tons of feces and doing the work which was meant for Sudras. I could have used my field crew to help Ram, but I was a young man with high ethical standards and believed that I should never use the railway staff for my private work.

I rolled up my sleeves, tied a handkerchief to my nose, grabbed a shovel, and started loading the wheelbarrow. In thirty minutes we cleared and washed the area.

"Where do these elephants come from?"

"They are the maharaja's elephants which go daily for their morning dip in the sacred river and pass our place at nine."

"Ram, why do they bless our place?"

"I think nine is their time to answer the call of nature. They slow down, pause for a moment, and dump their dung."

"That's horrible. I'm going right now to the palace and request the maharaja to order his mahouts not to stop here."

"Bir, control your temper and pay proper respect to the maharaja."

"Don't worry, I want to keep my neck and will be very polite and tactful."

I took my jeep and shot to the palace. The military guard at the gate stopped me, and I said, "I'm the engineer who is working to link your town with the railway and want to see the maharaja."

"You can't see his highness, since last Sunday he left for America with his new British wife."

"What about his Indian wife?"

"His Highness has a harem of ninety, and he can't take all of them."

I scratched my head and asked, "Well, who's in charge of the stables?"

"General Khosla."

"How many generals do you have?" I enquired.

"Eighty."

"What is the size of the royal army?"

"One sixty."

On discovering that fifty percent of the soldiers were generals, I had a hard time to control my chuckle.

"Where can I meet General Khosla?"

"Go straight and take the first turn to the left, and you will see the royal stables."

I thanked the guard and drove to the stables, where I found a tall, muscular man with a bushy mustache, strutting back and forth, while twirling a baton. The medals covering his chest jangled at each step. He twisted his mustache and barked his orders to the men who were preparing the maharaja's racehorses for the Indian Derby. I introduced myself and asked, "General, can I have a few minutes with you?"

"I'm busy."

"Sir, only ten minutes."

He caressed his mustache, looked straight at me, and said, "All right, five minutes."

"Sir, your elephants don't wear pouches and mess up my place everyday."

He grabbed his big paunch and burst into peals of laughter. "Young man, they are not horses. No one can make and then fit a pouch on the elephant's bottom."

My face turned red, and I took a deep breath. "Sir, I'll feel highly obliged if your mahouts can force the elephants from unloading in front of my house."

He wiggled his baton at me and said, "Look, these are royal elephants, and when they have to go, they go, and mahouts can't do anything about it."

"Sir, I've one suggestion."

"What's that?"

"Sir, if you order your mahouts to leave early, then the elephants will reach the river and seek comfort there. This will greatly help me and the public."

"I won't mind it, but the elephants can't leave without the blessings from our priest."

"Sir, how does the priest perform this ritual?"

"He throws the sacred water on the elephants, while chanting some mantras."

"Sir, can you ask him to change his schedule?"

"Impossible, only his highness can do that, and he's in America."

"Sir, can I approach the priest?"

"Yes, I've no objection."

"Thanks general, I'll try my luck," I said. "Sir, by the way, how many elephants do you control?"

"Twenty, but soon we're going to add eleven more."

"Sir, the maharaja uses them only once a year to go the temple on Diwali festival. Why is he adding more?"

He straightened his chest and a gleam danced in his eyes. "We have to beat the maharaja of Jind who has raised his herd strength to thirty."

"Sir, it's a great honor to control a herd of elephants."

"Certainly, it is," he said and looked at his watch. "Well, you've one more minute. Let me tell you something about elephants which had been great fighters in our ancient history. Alexander the Great attacked us with his horse chariots, but our elephants routed the horses, and Alexander had to turn back without achieving his goal of conquering Delhi. Our Maharaja's grandfather had one hundred elephants, and he offered those to President Lincoln to help in the Civil War. If Lincoln had accepted the offer, it would have saved many American lives."

He again checked his watch. "All right, your time is up."

I thanked him and drove to the temple.

221

I parked my jeep at the huge arched entrance to the temple, removed my shoes, and entered the marble temple which had a huge golden dome. I knelt before the statue and gave my offering to a potbellied priest who accepted it and made a red mark on my forehead.

"Holy priest, I'm an engineer with the railways," I said. "Can you spare a few minutes."

The priest nodded with a smile and deputed his assistant to relieve him. We walked out and sat cross-legged on the marble walkway surrounding the temple.

"Holy priest, I have one request."

"What's that?"

"Can you bless the royal elephants thirty minutes earlier?"

"No, the time is controlled by the heavenly stars, and I'm helpless."

Then he pointed to a ten-foot tall marble statue and said, "Did you make your offering to God Ganesh?"

I shook my head and gazed at the statue—it had a human body and a head of an elephant. Being a Sikh I was not familiar with this Hindu god.

He found me staring at the statue with confused looks and explained, "He's the god of learning, knowledge, and wisdom and is the eldest son of the mighty God Shiva and Goddess Parvati. His picture appears on every book and ledger of the state. Before starting any work, one must placate him to avoid bad luck."

I scratched my chin and questioned, "Why does he have the head of an elephant?"

"He was not born like that. He was handsome, and later on an elephant's head was attached to his neck."

"How did this happen?" I asked.

"He was leading God Shiva's forces in a battle against the Devils. One Devil chopped his head and disappeared with it. God Shiva defeated the Devils and found his son without his head. His wife, Goddess Parvati, hugged her son's headless body, wept, and begged her husband to restore the head.

"'Look, I'm the god of destruction and can only destroy. Brahma is the creator; you better approach him,' God Shiva said.

"Parvati flew to God Brahma's durbar, grabbed his feet, and washed those with her tears. God Brahma opened his eyes and said, "Parvati, what's tormenting you.'

"'I request you to restore my son's head.'

"'Where's the head I gave him?'

"'The Devils have stolen it,' she replied.

"'Go, and bring me a head of a child, and I'll attach it to your son,' God Brahma said.

"Parvati bowed her head and prepared herself to fly around the universe. God Brahma raised his arm and said, "Parvati, wait; there are some stipulations.'

"'What are those?'

"'You can cut off the head of a child, only when the mother is sleeping. Moreover you can't touch the child if his mother is sleeping with her face toward him.'

"'Can I bring the head of a grownup boy?'

"'No, it won't take root; I need a child's head.'

"Goddess Parvati gave her promise and flew around the world. She checked millions of mothers and none was sleeping with her back to the child. She was disappointed and reported this to God Brahma who told her to bring a head of some animal and warned her that his previous guidelines must be followed. She covered the universe and failed to find her target. While returning, she stopped at the river bank and washed her face. She noticed a herd of sleeping elephants and was delighted to find—all mothers slept with their backs to their offsprings. She selected the prettiest head and brought it to God Brahma who fixed it Ganesh's neck."

He paused to look at me and continued, "God Ganesh took his mother's advice and never touched any weapon after this. He devoted his entire life to learning, gathering wisdom, and teaching."

We walked to the statue. The priest took a deep breath, touched the ground with folded hands, and said, "Praise God Ganesh!"

I thought there was a window of opportunity for me, and if I made a big offering to this god, the priest could be swayed in my favor. I placed one hundred rupees at the feet of the statue, bowed, stood with folded hands, and prayed, "God Ganesh, please ask the priest to help me with my problem."

The priest patted my back. "Engineer, this trick won't work. God Ganesh knows about the strength of the stars, and he would never meddle in this affair."

I was devastated since I had wasted one hundred rupees without producing any results. With a heavy heart, I took my leave from the priest and returned home. Somehow I managed to convince Ram to give me a few more days.

Next day I confided the problem to my inspector who was the resident of the state and knew the priest and his family.

"Sir, the priest is inflexible, but he has one predicament, and we can easily exploit it."

"What's that?"

"His son has quit school and doesn't want to become a priest. You can give this young fellow a job in our survey party, and then he can approach his father."

I was delighted and said, "Get him; I'll appoint him as a chainman."

The chainman simply holds the chain, and this doesn't require any skill or training.

Next day the priest's son, Kishan, joined the survey team.

After two days I called Kishan to my office. Kishan arrived and stood with folded hands.

"Kishan, I can promote you to head the chain gang, but I have one condition."

"Sir, what's that?"

"If you can manage to send your father to the royal stables thirty minutes earlier than he's doing now, the job is yours."

"Sir, that won't be tough. Father goes to the temple at four in the morning, and Mother gets up at six and makes his breakfast. Father comes home at six-thirty. After finishing his food, Father prays for forty minutes and then goes to the palace stables. Tomorrow morning when Father begins eating his breakfast, I'll start singing movie love songs. Father hates them and will sprint out of the house, since he doesn't want to pollute his ears with dirty words. I'm certain that with this trick I can force my father to go to the stables more than forty minutes earlier than his normal schedule."

"All right, after he does that for seven days, I'll promote you."

Kishan bowed and left with a grin.

Next morning I stayed home and waited for the arrival of the elephants. At eight-twenty the elephants ambled in front of my house. I held my breath, watched their bottoms, and was delighted to find no dung. I followed the herd to the river and was thrilled to watch them seeking comfort in the flowing water. I glanced at my watch: 9:00.

After seven days I promoted Kishan. The priest informed the palace that owing to the recent changes in the solar system, he was forced to modify his schedule.

Ram agreed to stay and unpacked his belongings. Thus the crisis, created by the elephant dung in my life, was averted.

My Indian Mother-in-law

"I want you to invite your mother," I said.

"I'll never do that," my husband, Rughby, a tall man with trimmed salt-and-pepper beard snapped back.

"Why?"

"Emily, you won't be able to handle her."

"Don't scare me. In Cleveland High I manage forty rebellious teenagers in my class. Your seventy-year-old mother won't be any problem for me," I said with a determined stare.

"Forget it. She's a ruthless matriarch. Let's not destroy our happiness. Two days before leaving for America, we'll go to Amritsar and meet her."

"Rughby, don't be heartless. You're her first born, and she has not seen you for more than ten years."

"Look, you'll be handling a ball of fire."

I chuckled. "Don't worry. I know how to use a fire-extinguisher."

He uncoiled himself from the chair, lowered his head, and padded up and down the lawn. Finally, he scrunched back into his chair and said, "All right, you win. Remember, I warned you."

"You have done that many times. Get up and phone your brother."

He went to the study and phoned.

In 1960, I was teaching at Cleveland High and met a fellow teacher, Rughby, who had emigrated from India. We fell in love and were married in 1963. During the summer vacation of 1965, we decided to spend three months in Chandigarh. Rughby leased a bungalow along with the servants and car from a general who was visiting his son in America. Most of Rughby's relatives and friends lived in Chandigarh. Rughby's father passed away in 1960, and his mother stayed with his younger brother who was posted at Amritsar.

We didn't have to wait long for the results from Rughby's call. Next day Rughby went to the bank, and I trimmed the rose bushes. As I heard a rattling noise, I looked toward the gate, and noticed a big government car with shining plate: "Chief Engineer," crawling on the driveway. The car stopped and a heavy-set man, wearing a blue turban, emerged from the car. I recognized him: my husband's younger brother. He addressed me with folded hands, "Good morning, Bhabijee (sister-in-law)."

I laid aside the clipper and said, "Good morning."

"Brother phoned me to bring Bibijee (mother), so I've brought her."

Suddenly my courage failed, and I felt a knot in my stomach. I wanted to meet my mother-in-law while my husband was standing next to me, and here I was facing her alone. There was no way out, so I recovered my aplomb, walked to the car, and saw a tiny gray-haired lady gawking at me from the car's rear seat. I followed the Indian custom of touching her feet and helped her to wiggle out of the car. As she stepped out of the car, she groaned and grasped her walking stick. I held her other hand, and we shuffled into the living room.

"Cold drink or tea?" I asked the chief engineer.

"Thanks, I'm already late for my meeting. Bibijee, however, will like tea at this hour," he blurted, waved his arm, and shot out of the house. I observed the gleam in his dancing eyes and was sure the fellow was delighted to get rid of his burden.

I went to the kitchen and told Ramu, the cook, to bring tea for the guest in the living room. I sat facing my mother-in-law and tried to communicate through smiles and gestures, but she ogled me through her steel-frame glasses without showing any emotion or response.

The uneasy stance was broken, when Ramu placed the tea tray before her. She ordered Ramu to sit on the floor near her feet and chatted with him, while she slurped tea. Soon she yelled for the other two servants—the gardener and the driver, and made them sit near Ramu with folded hands. Now she was all smiles. I was excluded from the conversation and watched them without understanding a word.

I heard the squeaks of a vegetable-vendor's cart and his vociferous shibboleths. As usual, I took Ramu and bought fresh vegetables. On returning to the living room, I sat closer to the old lady, but she scowled at me and there was no change in her attitude. I was disappointed and felt like an outcast. I decided to go back to my flowers.

Rughby returned from the bank and met me in the garden.

"Bibijee has arrived," I said.

"Did you meet her?"

"Yes."

"Emily, how was your meeting?"

"Terrible! I tried my best to please her, but she ignored me, and the only thing she offered me was a big scowl. I think she hates me."

"I bet she does."

"Why?"

"You're a foreign-born and didn't bring her any dowry," he said and held my hand. "Well, I warned you, but you were adamant. Now let's work together to handle the tigress."

We went inside the living room and found the servants had left; Bibijee was dozing with drool dripping from her lips. We were afraid to disturb her and went to the study and read the newspaper.   At 12:30, Ramu came to us and said, "Sahib, lunch is ready."

Rughby and I went to the living room, and he touched his mother's feet. She blinked and blessed him by patting his head. She grabbed her walking stick, lumbered to the dining table, and sat cross-legged on the chair at the head of the table. Rughby sat near her and I adjusted next to him so he could translate the conversation for me, and I was away from her firing range.

I glanced at the table and was stunned to find that none of the vegetables I had purchased were on the table. Bibijee noticed the clouds on my face, yelled at Rughby, and stabbed him with her index finger. Rughby mumbled a few Punjabi words and nodded his head.

I whispered in Rughby's ear, "What's going on?"

He looked as if he had been mauled by a tigress. He leaned toward me and said under his breath, "Wait, I'll tell you later."

We finished lunch. Bibijee washed her hands in the finger bowl, took hold of her stick, and said, "I want to take my noon siesta."

Rughby escorted her to the guest bedroom, and she went to sleep.

"Let's go for a walk," Rughby suggested.

"Rughby, it's too hot outside."

"Well, I want to show you something."

Rughby took me to an enclosed dump, pointed to a heap of fresh vegetables, and said, "There are your vegetables."

"Horrible! How could they reach here?"

"Mother ordered Ramu to throw these here."

"Why?"

"To teach you a lesson that you can't buy anything without her permission."

"Rughby, I didn't know that I had to seek her permission for this."

"According to our customs, she's the head of the house."

"Well, what should I do now?"

"Forget about running the house and give her full control. Spend time with me, books, and the garden."

"It's fine with me. I wish she had explained instead of throwing away my purchase."

"Erase the whole affair from your mind. You can't help it. She will find fault with anything you do."

"Like what?"

"The way you walk, sit, speak, dress...."

"She'll make us miserable. Why not send her back?" I asked.

"Our dumb traditions; I can't do that."

"All right, then I'll find a way to get out of this fix."

"Let me try to humor her," Rughby said and left.

I relaxed in the lawn chair and closed my eyes. The vision of my father, a tall, red-headed Marine Officer appeared before me.

"Emily, remember when you face an enemy in the battle, you don't close your eyes and pray or try to run away. You fight with all your weapons," he said.

I rubbed my eyes. Dad's image vanished, but his advice was still ringing in my ears. I decided to give a chance to diplomacy, and if that failed, then adopt harsher methods to protect myself.

At eight in the evening, Bibijee sat cross-legged on the bed and recited her prayers. When she ended the session, I tiptoed in, touched her feet, and tucked her under the covers. I was frustrated to find no change in her frown, and she didn't utter a word.

During the night she snored like a pregnant frog, and the night passed without any incident. I heard banging of a stick on our bedroom door and looked at the luminous clock: 4:07. I shook Rughby and he opened his eyes.

"Get up and give me my tea," the voice at the door demanded.

Rughby stifled his yawn and said, "Bibijee, give us two minutes."

The grumbling voice, the sound of shuffling footsteps, and the thud of the walking stick, faded away.

Rughby held my hand and pleaded, "Please go back to sleep, and let me handle this."

"Why can't Ramu do this?"

"She will not accept morning tea from a servant."

I was surprised at her strange behavior and found Rughby mumbling in Punjabi. He always did this to control his anger.

"You better rest. I've learned how to brew the Indian tea from Ramu and will give her that. It will please her, and I might win her over," I said.

"That's a smart move; wish you good luck," he said.

I left the bed, went to the kitchen, prepared the tea, and took the glass to Bibijee's bedroom. I parted the door and saw her seated cross-legged on the bed. She raised her head and pointed her finger to the side table; I placed the glass on the gestured spot and moved out without getting a smile or words of thanks.

Crestfallen, I returned to the bedroom and tried to sleep. After ten minutes, we heard loud banging of a stick from Bibijee's bedroom, and Rughby dashed there. I could hear the old lady bellowing at the top of her lungs, and Rughby meekly saying hanjee (yes) all the time. I wondered how such a tiny person could raise such high decibels and scare a man double her size.

Rughby returned to me, wearing a factitious smile. I could see through the thin veneer and asked, "What lecture were you getting from your mother?"

"It was not a lecture; just a friendly conversation."

"Look, conversation means an exchange of words, but you never said any word other than hanjee, and I know what that means."

His joyful facade crumbled down. "Okay, she was complaining about your tea."

"I used the same material and process as used by Ramu in the afternoon tea, and she was ecstatic about it."

"Darling, there's a big difference."

"What's that?"

"He's the servant, and you're the daughter-in-law."

"Tomorrow come to the kitchen with me, and we'll adopt another approach."

"All right, I will be with you. Hope it works for us," he said.

Next morning Rughby got up with me at four. I made the tea, and he took the glass to Bibijee. I pussyfooted to her bedroom door, and watched through the narrow slit: When Bibijee saw her son with a glass of tea, she stopped chanting, held the glass with a smile, and took a big sip. I anticipated a yell, but instead I heard slurps followed by a syrupy voice, 'Good tea! Good! Good! Good!"

I was delighted, but after a few sips, her tone abruptly changed and I heard her chastising Rughby. I could easily understand from the pitch of her voice that she was mad at something.

Rugby came out, closed the door, held my hand, and we returned to our bedroom.

"I heard Bibijee praising the tea. Why was she so mad at the end?"

He forced a smile. "Well, she was exceedingly happy with the tea and talked about it."

"Don't prevaricate; come out with the truth."

"All right, she told me that I made a blunder in marrying a foreign-born girl who can't make a good cup of tea."

"I made the tea which she was ravishing."

"The trouble is she thinks that I brewed the tea."

"Tell her the truth." I said.

"I can't"

"Why?"

"Then she'll yell at me for cheating."

We sat wordless for a few minutes and then deiced to catch some sleep—there were still two hours for sunrise.

Next day, I decided to give the last chance to my diplomacy and took Bibijee for a stroll around the lake. I bought flowers and ice cream for her and tried my best to wiggle into her heart. She smiled one time, but when we returned, I saw fire emitting from her scolding eyes. I went to my bedroom, covered my face in the tent of my hands, and the tears trickled down my fingers.

"Stop crying; you'll never be able to please my mother. Damn the traditions; I'll take her back to my younger brother," Rughby said.

I dabbed my eyes and said, "Please give me one more chance; she needs a stronger medicine."

"All right, only one try."

In the afternoon, I went to my neighbor, Satwant, who had become my close friend, and shared my problem with her. We devised our plan.

Satwant came over and visited Bibijee for one hour, while I had gone to the library.

Next morning, seated in a garden chair, I was reading the newspaper. I saw Bibijee returning from the temple and kept my head buried in the paper. She came over to me, hugged me, and placed the marigold garland around my neck. Then she kissed my forehead several times and said in her mellifluous voice, "Emily, good girl."

She placed my hand on her heart and announced, "Me love big."

I was delighted at the success of my plan and thanked her with a smile.

She left the garden and shouted in a loud voice, so that neighbors and the servants could hear it, "Emily good girl, me love big."

Rughby, who was watering the plants in the kitchen garden, heard his mother's shouts, sprinted to me, and said, "Bibijee is completely transformed; I can't believe what I heard. She's no longer behaving like a tigress, but is acting like a cuddly poodle. How could you perform this miracle?"

"Satwant helped me."

"How?"

"As planned, Satwant told Bibijee that she shouldn't hurt the goose which is laying golden eggs for her son. Bibijee asked, 'How Emily is laying the golden eggs?' Then Satwant told her, 'Emily is a born American citizen, and she secured the citizenship for Rughby. According to the American laws, if she divorces him, she will get all the property and most of his salary as alimony. Rughby won't be able to support himself and will demand his share from the ancestral property.'

"You know your mother is a tightwad and will do anything to stop a leakage from her purse. From hence onwards she will worship me."

He held me in his arms and said, "I'm lucky to have married such a smart woman."

Next day Bibijee got up in the morning brewed her tea. During the day she made sure that I had proper rest and good food. She even hired a midwife who gave me a massage daily. She told all the relatives and friends, "My son is lucky to find, Emily, a rare gem."

Rughby's younger brother's wife, who was regularly tortured by Bibijee, asked me how I could win over Bibijee. I just smiled.

Three months slipped away, and we had to say goodbye to Chandigarh. At the airport, Bibijee hugged me and whispered in my ear, "Rughby good boy; no divorce."

God Parts Heaven for His Believer

"If you believe in Him, He will part the Heaven to grant your wish," our farmhand, Mann Singh, a towering giant, always sang this hymn in his melodious voice.

He paused to clear his throat with a dry cough and continued singing the same hymn; he was never bored by the repetition. He had a black flowing beard, rosy cheeks, and wore a saffron colored turban. He, however, was blind.

My village stood at the feet of majestic Himalayan Mountains, and we could hear the murmur of the waters of the sacred river. For eons my family had been farmers, and we loved the feel of the dark soil and the smell of the clean fresh air.

I was nine-years-old, when he joined our family. I clearly remember that day: My father and I were sitting on wooden stools, chewing sugar cane, and a tall man appeared before us. He greeted Dad in a firm voice, "Sat Sri Akal (Sikh greeting)."

Dad stopped chewing, laid the sugar cane on the ground, and returned the greeting.

"My name is Mann Singh, and I want a job," the visitor said.

"What can you do for us?" Dad asked.

"Protect and take care of your animals."

Dad looked at the lifeless eyes, hesitated, and said, "It's tough. An eight-feet-high mud wall, with steel gate, encloses my barn and the house. In spite of this, the thieves have managed to steal my horse and a bull."

"Well, give me the job for one month. If you're not satisfied, I'll leave without asking for any wages."

Dad was skeptical, but on finding a look of confidence on the face of the towering man, he agreed.

"Come on, let me show you the place where you will sleep and give you a tour of the barn," Dad said.

Dad took him to a room in the barn where there was one string cot, a cane chair, and a small wooden table.

"Here is the room for you. My son, Bir, will bring the bedding and towels."

Mann placed his backpack on the cot and said, "That's fine. Now I'd like to meet the animals."

Dad took him around and introduced him to two horses, one camel, five buffaloes, three cows, four bullocks, and a dog.

Mann gave a name to each animal and whispered in its ear. In a few days the animals were responding to his commands. Our favorite dog, Kalu, trailed him instead of running after Dad. All other farm hands who lived in the village respected and admired him.

His past history was a closed chapter, and none knew where he was born, and how he lost his sight. There were frequent thefts in the village, but after Mann took charge, no thief came near our barn. Dad was delighted, and Mann became a part of our family.

I enjoyed carrying dinner for Mann. We sat on the string cot, and he narrated stories from the Scriptures. We became good friends, and he taught me how to train my ears, eyes, and nose to watch, hear, smell, and detect things which are not perceptible to a normal person.

One day I asked him, "How did you lose your sight?"

"God gave it, and He took it away; I've no complaint," he replied and turned reticent.

I never popped the question again.

Eight years slipped away, and I graduated from high school. Dad wanted me to go to college which I abhorred.

One day I approached my father, "Dad, I don't want to go to college."

"Why? Education is good for you."

"I enjoy plowing the fields in clean air, singing to my buffalos while listening to the music of the crickets and the bells around the necks of my animals," I said.

"If you work hard at the books, you might become a Deputy Commissioner."

"I'm not good at the books and will end like Labhu."

"What's Labhu doing?" he asked.

"He obtained his college degree and got his job as a Babu in Amritsar. I visited him and found him sitting in a windowless room with mountains of files. Working there would choke me to death."

"I can understand you, but we can't survive on the land which I own."

"Dad, I don't ask you to give me any fertile land."

"What do you want?"

"Twenty acres of your barren land," I said.

"What will you do with it?"

"Dad, don't you remember our family adage?"

"What's that?"

"God is afraid to send a Jat (Sikh farmer) to Hell even, since He's afraid this fellow will till it and make it into a fertile ground."

Dad chuckled. "All right, if you don't want to go to college, you must follow our family tradition—join the army, retire after fifteen years, and then take care of the land."

"Why can't I stay in the village?"

"Son, I see the dark shadow on your upper lip which reminds me of our axiom."

"What's that?"

"When a boy gets black fuzz on his upper lip, and a calf starts digging with its front hoofs, both are entering volatile puberty, and only God can save them from trouble. To help you, tomorrow we will visit the recruiting center. The cavalry will take out all your wrinkles."

"I agree, anything is better than the college," I said.

Next morning I joined as a soldier in the First Sikh Lancers. My grandfather and father had served that unit. They joined at the age sixteen and retired with a full pension when they reached thirty-one and then worked on the family farm. I was late by two years, since I completed high school.

After one year I got my fifteen days furlough. When I arrived home, I found a great transformation in Mann. He was wearing a pink turban, his beard was tied, and he looked much younger.

As usual I took his dinner, and he asked me about the army. I told him about my horse in the regiment, and my winning the regiment rifle shooting competition. He was in a jovial mood and thumped my back. "Good job, keep it up."

"You're spruced up. What's the reason?"

"Bir, can you keep a secret?"

I grasped his hand and said, "We have been friends for ten years, and I never let you down."

"Do you remember the hymn which I sang?"

"Yes, God parts Heaven for His faithful."

"Bir, God did part Heaven for me and granted my wish."

"What wish?"

"Throwing a young girl into my bed."

I chuckled. "You must be dreaming."

"No, it was the real thing," he said. Then he took out an earring and showed it to me. "She left this to remind me of her visit."

"Come on, tell me the whole thing."

"Well, on March 29, I checked all the animals and went to sleep at eleven. Suddenly, God parted the Heavens and sent me a gorgeous woman. She lifted my blanket and embraced me. I felt her bottom; she was naked. I wanted to yell with joy, but she shushed me. She was trembling, and I felt her hot tears. I kissed and hugged her. She told me in whispers, 'My name is Taro. I have eloped with Billa, your neighbor's son. On hearing the arrival of the police, Billa took the ladder and made me climb the wall which separates your barn from his place. Then he ordered me to sleep with you. Please be quiet, since if I'm discovered, the police will arrest Billa and my father will kill me. So I'm here to please you.' We could hear the police shouting and searching Billa's barn and house.

"I asked, 'Why did you fall for Billa, a married man with two children.'

"'Billa lied to me and made me believe that he's a bachelor and is the only son of a rich landlord,' she replied.

"'You're in a big mess. Billa doesn't have much land and is always in and out of jail.'

"'The crook is handsome and a smooth talker,' she wiped her tears and mumbled.

"'I agree, but what are you going to do now?'

"'I can't go to my parents. The only choice I have left is to go the Golden Temple and serve in the kitchen,' she replied. 'Well, do you have a wife?'

"'No.'

"'Were you ever married?'

"'No, I did get betrothed, but my fiancée was killed in a bus accident.'

"'Sorry to hear that,' she said. 'How did you lose your eyesight?'

"'I met an accident.'

"'Did you see an eye doctor?'

"'No, I don't see any hope,' I said with a sigh.

"'Well, how old are you?'

"'Thirty-six.'

"'You look much younger. Anyhow, you are a young man and must look to your future,' she said. 'You come to the Golden Temple kitchen and meet me there. I'll take you to Doctor Sohan Singh who performs free eye operations for the poor.'

239

"'Are you serious or putting me on to escape the police?' I asked.

"'You're a real gem, and I will go anywhere in the world with you.'

"We were in Heaven and made love. Seven hours flew away, and at six we heard Billa whispering from the top of the wall. She got dressed, and Billa pulled her up."

"Did you ever hear from her again?" I asked.

"Oh, yes. I met her in the Golden Temple kitchen, and she took me to the doctor who examined me. I was ecstatic to learn that he could restore my eyesight. So next month the doctor will operate, and after that I'll leave your parents and go to my birthplace."

"What about your girlfriend?" I asked.

"She will be my wife. We'll get married at the Golden Temple."

I hugged him and said, "Next week I'm leaving for my unit and will see you after one year."

He patted my back. "I love you like my younger brother. Promise to visit Arjan in Pidi Village."

"Who is Arjan?"

"Bir, that's the name given to me when I was born."

"Why two separate names?"

"Actually, I have used five different names." he said.

"That's real exciting. Tell me all about it."

"I will, but first promise not to reveal a word of it to any living person."

I grasped his hand and said, "I promise."

He adjusted his shoulders, took a deep breath, released it through pursed lips, and said, "On February 8, 1908, I was born in Pidi Village. When I was fifteen I was engaged. My fiancée got killed in a bus accident. Then the society branded my birth stars as wife killers. I was the champion wrestler and weight lifter, but in our land, full of superstitions, I lost all chances to have a wife. I decided to renounce the world and left my home. I became a clean-shaven monk, adopted the name of Das, and joined Krishna Temple at Hardwar. In two years I found that the monks were more dissatisfied than normal humans and their cover of celibacy and depravation was a sham. Most of them slept with the temple Devdassies (Hindu nuns) and lady worshipers. I was disgusted with the hypocrisy, but struggled along," he said. "Have you ever heard the name Buta, the bandit?"

"Yes, he was a famous daredevil robber. He robbed banks and killed many constables. He could easily evaporate and the police from four provinces were chasing him. Finally he disappeared and the police never heard about him."

"I met Buta, when he came in a disguise to Hardwar to throw the ashes of his three men and his younger brother. He liked me, and we became friends. He revealed his identity and offered me a job in his gang. I was fed up with the life of a monk and this offered great thrill and adventure. So next day I staged my drowning and became Ganda. I used that name for two years and won Buta's complete confidence. Buta was killed in a police encounter. I cremated him and took up his name. Thus I became Buta. All of Buta's followers wanted to keep his legend alive, and they pledged allegiance to me. We robbed several banks and gave the money to the poor. One day a police party raided our hiding place. We killed many constables, but they kept on coming. Finally, we decided to discard the place and shoot through the cordon. We rode our horses and galloped through the bullets. I fell from the horse and tumbled down a cliff. Most of my men were caught. When I became conscious, I discovered I had lost my sight. I hid in the jungle and grew my beard and wore a turban. Now nobody could recognize me. I learned that your father badly needed a farm hand and joined his services as Mann Singh."

"You're a remarkable person. Wish you good luck."

"Bir, God has granted my wish. Now I want to raise a big family and will be an honest, hard working farmer with full faith in Him."

I embraced him and said my goodbye in a choked voice.

241

Next year, when I came on my vacation, I rode my horse to Pidi Village and met Mann who was known as Arjan. He embraced me and introduced me to his wife and two-months-old son. He winked at me and sang, "God always parts Heaven for His faithful."

Hindu Monk and Celibacy

"Mother Ganges, please save my soul; I'm sinking in sin," Gopal, a clean-shaven Hindu Monk, stood in knee-deep water, and implored.

It was freezing cold. The sun god, dressed in golden robes, struggled to get up from his comfortable bed behind the tall snow-clad Himalayan peaks, and its glimmering rays danced over the whispering ripples. Without the rambunctious worshipers, the place looked sedate and quiet. The tranquility, however, failed to quench the fire raging in Gopal's heart. He prayed for thirty minutes, bowed with folded hands to the rising sun, sighed, and donned his saffron-colored robe.

Then he sat cross-legged on the wet sand and chanted mantras. For twelve years, the chilling wind and icy water never bothered him, and he relished this ritual. Today, however, he failed to calm the turmoil in his heart. He became desperate and decided to meet his guru and seek his advice. He rushed to the marble temple and entered the private chamber of the head-monk. He found the head-monk, an emaciated man, with flowing white beard, seated cross-legged on a tiger skin, lost in his meditation. He touched the old man's feet and stood with folded hands.

The head-monk opened his eyes and said, "Son, what brings you here?"

"Guru, I'm losing control over my passions," he stuttered.

"Ram, Ram, Ram," the head-monk touched his sacred thread (cotton thread necklace worn to protect against sins) and said. "When you were fourteen you joined us and have been here for more than twelve years and never complained about it. All right, did you experience this trouble before?"

"Never, I always looked at every woman without any lust in my heart. Suddenly, I've become a voyeur and can't lift my eyes from young girls."

"Have faith and tame the wild horses in your brain. We all faced this battle and won it. Don't fail. It will disappoint us and shatter the hopes of your parents."

Gopal stifled a sob. "I know the implications. I opted to become a monk without anybody's coercion. When I entered the order, my mother touched my feet with tears running down her cheeks and said, 'Son, you're entering a noble profession which requires many sacrifices. Never drop out and stain our family name.' Her words always ring in my ears."

The head-monk sat wordless and snaked his fingers through his beard. After a few minutes he said, "I know you're facing a tough battle. To help you, I'll give you a page from the holy Scriptures. Keep that in your pocket and start reading it as the Devil attacks your heart."

"Thanks, I'll do my best. But I've one question."

"What's that?"

"Why can't I marry and still be a monk?"

"Impossible!" the head-monk yelled. "If we discover you're having an affair with a woman, we'll kick you out, and the world will despise and shun you."

"I still think that if I were a married man, I would do a better job in teaching the Scriptures. Why this cruel restriction?"

"Son, you chose this path yourself and nobody forced you into it. You have been a good monk, and all admire and respect you. Don't let us down and destroy yourself."

Gopal wiped his tears with the back of his hand and said, "I'll try. Please pray for me."

The head-monk patted Gopal's back said, "Go, God will protect you."

244

Gopal prostrated himself before his guru and rubbed his nose. He felt better, scrambled up, and decided to shut his eyes at the glimpse of any beautiful girl.

For three months he shunned the ladies and felt as if he had won the battle with his libido. But his bliss soon ended. One night, while he was cleaning the temple and picking up the flowers showered on the goddess, he noticed one garland had slipped from the neck of the statue. As he was adjusting it, his hand touched the nipple of the marble breast. The sensation fired his prurient hormones, and he tightened his dhoti to choke his excited lingam (penis). He wondered how a warm soft breast would feel. He took out the page from his pocket and began reading it aloud. This calmed him.

During the night, though, as he was lying on his hay bed, his thoughts turned toward the excitement generated by the nipple. His body caught fire and sleep left him. He rushed to the Sacred River, took a dip in the ice-cold water, and read aloud the page given to him. He felt better and continued doing that for several days.

One day, while he was sitting at the feet of the goddess and accepting offerings from the worshipers, he noticed a young girl coming with her offering. He tried to shut his eyes, but the shutters refused to close. She had milky skin, large almond-shaped brown eyes, and golden hair. As she handed him a garland and flowers for the goddess, he felt the touch of her silken hand. A current sparked his body, but he managed to kill his smile. As he handed her the temple Parsad, he noticed her rosy lips had curled up in a smile, and a gleam was dancing in her bewitching eyes. He closed his eyes and chanted a mantra, but his heart kept thudding.

Next day, to avoid the dangerous temptation of meeting the young girl, he pretended sickness and requested another monk to take his place near the goddess. While he was resting on

245

his bed, his thoughts turned toward the girl. Standing in the flickering candles of the temple, she looked like a goddess who had come from Heaven to bless him. The temple bells shattered his dreams. He slapped his head and began reading the Scripture, but this failed to help him. She had captured his heart and always appeared in his dreams and thoughts. He realized he was falling in love and had no control over himself.

One Sunday, while he was working in the garden, he heard the swish of the sari and the jangle of the tiny ankle-bells. As he raised his head, he saw the same pretty girl, and their eyes met. He dropped the sickle and stared at her with an open mouth.

"Namaste, Monk," she said in her mellifluous voice.

He struggled to melt the words which had frozen in his throat and managed to say, "Namaste, child."

She bowed her head with folded hands and asked, "Can I join your class?"

"Child, what class? I teach so many."

"Bhagavad-Gita."

"Child, you're welcome to join it."

She thanked him with a smile and left.

He resumed cutting hay, but his heart was chasing the beautiful figure that had wonderful curves and firm breasts. Now the lack of concentration resulted in an injury to his finger, and he rushed to bandage it.

She joined the class and asked many intelligent questions, and he was greatly impressed. One evening, when he had finished teaching, and all the students had left, she approached him and said, "Respected Monk, why don't you look into my eyes, while answering my question."

"Child, next time I'll do better."

"Why do you call me a child? You have not seen more years than I."

246

"Child, it's dictated by my profession."

"Well, can I see you alone for a few minutes, away from the temple?" she whispered.

He noticed a trap in her dancing eyes, but he was helpless. "Yes, child, come to the bank of the Sacred River at four in the morning in front of the Kali Temple. I always pray there."

He couldn't sleep during the night and was at the river bank early in the morning. When the wafting perfume and the chimes of the ankle-bells announced her arrival, he opened his eyes and stood up.

"Namaste, my name is Kanta," she said.

"Child, I know that."

"Can we talk like two young persons without this child business?"

"All right, I'll break this rule," he stammered. "Well, my name is Gopal."

"I know that. However, when a monk joins the order, he discards his old name and is given a new name by the temple. What name did your parents give you?"

He scratched his head for a few seconds and stuttered, "Vijjay."

"Vijjay, nice to know you."

He stretched his hand, but she turned it down. He was stunned.

"Look Vijjay, you're not supposed to shake my hand," she smirked.

"Why?"

"I'm a Sudra."

"You don't look like a Sudra," he mumbled.

"I'm not Mangu's daughter. I take after my real father."

"Who's that person?"

"I don't know his name, but he is a British soldier who raped my mother."

The ground slipped under his feet. He turned reticent and stared at the sky. He was breaking his vows for a Sudra girl, but his heart told him that she was only a half Sudra.

Suddenly, he grabbed her in his arms, kissed her, and said, "I don't care who you are. I love you, and I'm sure we were husband and wife in our previous births."

He had never kissed a woman before and this intoxicated him.

They held hands and talked for fifteen minutes. Then they found other bathers coming toward them. She covered her head with her head scarf and slipped away. He stood on one leg in the water and prayed.

When he reached his room, he was bubbling with joy. The touch of her silken lips and the feel of her firm breasts had supercharged his body. His stubborn mind, however, failed to overcome the guilt of touching a Sudra. He sprinted to take another dip in the Sacred River and begged forgiveness from the gods.

He knew he was sinking in a quagmire, but he was like a moth that flies to the flame, knowing fully well that it would incinerate it. Now he was not afraid of the future and wanted to possess and enjoy her.

He constructed a thatched hut on the isolated bank of the river and suggested that she should meet him there. Now he could hold her in his arms and feel the warmth of her body. He longed to enter her body, but the idea of mating with a Sudra sent shivers to his heart. His lifelong belief stood in his path, and he failed to dislodge it. Finally he developed a plan.

Next morning, he removed her clothes, and she closed her eyes. He covered her with a white sheet and sprayed it with sacred water, chanted a mantra, and his lingam pierced her through a hole in the sheet. He was ecstatic, since he had copulated without his body touching a Sudra skin.

She chuckled, "Vijjay, why did you cover me with a sheet?"

"Protect you and myself from a sin," he stuttered.

248

"You're a damn hypocrite," she snickered.

He threw away the sheet and said, "I was cheating you and myself. Let's elope and get married."

"What about your job?"

"I don't care a fig for it. I can go to Hell with you."

"How do you want to execute your plan?"

"Tomorrow night I'll fake my drowning in the Sacred River and then meet you at the railway station at nine in the morning. I'll be a wearing a white turban and have a long white beard. We'll board the train to Bihar Province, change our names, and get married."

"How will we earn our living?"

"Working in the coal mines." he replied.

"I'm all for it. My mother approves our union. She will announce that I have gone to stay with my elder brother in Madras. All right, I'll see you at the railway station, but I'll be hidden under a black burka."

He took her in a bear hug, and tears of joy trickled down their cheeks.

Next night Gopal failed to return from the Sacred River. The search party found his saffron robe and towel on the river bank and assumed the poor fellow had been swallowed by Mother Ganges.

*　*　*

In the labor colony of the Krishna Coal Mines, Bihar, two persons sang, as they returned from their shift. Their faces and clothes were covered with coal dust. While laughing, they opened the creaky door of their thatched hut. After washing their faces and changing clothes, she began cooking, and he sat cross-legged and sang hymns in his melodious voice. After cooking food, she joined him in the evening prayer. He thanked God and set aside a portion of the food for the needy. After dinner they walked to the temple, entered the shed housing the homeless sick, gave them food, and nursed them. They returned after two hours and stretched on the mattress on the floor. He kissed her and said, "Kanta, this is real Heaven on earth. I'm content and happy and find myself more in tune with God. To Hell with celibacy. That damned thing is a great hindrance in the path of reaching the Almighty."

"I'm glad you broke your celibacy pledge, and I have a wonderful husband," she said with tears in her eyes.

A Novel Ritual of Dumping Sins

"Mom, why have these people become lepers?" I pointed to the lepers who had bleeding sores covered with buzzing flies and asked.

My mother, a heavyset, middle-aged lady, threw coins at them and said, "They are sinners, and God has punished them for their sins."

The beggars scrambled to pick up the coins.

I was five years old and carried the offering for Lord Buddha's Temple. Mom patted my back and said, "I want you to avoid all sins, otherwise God will make you a leper."

I raised my head and said, "I'll never go near any sin."

Every morning, I went to the temple with my mother until I reached eighteen, and then I left for college. At college I lived like a celibate monk and avoided all forms of sin. When I graduated, my parents arranged my marriage. Actually, it was a dowry deal—my father had incurred a heavy debt in paying the dowry for my elder sister, and he accepted the hand of a girl whose father, a naturalized American citizen, offered a huge dowry. Thus I was hitched to a girl who was lame and ugly and moved to my in-laws who lived in Cleveland, Ohio.

I joined Ohio State University. When I saw American students eating beef, drinking beer, watching dirty movies, betting on games, and ogling girls who exposed most of their bodies in bikinis, I thought they were great sinners and God would turn them into lepers. After a few months, however, I became friendly with a few Americans, and was surprised to discover that they were normal human beings and were

251

happier and more content than I. I started doubting my conception of sins. Slowly the barriers, which I had erected in my heart, crumbled. I discarded my dhoti and started wearing American clothes. After graduating, I got a design engineer's job with Howard-Tammen Consulting Engineers. Now I began enjoying the beautiful things created by God: eating hamburgers; watching movies; going to the beach; and sneaking to the stripper bars. I even flirted with my fellow lady workers. At this stage, I had convinced myself that my old conception of sins was wrong.

My wife was not beautiful, but she was a good-hearted, devoted person, and I loved her. When she and my unborn child met a tragic death, I felt a big void in my heart, and my world crumbled. Now my Indian beliefs, which I had managed to bury in my heart, sprouted back. I felt the gods had punished me for my sins. During the night I dreamt Devils roasting me over hot charcoal and couldn't sleep. I tried to drown my worries in alcohol, but failed. Finally, I decided to take a long leave and go back to India.

On reaching my village, I decided to contact my close friend, Arjan, who was always cheerful with a positive outlook on life. We were classmates for ten years. After high school he took care of his lands, and I went to college. I walked to his house, and saw him seated in a wooden chair, chewing sugar cane. He noticed me, dumped the sugar cane, and rushed to hug me.

He thumped my back. "What a surprise! When did you come?"

"Yesterday."

"Come on, sit down and tell me all about your new country."

I slouched in one chair and moaned, "Sin is more rampant in that place."

"Are you a preacher there?" he asked.

"No, I'm designing bridges."

Arjan narrowed his eyes. "What do bridges have to do with sins?"

"Nothing, but when one is loaded with sin, one can't find happiness in any job," I said, dabbed my eyes, and turned reticent.

Arjan shot up from his seat and pulled me out of my chair.

"Why are you doing this to me?" I moaned.

"Getting you out of the chair which is loaded with melancholy bugs."

"Arjan, I don't see any bugs."

"They are invisible, but I'm sure this chair has acquired the anguish bugs from Svetlana."

"Who is Svetlana?"

"Stalin's daughter," he replied.

I peered into his dancing eyes and said, "Stop fibbing. Stalin's daughter in this chair—impossible!"

He grasped my hand and said, "I'm telling the truth. Do you remember my elder brother, Rajan?"

"Yes, he was a handsome person with a smart brain. What happened to him?"

"He was selected for the Indian Foreign Service and was posted in Moscow as first secretary of the Indian Ambassador. There he met Svetlana and could easily charm her. They were married without Stalin's approval and lived happily for five years. Then tragedy struck him."

"Arjan, I think God punished him for his sin of marrying a foreign girl. Anyhow, what happened?"

"Rajan died of a mysterious disease. We all think the KGB was behind this, but Prime Minister Nehru was Stalin's friend, and he dismissed those as false allegations."

"That's sad. What became of Svetlana?"

"Bir, she came here with Rajan's ashes. My parents and I welcomed her and took her to the sacred river. I clearly remember how she stood in knee-deep water and scattered her husband's ashes over the ripples. She folded her hands as a gesture of farewell and froze with tears running down her cheeks. We waited for a few minutes, and then my mother wrapped her arms around Svetlana's waist and dragged her out. Svetlana used to sit in this chair with misty eyes, gazing at the distant horizon where the river appeared as a silvery line, hoping that her husband would walk out of it. We couldn't help her to get out of this depression. I was glad when she left."

"You should have helped the poor widow," I said.

"Actually it was good for her. She would have withered away in this tiny village. I'm glad she was taken by the CIA to America, and there she married an American architect."

He deposited me in another chair, chuckled, and said, "Look, color has already returned to your cheeks. Relax now; let me get you some tea."

He went inside the house and returned with two steel cups. He handed one cup to me and adjusted himself in the adjoining chair. I crossed my legs, took a sip, and sighed. "The world is burning in sin. We must repent; otherwise we will become lepers and end as larva in human stools in our next birth."

"Stop preaching," he snickered

"Arjan, I'm serious about my load of sins."

"What are your big sins?"

"I discarded my dhoti and ate beef hamburgers."

He shook his head. "Ram, Ram, Ram, you ate the meat of our sacred mother."

"I'm sorry; I'll never do that again," I said.

"What other sins did you commit?"

"I drank beer, watched dirty movies, and hugged American girls."

"Did you fornicate with those girls?"

"No, but I kissed them."

"Friend, your sins are minor, forget them," he said. "Did you bring Kanta with you?"

I stifled a sigh. "She's dead."

"Sorry to hear that. How did she die?"

"After two miscarriages, we were delighted when Kanta became pregnant. One Friday evening I spent a few hours with my American friend. We drank beer and watched a football game. When I reached home, Kanta was having labor pains, and I decided to drive her to the hospital. This was my terrible mistake—I had too many beers and should have called a taxi. On the way to the hospital, I had blurred vision and banged against the bridge pier. She died instantly, and I suffered in the hospital for one month. When I was caged in a steel bed at the hospital, I realized that God had punished me."

"Bir, you can't die with the dead; you have to live your life now."

"How can I? I carry mountains of sins."

He closed his eyes and scratched his head. After a few seconds he blinked and said, "I know your problem. You are suffering from self-destruction by carrying the burden of sins on your back and never getting rid of it."

"When you sin, you have to pay for that; nothing can save you," I asserted.

"You're wrong there. I don't carry any sin for more than a few minutes. I get rid of it and feel free of any guilt."

"Don't kid yourself; that's not feasible."

He uncoiled himself, grabbed my arm, and yanked me out of the chair. "Come on, I'll show you something which will solve your dilemma."

We climbed the stairs and entered a small room on the upper story. As he opened the door, we were greeted by the fragrance of fresh flowers and the burning incense. He flipped the light and prostrated himself before the marble statue of God Brahma, and I bowed with folded hands. He pointed to a small earthen pot in the corner and said, "That takes care of my sins."

"Arjan, stop joshing; that's just a pot."

"Yes, it is, but it carries all my sins."

I scrutinized the pot and mumbled, "It's all empty."

"They are invisible, but they are there. When I commit any sin, I dump it in this pot," he said and again looked at the pot. "I think it's full now."

"What do you do when it becomes full?"

"I carry it to the sacred Ganges River and dump my sins there," he replied.

"You know I'm a Buddhist and don't believe in a river washing our sins."

"All right, forget about the Sacred River. Think about Lord Buddha who has created many beautiful things, and he wants you to enjoy them without feeling any guilt."

"I can't. Sin is a sin, and I'm doomed by their burden."

"Well, try my ritual as a medicine. I'm sure it will work and in one year you'll get rid of your high blood pressure, high cholesterol, heart problems, et cetera. Your cheeks will turn rosy, and your hair will start turning black. It will bring a lasting thrill in your life."

I didn't believe in this container chicanery, but at this stage my health was cascading downhill, and I decided to try his remedy.

I grasped his hand and said, "All right, I'm willing to give it a try."

"Tomorrow is the sanctimonious day to empty this pot. Come here at six in the morning, and we'll make the trip together."

I shook hands with him and walked to my father's home. My parents, being Buddhists, were not pleased with my decision, but thought it was good for me to enjoy the company of my old friend.

Next morning I reached Arjan's house at six, and gave a timid knock. Arjan rushed out, hugged me, and said, "I'm glad you've come: you'll be blessed to learn the sacred ritual of absolving the sins."

We went to the living room, and he locked the door. There I saw a pot of ashes and two bags in the corner. He gave me one bag and a Langota (a string bikini) and said, "Remove all your clothes and put those in the bag. Wear this Langota and rub those ashes on your body."

Grudgingly I complied.

He completed the same ritual, opened the door, and shouted for his wife who brought two steaming cups of tea. We sat cross-legged on the floor. Arjan chanted mantras, and we finished the tea. Now several people had gathered in front of the house. When we emerged in our string bikinis, the crowd placed marigold garlands around our necks and touched our feet.

I whispered in Arjan's ear, "Why are these people worshiping us?"

"We're undertaking the arduous task of crawling to the river, and they are going by buses, tongas, and bicycles."

So far I had been thinking of walking to the river, and the revelation of going on my belly sent shivers into my body; I was completely befuddled.

He looked at me and said, "Don't get confused; it's very simple—we will cover the path to the river with our bodies."

"How will you extend your body to cover ten miles?"

He smiled and said, "I won't; you've misunderstood me. You stand behind me, follow my example, and you'll learn it in no time."

I groaned and hated my decision, but there was no turning back.

He folded his hands and shouted, "Mother Ganges take the burden of my sins."

I mumbled the same.

He drew a line in front of his feet with his finger, sprawled on the ground, stretched his folded hands, marked the position of the tips of his fingers, and stood up.

With some difficulty, I managed to do the same.

We lifted our bags and repeated the process again and again.

Soon the Sun God, with its blazing heat, emerged on the horizon and started scorching poor Mother Earth. I felt blisters developing on my chest, belly, and legs—the parts of my body which were repeatedly hugging the singed ground. I, however, did enjoy the pretty women, when they bowed and threw flowers at us, and some managed to touch our feet. It was strange that I didn't feel guilty in watching them. We had to cover ten miles, and after five miles I begged for a break. Arjan agreed, and we stopped near a hand pump, drank water, and returned to the marked spots.

After eight hours we reached the river, and I breathed a sigh of relief. We placed our bags on the bank and sloshed into cold water. My body felt better, but the blisters cried. Arjan washed the earthen pot with the sacred water and prayed with closed eyes, and I stood near him. A few minutes later, he opened his eyes, carefully placed the pot in his bag, hugged me, and said, "Mother Ganges has taken care of all my sins."

I noticed a glow on his face. I was cringing with pain from the blisters, but somehow I felt happy.

He gently patted my back and said, "Rejoice; you have completed the worship and learned my ritual of storing and dumping the sins. Let's rest, pray, and appreciate God Brahma's beautiful creations."

Without waiting for my reply, he dragged me to the busy area where young girls, in diaphanous saris, were taking their dip. We sat cross-legged, and I closed my eyes to pray.

"Don't be dumb, keep your eyes half shut, and close them only when a person comes to touch your feet," he whispered.

I acquiesced with a smile, and he began reciting the Scriptures. The fear of sin disappeared from my heart, and I started enjoying the beauties whose transparent saris revealed and embellished their lovely contours. The young girls bounced up and down with stretched arms, gyrating their solid bumps, and I ogled them to my heart's content. We meditated for thirty minutes and then took our clothes from our backpacks and donned those.

A Novel Ritual of Dumping Sins

Arjan bought one earthen pot, gave it to me, and said, "Take this pot, throw all your sins in it, and don't worry about them."

"It's okay for you, but what will I do in America?"

"Bir, take a bottle of sacred water with you, pour a few drops on the surface of any flowing stream, and empty your pot. The water bottle will last you for two years and after that I'll send you a tin."

I was surprised, since somehow I had started believing in this sacred ritual and was feeling cheerful and relaxed.

Suddenly Arjan latched onto my hands and dragged me toward a group of tents.

"Why are you doing this?" I questioned.

He chuckled with a gleam in his eyes. "We've to perform a sacred ritual."

"I'm too tired to do anything; let's go home," I stuttered.

"We can't; we face a big problem."

"What's that?" I asked.

"Look, we can't carry the empty pots home."

"Why?"

"The Devil is always searching for an empty pot—a spotless noble soul. When he finds an empty one, he jumps into it, and then no sin can be dumped in it. We'll put in a small sin, and the Devil will never bother us," he explained.

"Where will you get this sin?"

He pointed to the tents. "A pretty girl in one of those tents will oblige you."

"Damn it, that's adultery, a big sin."

"Look, we're doing a sacred ritual to protect ourselves from the Devil and future sins."

"Well, in that case I'm all for it."

We came near the tents, and I found long lines in front of them. Based on his experience, Arjan picked the best place, and we joined the line with folded hands.

I looked around and saw men fervently praying to the gods, while holding their lingams (penises). A wrinkled old man, who appeared to have seen more than ninety-years-old, stood in front of me. He was clutching his stick and chanting mantras in a loud sonorous voice. On noticing me staring at others, he scowled at me and admonished, "Young man, close your eyes and pray to the gods."

I obliged; I didn't want to argue about anything.

The old man's turn came; he paid the money, discarded the stick, and dashed in like an excited bull.

Twenty minutes later it was my turn. Arjan pushed me toward the tent and whispered, "After you complete this ritual, exit at the rear, and wait for me."

I opened the flap and found a large bed covered with flowers, and a gramophone was playing the sitar music. A tall, gorgeous, naked girl in her teens greeted me. She had firm breasts and charming curves. My heart had not fully recovered from the fear of the fornication being a sin; I froze. She held my hand and said in her charming voice, "You appear to be new to this worship. Come on, you have to finish within the time you've purchased."

She removed my dhoti and langota. Then she patted my lingam which shot up.

I lifted her to the bed and entered her body. I felt no sin, but joy, since I had the pot with me. When my time was up, I donned my clothes and moved to the rear of the tent.

I gave her a long, sucking kiss.

She giggled. "You're a fast learner; hope to see you next year."

I kissed her again and said, "I'll try."

I cast a longing, lingering look behind, opened the rear flap, stepped out, and sat cross-legged on the ground. I felt joy and glow all over my body, and the pain from the blisters didn't bother me.

When Arjan emerged, he was singing the praises of the Sacred River.

"Bir, let me show you how to place your sin in the pot."

I nodded.

He sat cross-legged, placed the pot in front of him, chanted a mantra, and threw an empty pinch in the pot. I followed his example.

"Rejoice, you're free from your sin. Remember to make full use of your pot," he said.

We filled our bottles with the holy water, and started the homeward trek. Arjan's jubilant singing resonated in the air, and I dreamt about the girl.

When we were close to the house, he stopped singing and admonished, "Take good care of the pot and never carry the load of sin."

I nodded with a grin.

After dinner I took my leave with a great deal of hand shaking and back patting. I strolled back to my house, whistling a happy tune. I didn't want to show the pot and the bottle to my parents and concealed those in my luggage.

My vacation ended, and I flew back to America. When I returned to Cleveland, I placed the pot in my study near the portrait of my deceased wife. Whenever I committed any sin, I threw it in my earthen pot and felt free from guilt.

I adopted this ritual and became much stronger mentally, physically, and spiritually. With my heart full of peace and joy, I had benevolent feelings toward others and stopped branding them as sinners. All, including my enemies, were surprised, but I never revealed my secret.

Lynching of the Innocent

"Doctor, I can't sleep," I said.

On February 8, 1964, I was seated in the office of a famous psychiatrist, Dr. John Goldburg, 67 Main Street, Cleveland, Ohio.

He raked his fingers through his white beard and asked, "Did you try sleeping pills?"

"Yes, they didn't work. As soon as I drop off to sleep, I see flailing arms of flames rushing toward me. I try to run, but they wrap around me. My clothes catch fire, and my hair burns like a hay bundle. I feel excruciating pain, and I scream and jump out of the bed, trembling and drenched in sweat."

"Are you now facing any emotional crisis?"

"No, I'm very happy. I've a good teaching job and have met a wonderful woman. We are planning to get married on May 4. But with my mental problem, I had to postpone it. No woman will like her man crying like a baby at night and afraid to sleep."

"I see you have a serious problem," he said. "Were you ever hurt by a fire?"

"No."

"When did this trouble start?"

"On January 15, I was walking home and saw a building on fire. I noticed the flames and the entrapped people screaming for help. I was shook up, and when I went to bed, I saw the horrible dream which I had described to you. From then onwards this dream is haunting me. My work is suffering, and I've taken sick leave."

"You must have gone through a dreadful experience which you have buried deep in the layers of your mind. I've to dig it out. Let me hypnotize you," he said.

He conducted me to a comfortable couch, and I stretched on it.

"Well, after you're hypnotized, I'll tape our conversation. Once I find how and where your problem started, I'll solve it, and you'll sleep without facing this dream."

"That'll be great," I said.

The doctor swung a pendulum before me, and I entered into a trance. After thirty minutes, the doctor broke the spell.

"I've discovered the cause and have treated it," he said.

"What was my problem?"

"Let me play our conversation," he said and pressed a button on the tape. I listened to my following statement:

In 1941, I was a senior at Sanatam Dharam College, Hissar, India, and had come to my village during the summer vacation. One morning my father told me, "Bir, come with me to our village council meeting."

"Why?"

"Son, you're the first person from our village to enter college, and we can take advantage of your education."

"Do you know the agenda?" I asked.

"No, the chief suddenly called this meeting."

I took a yellow pad and pencil, and we rushed to the banyan tree near the village pond. This huge tree, with several trunks, had a large wooden platform, and I saw several men seated cross-legged on it. The boisterous jabbering of these men was matched by the ruckus of the polyglot birds. The placid cud-chewing buffaloes, unaffected by the noises of the men and the birds, were lolling in the nearby muddy pond. The sultry day was without any breeze, and the leaves stirred only when a bird shot out of them.

An old man, seated at the head of the group, flicked his rosary with closed eyes. He was the village chief. The perspiration had smeared the three horizontal white lines on his forehead and mixed them with the circular red mark. He looked like the picture of the holy saint painted on the walls of our temples.

We greeted the group with folded hands. The chief opened his eyes and gestured us to sit down.

"Chief, I've brought my son with me," my father said.

"Fine, we can use this smart college boy."

We removed our shoes, climbed the dais, and took our seats. I was excited, since this was the first time I was attending a meeting of the elders.

The chief raised his head, studied the group, stopped clicking his rosary, took a deep breath, and caressed his white beard. The coterie stopped chattering. The chief cleared his throat with a dry cough and addressed the group, "This urgent meeting is called to decide the fate of Labhu's daughter, Taro."

I held my breath, since Taro was the most beautiful girl in our village.

"What's wrong with her?" one member asked.

"She has eloped with a Sudra, and thus has brought shame and insult to our proud name," the chief announced. "She must be eliminated."

"Before we kill her, we must establish her guilt," an eighty-year-old member said.

"There is no need to do that. I've seen her leaving the village with Ganga, a Sudra," the chief asserted.

"Has anyone else seen her going with Ganga?" I asked.

All the other members shook their heads.

"I'm the chief, and I trust my eyes," the chief said. "Look, fellows, God made Sudras to serve us. They are untouchable and must be shunned. No girl from our village can dare to go near a Sudra. Our ancestors made clear rules: no Sudra can enter the village after sunset, and they must live in their huts outside the village."

I pleaded, "The world is changing, and the caste barriers are crumbling down. Sudras are human beings like us, and they do great service; in fact, we can't survive without their help."

The chief peered into my eyes and sermonized, "Young man, our Vedas clearly specify that God made the man and then created women, Sudras, and animals, to serve him. As ordered by the gods, Sudras are subhumans and must be kept in their proper place."

"The gods never ordered the caste system; it was conjured by a Brahmin, Manu," I said.

"Can you read Sanskrit?" the chief smirked.

I shook my head.

"The Vedas are in Sanskrit. I know Sanskrit and have thoroughly read them. It's clearly written there: the gods ordered the castes to keep the world in proper order," the chief explained. Labhu raised his hand and said, "Chief, I'll choke my daughter with my bare hands, but let's give her one chance to explain her action."

"No need to talk with the Devil. We must attack, burn the Sudra huts, and throw her and Ganga in the flames," the chief yelled.

I knew the chief's promiscuous father had been fornicating with a Sudra woman who gave birth to Ganga. The chief hated his half-brother who had fair skin and sharp features, without any trace of Sudra dark skin, blunt nose, and thick lips. Now the chief was trying to kill Ganga and Ganga's mother to eliminate his family shame. I thought of averting this tragedy and said, "Chief, I know Ganga, please give me one chance to meet him and clear the whole thing."

"Shut up. Your college education has spoiled your brain, and you've no regard for our traditions and family honor," the chief shouted. "Members, I want to hear from you."

One by one all the members, including my father, expressed their full support for the chief's noble task of punishing a Sudra.

I foresaw the coming catastrophe, slipped to the temple, and brought the priest. The priest tried to calm down the council members, but they were all fired up to eradicate this threat to their honor.

I made another desperate plea: "Chief, I don't dispute your decision. Please let me take Taro's three brothers, and we'll bring Ganga and Taro before you."

"It will take months, and we can't wait," the chief snickered. "Our daughters are not supposed to touch even the shadow of a Sudra, and Taro slept with Ganga. Her sin can't be ignored. We must attack Ganga's father's hut and burn it."

"We should punish Ganga and not his old father who has served the village for many years," I said.

"Ganga has disappeared, and we will never find him; India is a big country. We have no other choice but to penalize his family. If we don't do this, other young Sudras will seduce our girls, and we'll be finished," the chief raised his angry fist and screamed. "All those in favor of my proposal, raise their hands."

All ten members raised their arms. I was disappointed, since my father was one of them.

The chief recited a prayer with folded hands and then said, "Go and bring your weapons and gather other men to assist us in the holy job."

I tried to stop my father, but he was too inflamed to listen to any reasoning.

Soon the yelling mob, carrying spears, sticks, and swords, marched toward the Sudra colony. I was devastated.

The Sudras did the menial jobs and helped the farmers to raise the crops. They got low wages and were treated like animals. No Sudra was permitted to sit at the same level as the farmers. I hated all this inhuman treatment.

I thought of gathering Taro's three brothers and Sudra youths and facing the chief and his party. But my feet turned cold, and my courage collapsed. I, however, did the next best thing. I approached Taro's brothers, and they agreed to join me in helping the Sudras. While the chief was leading the group to Ganga's father's hut, we slipped to other huts, warned the Sudras, and helped them to escape to the fields. Then we slunk back into the chief's gang.

The mob surrounded Ganga's father's hut. The chief yelled, "Devils come out and face God's justice."

An old man, in his late seventies, emerged from the hut with folded hands and tears were running down his cheeks. Before the old man could say a word, the chief smashed his head. The old man fell down with a cracked skull. The cheering crowd set fire to the hut and threw the unconscious old man in the flames. I heard screams of an old woman and was sure those belonged to Ganga's mother. I saw a gleam in the chief's dancing eyes, as he heard the cries of a woman who used to sleep with his father.

The mob couldn't find any other Sudra in the remaining huts and returned to the village. The chief lead the group to the temple, rubbed his nose before god's statue, and thanked the god for helping them in their noble work.

When I watched the hypocrite exploiting religion and the caste barrier to achieve his goal, my heart cried bitterly.

Next day I cycled to the police station and reported all that had happened. The chief and ten members of his council, including my father, were arrested. The police, however, failed to get any eyewitnesses to the crime. All the villagers said that an accidental fire consumed the hut, and the old people couldn't get out. The police kept the prisoners for a few days for further investigations.

After two days Taro slipped into her house and found her mother working in the kitchen. She pussyfooted in, closed the door, and grabbed her mother's feet. The mother slapped Taro and asked, "Where the Hell have you been?"

Taro was prepared for this harsh treatment. She wiped her tears and said, "Mom, I had to do that."

"Why?"

After stifling her hiccups, Taro mumbled, "I was pregnant."

"Did Ganga do that?"

267

"No, he's a noble person who helped me. He acted like a brother to me."

"Why did you run away with him?"

"I was three months pregnant and was sure that my father and brothers, on learning this, would asphyxiate me. I sought Ganga's help, and he took me to a midwife in his cousin's village, and I had an abortion. When we learned about the murder of Ganga's parents, he left for the south, and I came here."

Mother took Taro in her arms and said, "What should we do now?"

"You can conceal my pregnancy and tell people that I went somewhere and Ganga happened to meet me at the railway station, and nothing transpired between me and Ganga. People will forget the whole thing and move on with their lives."

"I agree, but who made you heavy footed?"

"The chief," Taro stuttered.

The mother's mouth flew wide open. "The chief, Ram, Ram, Ram. How could he do that?"

"One morning I was praying in the temple basement. The chief slipped in, bolted the door, and gagged me with my head scarf. I tried to fight back, but he had a dagger in his hand and threatened to cut my throat. He removed my clothes and raped me with a grin on his face," Taro managed to say with a painful effort.

"What about the temple priest?"

"I think he was afraid of the chief. He must have heard the sounds of my struggle, but he never came to help me."

Taro's mother closed her eyes, covered her face with her hands, and tears ran along her fingers. She dabbed her eyes with the end of her sari and said, "Your father is in jail."

"I know that."

"Well, we'll not tell the truth to your brothers. If we confide in them, they will kill the chief's family and get into serious trouble. We'll inform them and the villagers that you went to

Hardwar to worship. Ganga saw you off at the railway station, and you were never emotionally involved with him."

"Mom, Ganga is a saint; he never even touched my hand."

"Wipe your tears, and let's meet your brothers," the mother said.

The mother opened the door and brought the brothers from the barn.

When the brothers saw their sister, they bit their lips and hissed like cobras.

"Calm down fellows, Taro went to sacred Hardwar, and Ganga helped her to board the train. She didn't even hold Ganga's hand. She is a good girl, and you must respect her."

The three brothers smiled and embraced their sister.

Next day, the three brothers approached me and told about Ganga's innocence, and how he helped their sister to board a train to the sacred city.

"What should we do now?" the eldest brother asked.

"Your father and my father did help the chief to kill an innocent man and his wife. We should make them pay for their crime."

"How?"

"Come with me, and let's record our statements with the police."

We cycled to the police station and gave our written statements. After one month the judge sentenced the chief for twenty years in prison with hard labor, and the ten members of the council were locked up for five years.

My vacation ended, and I returned to my studies. My mother was a forgiving lady; she pardoned me for my taking a stand against my father. Now I wanted to run away from my elders who exploited religion and caste barriers to torture and murder two innocent humans. After my graduation, I applied for admission to Ohio State University and was accepted. I did PhD. and started teaching in Cleveland High School.

Dr. Goldburg stopped the tape, patted my back, and said, "Young man, you're healed. Don't postpone your marriage."

I thanked the doctor, paid the bill to his secretary, and returned to my apartment. I had a wonderful sleep without any dreams.

She Defeated the Yammas

"Children, God is everywhere and nowhere; it all depends upon your faith. A statue is just to focus your mind on a tangible object. If you can develop a faith like your ancestor Baba Dhana, then you can force God to emerge from the stone and help you," a bald monk ended his sermon.

It was four in the morning and twenty worshipers had gathered at God Vishnu's Temple, in Pidi Village, Punjab, India. Sheila,
a seventeen-year-old girl with a charming, innocent face was seated cross-legged in the group. She touched her folded hands on the marble floor, stood up, and left the temple.

She arrived at her two-story brick home, went to the kitchen, churned the yogurt, and made butter and buttermilk. Her husband, Nathu, a tall handsome man, in his early twenties, stepped in and said, "Sheila, I'll have my breakfast before Dad and Mom."

"What's the hurry?"

"I want to check the farmhand."

Sheila served eggs, praunthas (freshly baked bread), fresh butter and buttermilk. Nathu finished the food, kissed his wife, and rode his black stallion to the fields.

Lal, Sheila's father-in-law, a seventy-year-old man, and his wife, Kanta, a hunchbacked old lady, entered the kitchen, and sat cross-legged on the jute mattress. Sheila served the breakfast.

"Sheila, I don't want you to walk barefoot to the temple, so early in the morning," Kanta said.

"I enjoy the worship, and God Vishnu is always with me."

271

Lal stood up and said, "I won't come for lunch, I've to preside over the village council meeting."

After her in-laws left, Sheila washed the dishes, and read the Scriptures.

As she looked through the window, she saw the black stallion entering the barn, and her husband was not riding it. She rushed to her father-in-law and informed him. Lal and Shiela rode to the fields and found injured Nathu lying under the banyan tree. They carried him into the house and sent for the village hakim.

Furniture was removed from the living room and Nathu was placed on a string cot. Nathu was unconscious, and his breathing was sporadic. A large earthen lamp was placed near the head of the cot, and its dancing wick made black tendrils which created ghostly figures on the walls. Another earthen lamp rested on the sill of the window. The hakim applied Brahmin-cow's dung mixed with his medicine to Nathu's broken neck, circled the cot, chanted mantras, and threw red peppers on the burning charcoal on his hand-held stove.

Sheila's heart sank to the bottom of the Indian Ocean. The awful smell of cow dung, the odor of the burning mustard oil in the lamps, and the irritating smoke of smoldering red peppers in the hakim's stove were choking her.

The hakim paused, checked the pulse, and moaned, "Chief, I could scare the Devils with the burning peppers and my chants, but I had failed to appease God Shiva; his Yammas (the carriers of the souls of the dead) are coming."

To announce the death of his only son, the chief snuffed the wick of the earthen lamp.

"Chief, Nathu now belongs to Mother earth, and let her embrace him," the hakim said.

The chief and hakim lifted the corpse from the cot and laid it on the floor. The cot was taken out of the living room, and a marble statue of god Vishnu was placed near the head of the corpse.

She Defeated the Yammas

The hakim dabbed his misty eyes, offered his commiserations, and left with his implements.

Sheila buried her head in her hands, and the tears trickled along her fingers. The henna painting on her hands was still fresh from the marriage ceremony. She had become a widow while in her teens and was facing a miserable life. She glanced at her in-laws: Her father-in-law whimpered under the tent of his hands, and her mother-in-law untied her braided hair and pulled them.

Sheila knew a wife is always blamed for her husband's untimely death and was preparing herself for the hard times of torture, humiliation, and insults.

The berserk mother-in-law rushed to wipe the red spot, the symbol of marriage, from Sheila's forehead, and yelled, "You're an evil omen; your marriage brought death to my son."

Then she spat on Sheila's face and shrieked, "You're a husband killer."

Sheila wiped the spit with the end of her sari and said, "Mom, I loved him and would have given my life to save him. We are helpless; everything is preordained in our karma. I beg you to give me ten minutes to be alone with my husband."

"Go ahead, you have already done your deed. We'll arrange the wood for the pyre and then go to the temple and bring the priest to prepare Nathu for the cremation," the old lady snarled.

The old couple shuffled back to the kitchen and then left. Sheila bolted the door, clung to her husband's cold body, and cried, "Nathu, why have you left me? You promised me seven sons."

There was no response from the corpse.

She heard the thumping footsteps and the swish of the robes. The wick of the lamp resting on the window sill fluttered, and she felt a cold draft. She was terrified. She didn't see any person entering the room and felt sure the Yammas had arrived. She prostrated herself before God

273

Vishnu's statue, rubbed her nose on the floor, and begged, "God Vishnu, please stop the Yammas from taking away my husband."

She had full faith in omnipotent God Vishnu who is the preserver of the universe, and she worshiped twice daily at his temple. Suddenly, the room was flooded with light, and she saw God Vishnu standing before her. The god placed his hand on her head and said, "Child, I can't stop the Yammas, but I'll provide you wings which can make you fly faster than them."

"Thanks, but I can't see the Yammas; how can I reach them?"

God Vishnu touched her eyes and said, "Now you will be able to see things which human eyes can't perceive. Get up and put up a fight. My blessings are with you."

A great surge of adrenalin began pumping through her body. She stretched her arms to touch the god's feet, but he had vanished. Then she felt her arms and found huge wings had sprouted along them. She slightly flapped the wings, and her head hit the ceiling. When she looked out of the window, she was surprised to see many miles beyond the horizon. After saying a prayer of thanks, she flew out of the window toward Heaven in search of the carriers of her husband's spirit.

In five minutes, she discovered the shadowy figures flying to Heaven. She winged faster. As she came close to them, she noticed four dark figures, with hooded black robes, transporting a stretcher on which her husband's spirit was strapped. These were Yammas who carried flashing spears in their one hand, while firmly gripping the stretcher with the other.

She stood with her extended wings and folded hands before the Yammas. Without saying a word the Yamma, nearest to her, pierced her with his spear. She felt sharp pain, as the blood shot out from her arm. She stopped the bleeding by bandaging it with a strip which she tore from her sari. Now she realized that there was no use in her begging these cruel and heartless Yammas, and she must approach God Brahma, the creator.

She prayed to God Vishnu who appeared and showed her the location of God Brahma's palace.

In a few seconds she entered the gates of God Brahma's court. She was dazzled by the glaring lights from the moon crescents in the god's black hair. She protected her eyes with her hands, and before the guards could spear her, she shot to the throne and grabbed the god's feet.

The commotion disturbed the god's meditation. He opened his eyes and saw a young girl with pleading tears and asked, "Child, what brings you here?"

"Devta, I want my husband."

"I created a beautiful specimen—more than six-feet-tall, muscular, chiseled features on a honey-colored face, radiant brown eyes, a good farmer, and a champion wrestler, and gave it to you."

"He was a wonderful husband, but he was with me less than a week. The Yammas are taking him away, and I want him back," she pleaded.

"It's beyond my jurisdiction. I make the creatures; Vishnu maintains those, and Shiva destroys them. We don't mess in each other's work. You should approach Shiva."

"Devta, where can I find God Shiva?"

"A few minutes ago, I found him leaving on his rounds."

"Did he ride the sacred bird?" she asked.

"No, he always prefers his favorite bull, Nandi."

She soaked God Brahma's feet with her tears and thanked him. God Brahma patted her back and said, "Child, my blessings are with you."

Suddenly she felt enormous strength in her exhausted body; she had the blessings of two gods. She flew out of the court with full determination.

Soon she heard the jangle of the bells and flew toward them. When she came closer, she saw a white bull, bigger than ten elephants, flying over the fields. God Shiva, with his mountain of black hair, decked with cobras, was enjoying the sight of his thousands of Yammas hauling in the dead. Different types of hissing snakes were coiled around his biceps and neck, and flames were shooting out of his nostrils. She knew that God Shiva had a cantankerous temper, but she had God Brahma's and God Vishnu's invocation which provided her with the needed courage. She flew straight to the bull and blocked its path with her large wings.

The bull snorted.

God Shiva yelled, "Get out of Nandi's path, otherwise I will turn you into ashes."

She kissed the bull's feet and begged, "Mighty Devta, please release my husband."

"I've instructed the Yammas to bring him, and I never withdraw my orders."

"Please show some mercy on a wretched girl."

"I can't. If I show compassion, I would never be able to do my job, and the world would become overcrowded. My agents collect millions daily, and I'm strict in the compliance of my decision."

Sheila refused to budge. God Shiva signaled his bull which kicked her, and she was thrown many miles into the sky. Now blood covered her face and soaked her blouse.

She was devastated—she was severely injured and had lost her appeal. The image of her grandmother, who became a sati by throwing herself on the burning pyre of her husband, flashed across her mind. She didn't want to take that cowardly way out, and resolved to die fighting with the Yammas. After wiping the blood covering her eyes, she took a deep breath, prayed to God Vishnu, and flew toward the Yammas who were carrying her husband. On reaching them, she jumped on the stretcher, clung to her husband's body, and the blood from her bleeding face covered the corpse. One of the Yammas grabbed her hair and threw her into the air. She felt sharp pain, but was undaunted and again returned to the Yammas. This time she noticed an old man with white beard leading the group. She remembered the Scriptures—this saint controlled the Yammas and appeared when the heartless Yammas were in trouble. She found compassion in the eyes of this saintly figure and caught hold of his legs. Taken by surprise, the saint pivoted and raised his arm to slap her, but he was hypnotized by the tearful, pleading eyes, and the blood covered face.

He lifted his rosary churning hand and said, "Child, what do you want?"

"The spirit of my husband," she begged.

"God Shiva has ordered me; I'm helpless."

"I beg for your mercy."

The saint ignored the plea and ordered his men to move faster.

On noticing the change in pace, she lowered her grasp from the legs to the Saint's feet and said, "You have to take me with him; nothing can stop me."

"Young lady, stop badgering us. We'll be late, and our boss has a fiery temper."

"He'll be glad to have two souls instead of one," she snapped.

"I can't, your name is not on my list."

She pleaded, "All right Babajee (a respectful moniker for an old man), I'll leave, if you grant me a tiny wish."

Frustrated by her persistent harassment, the saint grumbled, "All right, just one wish, other than releasing the spirit of your husband."

"Okay, grant me two sons."

The saint smiled and said, "I accede to your desire. Now release the iron grip on my feet."

She thanked the saint and disengaged her clasp.

The Yammas, lead by the saint, resumed their journey toward the gates of a huge hall where the spirits are checked with the ledgers maintained by the angels.

The saint ordered his men to hurry to make up the lost time. After one minute, he looked back and found Sheila still tagging them. He shouted, "Young lady, I granted your wish, and you gave me a solemn promise not to bother me. Why are you still chasing us?"

"Babajee, I'm requesting you to keep your word."

"I've granted you two sons, and you'll have those."

"How can I? You're taking away my husband."

The saint slapped his forehead and said, "Oh, I forgot you live in India where a widow can never marry again. Young lady, you tricked me. I can't break my promise and am forced to release your husband."

The saint ordered his men to remove the straps, and she noticed her husband's spirit shooting down to earth. Then the saint patted her head and asked, "Child, can you assist me?"

She bowed with folded hands.

"If my men go empty-handed, God Shiva will grill us. You can help me to get out of this fix."

"Babajee, I'm prepared to do anything you want."

"Well, the devil has captured one spirit which is running wild near your village, hurting many people. With the Devil's help, it evaporates from our nets, and God Shiva is annoyed with us."

"What can I do?"

"Help us to catch that spirit."

"Babajee, where is the spirit?"

"It lives in the banyan tree near your village cremation grounds. In the morning, your husband was riding toward his fields, and when he came near this tree, it scared his horse and placed a thick branch in the horse's path. The horse bolted, and the tree limb broke your husband's neck."

"How can I find the spirit?"

"Search the thick growth of bushes under the banyan tree, and you'll discover the skeleton of an old Brahmin priest. During moon-less nights, he used to rape young girls there. His heart failed while he was copulating with a minor. The terrified child ran to her home and didn't reveal it to anyone. This Brahmin had broken his priestly vows, and he didn't get proper funeral services. Thus he offered a perfect target to the

Devil who spotted and enslaved him. If you can cremate his body with proper rituals, then he'll lose the Devil's grip, and we'll nab him."

"We'll start in the morning," she said.

"No, you must begin right now; I want the spirit before sunrise, the end of our shift."

She nodded and the saint patted her head. She was hurled back on earth, found herself in her home, her wings had disappeared, her sight had normal range, and her injuries had vanished. When she gazed at the spot where her husband was lying, she found him standing up and folding the shroud. She rushed to embrace him. He kissed her, rubbed his eyes, and asked, "Sheila, what's all this fuss?"

"You were hurt, and we were taking care of you."

"I was riding near the banyan tree, something frightened my horse and it galloped. My neck hit a branch, and I passed out. I don't remember anything after that."

"Don't worry about it. How are you feeling now?"

"Fine, except for the sharp pain in my neck."

She grabbed his hands. "Let's go to that banyan tree."

"Not now, I'm too tired to go anywhere."

"I beg you. Do what I say, and I'll explain later. We can't waste a second; it's a question of life and death."

"Then let's move," he said.

Sheila and her husband slipped from the rear window and sprinted to the banyan tree.

"Let's explore the area under this tree," she suggested.

"What are we searching?"

"A skeleton."

With the help from a lantern they explored the thick vegetation and found a skeleton. He noticed the cotton turban, dhoti, and the sacred thread and said, "This belongs to a Brahmin priest."

"I know that. Hurry up; let's stack it on that pyre."

"We shouldn't mess with the pyre which is arranged for some other person," he yelled.

"Don't worry, please just do what I say."

Sheila didn't want to tell her husband that this pyre had been stacked for him.

They enclosed the skeleton in a white sheet which she had brought with her and placed it over the woodpile. He located the priest of the cremation grounds, gave him two hundred rupees and asked him to perform the sacred rituals. The priest recited the Scripture, poured sacred water over the sheet, pushed Brahmin cow's butter in the mouth of the skeleton, and broke an earthen pot near the head. The priest chanted a mantra and ignited the hay in the stacked wood. Flames, mixed with crackling sparks, shot out of the pyre, and she heard wailing and cussing in the twirling smoke—the Brahmin's spirit was battling the Yammas.

The chief and his wife returned from the temple with the priest. They didn't hear any sound inside the room and thought Sheila had fainted. The chief banged the door, but there was no response. Finally, they broke the door and were devastated to find no trace of Sheila or her husband's corpse, but the rear window was open.

"Let's rush to the cremation grounds. Sheila must be roasting my son's heart to enslave his spirit," the chief yelled.

The chief, his wife, the priest, and two other relatives ran to the cremation grounds. The chief saw the flames and shouted, "She's eating my son's heart. We must burn that witch."

When they came closer, they were amazed to find Sheila, Nathu, and a priest seated cross-legged with closed eyes near the fire.

The chief and his wife were stunned. They rubbed their eyes and dashed to hug their son and daughter-in-law.

Sheila looked up toward the sky and saw the saint flailing his arms. The four Yammas had strapped the Brahmin's spirit and were flying at full speed to their destination. She raised her folded hands toward the sky.

The group left the cremation grounds, returned to the village, and the dancing, singing, and merrymaking started.

At night when they were alone, Nathu asked, "How did you learn about the skeleton?"

Through her faith, she had experienced an unbelievable phenomenon. It would be difficult for her to explain the whole thing, so she smiled and said, "I dozed off while praying for you, and in my dream the Brahmin's spirit came to me and told me that it was sorry for hurting you. It begged me to end its misery by performing the proper cremation ritual. We've done the sacred services, and now I'm sure it will not hurt anybody."

Her Tragic Struggle

Thati Village, Bihar, India, 1945.

Bimla, an eighteen-years-old girl, heard the sounds of the shuffling footsteps and dry cough. She shot out of her bedroom and greeted her mother-in-law, Kanta, who placed the temple marigold garland around Bimla's neck and caressed her daughter-in-law's stomach.

"Ram, Ram, Ram. The gates of heaven are closed for me," Kanta dabbed her eyes with the end of her sari and moaned.

"Why are they closed?"

"I don't find any signs of a grandson who can open them."

"Mom, how can a child do that?"

"Bimla, when a grandson rings a tiny bell, while leading the funeral procession to the cremation grounds, the gods hear its sound and fling open the gates, and the Yammas (carrier of the dead) release the spirit."

"We'll hire ten priests who will blow conk shells, ring large bells, and play the drums. The gods will not miss their sound."

"Little girl, the gods are deaf to all other sounds and want to listen to the grandson's tiny bell," Kanta said. "Give me a grandson."

"Arun and I are doing our best."

"It has not produced any results. Our neighbor's son, Ramu, got married one month after Arun's wedding; he has one son and another is on the way. They are lucky; I'm going to burn in hell," Kanta lamented.

Her Tragic Struggle

Bimla was devastated and tears trickled down her cheeks. She had been a brilliant student and stood first in the district in high school and longed to go to college and become a doctor. Her dreams were shattered when her parents arranged her marriage. She, however, felt lucky, since her father had saved enough money for the dowry and could arrange her marriage to the only son of the Thati Village chief. The girls had no voice in their future. She pitied her friend whose father sold her daughter in marriage to a seventy-five-year-old man.

Kanta's loud sob ended Bimla's rumination.

Kanta grabbed Bimla's hands. "Look, you're a good girl, but if you don't give me a grandson in two years, I'll be forced to arrange another wife for my son," Kanta said. "Well, I'll go again to the temple and question our priest about this. Get busy and take care of your chores."

Kanta left, chanting mantras, and Bimla rushed to the kitchen, sat on a stool in front of a huge earthen pot, and started churning the yogurt. This process took thirty minutes. She enjoyed the splashing sound of the churner and recited Scriptures in sotto voce. When the churning became lighter, she checked the pot and found the butter had floated to the top. She removed the layer of butter and stacked it in a brass container. Then she ignited the wood in the Chullah (open hearth) and made the breakfast for the family.

The sound of footsteps reached her ears, and she covered her head with the end of her sari. One by one, her husband, father-in-law, and two farm hands arrived, and sat cross-legged on the jute mattress. She served them the breakfast with fresh butter and buttermilk. They stood up, washed their hands, and left. When she was cleaning the dishes, she heard the braying of the buffaloes as they were put in the yokes. Four pairs of buffaloes left the compound with the family dog, Kalu, barking at their heels.

Now Bimla was alone in the large two-story brick home. She took out a book and began reading it. After one hour, Kamla returned from the temple and addressed Bimla,

"Daughter-in-law, the priest told me his prayers had failed, and he suspects your birth stars are blockading the path of a child. He advised me to visit the village Jotshi (astrologer). Put on a new sari, and let's go to him."

Bimla changed her sari and accompanied Kanta to the Jotshi's house. She saw the Jotshi, an emaciated old man, rushing toward them while adjusting his slipping dhoti. They greeted him with folded hands. He returned the greetings, sat cross-legged on the mud floor which was freshly plastered with Brahmin cow's dung, and directed them to sit in front of him.

"Please read Bimla's hand, and let me know when I can expect a grandson," Kanta said and asked Bimla to show her hand.

Bimla extended her right hand.

"Child, give your left hand. The gods write the fate of men on their right hand," he said.

Bimla sighed and stretched her left hand.

She was disgusted: Even the gods favored men in writing their fate.

The Jotshi studied the hand for ten minutes and spoke to Kanta, "At present I don't find any line for a child on her hand. The lines, however, grow and disappear as ordained by the stars. Let me check her birth stars. Give me the time and date of her birth."

Kanta had already written that on a piece of paper and handed it to him.

He read it, spread his lunar and solar charts on the floor, and threw dice over them. He tried thrice, and then shook his head.

"The stars controlling her birth don't permit a child."

"Can you do something to change their minds?" Kanta asked.

"It's tough, but I can handle it. However, it will cost you two hundred rupees."

Kanta counted two hundred rupees and placed them on his extended palm.

He wrote down a mantra, gave it to Kanta along with a pouch of ashes, and said, "Before going to bed with her husband, your daughter-in-law must rub the ashes to her private part and recite this mantra fifty times. If she does that, you will find the results in thirty days."

Kanta thanked the Jotshi, and they left the place.

Bimla didn't believe in this whole affair, but she wanted to please her mother-in-law and was determined to show full cooperation. She could see the Jotshi was exploiting the situation and making big money from the rich chief's family.

At nine in the night, Bimla took her bath, sprayed perfume on her body, dressed in a diaphanous sari, and went to the bedroom. Her husband rushed to embrace her and passionately kissed her. He threw away his dhoti and jumped on the bed. She removed her clothes, sat cross-legged on the floor, and recited the mantra after rubbing the ashes on her pudendum.

"I'm waiting; what the hell are you doing?"

"Please be patient," she whispered.

She completed the ritual and told him how his mother had taken her to the Jotshi, and she was sticking to his instructions.

"If the gods don't give us a child, we can easily adopt one," he said.

"To please your mother, let's try this procedure for one month."

The ritual was practiced for thirty days. No results. The stars had refused to budge.

Bimla was feeling dejected. Arun kissed her and consoled, "Look, our farm hand, Kishan, had six children in six years, and his wife is pregnant again. I talked to him, and he said that I can adopt any one of his sons."

"I adore his five-year-old son, Gopi, who is handsome and intelligent."

"Great! Let's give this good news to Mom."

Arun and Bimla met Kanta in the living room.

"Mom, we have decided to adopt Kishan's son, Gopi," Arun said.

Kanta slapped her head and moaned, "Don't send me to a burning hell. The gods would never listen to the bell rung by a child who doesn't have my blood in it."

Kanta buried her head in the cups of her hands, but her tears slipped through her fingers.

Bimla wrapped her arms around Kanta and said, "Mom, we wanted to please you."

"Adopting a child will destroy me; never ever think about it."

"What can I do?"

"Follow my instructions, and I'll extract a grandson from you."

"Okay, I'll do whatever you desire," Bimla said.

"Good, I'll take you to God Shiva's Temple, and you worship the god's lingam (penis) which has blessed many infertile women."

Bimla nodded, and Arun grasped her hand. The disappointed couple left the living room.

Next morning, after the men left for the fields, Kanta took Bimla to God Shiva's Temple in a tonga (one-horse-drawn buggy).

They bought flowers and garlands at the gate and entered the marble temple which had a gold plated dome. Bimla saw the wicks flickering in many earthen lamps, and the smoke from the incense burning pots was curling toward the ceiling. When she made the offering to the potbellied priest who was sitting cross-legged near a cylindrical stone, she noticed lust in his eyes, as he touched her forehead to make a red mark.

"Child, are you seeking help from god's lingam?" he asked.

286

Bimla blushed and nodded.

He addressed Kanta, "Take her to the basement, and let her rub god's lingam on her productive part. Try this for ten days. If it fails, then I will perform the other worship."

Kanta thanked him. They went to the basement, performed the ritual, and returned home.

Bimla was confused—how can a stone give her a child?

At night Bimla told her husband about her visit to the temple, and asked, "My people don't worship God Shiva, and I know nothing about him. Can you explain how this stone happened to be part of God Shiva's lingam?"

"Yes, I can: One evening while relaxing on a gold bed, God Shiva became excited and wanted fun. But his wife, Parvati, was tired and had a headache, and she flew out of the bed. Our god didn't have to fly after her; he started extending his lingam and pierced her five miles from the bed. Parvati was in deep pain and cried for help. God Vishnu, the preserver, heard the screams; he threw his weapon which shattered the lingam into millions of pieces. Wherever a piece hit the earth, it turned into a stone."

"Hard to believe. Do you think this stone can give us a child?"

"I don't, but my mother firmly believes in it."

"All right, I will not break your mother's heart."

He kissed her and said, "Good, I feel obliged for your efforts to please my mother."

Ten days worship at the Shiva's Temple failed to produce any result. Bimla was frustrated. On the eleventh day, the priest told Kanta, "Now I have to perform a different ritual."

Kanta bowed with folded hands and said, "Thanks, on the birth of my grandson, I'll donate five thousand rupees to the temple."

The priest's lips curled in a smile, and he said to Bimla, "Child, follow me."

Bimla was scared. She took a deep breath and trailed the priest who took her to the corner room of the basement. She smelled the fragrance of the burning incense. There was a huge bed, and a cylindrical marble stone rested on it. He touched the stone with folded hands and placed it near the head of the bed. Then he asked Bimla to remove her clothes and stretch on the bed. With great trepidation she did that. He flicked sacred water over her private part, chanted a mantra, and rubbed the sacred stone on it. Suddenly, he dropped his dhoti, removed the gold statue tied to his lingam, and patted it. It shot up to an enormous size. She shuddered.

"Child, this lingam has sired more than one thousand children and will give you a son," he explained.

She jumped up from the bed and said, "Fornication is a sin. How can you dare to do this?"

"Don't be mad; I won't bless you. Look, it's in your interest to keep your mouth shut. If you reveal this, it will only hurt you and your family."

She donned her clothes, and they came to the upper level. The priest told Kanta, "Your daughter-in-law was good in performing the ritual. You're sure to get a grandson in nine months."

Kanta thanked the priest. Bimla glanced at him, but he avoided her eye contact. As they were returning to the village, jubilant Kanta was singing God Shiva's praises.

Everyday Kanta checked Bimla to find any indication of the morning sickness. After one month she told Bimla, "God Shiva's lingam worship has failed. Now I'm left with one choice."

"What's that?"

"Seek the devil's help," Kanta said.

"How are you going to do that?"

"We'll go to the devil's agent, Bhagwati."

"Where is she?" Bimla asked.

"She lives on the cremation grounds."

Bimla abhorred voodoo practices and pleaded, "Why don't we give up and adopt Gopi?"

"No adoption. I beg you to make this last effort," Kanta said with tears in her eyes.

Bimla took a deep breath and released it with a sigh. "Okay, to make you happy, I agree."

Kanta embraced Bimla and kissed her forehead.

Next day, they took a tonga to the cremation grounds and inquired about Bhagwati. The priest at the gate pointed to a thatched hut in the corner and said, "That's her place. Watch out, she's a devil's agent."

They threaded through the burning pyres, and Bimla saw tongues of flames shooting out of the burning wood, and smoke mixed with sparks twisting and rising toward the sky. The priests were adding wood and stirring the corpses with long bamboo poles. The air was filled with moans, sobs, and cries. She was terrified and grabbed Kanta's arm.

When they reached the end of the enclosure wall, Bimla saw an elephantine black lady, stark naked, dancing over a fire in front of a thatched hut.

Kanta folded her hands and said, "Bhagwati, I seek your help to get a grandson."

"It will cost you one hundred."

Kanta had come prepared. She laid one hundred rupees on the floor. Bhagwati picked it up and said, "Come in and sit down. Let me finish roasting this human heart."

Bimla and Kanta sat on the mud floor. Bimla was stunned to see Bhagwati eating the roasted flesh.

Bhagwati wiped her mouth with the back of her hand, dressed in a torn robe, and said, "I assure you that I can make any child enter a womb."

"How?" Kanta asked.

"I will give you human ashes. You take your daughter-in-law to the public square, make her dance naked and scatter them. Then she should take the child, she likes, to the river bank, make a devil's sign on the ground, lay the child on it, carve out his heart, throw the body in the deep water of the river, come home, and bring the heart to me. If you do that I assure you that she will become pregnant. When the child is born you can verify from his appearance and voice that he is the same child which you sacrificed."

Bimla was trembling and her heart was sinking. She was a pacifist who couldn't even swat a fly.

Kanta got the packet, and they sat on the tonga. On the way back, the terrified Bimla closed her eyes, prayed to the gods, and didn't speak a word.

When they reached home, Bimla cried, "Mom, I can't do this."

Kanta grabbed Bimla's feet. "I beg you. Look, you will be taking a child out of poverty and making him our grandson—a rich chief."

Bimla scratched her head and dabbed her tears. "I abhor it, but I don't want to break your heart."

Kanta kissed her.

Next evening Kanta enticed Gopi to her home. At midnight Bimla, Gopi, and Kanta went to the deserted public square. Bimla was hesitant, but Kanta peeled off Bimla's clothes and made her perform the dance. Bimla thanked God as no one entered the crossing while she was dancing. When they completed the ritual, a cycle came toward them. Kanta covered Bimla and Gopi with a sheet and concealed her face in the tent of her hands.

Then they rushed to the river. Kanta made the devil's symbol on the sand and laid five-year-old Gopi on it. Then she gave a dagger to Bimla and whispered in her ear, "Take this dagger and complete the ritual."

Bimla lifted the dagger and looked into the brown eyes of the child.

"Aunty, I love you," Gopi mumbled.

Bimla dropped the dagger and came to Kanta and said, "It's a great sin to murder a child; I'm scared. Let me take a dip in the sacred river to secure help from Mother Ganges."

"Hurry up, we can't afford to lose time."

Bimla waded into knee-deep water. She heard the whisper of the waves and saw several flickering candles floating on the surface of the water. She knew these were the leaf boats loaded with a burning wick and flowers, offered to the Mother Ganges at the temple which was located two miles upstream.

Every year ashes belonging to millions of persons entered the sacred river. A few months ago she had scattered her grandmother's ashes. Suddenly, she saw her grandmother standing on the water surface and addressing her, "Bimla, don't murder a child."

"Grandma, I'm in a fix and the only way out for me is to join you," Bimla said.

"I'll be glad to take you in my arms."

On hearing the whispering approval from her grandmother, she folded her hands to the river and said, "Mother Ganges, please accept my body."

She moved into deeper water and was swallowed by the roaring waves.

Kanta waited for fifteen minutes. When Bimla didn't come out of the river, she panicked. She rushed home and told her husband, "Bimla, Gopi, and I went for a dip in the sacred river. Bimla was dragged by a crocodile into deeper waters, and I couldn't help her."

The search of the river failed to produce Bimla's body. Four days later, Bimla's picture was cremated. Kanta lead the keening party who pummeled their chests, thighs, and cheeks, and blood was oozing out of her cheeks, as she scattered the ashes of the picture over the sacred river and said farewell to her obedient daughter-in-law.

*   *   *

Gopi's parents were delighted to get five hundred rupees for their son's help in the worship of the sacred river.

One year later, Kanta started arranging another wife for her son, but he became sick and was taken to Patna Hospital. He recovered. The doctors, however, found that he was incapable of siring a child: His semen didn't have live sperms. On learning the medical results, Kanta realized that the doors of heaven would never open for her. She banged her head against the wall and cried: "Ram, Ram, Ram. I'm responsible for the tragic death of my wonderful daughter-in-law. I should have allowed her to adopt a child."

Sledding

In 1995, my close friend, Ramu, and I graduated from the Delhi University and hitched on the long line of job-seekers. In ten months, we piled up hundreds of rejections. For getting a job in the Indian market, one has to posses four qualities: Good personality, political pull, computer skills, and top grades. We lacked all four. In desperation we applied for the jobs of sweepers in the city sanitation department. We were interviewed by the sanitation inspector. He was impressed with our qualifications, but before hiring us, he questioned, "Are you Harijans (Mahatma Gandhi gave this name to the Sudras)?"

We shook our heads.

"Sorry, for eons, this job is reserved for Harijans," he said. "Now, good pay is attracting higher castes, but I have to hire only Harijans."

With broken hearts, we shambled out of the office, sat on the wooden bench in the city park, and watched a shaggy dog fighting a losing battle with the crows for a tiny chicken bone.

"Look, like us, the poor dog is struggling for its survival."

"Forget the dog," he said. "Bir, I have a scheme which will make us rich and famous."

"Robbing a bank?" I said. "Buddy, the banks are now protected by armed police."

"No bank robbery," he said. "But I do have an ingenious plan."

"Your crafty plan will be like your previous shenanigans at the school," I said. "Do you remember what you did when we were in tenth grade?"

"Yes, it was lot of fun, and you enjoyed it," he said. "I gave laxative bars packed in candy wrappers to our class of thirty students. I handed you the real chocolate, which resembled the laxative bars, and ate a similar one before the class. After thirty minutes pandemonium prevailed. The whole class lined before one latrine, everyone holding his tummy, while shouting, screaming, and moaning. You and I joined the line and did our acting. Many dirtied their pants and the floor, and the school became a stinking mess."

"Well, that was for fun," I said. "Now we need jobs to feed ourselves."

"Calm down and listen," he said. "I want to represent India in the coming Winter Olympics."

"You are crazy," I said. "India has never done that."

"This time, I'll achieve it."

I stifled my chuckles.

"Okay, in what will you compete?"

"Sledding!"

I burst into peals of laughter.

"Buddy, have you ever seen a sled?"

"Yes, in TV, movies, and books."

"I think you took an opium pill today," I said. "Have you ever touched a sled?"

"No, but soon I will ride it."

"All right, have you ever walked on snow?" I asked.

He shook his head.

"You will slip and hurt yourself."

"I'm willing to take that risk," he asserted with a determined look.

"Well, India doesn't have ski ramps or indoor ice skating rinks," I said. "Where will you hone your skills?"

"Hanuman road."

"How on that busy road?"

"It has two thousand yards of a steep slope," he said. "My improvised sled can easily fly on it."

"That is a paved road and not a snow track," I said. "You must have some training on ice."

"I'll appeal to the patriotism of our public and the leaders who will force our Prime Minister to buy me a real sled and send me for training in the Swiss mountains."

"It's a big gamble," I moaned.

"Believe me, it will work," he said. "After returning from the Olympics, I'll be famous and run for the parliament from my district and easily win a seat. Then I'll get you a high paying job in the Federal Government, and our troubles will be over."

"It looks like an opium-eater's dream," I said. "Anyhow, it is better than starving."

"Then it is all settled," he said. "Sell your books and other things and raise five thousand rupees for our adventure."

"Okay, how much will you put in this?"

"Five thousand."

We shook hands and left for our homes.

Ten days later, we were ready with money in our pockets. We bought wooden planks and nailed them into a five feet long and three feet wide platform. Then we went to the city dump and purchased two broken children's tricycles. We attached their wheels to the platform and fixed the cycle's front wheel with a handlebar as the steering mechanism. After finishing our sled, we organized a meeting at the student union hall, where Ramu made a stirring speech: "Friends, we became free fifty years ago and have failed to send a team to the Winter Olympics. It is a big insult to our national pride. We are the biggest democracy in the world. I'm willing to sacrifice my life and money to achieve that goal."

Students stood up and gave him a thundering ovation.

Ramu raised his arm and said, "Fellow students, I want a few volunteers to help me. Those who are willing, please raise their hands."

Ramu and I listed three hundred volunteers.

Next day, we purchased two thousand Indian paper flags and collected two thousand empty beer bottles from the dump.

The announced day for running the sled arrived. Our volunteers blocked half of the Hanuman road with empty beer bottles which displayed tricolor Indian flags, and stood along the middle of the road with their large flags. Ramu and I carried our sled to the top where the incline started. Ramu was draped in our national flag and two flags fluttered from his helmet. Soon a large crowd assembled on both sides of our improvised track. We had invited the Speaker of the House to bless our enterprise, and he arrived with his big entourage.

Ramu sang the national anthem and then touched the feet of the Speaker who showered his blessings. Ramu flailed his arms and then sprawled on the sled. The Speaker gave the signal, and two volunteers pushed the sled. As the squeaky, rattling contraption moved forward and gained some speed, the crowd yelled. To our great surprise, it picked up speed of twenty miles per hour and reached the end of our track. Ramu tried to break it with his feet, but failed. The sled toppled, and he rolled over the embankment into a deep ditch. When the volunteers reached him, they found he was bleeding and his shirt was splattered with blood. I was delighted at the perfection with which Ramu accomplished this stunt, and no one noticed the concealed small bottle in which Ramu carried the chicken blood. When the Speaker arrived, Ramu again touched the Speaker's feet.

"Let's march to the Prime Minister and force him to buy a real sled and send this daring young man to Europe to get his training," the Speaker announced.

There was booming applause which muted all other noises.

After marching for thirty minutes, the procession of fifty thousand persons reached the parliament and the Prime Minister came out to address them. Blood covered Ramu was presented to the Prime Minister who patted him and said,

Sledding

"Young man, I admire your courage and will give you the needed help to represent our country in the coming Olympics."

The vociferous cheers, clapping, and whistles choked the air.

Ten days later, Ramu flew to Europe and from there competed in the race. All Indians were glued to their televisions and applauded, as they saw Ramu marching with the national flag. Yes, he did compete in Luge (French name for sled which is adopted by the Olympic Committee) races. Moreover he created a record—the slowest speed achieved by any sled.

After returning from the games, he borrowed a car, fitted his shining fiber-glass sled over its roof, and canvassed for the seat in the upper house. He trounced his opponent and became the MP.

Next month, I got a top salaried job in the Central Government. I've kept our old improvised sled in my living room. It was our passport to riches.

Jeeto's Sofa

As my guests step into my living room, they are astounded to see a battered maroon-colored sofa. Its teak frame has scratches and dents, and stains, patches, and worn spots cover its entire surface. Its imported British springs have lost their youth and creak and sink as people sit on it. Moreover, it is an eyesore in the shining new furniture surrounding it. All recommend its replacement, but I will never do that. Why? For fifty-two years, it has been my best friend, comforter, and solacer. It shared my laughter and joy, and at the time of distress, it offered me its shoulder to rest my head and shed my tears on it.

On March 12, 2007, my husband came from his morning walk, wrapped his arms around my waist, kissed me, and said, "Jeeto, you're still looking like the bride on our honeymoon." He stretched on this sofa, and I switched on the TV for him. He closed his eyes and left for Heaven in one minute. It appeared the angels were sitting on the sofa and gave him time to kiss me. I crumbled on the sofa and cried.

Our son is settled in America, and I live alone in a big house. I'm healthy and walk two miles to the temple daily and have a maid to help me. Now I pray to God to grant my only wish—before trapping my soul in their nets, the Yammas (carrier of the dead) should allow me to lie on this sofa and hug my husband's picture.

Let me describe, how this sofa entered into my life:

In 1947, I was eighteen and was studying in high school. I had reached the age at which the parents are supposed to arrange a husband for the girl. I heard the hushed discussion between my parents.

"Jeeto is eighteen. You must contact a marriage-broker and secure a husband for her," Mom said.

"Well, I did that yesterday."

"Could you find anything?"

"Yes, I met the boy in the college, and, also, contacted his teachers. He's tall, handsome, and a brilliant student. I met his parents and his mother agreed to visit us on April 9," Dad said.

"Good, I've seven days to spruce up every thing."

Next day, Dad called the masons to whitewash the rooms. Our yard was cleaned and the front gate was given a new paint. I was nervous, but I had to face this ordeal. However, I was glad my proposed husband was handsome and intelligent.

April 9 arrived; my parents were more unstrung than me. Mom dusted the living room several times. A car stopped in front of our gate, and Dad rushed to it. From the window, I saw an old hunchbacked lady stepping out of the car. She returned Dad's greetings with a frown. Dad escorted her to the living room, where Mom greeted her with folded hands. I saw no trace of smile on the old lady's face and realized I was sure of getting Hell from her. The servant shifted the side table in front of the old lady and laid the tea and sweets on it.

"Should I bring in Jeeto?" Mom asked.

The old lady shook her head with an angry scowl. "We must settle the dowry first."

"Kindly tell me your demands."

The old lady handed over a long list to Mom who passed it on to Dad.

Dad skipped through the list and his face turned ghastly pale.

"Please give us a few minutes to figure out everything," Dad said, stood up, and walked toward the dining room. I dashed out from behind the curtain and stood near the open window of the dining room.

"She's a greedy witch," Mom moaned.

"I agree, but the boy is good. He'll graduate and get a job away from home and Jeeto will be out of her clutches."

"How are you going to raise the money?"

"I'll sell my white stallion," Dad said with a sigh.

"You love it and will miss it."

"I've to sacrifice for my daughter."

Dad and Mom ambled back to the living room, and I returned to the curtain.

"Bibijee (respected old lady), we agree to give the dowry demanded by you," Dad said.

A tiny smile flickered on the wrinkled face, but it quickly faded away. "I want the top quality things. Have you noticed the list of the twenty relatives?"

Dad nodded.

"You have to provide each a heavy gold ring and silken dress."

"We will do that."

"I'm very particular to get the best sofa. It should have teak frame, Dhaka silk upholstery, and imported British springs. I'll not accept the cheap stuff on which I'm sitting here."

"Rest assured about it. I'll go myself to Kartarpur (town where sofas are manufactured)," Dad replied.

"All settled. Now you can show the girl," old lady said.

Mom came inside, escorted me in the living room, and I touched the old lady's feet.

"I accept her," she said. "Let her go back, and we can talk about the marriage details."

I left the room. Dad, Mom, and the lady discussed the nuts and bolts of the marriage: the size of the marriage party, the dinner, the breakfast, and the lunch.... November 10 was selected for the wedding.

On November 1, Dad sold his stallion, went to Kartarpur and brought this sofa in a truck. Marriage was performed on November 10, and I came with my dowry to my in-laws house. My mother-in-law checked the sofa and said, "I'm glad your Dad didn't skimp on it."

Jeeto's Sofa

I was lucky to get a wonderful devoted husband. He hated his ruthless mother, but the traditions forced him to obey her. He lived on the college campus fifty miles away, and I had to face his mother alone. Indian mother-in-laws are famous in giving tough times to their daughter-in-laws, but my mother-in-law was the limit. For two years I endured her tortures. After getting nasty rebukes from her, I sought comfort from the sofa and cried on its arm.

Two years later, my husband got a job in a distant town and we moved in our house with this sofa. Now this sofa witnessed laughter, joy, and love making. I had labor pains while I was resting on this sofa and my husband rushed in with a midwife.

When my son's in-laws came to our house, while sitting on this sofa I declared, "We are not accepting a penny in dowry. You're giving us the most precious thing in the world—your daughter."

Fifty-two years of wonderful married life ended at the death of my husband. Now my flight to Heaven is due anytime. As I was reminiscing on the sofa, I dozed off to sleep. I saw I was taken to Heaven by the Yammas and my husband was waiting for me at the entrance gate. He hugged me and took me to his unit. When I stepped into his living room, I was delighted to see my maroon-colored sofa. My husband lifted me, stacked me on the sofa, removed my clothes, and we enjoyed our Heavenly bliss.

My Struggle to Find Love

There are two categories of love: Carnal Love and Sublime Love. In Sublime Love, a person shows unselfishness, kindness, sacrifice, and noble feelings. The relationship between parents and children, brothers and sisters, gurus and disciples, and teachers and students exhibits such love. Helping the sick, needy, poor, and oppressed needs this love. We, however, spend most of our time in handling the Carnal Love which we enjoy with our senses. So I'm writing about Carnal Love.

God created humans, planted love into their hearts, and then gave them five organs to enjoy different types of loves: Mouth, to love food and drinks, and singing: Eyes, to appreciate and love beautiful things created by Him; Ears, to love music, sermons, and affectionate words; Nose, to love the fragrance of flowers, perfume, and incense; Sex organ, to enjoy, mate, and reproduce. A man can reduce, subjugate, eliminate, and sublimate the desire for all these types of Carnal Loves. However, the most difficult to control is the love to find a partner and propagate the human race. If this love had not been so strong, the human race had disappeared long ago.

Let me describe my struggle with the Carnal Love for the fair sex:

While reading the following, please keep in mind, this happened eighty years ago. Now India is completely changed. Coeducation was started in 1936. Now boys and girls can date and chose their partners. However, most of the marriages are still arranged by the parents.

I was born in Thati, a tiny village in Punjab, India. In my childhood, boys and girls played together in the village park. I hated girls, since they got more hugs from the mothers, and pulled their long braids. They shrieked and I enjoyed it. On their complaints, my father spanked me, but my hatred for the girls grew stronger.

When I became five-year-old, the girls and boys went to different schools, and I was glad to avoid the dumb creatures with long pony braided tails. However, when I turned ten, my feelings towards girls started changing. I noticed the bums on their bosoms and was attracted by their shapely curves. Now, at the sight of a girl my heart fluttered and danced in its cage. I, however, couldn't speak to any girl, since it was forbidden by our traditions, and the girls visited me, only, in my dreams.

One day, I met my friend, Darshan, who was fourteen, four years older than I, since he failed in four classes and had to repeat those.

"Darshan, how is life treating you?"

"Great!"

"Have you ever embraced a girl?"

He chuckled. "Many times, rather I had slept with five girls from the village."

"You're bluffing," I said. "Where could you do this?"

"I'm telling the truth. I rent a room near the Golden Temple, and the girls tell their parents they are worshiping at the sacred place."

"Hard to believe," I said. "Anyhow, how did you manage to seduce them?"

"I meditated three hours daily for four years near the cremation grounds and developed an amulet. I wear that and recite some tantras near the girl. She gets hypnotized and immediately falls into my trap."

"Wonderful!"

He smiled.

303

"Well, I want to only hug and kiss a girl and nothing beyond that. Can you help me?"

"It will cost you fifty rupees," he said.

"I have ten and can work for you for the rest."

"All right, give me ten and promise to polish my shoes for six months."

"I agree," I said and gave him ten rupees.

He handed over the amulet to me. "Keep this in your pocket. When you see a girl alone, grab her hand, lock into her eyes, and recite the tantra: "Chakar cheen batan doku." The girl will jump into your arms and will kiss you."

I repeated the tantras five times and pocketed the amulet. The village chief's daughter, Kamla was of my age. She had rosy cheeks on a honey-colored face and was taller and stronger than me. Undaunted, I started stalking her. One evening, I found her walking on a deserted road. I rushed, grasped her hand, peered into her eyes, and started reciting the tantra. She pivoted, slapped me, and I forgot rest of the tantra. I dropped on my knees and begged forgiveness, but she rushed to her home. Next day the chief and my father spanked me, and I couldn't sit on my bottom for twenty days. I had learned a good lesson and never tried the voodoo again. Later on, I learned Darshan had cooked up the amulet scam and had cheated many boys like me.

In my part of the world, infant girl killing had been practiced for eons. This has resulted in shortage of girls. For one hundred boys there were less than 80 girls. The unlucky boys had to become hermits, purchase dark girls from the South, or die as bachelors. I prayed hard for a wife.

One day, my grandfather caught me hiding in the sugar cane crop and ogling girls bathing in the ghat reserved for the ladies. I, however, was surprised, when he didn't punish me, but took me in his hut.

"Bir, as I study your face, I am reminded of our famous axiom: 'When a boy gets a black fuzz on his upper lip, and the calf digs with its front hoofs, both are in a great turmoil. Only God can save them from trouble.' You are fifteen and must be engaged to a girl to avoid you from jumping into a pit full of snakes."

"Sorry, Grandpa. I'm helpless, and I do feel great attraction for the girls."

"Promise to control your passions, and I'll ride to my friend and ask the hand of his granddaughter."

"I promise by the Holy Cow."

Five days later my engagement ceremony was preformed, and I was on the top of the world. My euphoria, however, lasted for two months. My betrothed was killed in a bus accident. Now I was labeled as a betroth killer, and people blamed my birth stars. I lost all chances of getting a wife from my community.

I learned Muslim fakirs have magical powers, and I went to their festival. I saw sixty fakirs had assembled in a big circle and beautiful whores were singing and dancing in it. The fakirs, high on drugs, clapped and danced with the gorgeous ladies. When the ceremony was over, they dispersed into their tents. I went to the fakir from my village and touched his feet.

"I beg you to secure me a wife."

He raised his blood-red eyes. "I can, but like us, you have to build a link with God, first."

"How can you establish it?"

"The beauties, you saw singing and dancing with us, help us to build a horizontal link in the world, and we slowly lift it up in the vertical direction and establish connection with God."

"Why don't you try direct link with God?"

"Impossible to link with an abstract thing which we can't see or feel with our senses."

"Well, I can't meet the whores," I said. "Can you give me some other method?"

"Yes, go and pray at our famous lover's shrine."

"What is the name of the lovers?"

"Sohni and Mahiwal," he said.

"I've read about them in my books. That young couple sacrificed their lives at the altar of love."

"Good, go there in full faith, and my blessings are with you."

I thanked him and returned to Khalsa College, where I was a senior. I took two days leave and went to the shrine. When I stepped in the mausoleum, I saw two marble graves, hugging each other and covered with flowers and coins. Dark room was dimly lit with two earthen lamps whose wicks were flickering and sending tendrils of smoke toward the ceiling. I looked up and noticed a big hole in the ceiling, above the graves and asked one mullah, "Why is there a hole in the roof?"

"Sohni and Mahiwal couldn't be confined to the graves. They are prophets of love for the whole universe. They opened the hole and flew out. We patched it twice, but they opened it again."

I thanked him, but it looked like a fairy tale to me. Suddenly the clouds started pouring rain. I was stunned to find that not a drop landed on the graves. I thought there must a glass covering the opening, which people can't see in the dark room and decided to test it. I made one round of the graves and threw flowers and coins on them. Then I intentionally fired a silver rupee toward the ceiling. It hit the opening and bounced back on the pile of the coins. I was devastated. The whole thing was a big hoax. I gave up my hopes for finding a wife and returned to my books. I worked hard and stood first in the college, and the mirror told me that I was tall and very handsome.

One day I was walking on the corridor of the Golden Temple, praying for a wife. I met my classmate, Rattan who was accompanied by a middle-aged man and a charming young girl.

"Bir, meet my uncle, Gurdit. He is settled in America," Rattan introduced me.

I shook hands with Gurdit.

"Uncle, Bir stood first in the university, and he is a good athlete, too," Rattan told his uncle.

"Are you married?" Gurdit asked.

"No."

"Engaged?"

I shook my head.

"Please excuse us for a few minutes," Gurdit said and took Rattan and his daughter away from me.

All returned with smiles.

"Let's sit here for a few minutes," Gurdit suggested.

We all sat cross-legged on the marble floor.

"Bir, meet my daughter, Amrit. She has done her B.A. from UCLA."

Amrit and I greeted each other with folded hands.

Gurdit placed his hand on my shoulder. "Bir, Will you accept the hand of my daughter?"

I nodded.

My heart started Bhangra (acrobatic Punjabi dance.)

"We are returning to America tomorrow and don't have time for a lavish wedding," Gurdit said. "Will you agree to a simple wedding at the temple?"

"I have no objection."

We went inside the temple and the priest on the second floor performed our marriage. I immigrated to America, did graduate studies in UCLA, and joined a big consulting firm. Amrit completed her M.A. and began teaching in Los Angeles.

As I write this, I had enjoyed a wonderful married life for twenty years. I found true love from the prettiest woman in the world, and the distant stars didn't kill her: It was all a dumb Indian superstition.

My Search for Life After Death

"Grandson, tell your father I stored carrot seeds in the pitcher which is fourth from the left end, in the third row from the bottom. Also tell your Grandma to stop crying. Look, my clothes are wet, and it is making things difficult for me," my eighty-year-old grandfather said.

Before I could say anything, he jumped on his black stallion and bolted away.

I was surprised at his strange behavior. I was his favorite grandson, and he always hugged me and patted my back. I thought he might be in hurry to get his pension at Amritsar, but his messages and actions baffled me.

I was studying at Khalsa College Amritsar and was coming home on the Diwali holidays. At six in the morning, the train, draped in smoke, steam, and dust, dropped me at the railway station. I gave the ticket to the stationmaster, snaked through the crops on a narrow path, and reached the village pond, where I met my grandfather who was watering his horse.

I reached the house and heard keening sounds. As I stepped into the living room, I found the furniture had been removed and people were sitting on the floor. My heart felt a sharp jolt; there was a death in the family.

My father took me in his arms and said, "Your grandfather passed away yesterday."

"Impossible, I met him at the pond."

"Son, you suffered a mental hallucination."

"No, I saw him with my own eyes, and I don't drink," I said. "All right, he gave me a message about the carrot seeds."

"He forgot to buy that seed, and I'm worried, since the planting season is slipping away," he said. "Anyhow, what's the message?"

"He did purchase the seeds and gave me the location where he stored them."

"Good, let me take some others with us and check it," Dad said and called three persons who were sitting in the living room.

We rushed to the barn, and I pointed the pot amongst forty earthen pots which were used to store things. When we removed the pots above it, we found it full of seeds.

Everyone was stunned and baffled.

"Son, you did meet Grandpa's spirit," Dad said. "Let's go home and take care of the funeral."

We went to the corner of the barn, where Grandpa had collected and stacked wood for his cremation. Logs were loaded in a bullock-cart which transported them to the cremation grounds. We made a pyre and returned home. Grandpa's corpse was carried on a wooden bier and laid on the pyre. Dad ignited the grass in logs, and I watched the tongues of flames consuming the great soldier, good farmer, and doting family patriarch. Next day we poured milk over the ashes, collected them in cotton bags, carried those to the sacred river, and scattered them over the shimmering ripples.

My vacation ended, and I went back to my campus. In two years I graduated from college and came to America for graduate studies. At the Gurdwara (Sikh Temple) I met Jeeto, an Indian girl from my community, and married her. We had one son, Paul, and thirty years of wonderful married life flew away. When Jeeto left me, I was fifty-years-old. I depended so much on her: my food, health, medicine, and recreation. I had trouble with my eyesight, and she drove me everywhere. She took a promise from me that if she died first, I wouldn't plan a funeral service; cremate her, and dump her ashes in the sacred river. To fulfill her wish of joining her ancestors, I kept her ashes and arranged my trip to India. Paul and his wife left for their home in Arizona, and I was alone in the big house.

I closed my eyes, and tears trickled down my cheeks. Then the incident of meeting my grandfather flashed across my mind and his message, "Tell your grandma to stop crying. My clothes are wet, and I'm finding it hard to adjust," buzzed in my ears.

I thought Jeeto must be sitting right near me, and my weeping would create difficulties for her. So I took a bath, seated cross-legged on the floor, and prayed. I pledged not to shed any more tears and try to meet Jeeto's spirit.

So far I had my doubts about life after death, and thought Grandpa's meeting with me was a freak phenomenon. I withdrew from the library several books dealing with the life after death. Among them was the book "Edmond" by Sir Oliver Lodge, the world famous British scientist called the father of the radio. He experimented with the spirit of his son, Edmond, who was killed in France, in World War I. I read it twice. I, also, studied the book by Sir Arthur Conan Doyle, creator of Sherlock Holmes. He gave clear details about contacting the spirit of his son. Now I was sure that there was a life after death. Heartbroken and down in the dumps, I thought, if I could meet Jeeto's spirit and ask her what should I do now, it would help me.

I was confined in the house, and once a month I took a taxi to the grocery stores. I felt, slowly and steadily I was dying in my heart, and my body was decaying and withering. I, though, longed for a quick painless death, but the idea of meeting Jeeto's spirit kept me going. In my theosophical search, I had discovered Anne Woods, the daughter of the famous British Admiral, changed her name to Anne Besant and did great research on life after death, and established a big ashram (center for learning, healing, and meditation) near Mt. Everest peaks. I decided to visit this ashram after scattering Jeeto's ashes over the sacred river.

I flew by Air India Airlines to Amritsar, and my younger
brother picked me up at the airport. Father had arranged the
Sikh funeral service—the continuous reading of the Holy
Book for four days. I thought Jeeto's spirit will find peace
through this, and our prayers will help her. After the service,
my brother drove me to the sacred river, and I scattered Jeeto's
ashes over the dancing ripples. Thus Jeeto joined the company
of her ancestors.

Next day, after breakfast, I sat near my father.

"Dad, I feel lonely and need someone to help me."

"Hire a good servant," he said.

"It's impossible to get a servant whom one can trust in
America, and I'm not rich."

"Son, come and join Narain."

"Who's Narain?"

"He used to be a professor, but now he feeds the hungry
and treats the sick."

I scratched my chin. "Did he not get his Ph.D. in America?"

"Yes, he taught at Khalsa College. His wife cheated on him
and eloped with a student, leaving behind a five-years-old
daughter. He didn't marry again, and after his daughter's death,
he resigned his job and made a treatment center and a free
kitchen on his family farm," he said. "Follow his example and
don't dream of marrying again; it's against our traditions."

I felt a stab in my heart and wished my father could
understand the pain I felt. I longed for a companion. I
managed to mumble, "All right, Dad, I'll go there tomorrow."

Next morning, I took a taxi to the Bias River. The taxi left
the Grand Trunk Road and traveled five miles on a dirt road to
reach Narain's place. I noticed the hospital had three wards
and a large outpatient treatment center. There was a big
kitchen with a huge dining hall adjoining it. The smoke from
the kitchen loaded with spices wafted toward me. I walked to
the office and was received by a young lady.

"Welcome to the Narain's Center," she smiled and said.

"I want to meet Babajee (respected old man)," I said.

"He's in the kitchen; you can go there."

I walked to the kitchen and found a tall man, with a flowing white beard, addressing a group of volunteers. When he finished talking, I approached him with folded hands and said, "Babajee, I want to speak to you for a few minutes."

"I'm free now, let's go to my cabin."

He conducted me to a one-room-home which had one small bed, two wooden chairs and a small table. As we adjusted in the chairs, I said, "Babajee, my name is Prem Grewal. I've lost my wife and am searching for a way out of my depression."

"You have my sympathy, but only you can fight your way out of it."

"I need help and advice."

"Pray and keep in mind that no one can escape the Yammas (carrier of the dead)," he said.

"I have one question."

"What's that?"

"Do you believe in Heaven and Hell?" I asked.

"There are no such things. We create Hell for ourselves on earth with the hope of entering a mythical Heaven."

"Babajee, where did you do your Ph.D. in America?"

"Purdue."

"Babajee, I'm a Boilermaker, too."

"Good, past is dead and gone. Forget it and live in the present."

"I'm trying hard," I said. "Babajee, please give me your frank advice to handle the present."

"Find a companion and live your life," he said. "Let me give you my example. Forty years ago, my wife left me, leaving me with a five-years-old daughter. I was thirty-six and strongly believed in our traditions, so I decided not to marry again and seek Nirvana."

"Were you able to secure it?"

"No, only Buddha secured it by torturing his body."

"What was your method in seeking Nirvana?"

"After finishing classes at the college, I walked to the Golden Temple, prayed there, and returned home exhausted."

"You covered twelve miles daily," I said. "Who took care of your daughter?"

"I sent her to a boarding school in Simla Hills. Anyhow, despite all the hardship, I felt even more miserable and discontented. My daughter grew into a beautiful lady. When she was eighteen, she asked my permission to marry a young man from my village. I refused," he said.

"Why?"

"The young man was a Sudra, and I couldn't break the traditions. Next morning, I discovered my daughter had committed suicide by taking a poison. I told everybody, she had a heart attack, cremated her in hurry, and dumped her ashes in the Bias River. I resigned my teaching job and opened my Center here. Daily, I feed more than five hundred hungry people, and my hospital treats one thousand sick."

"Babajee, you did suffer to uphold the traditions. Did you get any consolation from it?"

He sighed and shook his head.

"Not a tiny pinch," he said. "Don't fall into a trap like me, but feel free to do what suits you."

"How did you happen to start this hospital?"

"My high school classmate, Satwant, received her M.D. degree from Medical College Lahore, and her family forced her into a marriage with a rich landlord who was a womanizer and drunkard. The fellow died in a car accident, and she became a widow at the age of thirty-two. As dictated by our traditions, she couldn't marry again and endured a miserable life. When I opened this Ashram, she joined me."

"What is your relationship with her?"

"We're one in our souls, minds, and hearts. We are in Heaven right here on earth. We find God in each human being and are serving God's children."

"Do you believe in life after death?"

313

"I have my doubts; I'm a scientist," he said. "Prem, do good deeds on earth and enjoy Heaven here."

I thanked him, shook hands with him, and returned to my village.

As I had already decided, I left for Anne Besant's Ashram. I traveled light with just a heavy backpack and a handbag. The train carried me to Darjeeling, and from there I took a rattling bus to Thimpu. I reached the town late in the evening and was lucky to rent the last available room in the only hotel in the town. It was a dingy, small room with a string cot, a wooden table, and a cane chair. I opened the small window, filled my lungs with the clean fresh air, and enjoyed the sight of Mt. Everest and its sister peaks.

Next morning at seven, I went to the bus stand. A volunteer from Besant's Ashram was there. At eight the bus arrived and the volunteer greeted fifteen foreign tourists, and directed her sherpas to take hold of their luggage.

I approached the red-haired, tall volunteer and asked her permission to join the group.

"You're welcome; give your luggage to the sherpas."

"Thanks, I can manage that."

The volunteer addressed the group, "My name is Tresa, and I'll conduct you to our ashram. It's a five miles steep climb, and I'll move at the pace suited for you. You know Mother Besant passed away in 1940, and Mother Amrit has taken her place."

"Amrit is an Indian name; is she an Indian lady?" I questioned.

"No, like Anne Woods who adopted the Indian name Besant, she's a German lady and took the Indian name 'Amrit' which means nectar."

After four hours we reached the ashram. Tresa gave us a tour of the place and assigned us our rooms. We had dinner, and then Tresa took us to meet Mother Amrit. As I stepped in the meditation hall, I saw many flickering lamps and people seated cross-legged with closed eyes near them. We walked to the corner and saw a white-haired lady seated over a marble dais. There was a glow on her radiant face—she was Mother Amrit.

She raised her hand and said, "Children, you're tired now; take rest and meet me at five in the morning."

We bowed our heads and left the hall.

Next morning I stood in line to seek a private audience with Mother Amrit. When my turn came, I greeted her with folded hands and said, "I want to contact the spirit of my wife."

She opened her eyes and said, "Let me try."

I felt a cold blast and the wafting Indian perfume, Cahammeli, pleased my olfactory senses. This perfume had been my wife's favorite perfume.

"Your wife, Jeeto, is standing in front of you; you can speak to her," Mother Amrit said.

"Jeeto, how are you?"

"Fine, but you are creating problems for me."

"How?"

"Your tears are making a slippery mess for me."

From the tone of the voice, I was sure I was talking to my Jeeto. I also remembered that many years ago Grandpa's spirit had told me to inform his wife to stop crying. So Jeeto must be in the same predicament.

"I'll do my best, but I miss you very much," I said. "Well, are you in Heaven?"

"We're not allowed to talk about it," she said.

This reminded me what I had read: Sir Oliver Lodge and Sir Conan Doyle couldn't get this information from their sons. There is a strict discipline in the life after death.

"Jeeto, I feel depressed and lonely."

"Get out and meet people, pray, and take care of your health."

"I'm miserable, and need a companion," I said. "Would you mind, if I take a wife?"

"No, I want you to be happy, but you don't have much time left."

"How many years do I have?"

"Not years, but days," she said.

"Great! I'm delighted to hear that," I said. "Are you sure?"

"Yes, remember that in our world there is no limitation of time and space."

I recollected the experiments made by Sir Oliver Lodge and Sir Conan Doyle with the spirits of their sons. The spirits' predictions turned out to be correct.

"Darling, soon I'll join you." I said

"I'm waiting for you," she said.

I felt a soft kiss on my lips. The lamps flickered and the spirit left the place.

I thanked Mother Amrit, touched her feet, and moved out of the room, and the next visitor took my place.

I returned home, bubbling with joy. My family and friends were surprised to notice the sudden change in my mood—I hugged everyone and forgave the wrongs done to me. Finally, I took a bus to Ludhiana to meet Jeeto's parents.

*   *   *

Postscript: On March 29, 2005, the following news was published in the Indian newspapers: "At Amritsar, an overloaded bus crashed into a bridge abutment and burst into flames. One passenger was killed and ten injured. The dead person's name is Prem Grewal, and he is a naturalized American citizen. His parents took the charred body, cremated it, and scattered the ashes over the sacred river."

A Smart Polygamist

"Detective, I want you to find my daughter's missing husband," Natha Singh, a tall muscular man, with white flowing beard said.

"No problem, but before I undertake any job, I always record my conversation with my client," I said. "Have you any objections?"

He shook his head.

I stabbed the button on the recorder on the table.

"All set," I said. "What is his name?"

"Diljit Singh."

"Have you got his picture with you?"

"Yes," he said and laid the picture on the table. "This was taken at the time of the marriage."

I studied the photo of the couple in the marriage dress: It showed the bridegroom, a tall muscular man with reddish-brown trimmed beard and blue eyes, and the gorgeous bride having a beautiful oval face and rosy cheeks.

"When did he marry your daughter?"

"1998."

"Did you arrange the marriage?" I asked.

"Yes."

"Now tell me something about your daughter," I said.

"Her name is Kuldip, and she did her M.A. from the Government College, Ludhiana."

"Did she meet Diljit before the marriage?"

"No."

317

"Was any marriage-broker involved in it?"

He shook his head.

"How could Diljit secure her hand?"

"She is a good dancer and singer and was heroine in her college stage play. Diljit met her after the show, gave her 24 red roses, and introduced himself. She was impressed with this tall gentleman. Next day he came to my home and told me, he's settled in America and owns a big computer consulting firm. For ten days he came daily with gifts for Kuldip and rest of the family. I was impressed by his actions and agreed to his marrying Kuldip."

"How many guests did he bring in the marriage party?"

"Two," he said.

"Strange! No body brings less than twenty-five," I said. "What were those persons?"

"His grandfather and grandmother."

"What about his parents and his sibling?"

"His parents died in a car accident, and he was the only child."

"Looks suspicious," I said. "How many days did he stay after the marriage?"

"Thirty days."

"Did he visit again?"

"Yes, for three years, he came every year for one month, brought lot of cash and deposited it in Kuldip's name."

"How did he treat you?"

"He was polite and respectful," he said. "He was a good sycophant."

"Why didn't he take his wife with him to America?"

"Every year he promised to get the entry visa for his family, but later told us the immigration process is very slow."

"What happened this year?"

"He was supposed to come in January, but failed to do that. We waited, and Kuldip wrote letters to him, but didn't get any reply."

"Why didn't she phone him?"

"He never gave his phone number, but regularly contacted her from America."

"What's his mailing address in America?"

"2338 Rockwell Drive, Baltimore, MD 21228," he said. "We never used it, since he called every evening."

"There are many Sikhs in Baltimore," I said. "Did you ask anyone to check his place?"

"Yes, I asked my friend's son who is working in New York. He went to Baltimore and discovered the address given by Diljit was a vacant lot."

"Did you contact his grandparents?" I asked.

"Yes, they are befuddled and have not heard from him."

"He can't vanish," I said. "Don't worry, I'll dig him up."

I filled the contract papers laid before him, and said, "Please read these and sign them."

He skipped through the papers and signed at the bottom line.

"All right, I want to start my investigation with his grandfather," I said. "Give me his grandfather's name and address."

"Bachiter Singh, Gill Village, Ludhiana."

I noted down the information and said, "I'll go to that village tomorrow and let you know the results."

"After that I want you to go to America," he said. "You had worked with the world famous detective in America for fifteen years, and it would be easy for you to ferret out Diljit there," he said.

"I'll do my best," I said. "Well, I'll close the case in hand in ten days and then fly to America."

"I can wait that long," he said.

He stood up, shook my hand, and I escorted him to his car.

Next morning, I took my jeep to Gill Village. I entered through a large arched brick gate which had thirty-foot-wide wooden door. The bullet holes on the steel plates studded on the gate looked like a piece of modern art. In ancient times, the village was surrounded by a tall mud wall, and this gate was the only entrance. The mud enclosure with its four towers had disappeared, and the gate was the only thing left. I parked my jeep near a banyan tree and asked one villager about the directions to reach Bachiter Singh's house. After fifteen minutes, I stood in front of a three-story brick home. I knocked at the door. An old lady parted the flaps, and I greeted her with folded hands.

"I want to see Sardar Bachiter Singh on a very urgent matter," I said.

"Come in and sit on the sofa," she said. "I'll tell him about you."

I perched on the sofa, and she left through the back door.

I examined Diljit's marriage picture which was hanging on the wall. As an old man with snake-charmer's eyes, emerged out of the rear door, I stood up and shook hands with him. He sat on the recliner next to me.

"I want to know the whereabouts of your grandson, Diljit," I said.

"I've not heard from him," he said after inhaling a sigh. "It has broken my heart."

"Sad to hear that," I said. "How did Diljit's father meet his death?"

"He was driving his car to New Delhi and was smashed by a truck."

"I was told by Natha Singh that Diljit's mother was with his father."

"Yes."

"It was tragic," I said. "In this accident Diljit was lucky. He recovered, but his younger brother and sister died in the crash."

Tears trickled down his cheeks. "His younger brother, Balbir, and his sister, Amrit, died along with their parents, and I cremated four bodies."

I had been studying the old man's face muscles and the tone of his voice and found he was struggling to fabricate the lies. Now he was caught in the trap laid by me.

I flashed my badge before his eyes.

"Here's my badge as a detective," I said. "You have told me a bunch of lies, and I have corralled you."

"How?"

He started trembling and grabbed the arms of his chair to steady his hands.

"Diljit had no sibling."

"Sorry, I've become a senile, and my memory failed me," he said.

"Hell, you even cooked their names," I said. "Look, I'm going to get you arrested for taking part in a fraud."

Tear trickled down his cheeks, and he begged, "Please don't inform the police. I've not hurt anybody and am willing to tell you everything."

"Okay, give me the full details."

"I taught at Khalsa School Amritsar and used to live near the cantonment. Diljit's mother cleaned our latrines. She had blue eyes and blond hair. She dyed her hair black, but couldn't conceal the color of her eyes. It was a known fact that her mother was frightened by a British soldier while she worked in the barracks. Thus Diljit's grandfather was a Tommy. Diljit couldn't carry his Sudra parents and relatives in the marriage party, so he begged me to act as his grandfather."

"How much did he pay you?"

"50,000."

"You knew Diljit's family," I said. "Why did you lie about his sibling?"

"He did have a sister and a brother, and they died in a bus accident. I forgot what Diljit told at his marriage and got mixed up."

"Do you know where Diljit had gone?"

He shook his head. "He came here after the marriage, paid me, and I never saw him again."

"Give me the name of Diljit's parents, and where can I reach them?"

"His father's name is Amru, and he died five years ago. His mother's name is Gangee. Diljit bought a nice home in Ludhiana for her, and she leads a comfortable life under a different identity. She, however, will never admit Diljit is her son."

"What's her address?"

"233 Sangat Road, Civil Lines."

"Please don't send me to jail," he said. "I'm an old man and won't survive there."

"Well, if you've told the truth, you shouldn't worry."

"I gave you the truth, and Satguru is my witness."

I said my farewell and drove to Ludhiana. There I went to the police headquarters and contacted the police inspector and learned Diljit had no criminal record, and they didn't know his whereabouts. I left the police station and parked in front of 241 Sangat Road and entered Natha Singh's house.

I sat on a sofa next to Natha Singh in his living room and the servant served us hot tea.

"Did you find any trace of Diljit?"

"No, but Bachiter is not Diljit's grandfather," I said.

His mouth flew wide open, and he stuttered, "Holy Cow! How Diljit got him?"

"Diljit hired him for 50,000 rupees."

"Could you find his real parents?"

I shook my head.

I didn't want to destroy his happiness by revealing what I have discovered about Diljit; my job was to locate Diljit. Natha Singh would be demolished to learn that his daughter had been married to a Sudra, and Diljit's mother who was highly respected lady would be decimated.

It was a pathetic fallacy. The mother-in-law lived only four houses from Kuldip's residence, and Kuldip didn't know about it. The old lady saw her son's marriage and watched her grandchildren, but had to ignore them with a heavy heart.

"I want to get Diljit's fingerprints," I said. "Is there any item which was touched by him only?"

He snaked his fingers through his beard for a few seconds and then beamed, "Oh, yes. His prayer book."

"Don't touch it, and let me pick it up."

He took me to the prayer room. I lifted the book with my handkerchief, and we returned to the living room.

"What are your future plans?" he asked.

"Search in America."

I took my leave from Natha Singh and returned to my office in New Delhi. I was delighted, since with the help of my gadgets, I could lift Diljit's fingerprints from the prayer book.

Ten days flew away. On June 18, 2002, I took British Airway's flight to BWI. I stayed at Baltimore Inn and started my search. The best place to locate a Sikh was the Gurdwara (Sikh temple). Before doing that, I decided to check the address given by Diljit Singh to his wife in India. I rented a car and drove to 2338 Rockwell Road and found it was a vacant lot, and the persons living in the houses adjoining to it knew nothing about Diljit. I went to the Gurdwara and showed Diljit's picture to the priest. He told me the man in the picture is member of the congregation and his name is Gulshan Singh. He searched the register and gave me the address of Gulshan Singh's residence. He also told me, Gulshan had not attended the services for six months. I thanked him and drove to Gulshan's residence 2302 Westchester Ave., Catonsville. It was a two-story brick home with huge fenced yard in front of it. I stabbed the bell and a beautiful lady opened the door.

"I've come from Gulshan's parents and want to deliver him their message," I said.

"He's not at home," she said. "You can give me the message."

"My legs are hurting," I said. "Can we sit down?"

"Yes, come in," she said and opened the door.

323

I sat on the sofa.

"Gulshan's father was hurt in a car accident at Ludhiana, and he wants Gulshan to come for a few days."

"You're mistaking my husband for someone else," she said. "His parents live in London."

"Have you met them?"

"No," she said. "Gulshan had been very busy with his business, and he promised to take me to London next year."

"How many children do you have?"

"Four: three boys and one girl"

"How many days does Gulshan stay at Baltimore in a year?"

"Three months," she said. "He travels to his branches in other countries."

"Where are those?"

"Toronto, London, and New Delhi."

"This time, when did he leave your house?"

"On December 15, 2001. He told me he was going to an urgent meeting in London and took a taxi to BWI."

"Did you hear from him?"

She sighed and shook her head.

I didn't want to destroy her happiness and said, "Sorry, I made a mistake. I'll trace the Gulshan from Ludhiana."

I said my goodbye and returned to my hotel. An FBI agent, who worked with me in Los Angeles, was now posted in Washington, DC. I met him in his office. He revealed to me that Gulshan was running an international drug smuggling ring. His yachts smuggled drugs to America. On December 2, 2001, one of his boats was caught with ten million dollars worth cocaine and his men revealed his name. He was going to arrested, but his paid informers in our department leaked him the news, and he flew away.

"Did you check the airports?"

"Yes, but found nothing; he must traveled under another name."

I thanked him and returned to my motel. Now I decided to hunt him in Canada.

I flew to Toronto and went to my friend, Harjit Singh, at 80 Whitehorn Crescent.

"What's the reason for this sudden unannounced visit," he asked.

I showed him Diljit's picture and said, "I'm trying to trace this man."

"Look, he's a very pious man and is the president of our gurdwara."

"What's his name?"

"Labh Singh," he said.

"Has he got his family here?"

"Yes, a pretty wife and three children. He has a big mansion and keeps a yacht for his hobby of deep-sea fishing."

"Appears to be a god man," I said.

"Certainly, he is a gem," he said. "Why are you searching for him?"

My revealing the identity would have hurt an innocent family and many Sikhs, so I said, "He must be having his twin brother who is wanted for murder in India."

"Do you know the parents of his wife?"

"I don't know the name of his father-in-law, but he lives in Yuba City, California."

After lunch, I took a taxi to meet Labh Singh's wife. I stabbed the bell, and a gorgeous lady opened the door.

"Can I see Sardar Labh Singh?" I asked.

"He's not here," she said.

"Where is he now?"

"He left for his office in America and phoned me every evening. However, I've not heard from him since mid December, 2001," she said. "He must be very busy in his office in America."

I thanked her and left the place.

I checked the telephone records and found Labh Singh made frequent calls to Baltimore, London, and Ludhiana. I noted down the telephone numbers and the dates he called.

Next day, I reached Heathrow Airport and lodged in Imperial Hotel. With the help of the telephone directory, I could locate the place to which Diljit had been calling. I took a taxi and reached this house in the rich neighborhood. I prodded the bell, and a chubby, dark-skinned woman opened the door. She was dressed in flashy sari. I could easily guess, the lady with dark skin and blunt features was a Sudra.

I greeted her with folded hands, showed Diljit's picture and said, "I was told this gentleman lives at this place."

"Yes, this house belongs to him."

"Can I see him?"

"Why are you asking for it?"

"His grandfather has left him a huge fortune in India, and I'm the estate-adjuster."

"Mister, Satnam's pauper grandfather died twenty years ago."

"Sorry, I must have had a wrong information," I said. "Are you his wife?"

She nodded.

"When did you see him last?"

"He came on December 18, 2001. Next day, he went for swimming in Thames River and was swallowed by the river. I cremated his clothes which were left on the bank and did Bhog (funeral services) for him."

"Sorry, to hear your tragedy," I said.

"He was a good husband and great father to his five children," she said and dabbed her eyes.

I had met four families of Diljit Singh, but he was still missing or dead. I returned to India and told Natha Singh Diljit went for swimming with his friends and got drowned.

A Smart Polygamist

Though, I closed the case, yet I doubted the drowning of this cunning person. I always kept his picture and fingerprints with me. On November 7, 2002, I went to Lahore, Pakistan, to investigate a case. In the evening I went to the Shalimar Gardens. While I was walking along the cascading waterfalls and sprinkling fountains, I came face to face with a man who resembled Diljit. I dropped my book and requested him, "Sir, my back is hurt and I can't bend; kindly lift the book for me."

He picked the book and gave it to me. I thanked him and followed him to his car. I wrote down his car's plate number. When I returned to my hotel, I developed the finger impressions and photographed those. I compared those belonged to Diljit Singh, and those were a perfect match. So this Muslim was Diljit Singh.

I went to the motor vehicle department and bribed the clerk who gave me the name and address of the owner of the car which had the given plate number: Mushtaq Ali, 232 Civil lines. I reached this place and secured meeting with Mushtaq Ali.

"Mushtaq, I'm a detective hired by your father-in-law Natha Singh, and have traced you in Baltimore, Toronto, and London. You have four wives and fifteen children. FBI told me you are wanted for drug smuggling."

He shot up.

"Don't move or do anything foolish," I said. "I've loaded revolver in my pocket."

He crumpled into the chair. "Your getting me arrested will hurt the five families you have seen, and my sixth wife, Noor, who is expecting a child next month. I've been supporting all of them," he said. "I've left drug smuggling and am an honest banker now. You can check here."

"After December 2001, your wives have not received a penny from you."

"Sorry, I' was supposed to be dead and therefore couldn't send the money to them. I'll establish an anonymous trust

327

which will send 25,000 dollar to my each wife every year, till their deaths."

"All right, it is a deal," I said, and we shook hands. "Show me the papers tomorrow. I'll close the case and will never bother you."

Next day I checked the trust papers and left Lahore.

After completing my work in Pakistan, I returned to Ludhiana and told Natha Singh, "My friend in America, who is helping me to locate Diljit, phoned me that he had discovered the trust made by Diljit before his death and this will send 25,000 dollars to Kuldip every year.

"Thanks, she had already received the check for this year," he said. "God bless Diljit's soul. He was a devoted husband and a good father. My daughter won't face any financial difficulties in raising the children."

Cruel Hypocrites

February 8, 1955. Harijan Colony, Ludhiana, Punjab, India

"Light of my eyes, why are you crying?" Gangee, a tall Sudra lady, threw the cane basket from her head, lifted her seven-year-old son, kissed his cheek, and said.

Gurdita wiped his tears with his knuckles and replied, "Why my father isn't visiting us?"

"When you were six days old, he died in a bus accident."

"Don't have I grandparents or cousins?" he asked.

"Your grandparents passed away, and you don't have any cousins," she said. "Tell me what you learned at the school."

"School," he said. "I'm doing okay."

She opened the door of her one-roomed hut and said, "Let me cook your favorite food."

"Spicy grams?"

"Yes," she said with a smile.

"Great!" he said. "I've one question."

"What's that?"

"I don't look like a Sudra," he said. "My complexion is fair, and I've sharp features."

"You're not a Sudra," she said.

"What am I, then," he asked.

"Guru's child," she said.

"How could you get me from Guru?"

"I went to the Golden Temple, prayed there, and Guru blessed me with you. Therefore I named you Gurdita which means, given by Guru."

"That makes me really proud and happy," he said. "Mom, your skin is also white. Why do you darken your face and hands?"

She hugged Gurdita.

"I'm forced to do that," she said. "Stop bugging me. When you are in the tenth grade, I'll explain you everything."

"Okay, I can wait eight years," he said. "Don't worry, I'm going to study hard and will become a Deputy Commissioner."

"I'm praying for that day," she said. "Go out and play with your friends, and your food will be ready in thirty minutes."

Gurdita kissed his mother's cheek, wiped the black soot from his lips, and dashed out.

Gangee cooked the meal and shouted for Gurdita. They sat on a jute mattress and enjoyed the simple food. She tucked Gurdita in his bed on a string cot and tried to pray. She believed in God, but felt God had punished her too much for her one sin.

The Time God turned eight pages on his calendar. Gurdita, now called, Gurdit Singh, had grown taller than his mother, and a black fuzz had appeared above his upper lip. Hard labor had brought wrinkles on Gangee's face. She had stopped using henna to color her hair; those had turned gray. After dinner, Gurdit helped his mother in cleaning the dishes and they sat cross-legged on the mud floor.

Gurdit grasped his mother's hand and said, "Mom, I'm in the tenth grade and want to hear about my father."

"Forget the whole thing; it will hurt both of us," she said.

"You promised."

"All right, I'll disclose it to you, provided you promise not to reveal it to any person in the world," she said.

He raised his hand and said, "I give you my solemn word."

She took a deep breath, released it through her pursed lips, and said, "We are not Sudras."

"What are we then?"

"High caste Sikhs," she said. "My father is the principal of Khalsa College, Amritsar, and he's highly respected by the Sikhs."

"Can I go and meet him?"

"No, he will never accept you," she said.

"Why?"

"It will tarnish his pride, and he'll throw you out as an imposter."

"Why would he do such a cruel thing?" he asked.

"Wait, till you hear the tragic story of my life."

"I'm all ears."

"Son, my birth name is Kuldeep and not Gangee, and my twin sister's name is Amrit. We lived in a big bungalow with four servants. When Amrit and I entered college, we met Dad's favorite students who were cousins."

"What are their names?"

"Jodh Singh and Niranjan Singh. Jodh Singh was a tall, fair-skinned person who was a slick-talker. Niranjan Singh was chubby, but was a brilliant student. They courted me and Amrit, and helped Dad in his gardening. Dad liked them and encouraged their meeting us. Amrit, a cunning schemer, could trap Jodh Singh who was adored by both of us. She married him, and I wedded my second choice, Niranjan Singh."

"Did you love Niranjan Singh?" he asked.

"Yes, I gave him my full devotion."

"Mom, what happened after the marriage?"

"Jodh and Niranjan wanted to become the chief minister of Punjab, and they entered politics. Jodh Singh joined Akali Party, and Niranjan Singh entered the opposition, the Congress Party. As newly married couples, we rented homes in Ranjitpura, not far from each other. Jodh Singh, with his powerful oratory and knowledge of Sikh Scripture, became the head priest of the Golden Temple, which was his stepping stone to head the party which ruled the state. My husband wore hand-spun cotton clothes and started Export-Import Company. He made very good money and Amrit envied us.

"One day Niranjan told me, 'Kuldeep, to rise in the Congress Party, I've to start a political agitation and get arrested. When I come out of the jail, I'll knock out Partap Singh who heads the party.'

"'I can't live without you,' I cried. 'How long will you be behind bars?'

"'Not more than three months,' he said. 'I hate it, but this is a quick way to become the chief minister.'

"I agreed, and Niranjan led an agitation against heavy taxes on food products. He was arrested and jailed for three months. I was lonely in a big house, and Jodh Singh came daily to console me. He read scripture and sang hymns. I fell into his trap, and he seduced me."

"Didn't your sister object to her husband's coming to you daily?" Gurdit asked.

"No, Jodh Singh is very persuasive and could easily convince her that he was just helping her sister in the time of her distress. Anyhow, I slept with him one time and realized my mistake, and never permitted him to kiss me after that. Three months later, Niranjan was released from the jail. He came home, and I welcomed him with open arms. I prayed God not to punish me for my one mistake. But God ignored my pleas. After seven months you were born, and we named you Satnam. Two days after your birth, Niranjan made the calculation and could see he couldn't have sired the child; he was in jail at the time of the conception. Moreover, you resembled Jodh Singh, and he had learned from the neighbors that Jodh Singh had been coming to his house everyday. Niranjan hit the ceiling and threw me out of his house and announced that you were an illegitimate child, and I was not a faithful wife. I grabbed his feet and begged him to forgive me, and I promised to never cheat on him. He kicked me and spat on my face. I took you to my father's place. He kept me one night and then asked me to leave."

"Why was your father so heartless?" Gurdit asked.

"He wanted to save his reputation and the job."

"How could it affect him?"

"If I, a woman with an illegitimate child, stayed with him, he would have lost his job as the principal of the top Sikh college," she dabbed her eyes and said. "I was left with two choices. Either to become a prostitute or disappear under a different name. I chose the latter. I darkened my face, colored my hair, and rented a mud hut in Ludiana under my new name, Gangee."

For a few minutes, both sat wordless, dabbing their tears.

"I know Jodh Singh is the renowned and respected Sikh leader and in his sermons, he always stresses upon faithfulness to one's wife," Gurdit said. "What a rotten hypocrite!'

She sighed and wiped her tears.

"Should I contact him for some financial help," he said. "After all I carry his blood in my veins."

"Never do that, it'll hurt you. He has built his reputation as a saint. He never saw me or rendered any financial help, after I was thrown out. He'll not admit his part in my life," she said. "On the books you're the child of Niranjan Singh, and you can claim that right, but I advise you to forget everything and focus upon your studies."

"All right, I'll ignore those crooks," he said. "However, after I secure my degree, I'll give them one chance to redeem their mistakes."

"I dissuade you from doing that," she said. "I blame my own karma which destroyed my entire life for one silly mistake, and I had to endure this hell."

He hugged his mother and said, "In a few years, you will leave this mud hut and live in a big bungalow with many servants."

Four years slipped away. Gurdit stood first in the college in his B.A., and his mother was delighted.

"Mom, wish me good luck," he said. "I'm going to meet Jodh Singh and Niranjan Singh."

"Go ahead, but be prepared for disappointment. Niranjan has two sons and two daughters, and Jodh Singh has two sons. They might try to eliminate you to remove the dark spot on their lives."

"Don't worry, I'll be fully prepared to defend myself."

"Don't harm them," she said. "They are your fathers."

"I promise, I'll never hurt them."

Gurdit went to Amritsar and returned with dejected looks.

"Son, you look devastated; what happened?" Gangee asked.

"Jodh Singh is now the president of the Akali Party. I went to his office and introduced myself as Gurdit Singh. As I stood before his large desk, his eyes pooped out. He rushed to close the door and asked me to sit down.

"'Do you know me?' I questioned.

"He shook is head.

"'I said, 'Look again, you sired me.'

"He snaked his fingers through his long flowing beard and said, 'All right, Satwant, don't open the grave; you'll be buried in it. You better get out and never speak a word about Satwant.'

"'Look, I'm not afraid of dying for my mother. You created hell for her.'

"'All right, I admit my mistake,' he said. 'What do you want?'

"'Come and apologize to my mother.'

"'I'll never do that; it will destroy me,' he said and rang the bell. Two sewadars (peons) appeared. He told them, 'This young man has admitted to me that he had burnt our Holy Book. Take him outside and teach him a good lesson.'

"As the peons tried to grab me, I took out my revolver and fired in the air. They ran to the door. I told Jodh Singh, 'I can kill you, but let God punish you for your crime. My mother suffered terribly for your fornication.'

"He was trembling and begged me to spare his life and ordered his peons not to touch me. I left him and went to

Niranjan Singh. Niranjan, with his potbelly, looked like a Panda of Hardwar. He didn't recognize me. I told him I want a job in his firm. He made me sit on a chair in front of him and questioned me about my education and other details.

"I peered into his beady eyes and said, 'Sir, study my face again and let me know what do you find there.'

"'Nothing, I don't know you,' he asserted.

"'Do you remember your son, Satwant,' I said. 'I'm that person.'

"His face turned red, and he raised his fists to attack me. I, being much stronger than him, could easily subdue him. He begged me to keep my mouth shut and offered me fifty thousand rupees. I told him, 'Keep your money. I needed a father's love which you never provided me. Look, you destroyed my mother's life. She cleaned latrines to support me and herself. I know if I reveal this, you'll lose the chances to become the chief minister of Punjab. But I won't do that and leave the punishment in God's hands.'

"He buried his head in the tent of his hands and was completely befuddled. I left the miserable crook."

"Son, I'm glad you didn't hurt them. You have seen them. Now work hard to get a good job, so I can retire," she said.

Gurdit stood first in M.A. His mother died on the day he got his degree. He telephoned Jodh Singh and Niranjan Singh about the death of Kuldeep. They refused to attend the cremation. He stood alone with folded hands before the pyre of his mother and saw the shooting flames consuming his mother's tired wrinkled body. He took a pledge to punish the crooks who threw her into a burning hell.

He discovered the secret promiscuous rendezvous of Jodh Singh and Niranjan Singh. They had been making the fornication mistake almost every night. But they refused to pardon one mistake of his mother.

Gurdit took the Indian services competition, and was selected in Indian Police Service. After three years, he was posted as superintendent of police Amritsar.

His detectives informed him, Jodh Singh had seduced many young girls, but he could hush up the affairs with money and threats. He, however, had murdered one young girl who refused to get abortion and wanted to expose him. They were hot on his trail, but were afraid of the political pressure. He told them to do a thorough investigation, and he will withstand all the heat from the top. Soon they gathered enough evidence to convict Jodh Singh.

One day, Gurdit was surprised to see Jodh Singh in his office. Jodh Singh grabbed Gurdit's feet and said, 'Help me and hush up the case against me."

"I believe in justice and the rule of law," Gurdit replied.

"You have my blood in your veins," Jodh Singh said. "You should help the person who brought you in the world."

"Remember, what you did to my mother," Gurdit said. "You failed to recognize me, when I saw you last time."

"Forgive me," Jodh Singh said. "You must help your blood father."

Gurdit rang the bell and ordered the constables to take the old man out of his office.

Jodh Singh was hauled out.

Niranjan Singh's Export-Import Business was just a cover for his drug-smuggling. He kept horses on the bank of Ravi River which partitioned India and Pakistan. At night his horses crossed the river with tubes tied to their bellies. They carried liquor to Pakistan and brought back opium. One of his agents was caught, and he exposed him. He couldn't influence the government which was controlled the Akali Party. He thought of appealing to the noble side of his son and rushed to Gurdit.

"Son, I beg you to forgive my past mistakes," Niranjan said and laid bundles of rupees on the table. "Here's two lakhs for you."

"Look, you can't purchase me," Gurdit said.

"You're my dear son, and you shouldn't destroy your own father."

"You had no sympathy for me and my mother, when you threw us out of your house," Gurdit replied.

Gurdit rang the bell, and two constables dashed in. He threw the bills on Niranjan Singh's face and said, "Get out with your bribery money."

Gurdit gestured to the constables who shoved Niranjan Singh out of the office.

In four months, Jodh Singh got life sentence for the murder, and Niranjan Singh was sent behind bars for ten years for his smuggling operations.

Gurdit had kept his mother's ashes in a cotton bag. He hugged those and took them to the sacred river. He stood in knee-deep water, scattered the ashes over the murmuring ripples, and said, "Mother, God has taken your revenge. Now you can rest in peace in the belly of the sacred river."

The Sounds of the Last Farewell

On March 6, 1945, I slept on a string cot at the top of our house in Thati Village, India. As I awoke at five in the morning, I heard the sounds of the chirping crickets and the croaking frogs. Soon the singing bulbuls joined the chorus with their melodious tunes. Suddenly, one pair of hooting owls swished by me, and several cooing peacocks zoomed over my head. Then I heard the tintinnabulation of the temple bells and the pleasant blowing of a conk shell. I got up from the bed and looked toward the barn and heard the singing farm workers who were yoking the snorting buffaloes.

The sounds here were a big contrast to those in the city, where I was attending a college. There, I always heard the constant blasting of the horns, screeching and grinding of the tires, the cacophonous noises of the hawkers, and the ear-piercing sounds of the loud speakers. For a few minutes, I enjoyed the soothing sounds of the village and then climbed down the steps.

I had come to attend the funeral services of my grandfather who had died yesterday. My grandfather, who retired as a captain from the army, was a tall man with the build of a giant.

I reminisced over my visit to his house near the tube-well in the fields on Basant Holidays. After grandma's death, he built that small house and moved there. When I reached near the tube well, I heard the splashing sound of water which was gushing into a large concrete basin. One year ago there used to be a Persian well here. I missed the sounds of the bells from the neck of the buffalo which turned the water wheel, the clicking of the wheel locker, the swishing sound of the buckets

338

pouring water into the steel trough, and the singing of the drover. Those beautiful sounds had left this world forever. A sigh escaped my lips.

As I moved closer to Grandpa's house, I heard the sounds of sawing wood mixed with the singing of the hymns. Grandpa was sawing wood. I greeted him with folded hands. He placed the saw on the ground and said, "Bir, how are you doing in your studies?"

"Fine, Grandpa," I said. "Why are you sawing wood?"

"We all are transients on the earth. My time to leave this world is due anytime. I felled a dead tree and am stacking its wood for my cremation."

"Grandpa, you're going to live many more years," I said. "Anyhow, let me help you."

We sawed and chopped the wood for five hours.

"Thanks, Grandson. This wood will do a good job in turning me into fine ashes."

That happened six years ago, and today that wood was being carried to the cremation grounds.

My rumination ended, and I joined the mourning party in the living room from which all the furniture had been removed. Grandpa's corpse covered with a white sheet was lying on the floor. I heard the flickering sounds of the cotton wicks in the two mustard oil earthen lamps, placed near his head. I was annoyed at the overhead ceiling fan which was keening like a professional lady mourner who was suffering from a bad cold. However, it was a miserable sultry day, and we couldn't do without the fan. All the mourners sat cross-legged with smiles on their faces, since it was the time to rejoice and bid farewell to Grandpa who was ninety and still worked on the farm and had died in his sleep without suffering any pain.

The priest arrived. He said a short prayer, and a bier was brought near the corpse. Grandpa's lifeless body was laid on the bier, and four persons lifted it up. Now the procession to the cremation grounds was organized. My five-year-old younger brother led the party while ringing a tiny brass bell. The bier followed him. The priest suspended one small drum, called Dholki, from his neck and began beating it to keep consonance with his singing. Two hundred people, singing hymns in off-beat tunes, trailed the priest. After twenty minutes, the procession reached the cremation ground, a covered tin shed with concrete floor.

The wood had already been stacked in a four-foot-high pile; the bier was placed on it. The priest inserted dry hay at several places in the wood pile. Then he ignited one spool of hay, gave it to my father, and directed him to light all the hay spools in the wood. As my father touched the hay with his torch, roaring flames shot out and started consuming the corpse. Sparks cracked out of the wood and rocketed toward the sky. With crispy sounds the flames devoured the white shroud first. I heard the sounds of the exploding bones, the wheezing noise of the singeing flesh, and the crackling of the wood. When the flames reached the head, the hair burnt with a loud hissing sound. Now the tongues of the flames were engulfing the whole body. We all bowed our heads with folded heads and left the cremation ground. The cremation attendant holding a long bamboo pole took charge of the cremation. His job was to stir the wood and add more to complete the process.

On reaching home, our mood changed. It was the time for rejoicing and celebrating to thank God for giving Grandpa a long healthy life. I joined other young men in tying tiny brass bells to our ankles and wrists. A man arrived with a big drum and the loud beat of the drum resonated from the walls. We performed acrobatic dance while clapping our hands. The thudding synchronized sounds of our feet kept harmony with our clapping sounds. And the tiny bells, attached to us, joined the chorus with their enchanting music. After one hour the drum beat went dead, and the bells became silent. We sat cross-legged on the floor and food was served to us.

The Sounds of the Last Farewell

Next morning I accompanied my father and other relatives to the cremation ground. Fire had died down, but a few sparks were still glowing like tiny glowworms. We poured cow's milk on the smoldering fire and collected the ashes in a cotton bag. The old soldier weighing 275 pounds had turned into six pounds of ashes. Father drove us to the sacred river. We stood in knee-deep cold water and listened to the murmuring ripples welcoming the old soldier. With his prayers, my father scattered the ashes over the shimmering whispering waves. We said farewell to Grandpa who had joined his wife and ancestors. Many persons had lost their young relatives, and the sounds of their wailing, keening, weeping, sniffling, and crying choked the air. I was glad when we left the place and reached home.

As we entered the house, my father grabbed me in his arms and said, "I pray God daily to grant me the death similar to my father; I long to accompany the Yammas (Carrier of the dead) while still walking on my two feet. Son, you, too, pray for me."

"I will. Keep in mind you have to travel forty years more to reach Grandpa's age; take good care of yourself," I said. "Well, don't worry about your final farewell; we'll hire two drummers instead one."

Dad burst into peals of laughter, and I joined him.

I Fought Racial Prejudices

September 9, 1964, Teachers' Lounge, Cleveland High School.

"Emily, how was your trip to India?" Dorothy, a red-headed teacher, seated next to me, patted my hand and asked.

"I had a horrible start."

"What happened?" she peered into my eyes and asked.

"I had to battle the Indian racial prejudices."

"Strange, I never thought you would face that problem in India."

"I did."

"Why?"

"Dorothy, I was treated like a Sudra."

"I know India has a caste system, and the lowest caste is called Sudra, but you are an American."

"The problem is that for orthodox Brahmins, any person born beyond an ocean—white, brown, black, yellow or green, is a Sudra. I was in bigger trouble, since I was born beyond several oceans."

"Emily, those miserable sick minds. Do Rughby's parents believe in this?"

"No, they don't, but his grandmother, who is the family matriarch, strongly clings to her convictions."

"A tough challenge; how did you handle her?" she asked.

"Well, when we reached Rughby's father's house, we met our challenge—Grandma. She screamed and wanted me to be thrown out of the house."

"Did she succeed?" Dorothy asked.

"No, on the other hand, we broke her cocoon, and she welcomed me."

"That seems like an exciting adventure."

"Yes, it was."

I noticed four other teachers, who were eavesdropping, had laid down their papers, and were looking at me.

I addressed them, "Come on, let me describe my trip."

The group moved their chairs closer to me.

I cleared my throat with a dry cough and said, "First let me give you some idea about Indian racial prejudices: Many years before the birth of Christ, Aryans invaded India, captured the original inhabitants, enslaved them, and called them Sudras. The Sudras were treated much worse than American slaves. In 1935, Mahatma Gandhi started his struggle to improve the plight of the Sudras and gave them a new name—Harijans, meaning children of God. Slowly and steadily the situation started improving. In 1947, after independence, the government banned all racial discrimination and took steps to help the Sudras. Many Brahmin families, however, continued holding onto their old practices. Gandhi was gunned down by a Hindu fanatic who opposed the changes."

I paused for a few seconds to watch the reaction on their faces. They were spellbound. I continued, "I think racial prejudice is a Devil, who has flimsy legs and a closed mind. It swings its sword and butchers many hearts without caring for the pain and sufferings of its victims. The best approach to deal with it is to attack its foundations, and then it crumbles to pieces. Well, we did that."

"How?" Dorothy asked.

"This summer vacation I forced my husband, Rughby, to take me to India and introduce me to his family. He warned me about his archaic grandmother, but I thought it won't be difficult for me to handle an old lady and ignored his plea for postponing the visit till Grandma had entered the next world.

"Anyhow, we flew to Chandigarh, India. As we reached Rughby's father's home, a two-story brick bungalow, the

343

servant stopped us in front of the door. I was stunned. Suddenly the door opened, and I saw my mother-in-law, dressed in a multicolored sari and tons of jewelry, holding a brass pot full of water.

"'What's this?' I whispered to Rughby.'

"'I think Mother wants to give you our traditional reception. Be patient.'

"My mother-in-law raised her arms and circled the pot around my head. Then she took a sip, and Rughby stopped her. She did this five times, handed the pot to her daughter, and poured oil on the jambs of the door. After this ritual, we were allowed to step inside. My mother-in-law embraced me and kissed my forehead. Rughby's sister took me in a bear hug, and my father-in-law patted my head."

"'Did you learn the significance of this ceremony?' one teacher asked.

"'No, I asked Rughby. He was not sure, but thought that it might be a method to please the gods and chase out evil spirits.' "During the ceremony, I nervously watched the heavy pot going over my head, and Rughby's struggle to stop his mother from consuming too much water. It could have easily slipped from her hands and drenched me. With laughter and chuckles the ritual concluded, and we entered the living room which had two sofas and four cane chairs. I sat on the sofa. Rughby's sister sat next to me and wrapped her arm around my waist, and my mother-in-law occupied a chair near me. The servant brought hot tea with Indian sweets and placed them on the side tables. We enjoyed pleasant conversation, while sipping tea. Beads of perspiration appeared on my face, and I looked up at the squeaky overhead fan, which was fighting a losing battle with the Indian heat. My mother-in-law noticed this and started vigorously waving the hand-fan to cool me."

"Well, you got a royal reception. When did you face the racial problem?" Dorothy asked.

"Just coming to it. I heard a dry cough accompanied by a scuffing sound. Everyone's face became tense, and Rughby glanced at me with a worried look. I felt as if I was standing on the tracks, and the steam engine was approaching me. An old lady, with white hair tied in a bun over her head, shuffled into the room. She had a thin, wrinkled face, and her deep-set eyes hovered like a hawk.

"All shot up and stood with folded hands. I found a lull which always occurs before a big storm and tried to keep my aplomb under the facade of a nervous smile. Grandma raised her rosary flicking hand and gestured us to take our seats. She mumbled some greetings, removed the marigold garland dangling from her neck, placed it near her, and sat cross-legged on the sofa. Then she adjusted her steel-frame glasses and ogled my face. She wiped her glasses with the end of her sari and again eyeballed me with her open toothless mouth. All held their breath. She shook her head and shouted, 'Hari Krishna! A hemp-haired pale-face Sudra.' Then she slapped her forehead. 'I never dreamt to see such a thing in my family. What a curse!'

"My heart began thumping out of its cage, and my palms got soaked with sweat. I bit my lower lip to control my anger. Rughby's warning flashed across my mind: Grandma is a staunch believer in the caste system. For her, any person born beyond a long stretch of water is a Sudra. While walking on the street, if she was ever touched by the shadow of a Sudra, she sprinted home to take her bath and wash her clothes. At this stage I wished I should have avoided this trip, but it was too late. I had expected some trouble, but never thought she would attack me openly in such a rude manner.

"My mother-in-law's chin dropped, and I could see clear pain in her misty eyes. She touched Grandma's feet and said under her breath, 'Grandma, your grandson's American wife is pretty like our goddess, Parvati. She has chiseled features on a milky face.'

"'Where was she born?' Grandma yelled.

"'America.'

"'Isn't that beyond an ocean?'

"My mother-in-law nodded.

"'Then she's a Sudra. Vedas are clear about it,' Grandma announce with authority. 'I want her to leave right now and stay in a hotel. After she clears out, wash the whole house, particularly the sofa, on which she's sitting, with sacred water.'

"My father-in-law stood up, looked at Grandma with a rebellious stance, and said, 'I'll never do that.'

"Grandma's face turned red, and she twisted the end of her sari for a few seconds. On noticing the unyielding attitude of her son, she mumbled, 'Alright, she can stay for a few days.'

"'Thanks Grandma,' Rughby said. 'Times have changed, and we don't have any Sudras.'

"'Shut up. Do you know how humans were made?'

"Rughby shook his head with a sigh. I could see he was acting to please the old lady. I was sure he must have heard it many times.

"'Your grandpa was a great scholar, and he explained the creation of human life to me.'

"Now the sound of the over-head fan and our breathing filled the air. I braced myself for some offensive mythology. Grandma adjusted her legs and took a deep swallow followed by a cough and continued, 'Brahma Devta built the earth, but he could not create human life. He approached God to make human beings to inhabit this earth. God baked a specimen and offered it to him. Brahma shook his head in utter disgust and refused to accept it saying, 'My Lord, this is black, fully burnt; you have kept it in the fire too long.'

"'All right Brahma, give me more clay, but don't destroy my creation.'

"'Holy God, what should I do with this burnt stuff?'

"'He can serve your man.'

"Brahma gave the well-pounded clay to God who made a model and started baking it. After taking it out of the oven, he showed it to Brahma.

346

"Brahma again shook his head. 'Lord, this is half-baked. I don't want a pale-face.'

"'You are a perfectionist. Let me try again.'

"As God took out a light-brown face, god Brahma jumped with joy. 'This is what I wanted. Lord, what should I do with the pale-face?'

"'Throw it in some snow-covered region, and you won't notice him while making your rounds of the earth.'

"Grandma paused to fix her glasses and continued, "Well, so you see, we're the real people, properly baked, true Aryans, and the gods gave us India and banned us from crossing the waters and mingling with others.'

"All sat wordless, trying to find a way out of this awkward situation. I was surprised to hear this absurd theory of creation. My husband said in an appeasing tone, 'Grandma, that is only mythology.'

"'Shut up! You have polluted your mind and body by crossing the oceans which are forbidden by the gods.'

"'Grandma, I took my bath with the sacred Ganges water as soon as I arrived at New Delhi.'

I knew it was a concoction, since we never had a drop of sacred water.

"'Bhudo (idiot), you destroyed the sanctity of a Brahmin's home by bringing in a Sudra. The gods are sure to punish us. To save my family, I'll fast in my room and won't come out until the Sudra has left my house.'

"Grandma scrambled up from the sofa and scurried to her room, while chanting mantras in a doleful, angry voice.

"I glanced at Rughby. His face muscles were twitching, and he raked his fingers through his salt-and-pepper beard and stared at the ceiling. My father-in-law, a bald headed man in his late sixties, stifled a sigh, and addressed me, 'Daughter-in-law, I'm sorry. My mother lives in her own cave, and we're having a tough time to please her. After independence, the lower caste men are holding top jobs. My boss, the principal of the college where I teach, is a Sudra. I invited him to my home, but after his visit my mother rebuked me and washed all the floors and walls with Ganges water. Please excuse her strange behavior. She will soon calm down. We all are proud of you.'

"My mother-in-law wiped her tears with the end of her sari and hugged me. My husband's sister grabbed me in her arms and whispered, 'Bhabi jee, you are the best in the universe!'

"I noticed all were struggling to please me, but no one had the courage to challenge Grandma. Evidently, Indian traditions had tied up their thinking. After dinner Rughby and I went to the bedroom allotted to us. I felt a sigh of relief and said, 'Rughby, let's move to a hotel tomorrow. I don't want to be responsible for your Grandma's death.'

"'Darling, if we do that it will break my parents' hearts. I know Grandma keeps enough food—parched grams and sweets, in her steel box. She'll be okay,' he said, and his hand started wrestling with his mustache. 'Let's try to help my family.'

"'Rughby, what can we do?'

"'Break Grandma's cocoon.'

"'How?'

"'The only person in the world that can change her mind is my grandpa; I'll seek his help.'

"I was puzzled and mumbled, 'How? You told me your grandpa died ten years ago.'

"'Yes, but his spirit is still living, and Grandma strongly believes in life after death.'

"'That still baffles me.'

"'My friend, Ajit, is a great actor, and I'll discuss this with him. He can dress in Grandpa's clothes, appear in Grandma's bedroom in the middle of the night, and straighten her thinking.'

"'Looks difficult,' I mumbled.

"'I'm sure it can be easily accomplished.'

"'Well, wish you good luck.'

I Fought Racial Prejudices

"Next day we went to Ajit, and he gladly agreed to help us. We gave him Grandpa's picture and a few tapes of the sermons delivered by Grandpa. After three days of rehearsals, Ajit was ready and informed us.

"The D-day arrived. During the night Rughby brought Ajit and smuggled him into our bedroom, where Ajit dressed himself in grandpa's clothes: white turban, wooden beads, forehead markings, wrinkles made with grease, and old canvas shoes without laces. Ajit had the same height, and he took help from a pillow to make Grandpa's huge paunch. After the makeup, he looked exactly like Grandpa. I pussyfooted to Grandma's bedroom, heard loud snoring, and waved my arm. Rughby opened Grandma's bedroom window with the help of a tin strip, stepped in, bolted the window, and unlocked the door. He signalled Ajit, and we held our breath.

"Ajit ambled into Grandma's bedroom chanting Grandpa's favorite mantras, kicked the leg of the bed, and yelled, 'Sita, lazy bones, get up and pray to the gods.'

"Ajit, a professional actor, sounded exactly like Grandpa, and he scuffed and coughed as was the habit of the dead man. Grandma rubbed her eyes and squinted at the apparition who had penetrated the locked door. She gazed at the figure and realized the spirit of her dead husband was standing there. She jumped from the bed and touched the spirit's feet.

"'Swami, how are things in Heaven?'

"'Woman, I'm greatly disturbed.'

"'Why?'

"'I've discovered some mistakes in my teaching.'

"'Swami, what are those?'

"'I distorted and misinterpreted the Scriptures.'

"'How?'

"'I gave wrong reasons for the caste system.'

"'You told me the caste system is made by the gods.'

"'I was wrong. All men are created equal. To exploit the weak and the poor, Manu made the caste system, and we followed it with closed eyes and minds.'

"'Swami, could you verify it with the gods?'

"'Yes, I discovered my mistake after conversing with them.'

"Grandma was speechless for a few minutes. She took a deep breath and mumbled, 'I'm all confused. Do you mean that it's alright to touch a Sudra?'

"'Yes, they're humans like us.'

"Grandma let out a sigh and murmured, 'This will save me so many baths; it becomes tough in winter. What about those born beyond the oceans?'

"'They are like us, too,' Ajit asserted. 'Look, your grandson has married a foreign-born girl. Have you welcomed her?'

"'No, I thought she was a Sudra.'

"'That was a big mistake. Tomorrow embrace her and be nice to her.'

"After some hesitation, Grandma moaned, 'Swami, I'll try.'

"'Woman, clear your mind. No try business. It's my firm order. Now get up, take your bath and recite the mantras which I taught you. Always remember God has made many different colored flowers in his garden, and He loves them all.'

"Grandma grabbed Ajit's feet, started crying, and asked, 'When are you going to call me to your place?'

"Ajit patted Grandma's shoulders and said, 'Woman, I left you to help our son and his family. Do your best and don't worry. When the time is ripe, I'll summon you. Mind it, I'm watching you daily.'

"While singing Grandpa's favorite hymn, Ajit left the room and came to our bedroom. We thanked him, and Rughby let him out of the house.

"At five in the morning, I heard the clicking of the hand pump and splashing of water mixed with Grandma's singing. I was delighted at the success of our adventure. After one hour Grandma left for the temple.

"While Rughby and I were having our morning tea on the veranda, we saw Grandma coming from the temple with her face wreathed in smiles. As she came near us, we stood up with folded hands. I was not surprised when she placed the marigold garland around my neck, embraced me, and kissed my forehead.

"'Granddaughter, You're not a Sudra, and I welcome you into my family,'she rejoiced.

"I was delighted at this metamorphosis and made a deep bow.

"Then Grandma turned to Rughby and said, 'I met your Grandpa last night, and he cleared my brain.'

"'Grandma, you must be dreaming,' Rughby said with perfunctory disbelief.

"'No, he was there. The door was locked, and he walked right through it. I touched his feet, and he was wearing his old canvas shoes. He even patted my shoulder. I'm so happy.'

"Then Grandma wrapped her arms around my waist, winked at me and said, 'My grandson is a smart picker, and he picked the prettiest.'

"Grandma and I became close friends, and I walked with her to the temple daily. It was a pleasant morning walk, and I enjoyed ringing the temple bell and throwing flowers on the marble statue. One day I was surprised to see Grandma patting the Sudra lady who had come to clean the latrines and giving her sweets. Now Grandma was cheerful and happy, since the cloud of hatred and prejudice had vanished from her mind.

"Our vacation ended. I couldn't control my tears as Grandma hugged me, and I felt her hot tears on my shoulder. PAN AM brought us back to Cleveland. This is the end of my story."

All the teachers, frozen in their seats, had been listening to my narration. As I concluded, all applauded and shook my hand.

64905203R00200

Made in the USA
Lexington, KY
23 June 2017